APRIL SHADOWS

The Dollanganger Family Series
Flowers in the Attic
Petals on the Wind
If There Be Thorns
Seeds of Yesterday
Garden of Shadows

The Casteel Family Series
Heaven
Dark Angel
Fallen Hearts
Gates of Paradise
Web of Dreams

The Cutler Family Series
Dawn
Secrets of the Morning
Twilight's Child
Midnight Whispers
Darkest Hour

The Landry Family Series
Ruby
Pearl in the Mist
All That Glitters
Hidden Jewel
Tarnished Gold

The Logan Family Series
Melody
Heart Song
Unfinished Symphony
Music in the Night
Olivia

The Orphans Mini-series
Butterfly
Crystal
Brooke
Raven
Runaways (full-length novel)

The Wildflowers Mini-series
Wildflowers
Into the Garden (full-length novel)

The Hudson Family Series
Rain
Lightning Strikes
Eye of the Storm
The End of the Rainbow

The Shooting Stars Mini-series
Shooting Stars
Falling Stars

The De Beers Family Series
Willow
Wicked Forest
Twisted Roots
Into the Woods
Hidden Leaves

The Broken Wings Mini-series
Broken Wings
Midnight Flight

The Gemini Series
Celeste
Black Cat
Child of Darkness

The Shadows Series
April Shadows

My Sweet Audrina
(does not belong to a series)

VIRGINIA ANDREWS®

APRIL SHADOWS

POCKET
BOOKS

LONDON • SYDNEY • NEW YORK • TORONTO

First published in the US by Pocket Books, 2005
A division of Simon & Schuster Inc.
First published in Great Britain by Simon & Schuster UK Ltd, 2007
This edition published by Pocket Books UK, 2008
An imprint of Simon & Schuster UK Ltd
A CBS COMPANY

1 3 5 7 9 10 8 6 4 2

Simon & Schuster UK Ltd
1st Floor
222 Gray's Inn Road
London WC1X 8HB

www.simonandschuster.co.uk

Simon & Schuster Australia
Sydney

A CIP catalogue record for this book is available from the British
Library

ISBN 978-1-84983-307-3

Printed and bound in Great Britain by
Cox & Wyman Ltd, Reading, Berkshire

out of a bad mood or throw off this shroud of grouchiness. According to him, neither my older sister, Brenda, nor I could ever do anything right anymore, whether it was the way we made our beds, cleaned up our rooms, or helped Mama with her house chores. Mama started to call him Mr. Hyde from the story of *Dr. Jekyll and Mr. Hyde.* No matter how she protested, it didn't seem to bother him, which disappointed and surprised my sister and me. Up until then, when Mama complained about something Daddy did, especially in relation to us, he softened. He would rather walk barefoot over hot coals than see her unhappy. She was always our savior, but now she was like a fairy godmother who had lost her powers and her wings. She fell back to earth to wallow in the real world with the two of us.

"It's like water off a duck's back," she muttered when he turned abruptly away from her or just left the room after she had protested about something he had said or done. "I might as well have addressed the wall. He was never like this, never," she said, wagging her head like someone who wanted to shake out what she had heard and what she had seen.

It became worse than that for her, however. Eventually, Mama cried a lot over Daddy's new ways and words when she thought we weren't looking. As a result of all this, the three of us changed. Brenda became Miss Angry Face, leaving her smile outside the front door whenever she came home from after-school activities, and I felt too numb and frightened most of the time, never knowing when Daddy would explode with another burst of complaints. That was the year Daddy started to criticize my weight, too. He looked at me with such displeasure in his eyes that I felt my insides twist, turn, and shrivel. I tried to turn away, but then

APRIL SHADOWS

came his words, which were like tiny knives poking at my heart.

"Your face looks like a balloon about to explode. Maybe we'll have to have your mouth sewn shut for a month and feed you through a straw like someone with a broken jaw," he said, bringing the blood so quickly into my cheeks I'm sure I looked as if I had a high fever.

It got so I was afraid to put my fork into anything on my plate. My hand actually shook, and my stomach tightened until I could barely breathe. A few times, I actually threw up everything I had eaten. Mama got very angry at him then. She widened her eyes and stretched her lips so thin they turned white, but even that didn't stop him. Brenda protested on my behalf, and when she did, Daddy turned his anger and criticism on her by saying, "What kind of a big sister are you? You should be on her back more than anyone and especially more than me. You know what it means to be physically fit and how being overweight can cause so many health problems."

Brenda was an excellent athlete. At five-foot-eleven in her junior year, she was the star of the girls' varsity basketball team and the girls' volleyball team. She had already broken all the school's scoring records. Her picture was almost always in the weekend paper's sports pages. Scouts had come from colleges to watch her play. There was talk that she might have an opportunity to play for the United States volleyball team in the Olympics. Other fathers attended the games and sat watching with proud smiles on their faces. About the time Daddy became our own Mr. Hyde, he stopped going altogether and then started to ridicule Brenda by telling her things like, "You're not going to be a professional athlete. Why waste your time?" He told her he thought her grades could be higher, even though she ran a good B+ average with all her extracurricular activities.

"If you didn't waste your time with all these games, you'd have As instead," he said. "It's about time you got serious about your life and stopped all this childish nonsense."

He had never called it that, had never tried to discourage her from participating.

When he spoke to her like this, Brenda's eyes would become glassy with tears, but she would not cry or respond. Sometimes, she could be harder than he was, and she would stand there as still and as cold as a petrified tree while he rained his lectures and complaints down around her. She looked as if she had turned off her ears and turned her eyes completely around. I cowered in the corner or ran up to my room, crying as much for her as I did for myself and Mama.

Because of all this, our family dinners turned into silent movies. The tinkle of glasses, dishes, and silverware was like thunder. Brenda wouldn't talk about her games anymore, and Mama was afraid to bring up any subject because Daddy would either be sarcastic or complain. He would sit there scowling or rubbing his temples. If Mama asked him what was wrong, he would just grunt and say, "Nothing, nothing. Don't start nagging me."

I kept my eyes down. I was afraid to breathe too loudly.

After dinner, Daddy often retreated as quickly as he could to his law office, claiming he had work he had to finish, and on weekdays he was gone before any of us had gotten up for breakfast. He never used to do that. Mornings were a happy time for us once. We greeted one another as though we had been apart for weeks.

Soon there were days when he didn't come home at night at all, claiming he had to make trips to service clients or deal with business matters. It seemed he would find any excuse he could to avoid being with us, and when he had to be with us, he was there only the minimum amount of time possible. Although Mama was ashamed to tell us, there were nights when he didn't come to bed. Instead, he claimed he had fallen asleep in his office on the sofa.

At first, Mama thought that he had found a lover and he wanted to get rid of us. She theorized that in his eyes, we had become a burden, dragging him down into waters that aged and weakened him. She was sure he blamed us for every gray hair, every wrinkle, every new ache.

"Men go through their own sort of change of life," she rationalized. "It actually terrifies them. He'll get over it," she said. It sounded more like a prayer she wasn't getting answered, because neither Brenda nor I saw any signs of his getting over it. On the contrary, he was getting worse.

Mama spent hours and hours sitting in what we called her knitting chair, where she made our sweaters, gloves, and hats, only now she wasn't knitting. She was just staring at the wall or through the television set, no matter what we were all watching. She didn't laugh; she didn't cry. Her face, the face that people called *the porcelain face,* began to show tiny cracks around her eyes and her quivering lips. The sadder she became, the angrier Brenda grew, and the more frightened I was.

Eventually, we found out why Daddy had turned into Mr. Hyde. The revelation was a bright flash that lit up all our dark confusion. It was like lightning piercing the walls of our home and making the air sizzle around us. All of our lives were caught in mid-sentence. Our hearts tightened like fists in our chests. Even our tears were caught unaware and too far down, buried under layers of anger and disappointment, to come quickly enough to the surface. I thought the whole world had stopped in surprise and shock. Everything I had thought real turned out to be illusion, and everything I thought was just an illusion turned out to be real.

The hardest thing for us to learn and accept was that Daddy had done all he had done, said all the nasty things he had said, avoided us as much as he had avoided us because he loved us so much. To love someone so much that you would rather hurt them now than have them unhappy forever is a love so powerful it is beyond understanding.

Mama felt betrayed because he hadn't told her, Brenda hated herself for the things she had done and said to him, and I wondered what the difference really was between love and hate.

It took me a long time to find out, and I'm still not totally sure I know.

1

Sunny Memories

I used to feel as if it were Christmas every day, all day long, at our house. Mama's voice was so full of happiness whenever she spoke. Anyone who saw how we all woke and greeted one another in the morning would think we had expectations of gifts around a tree. Laughter and giggles rang like silver bells, and Mama's smile beamed so brightly that there were never dark days, even when the Tennessee sky was totally overcast and bruised, angry-looking clouds threatened to drench us in a bone-chilling rain.

I wasn't afraid to pretend, to dream, and to imagine anything. I'd blink and see sunlight glimmering off mounds of snow that looked like coconut, and Daddy seemed to know that those sorts of days, days that threatened to depress us, were days when he should bring home surprises, whether it be a bouquet of Mama's favorite baby roses, a new doll for me, or some game for Brenda. Back then, he bought her a Ping-Pong table and rackets, a Wiffle ball and bat, a new tennis racket, and a set of golf clubs. She played every sport well, even though she eventually favored basketball and volleyball because of her height and speed. As soon as Daddy realized that, he put up a basketball net and backboard in our driveway.

Mama said that back then, his friends kidded him about trying to turn his daughter into the son he didn't have. Mama and Daddy had stopped having children after I was born. I never asked why. Brenda told me it was because Daddy wouldn't be able to stand having three girls. He was already outnumbered so much. However, we couldn't help believing it had something to do with Mama's health, because I had been such a difficult birth, and in the end, she had to have a cesarean delivery. In the back of my mind, I couldn't prevent myself from thinking that if it weren't for me, Daddy might have had the son he wanted.

No one ever made me feel guilty about it. No one even so much as hinted at my birth being the problem. Despite it all, we were truly the perfect family in the eyes of all our neighbors and family friends.

I used to wish that we would be frozen in time. While most of my friends were hoping the hands would spin quickly over the faces of their clocks and watches so that they could drive their own cars, be able to stay out later and later on weekends, have dramatic heart-shattering romances, and collect boyfriends like butterflies, pinning their pictures on the walls, I tried to tread time the way I would tread water. I wanted Mama and Daddy to be forever as young as they were, still passionate about each other, always holding hands or hugging and kissing.

At an early age, I noticed that the parents of my friends didn't stand as close to each other, didn't touch or look at each other as much as my parents did. I would hover close by, believing that just being in their shadow, bathing in their laughter and their smiles, was enough to protect me forever and ever.

Brenda wasn't as sensitive to all this as I was, and she certainly wasn't interested in freezing time. She was anxious about trying out for college varsity teams and competing seriously in games where she could excel and win the appreciation and interest of people who could further her athletic career. Adolescence seemed to be more of a nuisance. She would get absolutely impossible when she had her period. On more than one occasion, she wondered aloud why boys' lives weren't equally interrupted. Why weren't their rhythms changed, their energy sapped, their moods depressed?

"If I could change my sex," she once whispered to me, "I'd do it in a heartbeat."

The very thought of such a thing made my own heart race. I had nightmares in which Brenda grew a mustache, but more frightening than anything was the idea of her having a boy's sex organ. Once, I dreamed of surprising her in the bathroom after she had taken a shower and seeing her cover herself just a second or two too late. That dream woke me, and I sat up quickly, my heart pounding, my skin clammy. I was only twelve then. Brenda was nearly fifteen and close to five-foot-eleven inches tall. She took after Daddy's side of the family. He was six-foot-three and his father had been six-foot-five. Mama was five-foot-ten herself.

I had fears of being so short people would think I wasn't really a part of the family or that I had been malformed. My body grew out more than up. I had bigger bones than Brenda and already wider hips. My weight went first into my thighs and spread around to my rear. It crept up my back and thickened my waist. By the time I was twelve, I was one hundred fifty pounds. Even though I was overweight from the age of seven on, neither Mama nor Daddy made much of it. Mama used to say, "She'll grow out of it as she gets older and taller."

I grew older, but I wasn't growing all that much taller. I was still five-foot-three, and it began to look as if when I had wished time would freeze, it had, but it had frozen only for me.

Another reason I felt out of place was that I was not half the athlete Brenda was. She didn't like to play any sport with me because I was so poor at it. I was no match for her in Ping-Pong, and I was pathetic when it came to basketball, half the time not even reaching the rim with a shot, and when I threw a baseball—or anything, for that matter—she would complain that I threw just like a girl.

What did that mean? I wondered. I *was* a girl.

Board games were my specialty. I could give her a challenge at checkers or backgammon, but she never had the patience to sit for hours playing board games. Through rain and snow, wind and gray skies, Brenda would be outside shooting baskets, practicing her putt for golf, or just running to stay in shape. She was driven. Daddy used to say proudly, "That girl has drive. She loves competition."

Brenda did love competition, and she loved winning the most. She never played for the fun of it. When she and Daddy played basketball, she would work hard at defeating him. He was good, too, so it was always a battle. If he so much as seemed to let her win, she would rant at him and tell him she didn't need his charity. That would get him angry.

"Charity, huh?" he would puff, and they would play harder, play for keeps, and if she beat him, which she often did, her face would fill with a satisfied glow that made him shake his head as if he didn't understand her at all, as if she weren't his daughter but some stranger.

Daddy had been a very good athlete in both high school and college. He had his certificates and his trophies, and staying in good health was very important to him. He was always exercising, claiming the physical activity helped him to be a sharper thinker and gave him more energy when others were faltering. In that regard, he was far closer to Brenda than he was to me, but when I was younger, he did think I was cuter, more lovable. He called me his panda bear, because I had Mama's coal-black hair and alabaster complexion, with ebony eyes he said were panda bear button eyes. One of the first stuffed toys he bought me was a panda bear. I kept it with me in bed, lying against the pillows when the bed was made. I kept it under the blanket with me when I went to sleep. I called it Mr. Panda and often carried on long conversations with it, rattling away as if I really expected the stuffed toy would suddenly come to life, like toys in the movies, and reply.

Brenda made fun of that when she heard me. Mama thought it was cute, and at one time, so did Daddy, but when he became Mr. Hyde, he mocked it and told me I should put my panda bear in a carton in a closet or give it to a younger girl.

"Where are your *real* friends?" he would demand. "You don't get invited to parties or anyone's house, and do you know why, April? I'll tell you why. You're too overweight. You won't have any social life. Go on a diet," he ordered.

He wasn't wrong. I didn't have any social life. I had never had a boyfriend, and the only friends I had at school were other girls who had never had boyfriends and had none now. No one asked us to dances or parties, and what bothered me a little was the fact that I had never had a heart-throbbing crush on any boy, either. It was a sensitive area for Brenda as well, and she was quick to come to my defense.

"People should be friends with her because of who she is, not because of what she looks like," Brenda told Daddy when he criticized me.

"Oh? And who is she?" he countered. "Mrs. Panda Bear?"

I could hardly breathe. My throat tightened, and my chest constricted. *Could a girl my age get a heart attack?* I wondered.

I quickly retreated to my room and closed the door. I wanted to be like Brenda and never cry in front of him, but it was harder for me. Maybe I just had more tears inside me than she had. Thank goodness I had my own room, my own sanctuary. He had stopped barging in on me after I was about ten. Mama had told him I was a young lady and that he had to recognize the fact. He wasn't upset about it.

In fact, his face lit up with happiness at the time, and he nodded at the three of us around the dinner table, declaring he had three beautiful women in his home. How could he go so quickly from that sort of a daddy to Mr. Hyde?

I imagined all sorts of fantastic answers. His body had become inhabited by some evil spirit, a poltergeist, or maybe even an extraterrestrial. Someone had cloned him, and the clone had an entirely different personality. Or maybe it was just as Mama had told us when it all began. "He is being this way now because he is afraid you will be too weak or we won't be perfect enough. He doesn't mean to be so cruel. It's just tough love."

Brenda smirked at that.

"Yeah, right," she said, which was always her way of saying *That's stupid*.

Her room was right next to mine. We lived in a sprawling ranch-style home with bay windows in the dining room and large picture windows in the living room. Brenda's and my bedrooms were on one side, and Daddy and Mama's master bedroom was on the other. Daddy had a small wood-paneled office off his bedroom, the living room was large, and the dining room was right next to the kitchen so that Mama had a pass-through window. Our furnishings were all contemporary. Mama liked what she called the clean, simple look. None of it was inexpensive, but in those days, Daddy rarely, if ever, complained about anything she bought. After he became Mr. Hyde, nothing she bought was right or sensible, even down to the brand of milk.

When Brenda and I were growing up, money was never a concern. However, neither she nor I was wasteful or ungrateful for the things we had. We never took anything for granted or whined for expensive toys or clothes. Brenda never even asked Daddy to get her a car when she was sixteen, even though most of her friends and teammates had their own cars, even ones who came from families far less wealthy than ours. She passed her driving test, got her license, and drove Mama's car whenever Mama told her she could. She rarely, if ever, asked Daddy for his car. He used to offer it to her, but when he became Mr. Hyde, he

wouldn't, even if he had no use for it and it meant
Brenda had to beg someone to pick her up for a special
practice or a game. A few times, she had to take the
bus.

Because our house was bigger than most nearby and
we had a larger lot in an upscale neighborhood of
Hickory, a suburban community ninety miles from
downtown Memphis, people and our classmates assumed we were very rich. Daddy was a successful
business attorney, as his father had been. I couldn't remember my paternal grandfather, because he died of
heart failure before I was two, and my paternal grandmother had died four years before that of cancer.
Daddy lost his older sister, Marissa, to cancer as well. I
was too young at the time to remember much detail,
and Mama shielded me more from the sadness, but
Brenda could recall how our aunt grew gaunt and pale.
She said she was like a room full of light darkening
and darkening.

"Every time I saw her, she looked smaller, but her
eyes grew bigger. It was like her body was becoming
more and more surprised by what was happening to it.
It was very weird," she told me. "It got so I was afraid
of going to visit her with Daddy and Mama. I envied
you because you were so oblivious and protected.
Daddy wouldn't take you along to visit like he took
me, so you didn't see firsthand how very sad he was
about it all. He tried not to be sad. He told me sadness
hardens like tar on your soul, and you carry the weight
of it forever."

Aunt Marissa was married but had never had children, and we had little contact now with her husband, my uncle Granger. He had left our area and
moved to Oregon, where he met another woman and
remarried.

Despite all this sorrow, Daddy held on to his optimism and happy personality. He had his own firm
with two junior partners and was seemingly always
busy. We took at least two vacations a year. Before
his Mr. Hyde days, Daddy was a skier and had taught
both Brenda and me how to ski. Mama was okay at
it, but almost immediately, Brenda was on the advanced slopes with Daddy, and I was left with Mama
to navigate along with the other insecure skiers and
children. We went to Aspen and Sun Valley, and
once, we all even went to Austria during a Christmas
holiday.

They took us to Disneyland and to Universal City in
California. We went to the Caribbean, where Daddy
and Brenda went scuba diving, and we took a train trip
through the Northwest and Canada. There was a pile of
vacation pictures in the living room and dozens of
family videos on shelves and in drawers.

Our Christmases and Easter holidays were always
happy and grand. The front of our house was decorated
with lights, as were the trees. Mama would have a
party for her and Daddy's friends and business
acquaintances. There was even a time when Daddy
pretended to be Santa Claus and surprised me on
Christmas morning. I was only four. That was when he
gave me Mr. Panda.

Mama loved to cook and bake. She had gone to
school to be a paralegal, and that was how she and
Daddy had met, but after Brenda was born, she
stopped working. She wasn't unhappy about it, and she
never thought of herself as some shut-away housewife.
She was active in community charity events and fre-
quently held teas and dinner parties. It seemed there
was never a dull moment or an empty hour in our
house.

Sometimes, I felt as if we truly lived a storybook life, and every day brought a new chapter full of fun and excitement and surprises. If any family was a success, ours truly was. So many of my school friends came from broken families or one-parent families, and a few lived with their grandparents. If they didn't say it, I could read it in their eyes when they saw us all together at a restaurant or at the mall or just walking in the street. *You're lucky. You can't fail.*

I wasn't as good a student as Brenda was, even with all her extracurricular activities, but I wasn't a poor student, either. There was always an expectation about me. I would lose weight; I would get better grades; I would burst out with some talent. I'd be socially popular. Soon. It was always soon.

Soon wasn't to come soon enough. Before it could, the darkness was to close in on us, folding itself over our happy home and then seeping in under the doors, through the windows, down the chimney, until it entered our very hearts.

If I were forced to pick any special moment and say, "There, that's when I remember it all becoming too hard to bear," I'd pick the day Daddy forgot it was Brenda's birthday—and her sixteenth at that! I knew Mama had reminded him enough times about it. I even overheard her tell him what she was planning to buy her. It was a very expensive mountain bike.

Brenda didn't want a Sweet Sixteen party. She was never that sort of girl. Oh, she enjoyed pretty things and pretty clothes and had her favorite music, but she never seemed distracted by any of it. I remembered when Daddy thought that was a wonderful trait. "It's good to be like Brenda," he would tell me. "It's good to be dedicated and fixed on a goal, to know your priorities and live your life accordingly."

I supposed he was telling me that because I didn't have any apparent priorities or interests, except that I did like to read. In fact, I loved to read. I could get so lost in a book that I'd lose track of time and even place. Both Daddy and Mama used to laugh remembering when they saw me lying outside on a chaise longue reading and not at all aware that it was raining. It wasn't a heavy rain, just a sprinkle, but surely enough to stain the pages of the book.

"April is truly into the book when she reads it," Mama said. "She's beyond the page, past the paper and ink."

Now, Daddy called that foolish and said I was absentminded, even lame-brained.

"Only dogs would stay out in the rain like that. Even cats are smarter," he would comment should Mama ever remind him of that time. He came very close to calling me retarded, and of course, I hurried away to hide my tears behind the closed door of my room.

I was so angry at him those days that I was happy he had forgotten it was Brenda's birthday. *Good,* I thought, *Now he's the one who looks like he's lame-brained, not me.*

He had come home expecting that Mama had prepared dinner and we would be eating almost immediately. Instead, of course, she had made reservations at what used to be our favorite family restaurant, Dickson's Steak House. She told Brenda and me to get dressed and ready, anticipating Daddy's arrival. She did comment that she wasn't sure about his exact arrival time because he hadn't returned her phone call to the office and all his secretary would say was that he was in conference. She left a message and jumped to go to the phone every time it rang, but it was never Daddy.

The three of us, all dressed and ready, sat in the living room waiting. Mama looked nervously at the clock.

"What could be holding him up?" she muttered.

"Why doesn't he call you?" Brenda demanded. "It's just plain inconsiderate."

Brenda's face had changed so from her younger days. It used to be rounder, more like mine, but with her growth spurt, as Mama liked to call it, her face narrowed and seemed even to lengthen. I suppose her best feature was her eyes. They weren't quite as dark as mine. They were almost charcoal but clear and striking and almond-shaped. Her hair was more dark brown than black. She wore very little makeup, barely some lipstick, never cared about trimming her eyebrows, and rarely, if ever, wore earrings. She was wearing some tonight and did brush her hair, which she had let grow a little longer, more, I thought, to please Mama than herself.

Tall and lean like Daddy, she had a small bosom, long legs, and long arms. Her fingers weren't exceptionally long, but she had a very strong grip. I could see it in the faces of the men with whom she shook hands whenever she was introduced to someone. They were always surprised at the strength in her hand.

Part of her ability to focus was the intensity in her eyes when she fixed them on something, whether it be a basketball net or a hurdle to jump on the running track. She could apply this same firm attention to people as well, and most could not look her in the eyes.

"Now, Brenda," Mama began, preparing to roll out one of her many excuses for Daddy's current disturbing behavior.

"No, it's just plain rude for him to do this to us, Mama," she insisted.

"Oh, I'm sure he has something terribly heavy on his mind. Some of his cases are so complicated, Brenda. We just don't appreciate how hard he works. He's so good at what he does, we take it all for granted," Mama said.

"Yeah, right," Brenda replied, and folded her arms under her bosom so tightly her shoulders arched. She glared at the doorway.

Mama glanced again at the clock.

"We're never going to make that reservation, you know," Brenda muttered. "Call his office and see if he left, at least," she insisted.

"I've called twice," Mama revealed, quickly swinging her eyes away.

"Twice? Since when?"

"It doesn't matter."

"He can't be that busy that he can't take out two minutes," Brenda pursued.

Mama was silent. Her face was in a battle, fighting to maintain its composure. She closed her eyes and took a deep breath. Finally, we heard the garage door go up.

Mama smiled and stood up.

The door to the garage was right off the pantry behind the kitchen. We all waited, our eyes fixed on the living room doorway. He didn't appear.

"Matt?" Mama called.

"In a minute," he said sharply.

He was walking down the hallway to his office. We could hear him. Mama winked at us and waited. Brenda

looked at her watch and sighed loudly. I hadn't realized I was holding my breath until I felt the ache in my
chest and sucked in some air.

"What the hell's going on here?" we heard.

His footsteps grew louder and faster, and a moment
later, he was in the doorway. He stood there looking at
all of us, the confusion clear on his face.

Daddy was always a handsome man. He had my
coal-black hair and my ebony eyes with his dark complexion that gave him the look of a man who worked
in the sunlight and not in an office. His chin was sharp,
with a firm, masculine mouth and a perfectly shaped
straight nose.

"What's happening here? Why are you all dressed
and sitting in the living room? Why haven't you made
dinner, Nora?"

Mama laughed nervously, hoping that he was kidding and that he would suddenly burst out with
"Happy Birthday" and reveal some surprise gift besides the mountain bike they had bought her. He was
always doing something like that.

"Well?"

Her smile sank into her face.

"It's Brenda's sixteenth birthday, Matt. Remember,
I told you this morning we have reservations at Dickson's Steak House."

His eyes blinked quickly, and then he turned on
Mama. "No, you didn't tell me that."

"I did, Matt."

"I said you didn't. I think I'd remember something
like that. You've been doing this sort of thing more and
more lately, making plans without first checking with
me. I've made arrangements to meet Bob Peterson at
eight back at the office. We have depositions on the
Morgan case to prepare."

"But . . . you certainly knew it was Brenda's birthday," she said.

He glanced at Brenda.

She stood up sharply. "I don't care about any stupid birthday dinner, anyway," she said. She put her head down and charged out of the living room.

My heart was pounding.

"But . . ." Mama looked at Daddy.

"Well, I can't help it," he said. "We'll have a birthday dinner tomorrow night. What's the difference? Just put on a steak for me here." He turned and left Mama and me staring at each other.

She pulled herself together quickly, sucking back her tears and taking a breath so deep I thought it had originated in her feet.

"April, do me a favor and cancel our reservation at Dickson's, please," she said. "Then come help me set the table."

"Mama, this is terrible. It's Brenda's Sweet Sixteen dinner!"

"Just do as I ask, please," she said.

She turned quickly so I wouldn't see her tears. I was glad about that. I didn't want her to see mine. I made the phone call and then set the table while she worked quickly to prepare a dinner for us. I could hear her sniffles, but I didn't ask her if she was crying or say anything. Instead, I went to Brenda's room and knocked on her door.

"What is it?" she snapped.

"It's just me."

"What do you want?" she asked without opening the door.

"Mama's making us dinner. We canceled the reservation at the restaurant."

"I don't care."

"I'm sorry, Brenda."

I stood by the door, waiting, listening. Brenda rarely ever showed me any sadness. I used to wish and wish I could be as strong as she was, but Mama once said something I never forgot. She said, "Brenda cries on the inside, and when you keep your tears inside you all the time, you have a better chance of drowning in your sadness."

"Can I give you your present from me?" I asked through the closed door.

She was quiet.

Then the door opened, and I saw she had changed back into her jeans and the school sweatshirt that Daddy said was practically her second skin because she wore it so much. When he had first said it, it was like a funny joke, but now it was more like a bitter criticism.

"I'm not in the birthday mood, April. I'm sorry," she said, her arms folded, her eyelids lowered like tiny flags of surrender.

"I'd still like to give you your present. I was going to hide it in the car and go out and get it while we were eating at the restaurant."

She swung her eyes, and then her shoulders relaxed. "Okay, give it to me if you want."

"I'll be right back," I said, and ran out to the garage where I had it hidden. Then I returned to her room and handed it to her.

She sat on her bed and opened the box. With Mama's help, I had bought her a beautiful athletic suit. It had black with spice trim boot-bottom pants, a black cap-sleeve sport top, and a matching jacket.

"This is great, April," she said, holding up the jacket. "It's beautiful."

"I picked it out myself," I said proudly.

"You did great, April," she said. She looked at me a moment and then reached out, pulled me to her, and hugged me harder and closer than she had ever done. She held me longer, too. I had the feeling she wanted to keep me from seeing any tears in her eyes.

Mama called to us.

"I don't feel very hungry," Brenda muttered. She rose and put the athletic suit on her dresser.

"Mama will cry if you don't come to dinner," I said.

"I know."

We left her room and went to the dining room. I helped Mama bring out the vegetables, the bread, and the steak she had prepared. Brenda got the jug of cold water, the butter, and some steak sauce Daddy liked. He still had not appeared.

"Matt," she called to him. "Dinner's ready."

"I'm on the phone," we heard.

Mama sat, and we all stared at the food on the table. It was nearly a good five minutes before Daddy appeared, hurrying to the table. He stabbed a steak, put it on his plate without speaking, and then cut it and grimaced.

"It's overdone, Nora," he moaned.

"No, it's not, Matt. It's just how you always eat it and how I always prepare it."

"I know when it's overdone," he insisted. He started to serve himself the vegetables.

I reached for a steak and then some bread, and when he put down the vegetable dish, I scooped out some of the mixed vegetables. Brenda just sat staring across the table at Daddy, who looked very distracted and in deep thought. Mama hadn't put anything on her plate, either. Daddy looked at her.

"What now, Nora?"

Her lips quivered. "We don't even have a birthday cake for her," she said.

He looked at Brenda as if he once again had just remembered it was her birthday. "We'll have one to-morrow," he said. Then he glanced at me. "Not that everyone needs it."

"I don't need it," Brenda said. "I don't need any-thing from you," she added.

"Brenda," Mama said.

"Don't get smart," Daddy warned.

Brenda looked away, and then she suddenly changed her whole demeanor, reached for a steak, and began serving herself as if she were famished. I knew she was doing it just to annoy Daddy and show him nothing he could do would change her. Mama held her breath.

We ate in silence. Daddy ate very fast, his eyes avoiding us. When he was finished, he literally jumped to his feet and mumbled about having to return to the offices in downtown Hickory.

"Do you really have to go back, Matt?" Mama asked him softly.

"What?" he asked her, acting as if he hadn't heard or had already forgotten the question.

"I'm just wondering if there isn't a way for you to postpone the work one night. We can still go some-where to have dessert and celebrate."

"Of course I really do. What do you think? I'd go back if I didn't?"

Mama said nothing. I could see she was having trouble swallowing. "Don't you want to give her our present first, Matt?" she managed.

"Our present?"

"You know," she said, nodding. "In the back of the garage."

"Oh. Well, you take care of it," he said.

Before she could argue, Daddy left the room, and then we heard the door open and close to the garage.

I looked at Brenda, who looked at me.

We both realized it at the same time.

He hadn't even said happy birthday.

Not once.

2

Mr. Hyde Days

I suppose the thing that made Daddy's new behavior at home and toward us scary was the fact that we had very little immediate family anymore. Both Mama and Daddy came from families that had only two children. Mama had an unmarried brother, who was now an entertainer, a traveling magician who called himself the Amazing Palaver. Although he was unmarried, he had a female assistant we simply knew as Destiny, and we all assumed she was his love interest. Destiny was one of the most unusual names we had ever heard, but Mama imagined it was because she was an entertainer, too. We had never met her, and we didn't see Uncle Palaver often, but when we did visit, we enjoyed seeing him and spending time with him. Whenever he visited us, he said Destiny was taking advantage of the down time to visit her family as well. Up until Daddy's Mr. Hyde days, he enjoyed Uncle Palaver, too. Even though he didn't approve of Uncle Palaver's lifestyle and career, he always found him amusing and sweet, and at times Daddy even had helped him financially.

Mama was very appreciative of that. Uncle Palaver was three years younger than she was, but they always had been close while they were growing up and remained in close contact even when she was in college and he was on the road trying to be an actor, a comedian, or whatever. Mama and Uncle Palaver had lost their father in a car accident when Mama was twenty-two and Uncle Palaver was nineteen. For a while, he remained at home with their mother, caring for her. She was the only grandparent Brenda and I had ever gotten to know. However, four years ago, she suffered a serious stroke and was now living in a nursing home that catered to people her age with her sort of maladies. We visited her whenever we could, but over the last six months, Brenda and I had gone to see her only once. She had reached a point where she didn't know whether or not we were actually there. We heard that from time to time, Uncle Palaver had visited her and put on shows for all the patients at the facility.

The only other relatives with whom we had any contact were second and third cousins who were children and grandchildren of our grandparents' brothers and sisters. We would see one another at weddings and funerals, and everyone would always exchange telephone numbers and addresses and promise to stay in touch. Few actually made any effort to do so.

In the end, we had only each other, and with Daddy acting as he was acting, the three of us felt like some poor Eskimos left floating on a layer of ice. The winds were cold; the days were bleak. Happiness and joy became like air seeping out of a tire, leaving us flat and lost in confusion and sadness.

With that as our setting, all three of us were overjoyed to hear from Uncle Palaver and learn that he was stopping by for a day or two on his way to what he called a "gig" in Raleigh, North Carolina, where he was going to meet up with Destiny after she had visited her family. Mama had had little to smile about during the past few weeks, and just talking to her brother on the phone was enough to restore some of the familiar and cherished gleam in her eyes and blush in her cheeks. She began immediately to plan a wonderful dinner for the day Uncle Palaver arrived.

In my heart of hearts, I hoped and prayed that Uncle Palaver's visit would soften Daddy and perhaps restore him to how he had been before all this meanness and avoidance had begun. Surely, he wouldn't be unpleasant while Uncle Palaver was here. No matter what was bothering him, he was never one to wear his heart on his sleeve, as Mama would say. He hated watching all those television shows on which people would reveal their most intimate and private information.

"The next thing we'll see is a show with a camera and microphones in Catholic confessional booths," he said. "The priest will turn to the audience and get a consensus about what punishment or acts of contrition the sinner should perform."

If anything bothered Daddy, he would never show it in front of other people, and on those rare occasions when we had private family problems, he would die before revealing the slightest hint of it at a dinner party Mama prepared or any other sort of social gathering.

"We're giving up so much of ourselves when we give up our privacy issues," he told us all at dinner once. "People don't even know what self-respect is anymore. They should feel shame and keep their problems to themselves. Being ashamed about something isn't all that terrible. It has some purpose. It works as a deterrent. Nowadays, kids aren't ashamed about poor grades or misbehavior. Their parents aren't ashamed about being caught in adultery, getting divorced, going bankrupt. They just visit one of these talk shows and spill their guts in front of millions of psychological and emotional voyeurs. I'd rather be caught dead," he muttered.

Mama agreed but had to admit she watched some of those shows. Brenda was more like Daddy and thought he was one-hundred-percent correct.

"People lay their troubles on you all the time in school," she said. "The locker-room gossip about parents, boyfriends, and brothers and sisters sickens me."

"Hey, there's a new show," Daddy piped up, laughing. *"The Locker Room."*

Brenda laughed, too.

Those dinners and days were beginning to feel like distant dreams.

In any case, we all felt confident that Daddy would behave more like the old Daddy we knew and loved when Uncle Palaver was visiting. Brenda said it would be like a prison camp being spruced up for an inspection by some international human rights agency.

"Maybe he'll smile again, but it will be like a mask, I'm afraid," she predicted.

As it turned out, I wished he had worn any sort of smile, mask or not. When he heard Uncle Palaver was coming, he muttered, "That's all we need now," and stormed off to his home office, closing the door as he had done so many nights recently. He would remain in there until bedtime. Because Brenda and I were in our rooms doing homework or Brenda was at an away game, Mama ended up sitting and watching television for hours alone. A number of times, I pretended to have completed my homework when I hadn't, just so I could keep her company. It broke my heart knowing she was sitting by herself, trying to knit or do some needlepoint project, the light of the television flashing over her. I failed a math exam and a history exam because I didn't study.

Actually, my grades, though not anything to rave about before, took a real nosedive during these days. I couldn't help being distracted in class, missing notes, not listening to the teachers. Something Daddy had said or done the night before usually haunted me all the following day. My best friend in all the world, Jamie Stanley, thought I had grown bored with her because nothing she said got me very excited or interested. Finally, one day when she asked me a question and I didn't respond, she slapped her books on the cafeteria table where we were sitting and told me she wasn't going to bother talking to me or calling me anymore. She picked herself up and moved to sit with some other students, and suddenly, I felt more alone than I thought possible.

Uncle Palaver's arrival loomed larger and larger on my hope and wish meter. I couldn't wait for him to come. He always brought Brenda and me some special and unique present he had found on his travels. I had an elephant that raised its trunk and roared when I pressed a button on its leg, a lobster that sang "Sea of Love", and a canary that chirped every time I was a half foot in front of it. Brenda had a bubble machine, a handheld massage machine that relaxed aching and stiff muscles, and, most cherished of all, a volleyball signed by the women's volleyball team from the last Olympics. Daddy expressed doubts about its authenticity.

"So much of what your uncle does and says is based on illusion," he remarked, but Brenda never showed any doubt about it and exhibited it proudly in her room.

But lately, it wasn't the gifts we welcomed as much as Uncle Palaver's cheerful, childlike demeanor. He had become a very good magician and could do wonders with a deck of cards and sleight of hand. Like a true magician, he said he would take the secret of how he did his tricks to his grave. Most exciting was to hear his stories from his travels. There didn't appear to be a state he hadn't visited. He had even gone to Alaska and entertained soldiers on some army base.

Uncle Palaver wasn't making a lot of money, but he was no longer in any financial trouble and actually had come to repay Daddy for a loan he had given him two years ago. From time to time, he sent Mama newspaper clippings about his Amazing Palaver show, and she had pasted them all in an album. At last, we finally had some pictures of Destiny, too. All of us were surprised to learn that she was African American. Uncle Palaver had never mentioned that fact. In all the pictures, she looked as tall as Uncle Palaver and very sexy, usually in a tight outfit or even a bathing suit.

"No wonder he's doing better on the road," Daddy quipped when he saw pictures that included Destiny. "In some of those boondock towns, that's pornographic. I guess your parents would be surprised."

Mama hushed him and told him never to say such things in front of Uncle Palaver or anyone, for that matter. Whenever she could take out her album to show one of her friends, she would. She never mentioned that Destiny might be Uncle Palaver's girlfriend, although it was easy to see people thought it. Whatever, it made him more interesting. I never imagined Daddy would be in the slightest way jealous of that. He was so accomplished and successful, how could he ever be threatened by the small accomplishments and attention Uncle Palaver had achieved? Lately, though, he was beginning to sound that sort of a discordant note whenever he referred to Uncle Palaver.

"You blow him up too much, Nora," he warned. "People will expect to see him on television or something."

"Well, that could happen someday, couldn't it, Matt?" she asked hopefully.

"Yeah. If he stands on one, it could happen," Daddy said dryly.

I didn't think that was at all fair. I could see Uncle Palaver appearing on television someday. First, he was a very handsome, charismatic man with wavy dark brown hair that was Mama's shade and hazel eyes with green specks. He had her small nose and was lean and tall like Brenda. The childish gleam in his eyes gave him a charm that brought a smile to the faces of many people as soon as they saw him, onstage or otherwise. He had a way of reminding everyone of their childhood faiths, their own imaginings and wonder. Sleeveless, his hands empty, he would reach up and pluck a coin out of the air as effortlessly as someone plucking a berry from a bush.

"If you can do that all day, you'll be rich in no time," Daddy once remarked in jovial tones.

"I'm rich already, Matt," Uncle Palaver had said.

Daddy had raised his eyes and smiled skeptically, but I knew in my heart what Uncle Palaver meant. He had his freedom, his love of what he was finally doing, his joy in pleasing and bringing smiles to the faces of the people he met. Yes, his life was very different from Daddy's now. He didn't have many responsibilities, no responsibility to anyone but himself since he wasn't

married to Destiny. However, he had taken on a different sort of burden. He had become a happy daddy for
thousands of children, a loving brother to thousands of
women and men. His audiences had become his extended family, and when he performed, he bathed in
their laughter and wonder. That made him feel very
wealthy.

He had no home as such, just a mailbox. Instead, he
and Destiny lived in a motor home with "The Amazing
Palaver" written in bold red on both sides, the image of
a top hat and a rabbit peeking out just under the words.
The motor home was his most expensive possession. It
was about twenty-eight feet long, built on a van frame
with an attached cab section. It had a sleeping bunk
atop the cab in addition to the bedroom in the rear.
Last year, Mama and Daddy let me sleep in the bunk.
It was like camping out, even though it was only in our
driveway.

When I was alone in there, I did peek into the closet
and saw Destiny's dresses, shoes, even the bathing suit
that she was in when the pictures were taken. I saw her
makeup and a collection of wigs. She seemed to have
twice the amount of clothing and shoes that Uncle
Palaver had. There was a good picture of the two of
them on the dresser in his bedroom. It was a closer
shot and clearer than the newspaper clippings. I hated
to say anything, but when I looked at her in the picture,
I didn't think she was as attractive as she was in the
newspaper.

I enjoyed being in the motor home. There was a
kitchen and a little dining area, but Uncle Palaver
could push a button and one side of the motor home
slid out and expanded to the size of the living room
and dining room. More magic, I thought. Of course, it
had its own bathroom equipped with a small shower

stall and a small tub. He had a television set that worked off an antenna on the roof.

Daddy had helped him with the down payment for the motor home, and it was that money that Uncle Palaver was returning on this trip. He had told Mama, and she had told Daddy, hoping that would please him about Uncle Palaver's visit.

"He didn't have to come here to hand me the money," Daddy said instead. "Why didn't he wire it or send it as soon as he had it?"

"He just wants to thank you in person, Matt."

"I can't even remember how much I gave him and how much interest I lost doing it," Daddy muttered, more to himself, I thought. He realized it immediately and snapped his head back. "I just hope he's not returning it and then asking for another loan," he declared.

Daddy's attitude made Mama very nervous. "I hope he doesn't say anything like that when your uncle is here," Mama told me later. "Entertainers are insecure as it is. They're so dependent on how people react to them and so sensitive to any negative looks or words. Warner was always a very sensitive child," she said.

That was Uncle Palaver's real name, Warner, Warner Prescott. She told me he always had hated his real name because it made him sound too pretentious. When he became a magician and reinvented himself, he loved his new name. He signed everything *Palaver* and even had Daddy change his name legally for him.

"I guess he thinks he's competing with Kreskin," Daddy remarked, but gladly did it. Back then, he had no problem doing favors for Uncle Palaver—or anyone, for that matter. Now, I was afraid to ask him to fix the leaking faucet in my bathroom, much less take me somewhere to meet a friend.

Mama's preparations for Uncle Palaver's arrival became more and more intense as the day drew closer. She bought foods she knew he liked and spruced up the guest bedroom. Even though he could sleep in his motor home when he visited, she insisted he sleep in the house.

"You're my family," she told him. "Our family, Warner. You don't sleep in the driveway when you come here."

She was so proud of him that she contemplated having some of her friends over to see him while he was visiting. At dinner one night, she proposed the idea to Daddy. He sat there, looking confused and troubled, and for a moment, I considered the possibility that he had actually forgotten Uncle Palaver was arriving in two days.

"When would you do that?" he finally asked.

"We could do it Saturday night, Matt. We haven't done anything with anyone for nearly a month. We turned down three invitations because of your work commitments. People are beginning to think we don't like them anymore or we've become snobs."

"Who cares what they think? I don't live my life to please them," he snapped back at her. "Saturday is out of the question," he added. "I'm going to Memphis on Saturday to meet with Byron Philips of Philips, Lancaster, and Dunn on the Shelton Concrete matter. We're on the verge of a settlement that would bring us some important money. I told you that."

"No, you didn't," Mama said.

"I did, but you don't listen to anything I say when your little brother is coming. You're all in a dither about his visit, as if he was some dignitary or someone. He's just a wandering gypsy, a hobo on wheels, hardly anyone to make a fuss over, Nora, and certainly not anyone to spotlight at a party here. What do you want him to do, amuse the Krongers, the Metzlers, the Dismukes, and the Renners by pulling dimes out of their ears or telling them what card they picked from his decks? These people fly to New York and go to Broadway shows or go to London. You'll make a fool of yourself and a bigger one of me for sponsoring such a stupid event."

Mama simply stared at him. Brenda and I looked down, but I raised my eyes and looked at Mama's. There wasn't anger in them as much as there was pain and disbelief. She was searching Daddy's face now with the scrutiny of a detective, looking for some clue to help her understand how the man she had given her life and soul, her identity and love, had suddenly turned away from her.

Brenda slapped her fork down on her plate so hard I was sure she had cracked it. Daddy's head snapped up.

"I don't think Uncle Palaver's tricks are stupid at all," she said. "I think you're stupid for saying such a mean thing, and I think we should have the party with or without you. I have some friends I'd like to have meet him. Maybe he'll be here in time to attend the volleyball game Friday afternoon," she added pointedly. "He could take your seat."

We all held our breath. Even Daddy looked as if he had frozen in place. The silence was deafening. It reminded me of the movie about tornados we had seen in science class. I felt as if we had moved into the eye of the storm and a deceptive calm was filling us with false hope.

"Maybe he will," Daddy finally said. He said it in a soft, sedated manner with little or no emotion. Then he turned to Mama. "Do what you want on Saturday night," he added. "I'll try to be back before eleven."

Although it sounded like a concession, it had an empty, "I don't care" ring to it, and I knew Mama would do absolutely nothing about having a party for Uncle Palaver. Brenda and I would urge her to do it anyway, but she had never in all my young lifetime done anything like that without Daddy's full blessing and agreement. She was so in tune with his thoughts and feelings that she could hear the slightest hesitation and drop an idea or a proposal, and it used to be that he was just like that with her. There had once been a time when each other's unhappiness, for whatever reason, was a burden neither could long endure.

I wondered if Uncle Palaver had a trick up his sleeve that could restore that bit of loving magic.

Before I went to sleep, I knelt by my bed and prayed that God would have mercy on us. *We're being pulled apart,* I told him. *We're shattering right before one another's eyes and we don't understand what terrible thing we have done to deserve it.* I prayed that Daddy would change back to being Daddy and that Mama's heart wouldn't crumble. I prayed that Brenda would stop being so angry and that I would stop crying.

I fell asleep with Mr. Panda in my arms. In the morning, as usual these days, Daddy was already gone by the time Brenda and I went to breakfast. Mama looked peaked and white and very tired. It wasn't hard to tell that she had been up all night. Uncle Palaver was arriving in two days. How would he find us? Would he see the turmoil, and would he try to help, or would he turn and flee from it? He was never one to contradict Daddy. He was too gentle and easygoing a man. Daddy's words would surely devastate him, I feared.

I couldn't recall a time in my life when I was more

nervous and distracted. I felt as if I were walking in a thick fog when I went to school, and sure enough, I got into trouble when Mr. Leshman asked me a question in social studies class and I didn't respond. I was lost in thoughts about all the turmoil at home and never heard him. I didn't even hear him repeat it, even though I looked as if I were paying attention, my eyes on him. It confused and annoyed him.

He raised his voice and stepped toward me, and finally, I blinked. He stared, waiting for a response. I gazed around the classroom and saw the way everyone was looking at me, each with an expression half of wonder, half of amusement. Some of the boys were already giggling, and that fed the fire of rage building in Mr. Leshman.

"Well?" he demanded.

"Well what?" I replied, and the entire class roared with laughter.

Mr. Leshman's face turned ruby red. "I'll tell you well what, young lady. You go see the dean this minute," he shouted, and pointed at the door. "Go on!"

I shook my head. "Why? What did I do?" I asked him, which made everyone laugh again.

"Get yourself to the dean's office," he said, pronouncing each word distinctly and holding his arm out, his forefinger pointed at the door.

There was a hush in the room while I gathered my books, closed my notebook, and rose. I hunched my shoulders to use my body the way a turtle uses its shell and hurried out of the room. The back of my neck burned with the embarrassment that scorched my spine. I could barely breathe, because my throat had tightened with a stiffness close to rigor mortis.

The dean's office was next to the principal's office. His name was Dean Mannville, and he looked like a former professional wrestler, with a physical presence that was intimidating and eyes that were unmerciful, eyes that looked as if they had witnessed capital punishment. He was bald, with large facial features. If he ever smiled, it was behind closed doors. The students actually believed he was a retired hit man. No one, not the meanest, toughest students, could stare him down—or eyeball him, as he would say. He had no hesitation about throwing someone out or turning him or her over to the police if he or she had committed any sort of criminal act. In his eyes, there was always a war under way in the building. A sign above his desk read: "This is a school. Anyone who prevents learning is the enemy and will be so treated."

His office was small, with no windows. When anyone was sent there, the dean would close the door and, according to students who had told me about it, he or she would feel very threatened. Sometimes, they were left sitting there for hours with the heat turned up. There was the story about one boy who had been violent and supposedly even attacked the dean, who then battered him in defense, beating him so much that he had to be taken to the hospital in an ambulance. The boy claimed he never attacked him, but once that door was closed, who would believe him? Some kids thought the story was an urban legend, something created to keep the mystique of the dean's unflinching hardness believable. Whether it was true or not, it worked.

Of course, I didn't think the dean would be physical with me, but this was the first time I had ever been sent out of class for disciplinary actions, and I was frightened, not only of what would happen to me but also of the effect it would have on my parents. Mama didn't need an ounce more grief, and here I was about to give a pound of it to her. And Daddy certainly didn't need another reason to be mean these days.

The dean's secretary told me to sit and wait when I informed her I had been sent out of class. Minutes later, one of my classmates, Peggy Ann Harkin, arrived with the referral form Mr. Leshman had filled out about me. She smiled with glee when she handed it to the secretary.

"Leave your body to science," she whispered as she walked past me and out the door.

The door to the dean's office was closed. I tried not to act frightened or upset. I really didn't understand why Mr. Leshman had gotten so angry at me. Other students in his class had done worse things and not been sent out. He had just taken my response the wrong way. I didn't mean to be insubordinate, which was surely what I was being accused of doing. I rehearsed my defense and waited, my heart thumping.

The dean's door finally opened, and a boy named David Peet stepped out with his head down, his shoulders turned forward and inward. He was a redheaded boy in the junior class and recently had been removed from the boys' basketball squad for vandalism at an opponent's school. He damaged lockers after a game. I didn't know what new offense he had committed.

The dean handed his secretary a slip of paper that looked like a parking ticket.

"Mr. Peet will wait here for his father to pick him up," he told her. "Put this in his file, if there's any room left," he added. He turned to David. "Sit down, and keep your mouth shut. I don't want to so much as hear you breathe too loudly."

David glanced at me and sat, keeping his eyes fixed on the floor.

The dean picked up my referral and, without looking at it, gestured to indicate I was to go into his office. I rose and walked into it. He closed the door behind himself and went around to his desk.

"Sit," he commanded. He then read the referral and smirked. I wasn't sure if he was disgusted with me or with the referral. He looked up at me and sat back.

"Okay," he said. "Let's hear your side of this."

"I didn't mean to be insubordinate. I didn't hear the question, and he thought I was being disrespectful, I guess."

"You think Mr. Leshman doesn't know when a student is being a smart-ass in his class? He's been teaching here twenty-five years. I would say he's seen just about everything."

"I didn't mean to be disrespectful," I said. "I've never been in trouble in class."

"There's always a first time. Showing off for someone, a boy perhaps?"

"No," I said quickly.

He leaned forward and clasped his big hands. "I know how that can be," he said suddenly in a softer, almost kind tone of voice. "Someone eggs you on, and you get in trouble for it. That what happened?"

"No. No one egged me on or anything. I was just . . ."

"What?"

"I was just thinking about something else and didn't hear him."

He stared hard at me and then glanced at the referral. "He asked you the same question a number of times, and you ignored him."

"Not because I wanted to. I was . . . thinking about something else."

"What?"

"Something personal," I replied.

He sat back, and the phone rang. Practically lunging for it, he lifted the receiver.

"What? Why am I being interrupted?" He listened a moment. "I'll be right there. Don't let anyone out of the bathroom."

He hung up the receiver and stood up. I thought he would rise into the ceiling.

"You can spend today in after-school detention thinking about whatever it was you were thinking about that was personal, and writing an apology to Mr. Leshman. I want to see it on my desk before you leave the building. The detention teacher will bring it in to me. You come back here again, and I'll lose my temper," he said. "Now, go sit out there until the bell rings for your next class, and be sure you don't think of personal stuff in that class."

He went to the door, ripped it open, and charged out.

I rose and followed slowly. David was still sitting there waiting for his father to pick him up. He looked up at me as I took the seat next to him.

"What did you do?" he asked.

"Nothing. I just didn't hear a question, and the teacher thought I was being disrespectful."

He grimaced in confusion. "That's it?"

"Sorry," I said, seeing how disappointed he was with my crime. "That's it."

"Dean Mannville told you to sit quietly without any talking," the secretary reminded David.

He stared hard at her a moment and then turned away from both of us.

Not ten minutes later, a short man with heavy-lensed glasses and light brown hair appeared in the doorway. He was in a dark brown suit and tie and, because of the folds in his forehead and the way he squinted, looked as if he had a terrible headache. David gazed at him but didn't stand up.

"You know, I had to leave work to come here," the man said.

"I didn't call you," David told him.

"Oh, you're so smart. Let's go, buddy boy, and you can forget the car for the rest of this year," the man who was apparently his father said.

David stood up and smiled down at me. "What's *your* father going to do, take away your scooter?"

I watched him leave, glanced at the secretary, and then closed my eyes. What *was* my father going to do? Perhaps he wouldn't find out. The school didn't always send letters home, and I'd only be an hour later than usual. *Brenda would find out, of course,* I thought.

She did before the day had ended and I walked toward the detention room. She was on her way to volleyball practice and caught up with me, pulling my arm to turn me around.

"I heard you were sent to the dean's office. What did you do?" she asked.

I told her everything. I thought she would be very angry at me, but her face softened, and she looked as if she would cry herself for a moment. Then she sighed. "Don't tell Mama," she said. "If she asks why you're home later than usual, tell her you were in the library doing research for something. She doesn't need this," she added, and I nodded, even though I could count on the fingers of one hand how many times I had lied to or kept something from Mama, and that was always for silly stuff.

"Won't the school call to tell her?" I asked.

"Probably not. If anything, they'll mail a copy of

the referral and the action taken, but it will be days from now, and maybe we can get to it before Mama sees it," she said.

Brenda saw the reluctance and despair in my face over so much deception.

"Sometimes, it's better to hide things and keep someone you love from knowing things that will hurt her more," she said. She said it with such assurance I had the distinct feeling she had done exactly that many times and might even be doing it at this moment herself.

I raised my eyebrows, and she saw my questions in my face.

"Go on. Don't be late for stupid detention," she ordered, and hurried off to the locker room.

I watched her for a moment and then took my seat in the detention room. The detention teacher gave me a sheet of paper almost immediately.

"You're supposed to write something," he reminded me.

With tears burning under my eyelids, I began my apology. I wrote the same things I had told Dean Mannville and then signed it with "I'm very sorry."

The late bus didn't take students directly to their homes. I was let off at a busy intersection in Hickory that was a good mile walk to my home. It wasn't the first time for me. I really had remained after school for research or for club meetings. Just as I started out, I saw what looked like Daddy's car coming down the boulevard. I stepped back and watched it pass. It was Daddy's car, and he was in it, but he wasn't driving.

He was sitting in the passenger's seat with a young man I knew to be Michael Kirkwood, one of his junior partners, driving. I caught a good view of both of them as they passed. Daddy had his head against the passenger's window, his eyes closed, and Mr. Kirkwood looked very somber. I had never seen anyone drive Daddy's car with him in it.

Oh no, I thought. *Something bad happened at court. Daddy will be especially upset and in a bad mood tonight.*

I walked with heavy steps, feeling as if I had a stone in my chest. Actually, I was feeling sorrier for Mama than I was for myself. At home, she was probably singing to herself while she made preparations for Uncle Palaver's arrival. Now, I wished he would postpone. Maybe the weather would turn bad and we'd have an ice storm or something.

It was certainly raining in my heart.

3

Pins and Needles

Of course, I was afraid that Dean Mannville had told his secretary to call my parents to tell them about the disciplinary action taken against me and she had already done so, but, fortunately for me, Brenda was right. There truly were more serious behavior problems to absorb the school's resources and attention.

Mama was so involved with her plans for tomorrow night's dinner, she didn't even notice that I was home later than usual.

"Your uncle Warner is just crazy about my chicken Kiev," she said when I looked through the kitchen doorway and saw her sitting on a stool and flipping through some cookbooks. "You know it's hard to get the chicken boned just the way I like it to be, the way they do it at Kaminsky's Russian Tea Room in Memphis. You know what I mean, with the wing bone and all. I'll have to see about that tomorrow morning. I thought I'd get some of that couscous he loves, too.

Then I thought I'd make his favorite dessert, chocolate cream pie. It's one of your father's favorites, too."

Mama made her pie crusts from scratch just the way her mother used to make it. Uncle Palaver claimed he had to travel clear across country just for her pie.

"Are you absolutely sure he's coming this time, Mama?" I asked. I would have hated to see her disappointed after such a buildup, and there were other times when he thought he would visit but was detoured by a last-minute opportunity to travel elsewhere for a show.

"Oh, yes. He called again today. Brenda will be so pleased. He is getting here early enough to go to her game," she said. "We'll all go. Maybe we'll get your father to go this time. Sometimes, he can get out of work early enough. Hopefully, we'll have a victory celebration right afterward. That's why I want to get as much as I can done now," she added.

Her eyes were bright from the glow of so much hope. She believed that in one day, in one dinner, she would restore happiness to our home. It was on the tip of my tongue to warn her about what I had just seen when Daddy and his junior partner passed by on the boulevard. I should tell her how unhappy he looked and what a bad mood he might be in when he did come home, but it would be like telling a four-year-old that Santa Claus was not real. I nodded and left her.

I went up to study. My redemption would be my getting a very good grade on tomorrow's social studies quiz. It would help me convince Mr. Leshman it had all been a terrible misunderstanding and I had no wicked intent in my behavior. Perhaps he would stop the school from sending home the referral. Was I a dreamer, too? Was it like a disease in this house now to hope for things that would never come true?

Brenda was home before Daddy. Usually, when he was going to be very late, he would call Mama to let her know. With all her attention and concentration focused on Uncle Palaver's arrival, the big dinner, and what she hoped would be a wonderful family weekend, she had decided to order in Chinese food. Brenda came right to my room to find out if the school had called.

"I knew they wouldn't," she said when I told her that as far as I knew, they hadn't. I then told her how I had seen Daddy being driven in his own car.

"I don't know why someone else would be driving his car. He looked very upset," I said.

"So, what's new? I was going to take that picture of him and me when I received the basketball trophy last year and pin it on the front of our door so he would remember how to smile."

"You wouldn't, would you?" I asked, afraid of how he might react.

"I would if I could, but I couldn't find the picture. It used to be on his desk in his office. You haven't seen it anywhere, have you?"

"No."

"Forget about it. Just don't mention anything about seeing him before," she told me.

We joined Mama in the kitchen, where she repeated most of what she had already told me and then suddenly realized what time it was and the fact that Daddy hadn't called or come home. She went to the phone, but Daddy's office was already closed for the day, and the answering service took over. They patched her through to his private office line, but he didn't pick up.

"He's probably on his way home," she said. "I'll order the food. I know what he likes, anyway."

She took out the take-out menu we had from the

Fortune Cookie restaurant, and for the next few minutes, we debated what we should get and how much we should order.

"Maybe that's too much. Oh, I guess I can eat leftovers for lunch," Mama concluded.

Her eyes kept swinging toward the wall clock. We had yet to hear the garage door go up and Daddy drive in. I could see she was growing increasingly nervous.

"I'd better call the restaurant," she decided. "It takes a while, and he'll be disappointed if he has to wait too long to eat."

Brenda and I looked at each other, both of us thinking the same thing. *Who cares if he is disappointed? What about our disappointment in him?* Unfortunately, we were growing accustomed to Daddy's being late, Daddy not calling, Daddy not thinking first about us, as he used to. However, that didn't make it any easier to accept. To pass the time and not think about it, I returned to my room and my homework. Brenda did the same. A little more than an hour later, we heard the doorbell. We both came out of our rooms and went to the front door to see Mama accept the Chinese takeout and pay the bill.

She brought it into the kitchen, set it on the table, stared at it a moment, and then pressed her lips together and sucked in air through her nose.

"He's still not home, and he still hasn't called, Mama?" Brenda asked.

"No. I'll just get everything a bit warmer," she said, nodding at the bag of food. "I'm sure he'll be here any minute. Set the table, girls."

Without uttering a sound, Brenda and I did what she asked. Daddy was now hours past the time he usually came home. He was even past his record for being late. Mama told us to sit, and she brought in the food.

Daddy's dish was left over a small fire to keep warm. We ate, but we were all listening so hard for any sign of his arrival that no one dared talk much. Brenda tried to keep our minds off things by describing the game, her practice, their chances to win the first-place title. Mama listened politely, but it was easy to see she was looking through us both, the words merely brushing over her ears.

Finally, the phone rang. We all jumped inside our own bodies. It was as if a bomb had gone off. Mama leaped out of her seat and went to the phone in the kitchen. Brenda and I rose and went to the pass-through window to listen.

"But why didn't you call me, Matt? I've been worried sick about you."

She listened some more.

"I don't understand," she said, her voice finally permitting some anger to show. "You could have had John call for you. You've done that before. I don't understand," she repeated. "The three of us are just sitting here like idiots waiting on pins and needles. I don't care. Do what you want," she concluded, and hung up abruptly.

She must not have realized we were standing by the pass-through window. We saw her press her forehead against the wall phone, and then we saw her shoulders start to shake.

"Mama!" I cried, and ran around first to hug her.

Brenda followed, her arms folded, and stood by as Mama turned to embrace me.

"What did he say, Mama?" Brenda asked, her face glowing with rage.

"He said . . . ," she began between deep breaths and sobs. "He said they had a crisis with a case, and he went to Memphis to meet with attorneys. He said the meetings are continuing, and he will remain in Memphis overnight for a hearing in the morning in federal court about some bankruptcy motion or another."

"Why didn't he call to tell us?" Brenda followed.

"He said he didn't realize he would be so involved so long."

"Doesn't he still have a watch on his wrist?" Brenda pursued.

Mama nodded and then continued to cry. "Go finish your dinner," she said waving us away.

"I'm not hungry."

"Me, neither," I said.

"I'll help put it away," Brenda told her, and urged me to leave Mama be.

"Why is he being so inconsiderate?" I asked Brenda when we returned to the dining room.

"I don't know, and I don't care. When I see him, I'm going to let him know it, too," she said.

After we cleaned up, I tried to keep Mama company, but she shooed me away and told me to do my homework. She didn't watch television or do any of the things she usually did in the evening. Instead, she went to bed early herself. It broke my heart to see her bedroom door close. I knew she was crying and feeling miserable. Now, more than ever, I hoped and prayed Uncle Palaver would bring some of his magical rainbows into our lives.

Mama was up before Brenda and me in the morning. It wasn't hard to see she had cried herself to sleep, but she fought back depression and tears and talked only about Uncle Palaver's impending arrival.

"Probably, you should just remain at school, April," she told me. "The game is at four, right, Brenda?"

"Yes, Mama. She can hang out with me," she said.

Actually, that idea excited me. I wanted to hang out

with the junior and senior girls. Just listening to them talk about themselves and their social lives was entertaining. I had done it a few times before and felt like a fly on the wall, hearing about this one's romance and that one's breakup. They had no inhibitions when it came to talking about their sexual behavior, either. Girls who had shared experiences with the same boy made shocking comparisons, rating this one and that one for his love powers, as they called it. I noticed how Brenda ignored them and made no comments at all, even when some of the girls told her some boy had expressed interest in her.

"I can fix you up any time you'd like," Shelby Okun told her. Brenda glanced at her and shook her head.

Brenda wasn't that close with any of the girls in her class. She rarely attended any of their parties. Her social life was built completely around her sporting events. Occasionally, on weekends, she joined two other girls who were her teammates and went on hikes or long bike rides.

She went out on a date once in a while, but she hadn't met anyone she said she liked or with whom she would go on a second date, and as far as I knew, she had yet to go out on a single date this school year. She did attend pep rally dances, and Mama was hoping she would attend the junior prom. She talked about it with Brenda often, recalling her own high-school social life. She loved to show us her pictures, especially the ones taken during her prom. Although Brenda listened politely, she didn't seem to be at all excited about it. Her only interest in boys these days, in fact, was in beating them at various sporting events. On more than one occasion, I heard boys teasing each other by saying, "Brenda Taylor could whip your ass," in whatever sport they meant.

I heard them say other things about her, too, nasty things, and some even teased me with comments like "What's your sister do for sexual excitement, sit on fire hydrants?"

I fled from their laughter and smiles, my heart pounding. How I wished Brenda had a romance and could wipe those smirks off their faces. I wished it for her more than I wished it for myself. In my heart of hearts, I thought I wouldn't ever have a boyfriend until I lost weight. I made the mistake of telling that to Jamie Stanley once. She thought a moment, and then, as if she were afraid I would have a boyfriend before she did, she said, "You probably will never lose weight. You're afraid of having a boyfriend."

Was I?

Could such a thing be true? I wished I had someone I could ask. I was afraid to ask Mama, afraid I would make her think less of me, and I had never had any such conversation with Brenda.

Despite all the distraction and worry that hovered about me all day, I knew I did well on the social studies quiz. I was as attentive as could be in Mr. Leshman's class as well and tried to look repentant and sorry. He had my written apology on his desk, but he said nothing more about it. The only interest any of my classmates had in my unfortunate episode was to hear how mean Dean Mannville had been to me. I could see they were disappointed in my description, and soon no one wanted to know anything more.

Brenda let me sit with her and her two teammates with whom she usually sat at lunch, Nicole Lawford and Natalie Brandon, both girls almost as tall as she was. The importance of the upcoming game was all they talked about. They had to win to stay in contention for the league title. Their entire conversation was about the best and the weakest server on their team and how they would try to work off one another for offense. Although it was boring to me and nowhere near as interesting as the usual locker-room gossip, I tried to look interested.

At the end of the day, I joined Brenda again in the gym and followed her to the locker room. None of the other girls took much notice of me. I sat on a bench and watched Brenda change. Although she hadn't said anything more about Daddy, I was sure she was think-ing the same thing I was: Would he appear at the game with Mama and Uncle Palaver?

I watched Brenda and her teammates limber up for the Death Match, as they called it, and then, with them, I observed the arrival of the opposing team. The girls on that team seemed bigger and older. I knew from listen-ing to Brenda and her teammates talk that they, like our team, were undefeated. I was caught up in the excite-ment and for a while didn't think about Daddy at all.

The crowd of supporters for both sides began to ar-rive at about three-thirty, and the gym started to fill up quickly. I was nervous about finding good seats for Mama, Uncle Palaver, me, and maybe Daddy. It was hard to save that many spots in the bleachers. Finally, Mama arrived with Uncle Palaver at her side but with-out Daddy. My heart did a flip-flop, happy to see Uncle Palaver but so disappointed in Daddy's failure to appear.

"Look at her!" Uncle Palaver exclaimed as soon as he saw me. "You grew a foot since I saw you last."

"Did not," I said. "At least not upward."

He laughed and hugged me. I looked carefully at Mama to scrutinize her face. She was smiling, but there was an emptiness in her eyes that chilled my spine.

"Where's Daddy?" I asked her.

"We'll see him later," she replied, and glanced quickly at Uncle Palaver, who slapped his hands together as we sat, him in between us. He rubbed his palms, and when he lifted them apart, there was a girl's wristwatch in his left palm. It had a circular face with little hearts that popped in and out.

Mama laughed.

"I'll be doggone," Uncle Palaver said. "What's this?"

He plucked the watch out of his palm and held it up.

"Must be yours," he said, turning to me. "Try it on."

It fit tightly on my wrist, but I pretended it didn't matter.

"Thank you, Uncle Palaver," I said.

He sat back and pulled in his jaw. "I didn't give it to you. I have no idea how it got there," he said.

We heard a whistle blow. The teams were introduced. Brenda looked our way and saw Daddy wasn't there. I noticed the way her shoulders hoisted when she turned away. Anger had replaced pain and disappointment. What she was able to do, however, was place all that fury into her game. When she spiked the ball over the net, it looked as if it would drill a hole in the floor. The crowd watched her in wonder, and the applause began to build and build, our side's cheering voices drowning out the opponents' supporters. In awe and amusement, Uncle Palaver watched Brenda play.

"Don't get on that girl's bad side," he said when she stopped the opponents' lead player from delivering a return. The ball bounced off the poor girl's head, and she fell on her rear end. The laughter embarrassed her and affected the rest of her game. Brenda was intimidating.

We had a hard-fought but sweet victory, and there

was no doubt in anyone's mind that it was all because of Brenda. I could see the pain in Mama's eyes because Daddy hadn't been there to see her play. Uncle Palaver tried his best to make up for it, lavishing praise on Brenda. He tried to cheer her up by plucking a watch for her, too, this time out of her own closed fist.

"How did you do that?" she cried, laughing.

Uncle Palaver shrugged.

"I didn't do anything," he said. "I saw it peeking out between your fingers. That's all."

For a while, we were all distracted. On the way home, he talked about his latest trip and some of the shows he and Destiny put on. They had been part of a variety show last week, and he said there were jugglers and acrobats like he had never seen.

"And there was this dog that could understand words. I swear. He knew colors, numbers. It was incredible. Now, *that's* magic," he told us.

"When am I ever going to meet Destiny?" Mama asked him.

"Oh, one of these days our schedules will coincide," he replied quickly.

"Maybe she's another one of Uncle Palaver's illusions," Brenda quipped.

Uncle Palaver laughed, but he sounded more nervous than usual.

It wasn't until we arrived at the house that Brenda actually asked after Daddy.

"He said he was stuck in court all day," Mama said. "We'll start dinner without him, because he could be very late," she added.

Brenda looked at me and then at Uncle Palaver, whose eyes told her he was worried about Mama.

"Well, not to worry," Brenda said. "We have Uncle

Palaver. He could make Daddy appear whenever we want him to, right, Uncle Palaver?"

"Right, honey," he said, but I could see he didn't want to linger on that topic. "What a game you played. I was very proud of you."

"Thanks," she said. She flashed a smile and headed for her room to change for our wonderful dinner. Maybe no one else could tell, but I could from the way she walked and held her shoulders and her head: pain and disappointment had won back their position in her heart and pushed anger away.

She was crying inside again. Drowning in her own sadness.

Mama's dinner was so good, however, that we were all somewhat restored. Just as she was about to bring out our dessert, we heard the garage door go up. Daddy was home. I think we were all holding our breath. It was truly as if the world were made of thin glass and could all shatter in a moment, raining shards down upon us.

Daddy appeared in the dining room doorway. I had been building my angry onslaught against him as well, but when I saw him, my darts suddenly lost their points, and my anger turned to fear and even sadness. I couldn't remember seeing him look so tired and so defeated.

"Hi, Matt," Uncle Palaver said quickly.

Daddy nodded. He looked at Mama a long moment, and then he looked at Brenda.

"How did the game go?"

"We won," she said without a smile.

"Good. At least there's one victory in the house," he replied.

"I kept everything warm for you, Matt," Mama said.

"It's all right," he told her. "I had something on the

road with Jack. I've got some things to do," he added, and walked down the hallway toward his home office.

I was afraid to look back at Mama. Brenda had her eyes down, burning holes in the table.

"He's just tired, I guess," Uncle Palaver said. "I know what it's like to be working and traveling. Cuts down on your appetite something awful. Why, I've had days when I've eaten barely enough to qualify for one meal."

"Maybe I need to be on the road, then," I muttered. "Daddy would like that."

When I looked up, I was surprised at how cold and steely-eyed Brenda was. She was glaring at me so hard it made me cringe.

"When you hate yourself," she said, "you'll end up hating everyone else as well. Don't let him do that to you."

I could barely swallow. I looked at Mama, whose eyes were drowning. She rose quickly and began to take dishes into the kitchen. Brenda and I got up and started to help clear the table.

"Hey, hold on there, Brenda," Uncle Palaver said when she reached for the bowl of couscous. He leaned over and lifted it slowly. There were two silver dollars under it. "I thought so," he said.

Brenda shook her head and smiled. "Now, when did you do that?"

"Me? I didn't do anything. Those must be for you two," he said.

We laughed and continued to clear the table.

"Later," Brenda whispered, "I'm going to ask him to throw a sheet over Daddy, mumble some mumbo jumbo, make this man we call Daddy disappear and bring back the father we once had. That will prove whether he's a really good magician or not."

I smiled nervously. I couldn't deny that Daddy had become a stranger to us all. Brenda's wish was my wish, too, but as it turned out, we didn't need Uncle Palaver to make anyone disappear. Daddy decided to disappear entirely on his own.

It happened that night. After dinner, the four of us went into the living room, and Uncle Palaver continued to entertain us with some of his new sleight-of-hand tricks and some incredible card tricks, especially the one where he asked me to think about a card and then asked Brenda to pick it out of the deck, and she did. I really began to wonder if there was indeed magic involved. We were so distracted that we didn't notice for some time that Daddy had yet to come out of his office. Mama realized it first and went to see what he was doing. I followed to the living room doorway and watched her go down the hall. I saw she was surprised to find his office door locked. She knocked and called to him. He said something; she stood there a long moment, and then she returned to the living room.

"He'll be right along," she told us, forcing a smile onto her troubled face.

Uncle Palaver continued to entertain us with stories about the different characters he had met on the road. He had performed on a number of college campuses, too, and Brenda was interested in what he had to say about them. She was beginning to consider colleges to attend, and foremost in her mind, of course, was what athletic opportunities they offered young women.

I was the first to give in to a yawn, but it triggered everyone else. Uncle Palaver had gotten up very early and had traveled all day just so he could make Brenda's volleyball game. Mama admitted to being tired herself.

"Tomorrow's Saturday," Mama said. "I'm sure Matt

will have lots of time to spend with us all. Perhaps we'll go to lunch or maybe to dinner," she added, that little candle flame of hope still burning in her eyes.

"Sure. He works hard," Uncle Palaver said. "We know now where Brenda gets her determination and dedication, huh?" he added, smiling at her.

Brenda was not in the mood to be compared in any way to Daddy. She grimaced. "It seems to me the one with determination and dedication here is Mama," she told Uncle Palaver.

He held his smile, but I could see he was very upset as well. "Okay. Let's all have a good night's sleep," he said. "Nora, thanks for that wonderful dinner."

He kissed her good night, and for a moment, a longer than usual moment, I thought, she clung to him. Then he kissed each of us and went to the guest room.

"I'll go to bed soon," Mama told Brenda and me. We knew that meant she would wait for Daddy to come out of his office.

"I'm going to have it out with him tomorrow," Brenda warned me at my bedroom door. "I'll try to get him away from Mama. When you see me do that, you keep her busy."

"I should be with you," I said.

"Don't worry about it. You'll be with me. He'll know it's not just me talking," she promised.

"You were great today, Brenda. I was very proud of you."

She smiled and hugged me. "It was easy," she said. "Every time I had to hit the ball, I just imagined Daddy's face on it."

I thought she would smile or laugh after saying that, but she didn't. That, more than anything else that had happened during the Mr. Hyde days, made me feel sad and then afraid. Feeling so weighed down by the disappointments and tears, I went to bed thinking I would toss and turn, finding it impossible to get myself comfortable enough to sleep. Instead, I sank into the mattress. I hadn't realized just how exhausting all the emotional tension had been. To my surprise and delight, I fell asleep quickly.

The sound of a door slamming, followed by a wail and the horrible rhythm of constant, loud sobbing woke me abruptly. For a moment, I thought I might be in a dream. I glanced at my clock and saw it was two o'clock in the morning. The light flowing under my doorway from the hall told me someone was wide awake. I rose quickly, slipped into my robe and my slippers, and went to the door. I saw immediately that Brenda was out of her room. Her door was wide open.

I realized the sobbing was coming from the living room and hurried there. I was shocked to find Brenda, Mama, and Uncle Palaver also in their robes. Brenda and Uncle Palaver were seated beside Mama, who was looking down on the coffee table, where columns of papers were neatly arranged.

"What's going on?" I asked, my heart pumping so hard I thought my chest would split beneath my budding breasts.

"Daddy's gone," Brenda said, and Mama fell back into Uncle Palaver's embrace. She closed her eyes.

"Gone? What does that mean, gone?" I asked, embracing myself. A terrible chill had come over me like a splash of ice water.

"Gone means no longer here," Brenda said dryly. "It means good-bye."

"I don't understand," I said, now unable to stop myself from crying, too.

Brenda looked down. Mama sucked back her sobs and sat up, wiping her cheeks.

"Your father has left us, April," she said, speaking with such a lack of emotion it made me shudder to hear. "He has been planning this departure for some time, apparently. He sold his practice, for example, without my knowing anything about that, and all those cases he was supposedly working on were not true. He has provided us with a considerable flow of income. All the paperwork is right here," she said, touching one of the piles. "Neatly and competently arranged. I don't suppose there is a question unanswered when it comes to any of it.

"He left like some rat deserting a ship, in fact," she continued with bitterness infecting her tone. "He didn't bother taking much of his own wardrobe. He left instructions for that, too, however," she added, pulling one folder from a column. "Uncle Palaver is welcome to whatever he wants, and the rest goes to the Angel View Thrift Shop to raise funds for needy sick children. He even left most of his personal jewelry."

I walked farther into the living room and gazed down at the papers. I looked at Brenda, who turned away.

"When did he do all this?" I asked through my quivering lips.

"When? Much of it was done over the last month or weeks, I guess. Last night, I waited up for him, but he was busy arranging all this in his office. I finally knocked on his door and told him I was going to bed, and he said . . ." She started to cry again. Uncle Palaver held her firmly and kissed her hair.

"Easy, Nora, easy," he urged softly.

She got enough control of herself to continue. "And he said, 'Good night, Nora. Don't wait up for

me.' Don't wait up for him. Don't wait up," she repeated.

"Why did he do this? Where did he go?"

"Don't be stupid," Brenda said, her voice dripping
with venom. "Where do you think he's gone? He's off
with some other woman."

"But he can't be!" I cried. I looked at Uncle Palaver.
His expression held no hope of it not being so. No
matter how silly or inconsequential Daddy had thought
Uncle Palaver's life to be, he was still a man of the
world to me. He could and would see the reality of
events I would or could not.

He just shook his head in utter disbelief himself.

"How could Daddy just walk out and forget all
about us like this?" I moaned.

"That's not the amazing part to me," Brenda said.

"What is, then?" I asked quickly.

She looked at Mama. "Tell her, Mama. Tell her
what you discovered after you found all this."

Mama looked up at me, her eyes so red I thought
she would cry blood soon. "He's been going through
all the albums in the house. He's destroyed every picture of himself and cut himself out of every picture
with us or with me, even our wedding photograph!"
she shouted.

It roared in my brain like a clap of thunder.

I turned and looked over at the fireplace mantel.
The picture of her and Daddy from their courting days
was gone.

"All of our family vacation videos are gone, too.
I've looked everywhere. I did find the family albums
in his office," Mama continued, taking deep breaths.
"It was the first thing I saw when I realized he
hadn't come to bed and had gotten up to find him.

The office door was open, and the albums were there on the floor beside his desk. I went through the house looking for him and saw all these papers on the table."

"I heard a cry," Uncle Palaver said, "and came out as fast as I could."

"I did, too," Brenda told me. "Now I know why I couldn't find that picture I was describing to you earlier, the one where I received the trophy. I was going to put his smiling face on our door, remember?"

It was as if they were reporting the actions they had taken after a major crime had been committed. I sank slowly to the floor to sit and stare at the papers on the coffee table.

"He left a letter for us," Brenda added, the corners of her mouth dipping. She pushed the letter toward me.

"A letter?"

Mama started to cry again.

I looked at her and then picked up the letter and read it.

Dear Nora, Brenda, and April,

After a good deal of thought, I decided this was the best way to handle the situation. What I would like the most is for you all to forget me as quickly and as painlessly as you can. I know it's a strange request to make, but it has to be made for your sakes more than for mine.

As you will see, you are well taken care of financially and should have no worries on that score.

I realize I cannot do more than give you all grief and unhappiness, and that would be unfair to you.

It is better that you go through a short period

of sadness and even anger than live the way we are all living now.

Matt

Matt?

He didn't even sign it Daddy, I thought. The letter shook in my trembling fingers. I put it down so quickly someone would have thought it burned. It did burn, but it burned in my heart. No one spoke, and then Brenda suddenly began to laugh. She laughed so hard tears came into her eyes and ran out the corners.

"How can you laugh now, Brenda?" Mama asked, astonished.

Brenda continued to laugh.

"Brenda!" Mama cried.

Brenda stopped laughing and took a long, deep breath. "Don't you see, Mama? Don't you see?"

"See what?"

"Uncle Palaver did it. He made the stranger disappear. He's a wonderful magician after all."

4

Daddy's Secret

Anyone who would have stepped into our home or seen our faces would surely conclude we were a family in mourning. Even Uncle Palaver, who seemed always to move within a bubble of childlike innocence coated with optimism and joy, held his head down, his eyes dimmed and dark. He did all he could to comfort Mama, but she was inconsolable.

Despite what he had done, I didn't want to hate Daddy. I tried hard to push away those feelings. I felt more like someone who had been struck in the head, stunned, confused, and very lost. On the other hand, Brenda hardened even more, trailing bitterness behind her like someone tracking in mud wherever she went.

"Let this be a real life lesson for you, April," she told me the following day. She was sitting in the living room, gazing out at the driveway and the basketball net and backboard where she and Daddy had played so many times. As if it knew how to dress our mood, the day was overcast and dreary. Shadows splashed all around us in a melancholy downpour.

Brenda didn't look at me when she spoke. She kept her eyes fixed on the memories, I imagined, because I saw a different scene out there as well. I heard Daddy's laughter, saw him shake his head with surprise when Brenda dribbled past him or made an almost impossible shot.

"We've got a real WNBA star here, April," he told me.

I was jealous of their relationship, even though it was full of competitiveness. At least they were doing something together. All I could do was fetch the ball when it bounced off to one side or another and pass it to them. I was like a puppy waiting for a pat on the head. Sometimes it came; sometimes it didn't.

"The worst thing you can do," Brenda continued, with her eyes still fixed on that basketball net, "is give yourself completely to anyone like Mama did. You can see what good that's done her. The truth is, there is no such thing as a perfect love."

She turned to me. I was afraid to speak or move. I had been wandering about the house all day, standing for minutes at a time in the doorway of Daddy's office, staring in at his desk and his books. He had taken or destroyed pictures of himself, but the room still said *Daddy* to me, even though it was resoundingly empty; it was truly as if Uncle Palaver had made him disappear.

How could I still sense him so strongly if he wasn't going to reappear? I thought hopefully.

"You want to know why there can never be a perfect love, April? I'll tell you why," she said before I could utter a sound. "We're all too selfish. That's why. Down deep inside, we're all too selfish. We can't resist pleasing ourselves. Just remember that, April. Brand it into your very soul," she told me, and turned to look out the window again.

Mama was in her bedroom, the door closed. Uncle Palaver was in the guest room, probably trying to come up with some plan, some way to rescue the situation. I had cried as much as I could. My eyes were bankrupt.

"Maybe we can find out where he went," I said.

Brenda turned to me again, and for a moment, I thought I might have made a good suggestion. She looked as if she thought it was possible. Then she smiled, but it was that cold, plastic smile she could put on to signal she was about to throw a ball of thorns into someone's face.

"What for, April? To beg him to come home? Do you even want him to come home after this? Well? Do you?"

What could I say? I did. I wanted him back so we could change him, make him see how wonderful we were and how wonderful his life had been with us. I still believed in us.

"This is one of those life experiences that should help bury your childhood, April," Brenda said. "The days of candy canes, gumdrops, and bubbles are gone. You're going to grow up very quickly now. When you realize how alone you really are in this world, you grow up or you perish.

"It's a lot like that out there on the basketball and volleyball courts. You depend on your teammates, but you have to deliver, and they have to deliver, or you lose. It's as simple as that, winning or losing. In the end, you know what only matters? The score. That's it, April, the score. All the rest of it is . . . is baloney. Forget that stuff about 'It's not whether you win or lose but how you play the game that counts.' It doesn't count in the end. People respect winners, not good losers.

"We're not going to be good losers," she vowed. "Believe me, what Daddy has done is not going to make me a loser." She looked away, and then she turned back to me quickly, suddenly looking more like grouchy Daddy. "I don't want to see you moping about here and crying in the corners, either. Mama doesn't need it. Not only are we going to hold together; we're going to be better than ever. You hear me?" she practically shouted at me.

I nodded.

"Good. Anyone asks what happened, you tell them the truth, and go on doing whatever it is you have to do. You don't fail your tests and get into trouble in school like everyone will expect you to do, April. You study harder. I'm going to play harder," she said. "I'm going to win every trophy I can, because, in the end, that's what will tell Daddy what we really think of what he's done and what we really think of him. Understand? Do you?" she followed, her voice verging on out-and-out hysteria.

"Yes, Brenda."

"Good. Good," she said, and blew air through her lips. She got up. "I'm going for a run," she said, "in case anyone asks where I am."

She went to change into her running clothes and shoes, and I went to my room to do my homework. Usually, like everyone I knew, I left it for the last moment, but I wanted to be so occupied I couldn't think. A part of me continued to believe it was all just a bad dream or a misunderstanding, anyway. This couldn't be the end, the conclusion to all this. There had to be a better explanation and a better solution.

In the late afternoon, Mama came out to work on

our dinner. I went to help her, and Uncle Palaver sat at the kitchen table to watch and talk.

"I've decided to hang around a little longer, Nora," he told Mama. "If that's all right with you."

She stopped what she was doing. She wasn't crying anymore, but her face looked so drained and tired she seemed to have aged years in hours.

"No, Warner. I don't want you canceling your show dates to stay here and babysit me. I'll be fine," she said, "and it would only add to my unhappiness to know I was keeping you from developing your career."

"My career," he said disdainfully.

"It's what you enjoy, Warner. Don't put yourself down just because . . . because some other people did that. If you can make a living at what you love to do, you're a success," Mama insisted.

Uncle Palaver smiled. "You were always my best cheerleader, Nora."

"And I still am, so forget this idea about moping around the house."

He nodded. "I can come back on my sweep west," he said.

"Don't do anything that takes you off your track, Warner. I'm warning you."

"Okay, okay."

"When are you leaving, Uncle Palaver?" I asked.

"I'm supposed to be in Raleigh tomorrow evening," he replied.

"What about Destiny?" I asked.

"She's meeting me there."

"Then you'd better get an early start," Mama advised. "This weather isn't improving. They're predicting some storms."

He nodded. "I'll call you whenever I can," he promised.

"We'll be fine," she said, and turned back to her dinner preparations.

Uncle Palaver looked up at me and smiled. "Sure you will. You have two terrific young women at your side," he said. He pushed back the sleeves of his shirt. "Okay, April," he said, sitting forward. "Here we have a salt shaker and a pepper shaker."

He put them together on the table.

"I want you to move them to any place on this table," he told me, lifting them and handing them to me.

Mama's smile made me move quickly to take them.

"Go on, anywhere," he said.

I put them down at the other end as far from him as I could get them.

"Okay, let me concentrate a minute," he said, and closed his eyes while he squeezed his temples with his thumb and forefinger. Then he nodded. "I got it. Lift the salt shaker first," he said.

I looked at Mama. What was he doing? She shrugged, and I lifted the salt shaker. There, beneath it, was a shiny new penny.

"How could . . ."

"Lift the pepper shaker," he told me, and I did the same, and there on the table was another shiny new penny. "Those are lucky pennies," he said. "Check them out."

I looked at them. There didn't seem to be anything different about them. Neither one looked like part of some trick but, of course, I had to be skeptical.

"Mama, are these our salt and pepper shakers?"

"They are," she said.

"How did you do that, Uncle Palaver?"

"A real magician never tells," he said. "But I will this one time. I did it with magic."

Mama laughed.

It sounded so wonderful that it brought tears to my eyes. How I wished Uncle Palaver could stay with us just to make us laugh again and again, but Brenda was right. We had only ourselves now.

As always when Brenda did something athletic like going on a long run, she looked revived, not drained—stronger, not weaker, and certainly not tired. She looked more fortified than ever. It was easy to see she was determined not to cry or even look upset. I had never seen her as talkative as she was at dinner that night. It was as if she were out to make sure there were no long, melancholy pauses in the conversation among us. She talked about her upcoming game against the champion of the North Carolina league and then, for the first time, revealed some career plans.

"Of course, I hope I make the United States Olympic volleyball team someday, but I want to be sensible, too. I'm going to be a physical education instructor, only I'd like to be one at a college and not a high school. There are more dedicated young athletic girls in college. I'll enjoy that more. What do you think, Mama?" she asked, and Mama looked up with some surprise. We could see she wasn't prepared to involve herself in these sorts of serious questions yet. It was usually something Daddy initiated. He had the strongest opinions about it all, but she struggled to clear her mind and think.

"Sure, Brenda. That sounds very good. It's what you love, and like I told your uncle today," she added, looking at Uncle Palaver, "to do what you love and make a living at it is what I would call being successful. I guess, in fact," she continued, now that Brenda had forced her to think about other things beside

Daddy, "I guess I'll consider returning to work myself."

"That's a great idea," Brenda said, and looked at me with eyes that urged me to speak up as well.

"Yes, Mama, that is a good idea."

"I might even return to college myself one of these days and continue pursuit of a law degree," Mama added, buoyed by our enthusiasm.

"You could pledge a sorority," Uncle Palaver joked.

Was it a miracle? For a while, we were laughing, smiling, actually enjoying our food and one another's company. I was happy about that, but I also felt funny about it. I couldn't help listening for Daddy's car, for the garage door going up. I couldn't help imagining him stepping into the house and into the dining room doorway. The Daddy I was imagining was the old Daddy, the one who would joke and pretend to be upset that we had begun dinner without him.

What's this? I heard him say. *Did you really believe all that? Did you really believe I could leave my three girls?*

Brenda saw the way my gaze went to the doorway, and her eyes grew small with reprimand.

There was a pause in the conversation and laughter.

"Well," Mama said, reaching deeply for a long sigh, "I guess I had better prepare myself for the phone calls. This is a small community. You know how gossip flies. Of course, they'll all wonder how this could happen without my realizing it was going to, how he could leave his practice, set up another life, whatever he's done. I suppose I'll look like some stupid, vapid fool."

"No," Brenda said. "He'll be the one who looks like a fool. Don't dare blame yourself for any of this, Mama."

"No!" I cried.

Mama smiled. "My cheerleaders, Warner," she said to Uncle Palaver.

"I wish I had them with me," he said. He thought a moment. "The man has to be out of his mind to leave them behind. Brenda's right. In the end, people will pity him more."

Like a prophecy, his words hung in the air to contemplate and consider.

Although Brenda wouldn't show it, she was as sad as I was, if not sadder the following morning when Uncle Palaver prepared to leave. He gave us a tour of his motor home to show us some of the new things he had bought for it. I sat in the driver's seat and pretended I was on the road, unwrapping states and scenery like Christmas presents as I crossed the country. Never did Uncle Palaver's life seem as attractive to me as it did at that moment. Yes, he had no family to cart along and be responsible for. At least, no family yet.

Perhaps he would have one someday with Destiny, although he never did speak of her as his girlfriend or fiancée. Was he ashamed to admit he was in love with an African American woman? Or was he afraid she might disappoint him one day? Did he want to remain forever unattached? Was he the free soul he appeared to be, carried along by whatever whim or notion he had, accepting or declining invitations as he pleased? Every day brought some unexpected surprise. There were defeats and unhappy experiences, but all he had to do was get behind this wheel, start the engine, and drive off, leaving anything unpleasant behind him as forgotten as an old bad dream.

He would surely do the same soon after he left us, I thought. Oh, he would worry about Mama, but he would be so occupied with his work and his travels that he would not feel that worry as intensely as he felt it here with us. I didn't resent him for that; no, I envied him.

Take me with you, I dreamed of asking.

"Well, Nora," he said when we were all standing outside his vehicle. "I brought this to give to Matt, but I'll give it to you now." He handed Mama an envelope with the check in it to repay the loan Daddy had given him some time ago.

"You don't have to give me this now, Warner," she told him.

"Sure I do. I don't want to owe anyone money," he said. We knew he meant he didn't want to owe Daddy. "Brenda, you keep copies of all the news clippings from the sports pages. I'm going to brag about my niece everywhere I go."

"Thank you, Uncle Palaver. I will."

"And April, you keep looking under things. Magic happens when you least expect it," he told me.

Brenda and I hugged and kissed him, and then Brenda looked at me to tell me we should leave him and Mama alone for a few moments.

"I've got to get to my homework," she said.

"Me, too," I added, and we went into the house.

We both stood inside the doorway and looked out through the window on the side. Mama had her head down, and Uncle Palaver was talking to her. Finally, he just reached out to embrace her and held her. He kissed her forehead, turned, and went into his motor home. Mama stood there with her arms folded and watched him pull away. She looked so small and alone to me, it took all my power to stop myself from charging out to embrace her as well.

"Let her be," Brenda said firmly. "The more you cry in her arms, the longer it will take for her to get back on her feet. When we lose a game, we feel bad for a while, but we look forward to the next, April. Otherwise, we might as well quit. Understand?"

I nodded.

"C'mon," she said. "I'll challenge you to a game of checkers. The way you are right now, I might just beat the pants off you."

"No, you won't," I said.

The smile began in her eyes. I could hear her thinking, *That a girl. That's my sister.*

Mama was right about what would soon follow. The news of Daddy's departure spread very quickly, and the phone calls began and continued all the following week. Most of the women who called her used the excuse of just seeing how she was holding up and if there was anything they could do to help her in any way. What each wanted was to get closer, be on the inside, so she could be the one with the news bulletins. Fortunately, most of these calls happened while Brenda and I were in school. When we were home and we did hear her answer the phone and talk, her voice was always so thin, so low, so full of pain.

Despite her brave declarations about how she would carry on, she didn't look for work or even entertain the idea if someone else brought it up. Returning to college was as distant a dream as anything could possibly be. She left the house only to do what had to be done, and every night she greeted us with a new revelation about something Daddy had done, something good. It was easy to see that was how she held on to hope.

"Your father arranged for all our stocks and bonds to be handled by a money manager. I don't have to worry about any of it," she told us. "He arranged for the man who takes care of his offices to look after our house needs and problems, too. I really don't have to do anything, be anywhere. All the bills are being paid electronically! I don't even have to go to the bank," she said after we urged her to get out more often.

Both Brenda and I quickly understood that she wanted to be near the phone in anticipation of Daddy's calling, apologizing, begging to return. That call never came.

At school, Brenda was less bothered than I was by other students, especially girls on her team who had questions or comments about what was going on in our lives. Even without these events, she was not as approachable or as vulnerable. It was truly as if her skin were tougher than mine. Her aggressiveness on the court carried over into the classrooms and hallways of the school. Most girls were nowhere as competitive as she was, and most weren't interested in challenging her. They surely talked about her behind her back, but Brenda never cared. She seemed above it all, moving on her own plane, her own level, years beyond the others. It was as if she had left long ago and her body still had to work at catching up.

Those who always made fun of me because of my weight or whatever were eager to tease me about Daddy. The boys said things like, "He had to leave to get something to eat. You probably ate everything in the house." I would never say it wasn't painful, but Brenda's admonitions were stronger. I didn't talk back or fight back. The last thing I wanted to do was get into any trouble now. After a while, I was returned to the shelf of disinterest. I was too boring a subject, after all, and what little they gained or enjoyed wasn't enough to sustain the teasing.

I devoted my energy to my studies, and to everyone's surprise, including my own, my grades began to improve seriously. Even Mr. Leshman stopped me on the way out of his class one day to tell me how pleased he was with my grades.

"I'm very happy for you," he said, which struck me as a very ironic and strange remark. How could anyone be happy for me for any reason these days? Of course, few realized how hard it was back home, with Mama slowly fading away. She was losing weight, and she wasn't taking anywhere near as much care of herself as she used to take, whether it be her hair or her makeup or her wardrobe.

She spent so much of her time cleaning the house, I thought she would vacuum the rugs into threads. Not a speck of dust was permitted, not a smudge on a window or a glass. It was almost as if she blamed poor housekeeping for her problems and was out to change it dramatically. Somehow, she had disappointed Daddy by permitting a stain to linger or a smudge on a window. No matter what time Brenda or I returned from school, she was at one house chore or another. And when the house was spotless and shining everywhere, she turned her attention and energies to the garage.

Despite Daddy's suggestions, she did nothing with his clothing, and Uncle Palaver had refused even to look at any. She went into his office to clean and polish, but she didn't put anything away or take anything out. The truth was, she was living and working as if she really expected he would appear one day. She practically admitted it, telling us, "Your father isn't one to just pick up and leave like this. It's one thing for him to stay away for a day or two on business, but another to start a new life. I've spoiled him. No woman is going to spoil him like I did, especially not one of these modern women."

"What's a modern woman?" Brenda asked quickly.

"You know, one who wants a cook and a maid to do

all her housework and expects expensive gifts regularly. They never put themselves out of joint for anyone."

"That's ninety percent of the mothers of kids at our school," Brenda told her.

"Exactly."

"So what do you think, Mama?" Brenda continued. "He's going to show up and declare he had amnesia or something?"

"I don't know. I just . . . I don't know," she said.

Brenda was ready to keep pouncing on her, but she stopped, shook her head, and left the room. Mama looked at me and sighed.

"I know she wants me to hate him, April. I know I should, but I can't get myself to hate him. I'm angry and hurt, but it's just not in me to hate."

"Me, neither, Mama," I revealed.

"Maybe we should be more like Brenda. She's so strong. She'll never be hurt, and if she is, no one will ever know it."

"Is that good, Mama?"

Mama shook her head. "Right now," she said, "it seems wonderful to me. Go on, April. Do your homework, talk to your friends on the phone, do anything but hang around and moon around this house with me," she said.

"I want to be with you, Mama."

"I know, honey. But I don't want you to be sad. Please," she begged.

Reluctantly, I left her.

Our lives soon took on a strange ethereal quality. It felt as if we were floating through our days, and the things we did, we did mechanically, almost entirely without any thought. It got so we fled to our separate corners, afraid that if we did spend too much time with one another, we would crack and crumble into dust. I dreamed of that happening to Brenda and me and Mama simply vacuuming us up before turning the vacuum cleaner on herself. The empty house echoed with the sound of ghosts sobbing.

Mama never went outside for the mail. Usually, because of the later hours Brenda kept at school, I was the one to bring it in, and of course, my fingers trembled when I opened the door to the mailbox and slowly gathered the envelopes together. My heart thumped in anticipation of seeing Daddy's handwriting. I fantasized about a letter from him, one in which he begged for forgiveness and asked to return.

It never came. Weeks turned into months, and then, one day, there was a crack in the walls that had fallen with the weight of steel around us, and a piece of correspondence slipped through. Mama almost didn't see it. When I brought in the mail, I would leave it on the counter in the kitchen. Sometimes it just piled up for days, and sometimes she took it off immediately.

Lately, she had taken to bringing the mail into Daddy's office and sitting at his desk. Brenda looked at me, and I looked at her, but neither of us said anything about it. Was it a good thing or a bad thing? We both wondered. At first, she had treated everything that belonged to Daddy as sacred things. They couldn't be boxed or packaged or given away. Nothing could be changed. She had gone into his office only to clean it the same way she used to before he had left.

Was she in there now because it helped her remain close to him? Or was it because she had finally accepted he was gone, and as Robert Frost told us in his famous poem, nothing gold could stay? Was she finally conceding and facing reality, or, as Brenda so coldly put it, had she finally gone to the cemetery? A part of me wanted her to do that for her sake, so she could go on and do something with the rest of her life, but another part of me hoped it wasn't true. I couldn't help it; I wasn't Brenda. I had to cling to some hope.

One night, Mama was sitting in the office, mindlessly tearing open envelopes and filling files with documentation, when both Brenda and I heard her scream, "Oh, my God!"

We both came to our doorways at the same time and looked at each other. Then we charged down the hallway to the office. Mama was behind the desk, her hands over her eyes, her elbows on the desk. She looked like someone who was told to keep her eyes closed until the surprise was ready to be shown. Daddy's computer and monitor were turned on beside her. Although she knew how to use it well and often shopped over the Internet, as far as we knew, she had not done that since he had left us.

"Mama?" Brenda asked.

Slowly, she lowered her hands and looked at us. For a moment, she looked like a stranger. Her face was so contorted and changed, wearing an expression I had never seen. It looked like a composite of emotions: shock, sadness, but relief of some sort as well.

"What is it, Mama?" I asked, stepping into the office. Brenda followed.

She sat back and held up a letter.

"What is that?" Brenda asked.

Mama took a deep breath first and then spoke. "As you know, all of our business correspondence, every bill of any importance, legal documents, and so on, goes through the money manager your father had appointed before he left us. I get a monthly report, but I haven't paid all that much attention to it. The summary is all that matters to me. We've always been in the positive column; our income always exceeds our expenses, and there are trusts set up for both of you."

"Are we in financial trouble?" Brenda pounced. "Is that it? Was all that Daddy had done just window dressing?"

"No, honey, far from it."

"Then what is it?"

Mama looked at the paper and sat forward. "This comes from a health insurance company. Apparently, some time ago, your father contracted with an insurance company different from the one we've always had, the one that covered our family. This one was for him only, and that was why I never saw anything on it or about it before this."

"Why would he do that?" I asked.

"He was trying to hide something from us," Mama replied.

"What was he trying to hide?" I asked.

"I'm not sure exactly, but whatever it is, it's a very, very serious thing. This," she said, holding the letter up again, "is a letter approving the insurance coverage for his stay at a facility."

"What sort of facility?" Brenda asked.

"I looked it up just a few moments ago," she said, nodding at the computer.

"And? So?" Brenda pursued. "What is it?"

"A facility for the terminally ill," Mama told us.

No one spoke. It was as if we had all gone mute. Brenda finally stepped up to the desk and took the paper from Mama's hand to read. I stepped up beside her and read it, too.

"It's just outside Knoxville," Brenda said, and put the paper down on the desk.

"I don't understand," I said. No one spoke, so I whined, "I don't."

"None of us does, April," Brenda snapped at me, "so stop saying that."

I started to cry. I couldn't help it.

"I'll have to make some phone calls," Mama said.

Brenda and I sat on the leather settee and watched and listened.

Mama began by calling the facility. She asked if a patient named Matthew Taylor had been admitted. Whomever she spoke to didn't want to give her an answer immediately and passed Mama on to another person, who told her they didn't give out information about any of their patients over the phone.

"But I have to know if he's there. I'm his wife," Mama insisted.

"I'm sorry. That's our policy," she was told.

Frustrated, she hung up and thought, and then she looked up our family doctor's number. Of course, his office was closed, but he had an answering service. She told them it was an emergency and demanded that the doctor call her. The service told her they would contact our doctor, Dr. Brimly.

In the meantime, she called our financial manager and demanded to know how long payments had been made to this new health insurance company. He told her he had no information about it and that she would have to let him look things up when he got to his office in the morning.

"You know about it," Mama told him. "I know you know about it, Nick."

After she hung up, she nodded and told us he hadn't denied it.

"Why would he do this?" Brenda asked, shaking her head. "It's like some kind of conspiracy."

"A conspiracy of silence," Mama said, nodding.

The phone rang. It was Dr. Brimly. Mama immediately confronted him with questions about Daddy. She was crying as she asked the questions.

"What do you mean?" she cried, and just listened for the longest time. "I see," she said. "Thank you," she said, and hung up.

For a moment, we thought she wasn't going to tell us anything.

"Mama?"

"He said your father first came to him about having constant headaches. He started to treat him for migraines but very quickly realized it was more serious. He sent him to a specialist in Memphis, a Dr. William Kay, and that was the extent of his knowledge of your father's problems. He said apparently your father ordered Dr. Kay not to give him any information. He said . . ." Mama hiccupped, trying to catch her breath. "He said he was sorry, but it all just fell through the cracks, and he never followed up. He said he had heard Daddy had left us, of course, but he didn't put it together with anything."

"Headaches?" Brenda asked.

Mama nodded.

"Well, what did he think was wrong with him? Why did he think it was more serious?" Brenda asked.

"He suspected he had a brain tumor," Mama said.

She turned and looked out the window into the darkness. There was no moon, and the overcast sky had put a blanket over the stars.

"Mama?" I said, standing.

I could actually feel the floor trembling beneath me. Of course, that came from my own unsteady legs.

Mama turned slowly and looked from Brenda to me, her eyes dark with sadness.

"He was dying," she said. "He wanted to keep it a secret from us. That's why he left us like that."

"Why?" I asked, unable to control my streaking tears. "Why was he so mean to us?"

"So we would hate him," Brenda said.

I turned and looked down at her. "What did you say?"

"So we would hate him and not suffer. That was why he took away all the pictures of himself he could find, and why we can't find the family vacation videos. He tried to die for us before he really did. I'm right, aren't I, Mama?"

Mama nodded.

"But now," Brenda said for all of us, "we'll suffer more because of how angry we were at him."

Mama lowered her head. It was as much as confirming what Brenda predicted. Our true suffering had yet to begin, and what it would do to all of us was something we couldn't anticipate.

I pressed my hand to my heart to keep it from pumping through my chest.

And Brenda, lifted with new rage, stomped out of the room to cry where no one could see.

5

Conspiracy of Silence

All of this had left me feeling very frightened. There was no question that despite what Daddy had done, the very thought of his death continued to rattle my bones and make my heart tremble. Afterward, I was afraid to close my eyes and sleep because of the impending nightmares. None of us was able to get much sleep. I heard Mama moving about the house very late at night. It sounded as if she was opening and closing drawers in the office. Brenda didn't come out of her room, and I didn't go out to see what Mama was doing.

Some time before morning, I did finally fall asleep. I woke right after the sunlight brightened the edges of my shaded window. Passing clouds made it seem like God himself was taking pictures of the earth with a flashbulb on his camera. Each click of brief brightness finally nudged my eyelids open.

I rose slowly and listened for the sounds of Brenda or Mama or both. I heard nothing, not a peep. It was as if the house itself were holding its breath, awaiting the next bit of shocking news. I scrubbed my face vigorously with my dry palms to bring some blood to it and wake myself even more. Then I rose, put on my robe, and slid into my slippers. When I stepped into the hallway, I saw Mama's bedroom door was open. Gazing in, I realized she was up, and so I started for the kitchen. Brenda's door opened, and she, also in her robe and slippers, came out.

"Mama up?" she asked.

"Yes," I said, "but I don't hear her. Maybe she's gone somewhere."

Worried that she had left without us to find Daddy, we went looking for her quickly and found her still dressed in her nightgown and sitting in the kitchen, her hands around a mug of coffee. She looked up at us, her eyes so full of fatigue and sadness they looked as if they might slam shut forever and ever. Her hair fell wildly about her face. She gazed at us with a distant look that frightened us both.

"Mama?" Brenda asked. "Are you all right?"

"I've decided there's no point in pursuing all these people who seem to have been involved in your father's conspiracy of silence," she began. "I started to look for more evidence of what he had done, and then I stopped and realized what difference does it make anyway now? I want to go directly to that facility to see him."

"We do, too," Brenda said quickly.

"Yes, Mama."

She nodded. "You girls have breakfast, dress, and each pack a small bag for overnight or so just in case. We'll go right away," she said. "Brenda, you'll drive. I don't feel up to it," she said in her take-charge voice.

"Of course, Mama."

"While you're having breakfast, I'll start getting dressed," she said, rising.

"I'm not hungry," Brenda said.

"Make yourself something, if it's just some toast. It's a long trip, Brenda. We're going to need strength for the journey and . . . for what's to come," she added.

Brenda nodded. Neither she nor I needed to be told exactly what that meant. Mama walked toward us, paused, and then reached out, her arms embracing us both and pulling us toward her. She held us for a moment.

"Thank God for you two," she whispered, and then let go and went to her bedroom.

Brenda didn't shed a tear. She glanced at my tear-streaked face and went right to work getting us juice and preparing some toast and soft-boiled eggs. I set the kitchenette table, and she poured herself some coffee. I did, too. Neither of us spoke. It was good to have things to do, to keep ourselves moving and busy.

We ate quickly, almost in total silence, just asking each other for the salt and pepper. After we finished, I asked Brenda how long she thought the ride would take. She estimated five hours. She told me to go shower. She would look after cleaning up.

"What should I wear?" I asked her. For a moment, I thought she was going to laugh at the question, but then she looked thoughtful. After all, we were going to see Daddy in a hospital, maybe for the last time.

"Wear that pretty blue dress they bought you for your last birthday," she advised, and I hurried off to do what she said.

She didn't wear a dress, but she wore one of her nicest pants suits. Mama was waiting for us in the kitchen, just standing and gazing out the window.

"Good," she said when she saw us. "Let's go."

We got into the car. Mama decided to sit in the rear, so I sat up front with Brenda. Moments later, we were on our way.

"I didn't even ask you if you knew how to go, Brenda," Mama said once we left our street.

"I went into the office and got directions from the computer," Brenda said, and held up a sheet she had printed. "April will be the navigator." She handed me the printed directions to follow.

Brenda was right about the time it would take. We made a decision to stop for something to eat, if just to break up the journey. Brenda wanted us to do it so Mama would eat something. We both knew she hadn't had anything but coffee. She fell asleep for most of the trip and woke when we stopped at a roadside diner. She at least had some soup and a buttered roll. A little more than an hour later, we entered the small community in which the facility was located. I read the directions Brenda had printed from the computer, and about ten minutes later, we saw the address printed in gold lettering on a large, square, rust-brown pilaster by the entry gate. The building was considerably back from the street and off to the side a bit, and you would have to stop to see it well. The gate was open, so we drove right onto the property.

The long driveway was lined on both sides with long-leaf pine trees neatly spaced. The grounds of the property were very well manicured, the grass and bushes trimmed. We saw some fountains, and stone benches I was sure no one ever sat on. There was no one in sight, and it all had a peaceful, tranquil atmosphere. Even the birds seemed to fly slower, gliding as if they were in a dream before they rested on branches or the fountains and benches. I hesitated to say it was beautiful. I hesitated to say anything nice about a place in which my daddy was dying or in which he had already passed away.

The three-story building itself was so different from any I had seen. It had a light gray cladding with a centered gable and an accentuated front door supported by pilasters, a hipped light blue roof with three dormers, and rectangular windows with double-hung sashes. There were three chimneys. What made it very unusual was the wing set at an angle. It had a separate doorway and looked as if it had been added on some time after the original structure was built.

There was absolutely no name on the building to identify it. It looked more like someone's old mansion. Whatever automobiles were there were parked behind the building, even though there was a distinct area off to the right in front of it for visitor parking. We pulled into a space, and Brenda turned off the engine. For a moment, none of us moved.

"I guess this is it," Brenda finally said. "That was the address."

Mama dabbed her eyes with her handkerchief and opened the car door. We all got out and walked slowly toward the main entrance. It was odd, because for an institutional facility that was really a hospital, it had a doorbell to ring. Brenda had tried the door and found it locked. What sort of a place was this? I wondered.

We waited. It was still quiet, not a sound coming from inside, not a soul outside, not even a groundskeeper. The street from which we had turned in was still, too, with not a car passing by since we had arrived. It was truly as if we had entered a way station between this world and the next. It gave me the jitters.

Brenda pressed the buzzer again. We could hear it ringing inside. She looked at Mama, who was obviously battling back her own hysteria and trembling in her clothes. Finally, the door opened, and a tall woman with very short dark brown hair specked with gray stood before us. She wore a nurse's uniform, but it was more gray than white and had her name in black sewn into the right breast pocket: "Ms. Luther." She wore no makeup, not even lipstick. A fine trickle of lighter brown hair ran down her temples to the top of her jawbone. She pressed her thin lips together before speaking, and her somewhat bony nose dipped and came up as she finally did speak.

"Yes? How can I help you?" she asked.

"We're here to see Matthew Taylor," Brenda said. "We're his immediate family."

Ms. Luther scrutinized the three of us as if she could tell just by looking at us if we were telling the truth.

"That patient specifically has written on his admittance form that there would be no visitors, and no visitors are to be permitted," she replied. She looked as if she would slam the door closed as well. Her hand tightened on it.

Brenda, being the athlete she was, pivoted her left foot quickly to make that impossible and stepped forward. Mama came around on her right.

"Matthew Taylor is my husband," she said firmly. "These are his daughters. We just recently learned he has checked himself into this . . . this place, and we insist on seeing him."

"This place, as you call it, is special because we guarantee that we respect the wishes of our patients. It's very, very important to them and to their families. You'll have to contact Mr. Taylor's trustee to see about any possible changes, and then . . ."

"We're not leaving here until we see him," Brenda asserted. "If you want to have a scene, we'll have a scene. When people are very ill, they make decisions that they would not make if they were well. We don't care who his trustee is or what he says. That's our father, and that's my mother's husband in there. I'm sure this situation will interest newspaper and television people, and that's where we'll go, not to any trustee," she added.

Even Mama was surprised at Brenda's strength. I saw the way she lifted her eyebrows when Brenda finished. My own heart was thumping the way the heart of a coward would. I was ready to turn and bolt for the car. Brenda looked ready to grapple with the woman.

Ms. Luther saw that as well in Brenda's face. She pulled her head up, tightening the skin on her neck and lifting her narrow shoulders against her uniform.

"I am warning you," she said. "I don't intend . . ."

"Go on, call your security, and start the festivities," Brenda challenged.

"This is outrageous," Ms. Luther said, but I could see that she was weakening. Her shoulders sagged, and her hand loosened its grip on the door. "Mr. Taylor is in a coma and has been for days," she added. "He is off any life support as well, as he dictated in his admittance papers, and before you threaten any lawsuits, I want to assure you, it was all done through an attorney of his choice and properly assessed. That is the only way we accept any of our patients."

"Why do you call them patients?" Brenda asked her. "They're here to die, not to be treated and get well."

"Please," Mama pleaded. "Let us see him. If he is as you say, there is no possible harm done, anyway."

Ms. Luther turned her attention to Mama, since she had the more reasonable and far less threatening voice and look.

"Very well, I'll make an exception to our rules, but

only for now. If you return, you will have to have the trustee go through a proper legal procedure."

She stepped back, and we entered. The lobby was bare. The chairs and sofas looked vintage but rarely used. On the table between them was a brochure of some kind. There was an unlit pole lamp beside one of the chairs. Against the far wall was a desk with nothing on it and a dark cherry-wood grandfather clock against the wall to the right of that. The lobby walls were otherwise bare, except for a sign that read "No Smoking."

Ms. Luther turned to her right to lead us to a door. The floor was black marble with light white streaks that reminded me of the Milky Way. Our footsteps echoed because the building was deathly silent. It was truly like walking into a giant tomb, and it gave me the chills.

"Please be as quiet as possible," she said.

Mama reached back to put her arm around my shoulders to bring me alongside her. Brenda was right on Ms. Luther's heels, her hands clenched, her body poised and arched slightly forward like a bow about to shoot an arrow. Ms. Luther opened the door to a short corridor, at the end of which was a typical-looking nurses' station that you could find in any hospital. The two nurses behind the counters looked our way curiously. The air had the scent of detergents used to scrub floors and walls. Everything looked surgical-room aseptic.

Ms. Luther stopped at the third door on the left, put her hand on the doorknob, and turned to us.

"I ask only that you respect my situation and don't stay longer than a half hour," she said, and waited for some response before turning the doorknob.

Brenda looked as if she would lunge at her.

"Okay," Mama said quickly.

Ms. Luther opened the door and stepped to the side. The room also resembled a typical hospital room, the walls a light blue, a set of windows to the right and the left of the motorized hospital bed. There was an intravenous bag on a stand, still with some liquid, detached but still at the side of the bed. A heart monitor beeped on the right. The floor was of the same tile that was in the lobby. It was all Spartan without a painting, a vase of flowers, anything to add color and warmth.

Daddy was slightly propped up, his head lying a bit to the left, his eyes closed. Despite his condition, his complexion was surprisingly robust, I thought. It gave me a surge of optimism. Maybe he had begun a miraculous recuperation.

"What are you doing for him?" Brenda demanded, as if she were thinking the same thing.

Ms. Luther, who remained at the doorway, smirked. "There's nothing more to do for him under the circumstances," she replied. "I'll give you the contact number for his trustee, and you can have him put you in touch with Dr. Blocker, who administers to our patients."

"Administers what?" Brenda fired back at her.

"Peace and tranquility at a most troubling time," she answered without flinching. "A half hour," she added, and stepped out, closing the door behind her.

"That woman must be a direct descendant of a Nazi commander who ran a concentration camp," Brenda muttered after her.

Mama moved slowly to Daddy's bedside. Brenda brought the one chair in the room to her, and Mama sat, taking Daddy's hand in hers. I stood there looking down at him. Brenda moved to the window and gazed out, her body still very tight. I noticed her hands were clenched into fists that she kept at her side.

"Oh, Matt," Mama began, rubbing his hand softly. "This was so wrong, so wrong. I know what you hoped to do, but you didn't protect us by doing this. I believed in my vows, for better or for worse, in sickness and in health. We love you, Matt. It's not and never has been a one-way street when it comes to that. We should have been at your side all the time, throughout this ordeal."

I looked at Mama. She was gazing at Daddy and talking to him as if she believed he could hear every word, as if they were having one of their normal conversations at dinner. Brenda listened but didn't turn to look. She kept her shoulders high, her head slightly back, as though she were experiencing a whipping.

"Now you're in this horrible cold place with people who never saw you as we did. Why?" Mama asked, her voice cracking. "Oh why, my love?"

She lowered her head until her forehead could rest against his hand. I tried to breathe, but my chest had hardened into cement. When I looked at Daddy, I thought he appeared just as he would in any deep sleep, without Death slipping in beside him and entering his body to claim it.

Why did Death want to claim it? Why couldn't he leave us alone until Mama and Daddy were old and gray and tired of struggling against maladies of age, like so many other elderly people? Why couldn't he let Daddy live to see Brenda and me marry and have children of our own? What had he done to deserve this? I felt the need to shout, but I swallowed it all back.

The heart monitor continued its slow but regular beep.

Brenda finally turned and looked at Mama. "Look at her. We shouldn't stay here more than a half hour, anyway," she whispered to me. "It's too much for her."

From where did she get the strength? I wondered. Was it that she never stopped being a competitor? She could even compete against Death? Or did she really mean, *It's too much for me, for us?*

She walked around to Mama's side and put her hand on Mama's shoulder. Mama slowly raised her head and looked at her and then at Daddy.

"He's so peaceful," she said. "Maybe this was the best way."

"Not for us," Brenda insisted.

I knew what she meant. We all knew now Daddy's purpose for what he had done, but what he hadn't anticipated was how much we would hate ourselves for how we had reacted to it. We now knew the sickness had turned him into the monster. We now knew that the man both Brenda and I had called Daddy and Mama had called her husband had died long before he had begun this attempt to stop us from mourning his death so bitterly.

Mama took a deep breath and nodded. She rose, leaned over to kiss Daddy's cheek, and then turned sadly away. I was next. His cheek was still warm and soft to me. I wanted to whisper something. What? What could I say to him now? It came to me in a flash that began somewhere deep in my heart and my memory.

"Good-bye, Mr. Panda," I whispered.

Brenda heard it. I saw her eyes flinch and saw the way she raised them quickly toward the ceiling.

"Let's go," she forced herself to say.

Wasn't she going to kiss him? Couldn't she find it in her heart to forgive him?

I waited. Mama started for the door. Brenda stood there, staring down, and then she went to his side, took his hand in hers, and lowered herself to whisper, too. I didn't hear what she said, but as we left the room, I asked her what it was.

"I told him he was doing this just to prevent getting his ass kicked on the driveway basketball court," she said.

I looked up in surprise. Was that it? Were those all her possibly last words to him?

"And then I told him I loved him," she added.

Ms. Luther was waiting for us in the hallway and hurried to escort us out.

"Where will you be?" she asked, showing some sort of remorse and understanding.

Mama looked stunned by the question and shook her head. "I don't know yet. I . . ."

"We'll stop at that motel we saw on the way here," Brenda suggested quickly.

"Oh, yes."

"Here's the number of your husband's attorney, and here is our number," she added, giving Mama a card with the numbers written on it.

"Weren't you at least given instructions to call us in the event of his passing?" Mama asked.

"That's why I'm giving you these numbers," she replied.

"Gee, how considerate," Brenda muttered loudly enough for her to hear.

"We do only what we are instructed to do," Ms. Luther snapped at her.

"Only following orders? Where have I heard that before?" Brenda mused aloud.

Mama turned her toward the front entrance.

"Let's just go," she said, and we walked back through the lobby and out the door.

We drove directly to the motel we had passed and got two rooms since there wasn't one big enough for the three of us. Brenda and I shared one, and Mama took the one adjoining. As soon as she settled in, Mama called the attorney and spoke with him. We sat on her bed and listened to the conversation.

"Well," she said, turning to us after she was finished talking, "you heard some of it. Your father's plan was to keep us away from all the horror and misery he was going through. He was diagnosed some time ago and given little hope. When his symptoms grew worse, he made a decision to get away from us before they grew severe. The condition did affect his personality, his tolerance level, and his ability to do things for himself. He didn't want us to witness all that degeneration. There are instructions for afterward that included us. I guess the theory was that we would have all the sadness in one blow rather than a prolonged period of it.

"I could never hate him for this," she added, looking more at Brenda than at me.

"I don't hate him, Mama. I hate what's happened to him," Brenda said.

Mama took a deep breath. "I'll just get some rest, and then we'll see about finding a nice place to eat. We should have a good dinner," she said.

Good food always brought some comfort, helped you to feel better inside, I thought.

Brenda and I went to our room to rest, too.

"Did he have to go and hide the videos and take all those pictures from us?" I asked her, still stunned by the events as they were unfolding.

"He didn't know what he was doing by then, I'm sure," Brenda said. "The disease made him crazy. Just forget all of it. It didn't happen," she said.

Didn't happen? How could I ever convince myself of that? How could she?

I didn't think I would fall asleep when we both lay

down to take a short nap, but I did. Emotional exhaustion was harder and greater than physical, I decided. Brenda actually had to wake me to get ready to go to dinner. Mama had woken and called our room, but I didn't hear the phone ring. She had already located what the motel manager described as a good Italian restaurant nearby.

"Italian food is your father's favorite food, actually," Mama told us on the way there.

It was strange to hear her talk about him as if we didn't really know him. Of course, we knew that was his favorite food. Also, it was almost as if she were expecting he would meet us at the restaurant. He would have woken from his coma, gazed around, and thought, *What am I doing here?* He would have gotten dressed, found out where we were going, and gotten there ahead of us. I dreamed he was sitting at the table, smiling.

"I'm sorry, gang," he would begin. "I put you through all this unnecessarily. Let's just have a great dinner and all go home, okay?"

Oh, how okay that would be.

Maybe Mama was dreaming a similar sort of dream. In her mind, he would be up and ready when we visited him again. She was in what I would call a faux happy mood. She had a cocktail before dinner and talked incessantly, remembering happy times she had with Daddy. She talked about their courting days, their dates, their vacations before we were born. Recalling these joyful events invigorated her. Every memory was another brick in the wall to keep the tragedy and the horror about to befall us away for a while longer.

Unfortunately, that wasn't much of a while. Mama had called the facility and spoken with Ms. Luther. She gave her the phone number at the motel, and two hours or so after we had settled in for the night, the phone rang in Mama's room. Brenda told me she could hear it ring through the walls and woke up as well and could hear Mama's wail.

I was in a very deep sleep, burying myself in it as someone would bury herself in a few warm blankets. I didn't wake up until I heard sobbing and turned, wiped my eyes, and looked at Mama and Brenda holding on to each other. I dropped my head to the pillow and cried myself.

"At least we got here to see him," Mama said through her tears. "He waited for us. I know he did."

Even Brenda looked as if she believed that was what had happened.

In the morning, we headed back home. Daddy, in his careful preparations to lessen the impact of his death upon us, had made all the arrangements for his funeral and burial. We literally had nothing to do but dress and attend the church service and the internment.

Uncle Palaver had been calling us and reached us the day after we returned. Mama said he didn't seem all that surprised about what Daddy had done. He said he, too, had felt there was something unreal about it when he first learned of Daddy's leaving us but soon realized it was all true, terribly true. Now that he knew the whole story, he saw it as just another kind of sleight of hand. It would take him too long to drive back, so he flew back on a small commuter airline and was there at our side throughout. I wondered why he didn't bring Destiny, but Brenda thought he had decided it just wasn't the right time to make new acquaintances.

"She would be too uncomfortable. I know I would be," Brenda said. Of course, I agreed.

I was sure that people, friends and some distant rel-

atives who came, all thought it strange that we cried
little at the services. The truth was, we had already
cried out our tears. That was why we were so still and
vacant-eyed at the funeral. I knew people wouldn't understand. They all thought we were still angry about
his running off, perhaps. I could see it in their faces
when they offered their condolences. They disap-
proved, and that disapproval diminished their sympathy. Daddy never thought of that either, I realized.

In one sense, he certainly did make things easier.
The transition to life without him had already taken
place. After Uncle Palaver left to resume his touring
with Destiny, both Brenda and I returned to school as
quickly as we could. Teachers and friends offered sympathy, but Brenda barely acknowledged it. If anyone
thought she walked about with a chip on her shoulder
before, they were convinced that chip had grown now.
The anger that festered inside her continued to emerge
in her athletics. She was far more aggressive on the
courts and always looked like a bomb about to explode.

Mama again talked about returning to work but
never made a real effort to do so. She was shrinking inside, and she lost more weight. When I voiced my
worry, she told me it was expected after the loss of a
loved one and not to worry. She would get on her feet
soon. Why didn't I have the same reaction? Why didn't
I lose weight? I think I ate more out of depression and
sadness and gained more weight.

I moaned and groaned about myself as if I were
talking about someone else.

"You'll change," Mama assured me. "Soon."

There was that word again, that word built on a
foundation of promises: *soon*. It had been following
me all my life. In the next weeks and months, little, if

anything, changed, however. I went to a party but felt I was being invited out of sympathy and not desire. Even the girls who were not very popular avoided me. In the food chain, I guess I was the lowest of the low, and their disdain for me helped them feel a little better about themselves. If any boy looked at me, I quickly looked away, afraid that all I would see in his eyes would be either disgust or pity. Here I was nearly sixteen, and I hadn't as much as held hands with a boy, much less kissed any.

That summer, Brenda decided to take two of her senior year's required courses in an advanced study program the school had created. Her grades were just high enough for her to qualify. It made her eligible for early graduation. There were college scouts and representatives vigorously inquiring about her now, and before the high school year had ended, she had received two offers of full scholarships. If she completed her summer courses successfully, she would receive her diploma in mid-August and be able to leave and go to college in time to play for the girls' basketball teams. It was only a matter of deciding which one she wanted to attend.

The very thought of Brenda's leaving home so quickly depressed me. How hollow and empty the house would become without her, even though she spent so much time outside. During the summer, she also gave me more attention.

"You have to get hold of yourself, April," she said, finally echoing Daddy's warnings, the ones he made during his Mr. Hyde days. "Daddy wasn't all wrong about that. It is unhealthy for you to carry so much weight. You're going to start running and exercising with me," she commanded.

I was afraid I would look too foolish, but she was

more tolerant and patient with me than ever. I had the sense she had decided she owed this to Daddy, more than she owed it to me. One day, she even ransacked our kitchen pantry, emptying it of what she called high-calorie, low-value foods. She got Mama to stop making rich desserts after dinner, and she constantly cross-examined me about what I had eaten while she was away at school.

Before the summer had ended, I had gone a good ten pounds below my weight since Daddy had died. Brenda had me take tennis lessons, made me carry her golf clubs when she played golf with two of her teammates at a country club one of them belongs to, and nightly put me through a series of stretching exercises. We did some yoga together as well.

For the first time ever, I felt more like her sister. I think that motivated me more than my own desire to look better and feel better. It was important to please Brenda, to keep her interested in me, believing her efforts with me were worthwhile. With her going off to college, I wondered if I would just slip back into my couch potato rut and regain all I had lost.

"You better not," she told me before she left when I wondered about it aloud. "You have to take better care of yourself so you can look after Mama better, too," she warned.

Mama needed looking after. She had withdrawn into herself so deeply we both thought it would be difficult, if not impossible, to bring her back out.

"We're all she has now," Brenda said. "You've got to get her to think about herself. Be cheery, upbeat. Join something like the drama club, if not one of the teams. Make her come out to see you do things. You understand, April. It's going to be up to you now."

I nodded, terrified of the responsibility.

"Maybe Uncle Palaver will be back soon," I said.

"He won't, and besides, he won't be here long if he is. That's not the solution, April. Mama is our problem."

She smiled.

"You'll be all right. You'll see," she said. "I'll call often, and you'll come visit me when you can."

"Really?"

"Of course," she said. "I'll want you to bring Mama to the big games, too."

I didn't think I would cry the day she left. I was older now, not only because of time but because of what we had experienced. I wanted to be more like Brenda. I wanted to have her strength and her steely eyes and stoic face when I would most need it.

Mama had given Brenda her car, since we had Daddy's car now, too. I watched her pack and helped her load the car. When it was time for her to go, Mama and I walked out to the driveway to hug and kiss her good-bye.

She glanced at the basketball net and backboard. She squinted, and, like her, I could hear Daddy's laughter.

"I'll tell you both a secret," she said, still looking at the net. "It didn't matter that he wasn't there at the end, that he didn't come with you to the games and cheer with you."

She looked at me. Her gaze was firm, her eyes assured and focused the way she could make them when she put her whole heart into what she would do or say.

"He was always there. I saw him."

"Yes," Mama said, nodding and smiling.

"Don't you go gaining back a single ounce, April. I'm warning you," she said.

"I won't. I promise."

She got into her car and started the engine.

"Be careful, honey," Mama said.

Brenda nodded and winked at me. My big sister winked at me, and then she drove off slowly, turning out of the driveway and moving until she was gone.

Mama shook off a sob and put her arm around me.

We stood there staring after Brenda, both of us scared to admit how afraid we were of the silence that lingered.

Both of us scared of tomorrow.

6

Celia's Visit

Summer seemed to take forever to end after Brenda left us. I would sit on the grass and then lie back and look up at the sky, just watching the wind move clouds lazily. Sometimes I did it right after one of my runs. I tried having the same enthusiasm about the exercise that I had when Brenda was running beside me or just ahead of me. It was harder to keep it up, but I wanted to do it for her as much as for myself. I couldn't disappoint her. I didn't want her to give up on me.

But it was a lonely time for me. The few friends I had were away for the summer at camps or on family trips. It got so I wanted to sleep later so there would be less time to be awake and the day would pass faster. I was actually glad when school finally began, even though I had a hard time getting back into a regular schedule of activities. I just wanted to drift like those clouds I watched.

My English teacher quoted Henry David Thoreau

one day and said, "Time is the stream I go a fishing in." We were learning how different authors treated the concept of time in their works. Thoreau, he said, didn't live his life according to any schedule or any clock. He didn't have appointments hanging over his head. He ignored it all and enjoyed life. When I heard all this and read some of it, I became envious. How wonderful not to care about anything but the moment, to be able to relax and daydream with no one standing over me, reminding me of my responsibilities.

I also wondered, why teach us about Thoreau? Why torment us? How could we escape from reacting to the ringing of bells, being late, worrying about tomorrow and the days left until an assignment was due? How could we escape from torturing ourselves about our future, our graduation day? For us, the clock was ticking like a time bomb. Time wasn't a stream. Minutes weren't drops of water. They were little bees stinging us every time we dared slack off.

And then I thought about Uncle Palaver out there on the highways of America, driving at his own pace, accepting this date or that if he wished, or not accepting any and just drifting, or parking by a beautiful scenic area and just taking in nature. Suddenly, despite all that Daddy had said about him, I envied him. Time was truly a stream for Uncle Palaver, and yet he was an adult in an adult world. He had to pay taxes and bills and worry about health insurance and all that, but maybe being able to hold on to part of Thoreau's dream was Uncle Palaver's greatest magical achievement.

For Mama, time appeared to have come to a standstill. She, too, lost interest in dates, schedules, obligations, and calendars. She was adrift in a different way, sort of in limbo. The days could come; the days could go. It didn't matter to her. She forgot her own birthday, in fact, and was genuinely surprised to receive gifts from Brenda and me.

I was told by more than one sympathetic mourner that time had healing qualities. Every tick of the clock was supposed to be another step away from the sadness, and soon it would take us so far that we would no longer cry or suffer such great sorrow. However, it wasn't working that way for Mama. She refused to accept tomorrow. She refused to forget. For her, the clock had stopped.

I wrote often to Brenda, and whenever I could, I spoke to her on the telephone about my concerns for Mama. Brenda had opted to attend Thompson University in Memphis because it had such a well-organized and impressive female athletic department. It was a small college with only a little more than a thousand students, but its record on the basketball and volleyball courts, as well as women's field hockey, was impressive thanks to its recruiting. One of its graduates, Mona LePage, did get chosen for the women's Olympic volleyball team, and the school was very proud of her.

Since the college was in Memphis, most of the students commuted, but there was a small, two-hundred-population women's dormitory on the campus, and Brenda shared a room with a girl three years ahead of her, Celia Harding. Apparently, they had met at Brenda's registration and had hit it off so well so quickly that they decided to be roommates. In all her letters and phone calls, Brenda praised and raved about Celia Harding. In fact, she talked so much about her I couldn't help but be jealous. I was surprised, too, when she told me she was bringing Celia home to spend Thanksgiving with us.

First, I thought it was too soon to have an overnight guest, and second, I was afraid Mama wasn't strong enough to entertain a stranger, but Brenda had already discussed it with Mama, and Mama had agreed and even sounded a little excited about it. I relented and admitted to myself that it could be a good thing. It would take Mama's mind off the sadness and give her reason to do a full-blown Thanksgiving dinner. In my heart of hearts, I hoped and prayed that somehow Uncle Palaver would show up as well. He had been at our home only once for Thanksgiving, and I was just five years old at the time and barely remembered.

He called more often now. Mama would get all choked up on the phone, and I would take over and talk to him and hear about his adventurous life on the road. I kept prodding him about Thanksgiving. I didn't want to come right out and say Mama needed him or I needed him, but I came as close to doing that as I could. For a while, I did think he would come, but two weeks before Thanksgiving, he called to tell us about a wonderful opportunity he was given if he went to California. He was going to be featured on more than a dozen regional television shows, and his manager thought it could be just the break he needed to get onto a national television stage of one sort or another.

There were so many talented entertainers out there trying for the big breaks, and so many really deserved one. The competition was fierce, and opportunities like the one presented to Uncle Palaver so rare.

"It would be cruel and unfair to Warner to pressure him to come back here for Thanksgiving and miss his chances, April," Mama told me when I whined a little too much about it. "He has worked too long and too hard."

Of course, she was right, so I stopped talking about

him, and when he called again, I wished him luck. He promised to have a copy of one of the television appearances sent to us on video tape.

"Maybe I'll be there for Christmas," he offered, but I did recall him mentioning the possibility of his being hired to do a ten-day cruise out of Los Angeles and down to what was called the Mexican Riviera over Christmas and New Year's Eve. I didn't ask him, but I wondered if all of these bookings included Destiny as well. I imagined if she was part of his act, she would accompany him. Besides, I was sure he would want to be with her on New Year's Eve.

Just the thought of spending a New Year's Eve after Daddy's death was terrifying to me. Mama would be so lost, I thought. Maybe I could talk her into our going away, too, I decided. I tried, and she said she would think about it, but I knew it didn't go longer than a few seconds in her mind before floating away and disappearing like smoke.

The day before Brenda was to arrive with Celia, Mama showed some of her old energy. She changed the curtains in the guest room and bought a new area rug to put next to the bed. That afternoon, she decided the bedding now didn't fit the decor and, almost in a panic about it, had me go with her to buy new bedding. There wasn't a spot in the guest room she didn't polish. She washed down the bathroom as if she were out to prevent some sort of infectious disease. I kept asking her to slow down, to rest, but she told me she was fine.

She was still in there diddling about with one thing or another in the evening until she finally decided it was good enough and went to bed. The next morning, she was up before I was and working on the Thanksgiving dinner. She had me do all sorts of cleaning up around the house. I told her I had already vacuumed the living room, but she didn't remember, and she didn't believe it was good enough even if I had done it.

"We'll be exhausted by the time Brenda and her roommate arrive, Mama," I protested. "What good will that be?"

"Stop exaggerating," she told me, and had me wash the windows by the front door.

"Who's coming, the queen of England?" I muttered. She overheard me.

"Your father and I always treat our guests like royalty," she said. "We're old-fashioned that way."

I turned and looked at her. She was smiling, but it was different. That, plus the use of the present tense in relation to Daddy, sounded a small alarm in my heart. Later, it sounded again when I looked in at the dining room table and saw there was one more place setting than we needed.

"Mama," I said softly, entering the kitchen and coming up behind her while she prepared her sweet potato pie, "you put out too many plates."

"What?" she said, turning and grimacing with confusion. "What are you saying?"

"There are only four of us for dinner, not five, unless you invited someone else without telling me."

"Oh," she said. "I put out five?"

"Yes, Mama."

She shook her head. "Old habits die hard," she said, and returned to her sweet potato pie.

"I'll fix it," I told her.

She didn't reply, but I went into the dining room and rearranged it all. I left the place at the seat that Daddy always occupied empty, just as we had been doing since the day he left. Too many times, I had caught Mama looking at that empty place. Sometimes, she seemed to be seeing him there. I wouldn't say anything. I would pretend not to notice.

To keep my mind off it all the day Brenda and Celia were to arrive, I went into the living room and began reading my English novel assignment. I gazed at the clock from time to time in anticipation. Brenda had told us that she and Celia were meeting with some of their friends first to celebrate a bit and then heading to our house. They were supposed to arrive at one.

Mama was baking two pies, an apple and a pumpkin. Those had been Daddy's favorites, especially on Thanksgiving, and twice this morning, she had told me that.

"We've always had a nice Thanksgiving," she concluded. "Your father once said, 'I think I married you for your Thanksgiving dinners.'"

She laughed. I was happy to see her do that, but the way she looked when she said these things still bothered me. I couldn't explain why, but it did. For that reason, as much as anything, I couldn't wait for Brenda to arrive. She was already more than a half hour late. Impatient, I couldn't continue reading. I got up and paced about the house, going to the front door to look out every five minutes or so. Finally, I saw her car turn into the driveway, and a surge of excitement and happiness filled my heart.

Wait until she sees me, I thought. I had lost another ten pounds. *She'll be so proud of me.* Days before Thanksgiving, I was running and exercising more often and even contemplated going out for the girls' volleyball team.

I didn't want to be caught standing and looking out the front window, but I couldn't contain my bulging curiosity about Celia, after all Brenda's letters and all her conversations in which she praised Celia. I had never seen Brenda so taken with any other girl the way she was now taken with Celia. Who was this wondrous person?

When they stepped out of the car, I couldn't take my eyes off Celia Harding. She was taller than Brenda and more shapely, with long hair the color of a new penny. She had it tied in a ponytail. I had been hoping she would be short and plain-looking, even as overweight as I still was. As they drew closer, I saw she had beautifully shaped olive-green eyes and a soft, angelic smile, with tiny freckles on the crests of her cheeks. They giggled and brushed shoulders. I opened the door before they got to it and stood looking out at them. It took them by complete surprise.

"April!" Brenda said, as if she never expected to see me. "What were you doing, waiting at the door?"

She turned to Celia and laughed.

"This is my little sister, April. April, meet Celia Harding."

"Hi," she said. "I've heard a lot about you, April."

"Hi," I said. I didn't want to say I had heard a lot about her, and I didn't like being called a little sister.

"Are you going to let us in?" Brenda asked.

"What? Oh." I stepped back, and they entered.

"What a sweet-looking house," Celia said.

Sweet-looking? What kind of thing was that to say about our home?

"Where's Mama?" Brenda asked me.

"In the kitchen. She's been there most of the day," I said, "working harder than usual because we have a guest."

"Mama!" Brenda shouted, and walked by me. Celia smiled at me and followed.

I stood out in the hallway and listened to Brenda's introduction of Celia, and Mama's happy voice. In moments, they were all talking at once about the food, their trip, college. It was as if I were completely forgotten. Brenda didn't ask me a single question about my activities or what I was doing at school. Mama was totally absorbed in everything Celia was saying. She sat there with a smile on her face, a smile I hadn't seen so bright and alive for some time. I went back to the living room, picked up my book, and flopped into the big chair that used to be Daddy's chair. It was soft, with thick arms, and you could push back on it and bring up a footrest. To me, it felt as if I were in Daddy's arms again.

My eyes ran off the pages of the book. I really didn't absorb any of it. Instead, I continued to listen to the chatter among Mama, Brenda, and Celia. It was as if Celia had been an old friend or even a long-lost sister or something. Their laughter annoyed me. Finally, I heard them start down the hallway to show Celia the rest of the house and her room. They paused in the living room doorway and looked in at me.

"April," Mama said, full of surprise. "Did you meet Brenda's roommate?"

"Yes," I said. "I met them at the door, and I was in the kitchen just before, too, Mama!" I practically screamed.

"Were you? Well, what are you doing?"

"I'm reading my English assignment," I said petulantly. I was still waiting for Brenda to make some comment about my lost weight.

"Oh," Brenda said to Celia instead, "I've got to show you my scrapbook. It's in my room. Let's get you settled into yours," she added, and the two of them continued down the hallway.

"I hope it's all right," Mama cried after them. "I had so little time to prepare." She glanced at me again and then returned to the kitchen.

I sat there sulking until I got bored and rose to see what everyone was doing. Mama had the radio on in the kitchen and was listening to music, which was something she hadn't done for some time. I glanced in at her and saw her checking on everything in and above the stove.

As casually and seemingly as disinterested as I could pretend to be, I strolled down the hallway to Brenda's room and the guest room. The door to the guest room was open, and Celia's bag was still unopened on the bed. The door to Brenda's room was closed. I stood there, listening as hard as I could. They were talking, but not very loudly and occasionally, I heard a ripple of laughter from both of them.

Brenda had never had a close girlfriend in the sense most of the girls I knew had. I couldn't remember a time she had ever invited anyone to sleep over or have dinner with us, and she was never invited to anyone else's house, either. She palled around with her teammates in school, but they never did anything else together. *Perhaps that was why Mama was so excited about Celia,* I thought. Still, it was odd that I had never given it much thought until now. Even I, who was probably tied for the most unpopular girl in history, had girlfriends over on occasion. It didn't create a close, best-friend relationship or anything, but it was something.

I thought about knocking on Brenda's door. It had been months since she had left, and although we wrote to each other and spoke on the phone, we still had a lot of catching up to do. Why wasn't that as important to her as it was to me? Celia was probably just demanding so much attention, I thought. She looked like a spoiled woman, I concluded, although I had no way to defend or explain that. I knocked on Brenda's door.

"Yes?"

I opened the door and looked in. They were both on Brenda's bed, lying side by side and turned toward each other. The sight of someone else in Brenda's bed stopped me cold. I had never slept with her or crawled in beside her, even when we were in mourning. Brenda leaned on her left elbow and looked my way.

"Mama need us?" she asked.

"No, not yet," I said.

"What's up?"

"Um. I spoke to Uncle Palaver yesterday," I said, searching for something quickly.

"Yeah, Mama told me when I called. Uncle Palaver," she explained, "is my mother's younger brother."

"Oh, yes, the magician. I was hoping to see him," Celia said, sitting up.

She had untied her hair and shook her head so the strands would fall loosely about her shoulders. Her hair looked so soft and light I thought the strands could float. My own hair always felt coarse and rough to me, no matter what wonder shampoo and treatment I employed.

"I was hoping he'd tell us how to make Ms. Gitalong disappear," Celia added, and they both laughed.

"Who's Ms. Gitalong?" I asked, grimacing.

"She's the dorm mother. Her real name is Gitman, but everyone calls her Gitalong because they'd like her to git along," Brenda explained. "Celia gave her the name, and it's stuck."

The two of them laughed again.

"It doesn't sound like you're enjoying being there," I said, not hiding my hope that it was true.

"Oh, we find ways to enjoy ourselves," Brenda said, and they giggled.

I had never heard Brenda laugh so much or giggle. It was growing even more annoying.

"I'm thinking of going out for the girls' volleyball team this year," I said. "I didn't tell you on the phone because I wasn't sure, but now I am."

"Great," Brenda said. She turned back to Celia. "I think we should get ready for dinner. Why don't you ask Mama how much longer, April? Ask her if she wants us to do anything," she added.

"She doesn't," I said. "You know she doesn't. I'll ask her anyway," I said, relenting quickly, and looked at Celia, who held her smile on me like a flashlight.

I turned and hurried out to the kitchen.

"Brenda and her friend want to know how much longer, Mama," I said, making it sound as if Celia were the one being more demanding.

"Oh, tell them not to rush. I'll have everything set in an hour," Mama said. "Isn't Brenda's friend nice and very pretty?"

"She's very pretty," I admitted. "I don't know how nice she is yet."

I walked back to Brenda's room. She was in her robe, and the door to her bathroom was closed, but I could hear the shower going.

"Mama says in about an hour," I said. I looked at the bathroom door. "Why doesn't she use the shower in her room?"

"That's just a tub shower. My stall shower is so much better," Brenda said. "Don't worry. We're quite used to sharing everything."

She stood by her open closet, considering what to wear.

Finally, I had to say it.

"I lost ten more pounds, Brenda."

She turned and looked at me. "Why, yes, you have,"

she said. "That's wonderful. Now, don't go gaining it back like you did last time you lost weight," she warned.

And then she turned back to her closet. The shower stopped running, and a moment later, Celia opened the door. She stood completely naked, not even using the towel to cover herself. She had the figure of a professional model, her breasts round and firm and her waist small, with a stomach as flat as a sheet of paper. She didn't seem at all self-conscious about her nudity in front of me. She gave me barely a glance.

I'll never have a figure like that, I thought sadly.

"Brenda, stupid me. I forgot my electric toothbrush."

"No problem," Brenda said. "You can use mine."

Ugh, I thought. *They even share toothbrushes. If I have to share a dorm room with another girl like this, I won't go to college.*

Celia smiled and shrugged. "Thanks," she said. "Nice shower. Hi, April," she added, laughed, and closed the door.

"Aren't you going to dress for dinner?" Brenda asked me. "It's special for Mama."

"What? Oh, yeah, sure. I have something new to wear since I lost weight," I said, fishing for a compliment.

Brenda nodded. "Good," she said, and turned back to her closet.

I should have invited someone to dinner, too, I thought angrily, even a homeless person, a stranger, so I wouldn't feel alone.

At dinner, Celia took over some of my duties without Mama asking. She helped serve, and when Brenda tried to get up to do something, Celia insisted she sit.

"I have to earn my keep," she said, and Brenda laughed again.

Did they always giggle at whatever each other said?
I wondered. I had never seen Brenda act so immature.

"You don't earn your keep at the dorm," Brenda
teased.

"Oh, and you do, I suppose," Celia countered,
bumping her hip against Brenda's shoulder.

That got Mama started on questions about the dorm.
She started to tell stories about her own college experiences,
stories I had never heard her tell. Because I had
yet to attend college, I couldn't contribute anything to
the discussion.

"I'm going to go to college as far away as possible,"
I finally blurted. Everyone turned to me. "I'd like to go
to college in Europe, in fact, so I can meet interesting
people who are different."

"You?" Brenda said. "You've never slept anywhere
but here, never been away except on family vacations
when you were much younger. We haven't gone anywhere
like that for almost two years, in fact."

"Yes, we have," I said, my eyes burning. "When we
went to see Daddy."

How she could forget that irked me. I saw her flinch
and blink as if I had thrown a cup of hot water in her
face. She glanced at Celia, whose smile quickly evaporated.
Mama's forehead creased, and her eyes grew
small.

"I don't mean something like that, April. I mean
going away for fun, sleeping over at a friend's house or
something."

"You never did, either, Brenda."

"But I'm not telling everyone I want to go to college
in Europe. You are," she said so sharply it brought
tears to my eyes.

"Well, I do," I insisted. "In fact," I added, quickly
fabricating, "Uncle Palaver invited me to join him and

Destiny on his tour one of these days, and I might just do that this coming summer."

Brenda started to laugh.

"I might!" I said.

"Okay, good for you," Brenda said. "Don't get so emotional."

"It's all right," Celia said softly to me. "I can't say I wasn't high-strung when I was a kid."

"I'm not a kid. I'm fifteen, nearly sixteen, and in some countries, women are married at my age and already have children of their own."

Everyone stared, and then suddenly, they all laughed. Even Mama looked hysterical.

"They do!" I cried, which made them laugh harder. "Stop laughing at me!"

"We're not laughing at you," Mama said. "It's just funny to hear."

"Or to imagine you caring for children," Brenda said.

I glared at Celia and then lowered my eyes to my plate and continued to eat.

"This all so wonderful, Mrs. Taylor," Celia told Mama.

"Weren't your parents disappointed in your not going home for Thanksgiving?" Mama asked her.

I looked up quickly. That was a good question. How could she come here? Why was being with Brenda, someone she was with all the time, anyway, more important than being with her own family? Mama wouldn't approve of that. Mama always considered family very important. *She's finally realized it,* I thought, and looked gleefully at Celia, who first threw a glance at Brenda.

"My parents were divorced, Mrs. Taylor," Celia began. "They divorced when I was only eight. My father had a girlfriend on the side, and my mother found out."

"Oh, I'm sorry," Mama said, bringing her hands to the base of her neck. She fingered the ruby necklace Daddy had given her on her birthday two years ago.

"My mother took it very hard. She thought it was her fault somehow, and no one, no therapist, anyone, could convince her otherwise."

Mama shook her head sympathetically. "How is she now?" she asked.

"She's dead," Celia replied. "She took too many sleeping pills one night, and it was too late to do anything by the time I found her. I went to live with my father's mother, actually. My father remarried, and his new wife wasn't keen on having me move in with them."

"How horrible for you," Mama said, practically coming to tears.

"My grandmother passed away last year," Celia continued, "and I really don't have anything more to do with my father. I think he's responsible for everything terrible that's happened, and he knows that's how I feel, so going to his home for Thanksgiving wouldn't be very pleasant. I was grateful for your invitation."

"Oh, of course. We're so happy to have you," Mama said, nodding at me.

I didn't say anything. What could I say? Despite all the sad and terrible events of her life, Celia Harding was a vibrant, cheerful, and beautiful young woman. Maybe that was why Brenda was so fond of her. She gave her hope about herself, not that I ever thought Brenda was too weak to overcome the sorrowful events of our lives. I supposed they were good for each other, and although I was jealous, I had to accept it reluctantly and be happy for them both.

The conversation at dinner changed to happier topics. Celia told Mama about her plans to become an advertising executive. She had taken a number of courses in psychology, and she loved marketing and how images and words manipulated and controlled the way people thought and lived their lives. She did make it sound very interesting. She said she wanted to begin by working for some magazines and gradually get to the point where she had her own advertising firm. Mama sat there nodding as if she expected nothing less. No goal was beyond the reach of such an intelligent and attractive woman.

"I'm thinking of getting back into the working community myself," Mama said. To me, it sounded like an echo. I couldn't count how many times Brenda and I had heard her say that before.

"That's good, Mrs. Taylor. You should. It would enrich your life."

"Oh, please, don't call me Mrs. Taylor. Call me Nora," Mama said. "You'll make me feel old."

They three of them laughed.

I rose and began to clear the table.

"April has been such a help to me," Mama said, putting her hand on my arm. "I don't know where I'd be without her. Half the time, she's the one preparing our dinner, and she's becoming a better cook than I am."

"Mama!" I said. For some reason, it embarrassed me to have Mama tout my good qualities in front of Brenda's friend. I glanced at her and saw her smiling up at me.

"As long as she doesn't end up looking like a plump chef," Brenda commented.

I felt myself redden and quickly retreated to the kitchen to put the dishes and glasses into the dishwasher. Celia offered to help, too, but Mama insisted she and Brenda go relax in the living room. When I finally entered the living room, they were making plans for the next day. Brenda was going to show her around Hickory.

"What's there to show her?" I interjected.

"I'd like to see where Brenda grew up," Celia told me, and then smiled at Brenda. "Where a person lives tells you a lot about her, not that I don't know a lot already," she added, and once again, they both giggled like teenagers.

"If you want to, you can come along," Brenda told me.

I shrugged and plopped into Daddy's chair and listened to them chat about other girls at the dorm, some of the events that were coming up at the college, and Brenda's achievements on the basketball team. Even though Celia didn't strike me as the athletic type, she seemed well-informed about the league and the upcoming games leading to the championship. They were in contention, and from what Celia was saying, Brenda was a big reason why.

"I didn't attend any of the games until Brenda came to play for our school," Celia admitted.

Mama came in and listened to them talk, too. She practically said nothing for a long while, but just sat there with that smile frozen on her face. When they laughed, she widened her smile or giggled as they did. Once again, she began to tell some of her own college stories, even one about a boyfriend she had.

"You never said anything about him before, Mama," I interjected.

She laughed lightly like someone caught fabricating. "Your father is not one to appreciate hearing about my past love affairs, if you could call it that. It was just an infatuation."

I looked at Brenda to see if she was as disturbed as I was about Mama using the present tense in relation to Daddy, as if he were still alive and in the other room. She seemed not to hear. I don't think she heard anything. She was just staring at Celia with a smile on her face that mimicked Mama's.

We watched some television together, but Celia and Brenda interrupted everything with their silly comments. I was glad when they decided they were tired. Mama admitted to being tired herself, and everyone went off to bed, leaving me staring at the glowing box, not seeing or hearing anything in particular. I just wanted to be defiant and stay up longer than the rest of them. I wasn't going to sleep simply because Celia yawned. That was for sure.

Finally, I gave in. I didn't realize just how exhausted I was until I crawled under my blanket. I think I was asleep less than a minute after my head hit the pillow, but for some reason, my eyes snapped open about two-thirty in the morning. It was almost as if someone had nudged me.

My room wasn't that dark, because there was a full moon, and it was just in position to send its rays full blast at my side of the house. The shade lit up, and shadows from the weeping willow tree outside danced over it, taking odd shapes and holding my interest.

Then I heard the distinct sound of a door opening. I listened hard and heard what I was sure were voices. Curious, I rose and went to my door, opening it slowly to peer into the hallway.

Celia was standing in Brenda's doorway. She was in a nightgown, her hair down over her shoulders and back. She was barefoot. I could just see Brenda inside. She was naked. It surprised me because I never saw

Brenda sleep naked. If anything, she liked to wear Daddy's pajamas and, as far as I knew, still did.

I kept quiet. I couldn't make out anything they were saying. They were whispering now. Celia laughed and then quickly covered her mouth, and they both giggled. *When would I ever have a friend like that?* I wondered sadly. I was about to close the door and return to bed, when Celia leaned toward Brenda, and they kissed.

Only, it wasn't a good-night best-friend kiss on the cheek. Oh, no.

It was a kiss on the lips, a kiss like a kiss between a man and a woman, romantic and held much longer than a good-night kiss should be held.

My own breath stopped.

Celia turned and looked my way. I felt the blood rush up my neck and into my cheeks. I froze. I couldn't close the door. Her gaze held mine for a moment, and then she smiled that angelic smile and returned to her bedroom.

Brenda didn't see me.

She closed her door softly.

Celia closed hers.

And the only sound I heard was the drumbeat of my own heart as it marched my blood around my trembling body.

7

The Party

❧❖❧

Perhaps because of what I had seen and its effect on me, I fell into more of a coma than a sleep and didn't wake up until much later than usual. I had no real reason to make so much of what I had seen Celia and Brenda do. It was just a kiss. Maybe the way they kissed was their private joke. I had heard college changes you, and such unusual behavior could be something silly college girls did. I couldn't stop thinking about it, however, because of all the dirty jokes and nasty things boys said to me about Brenda in school.

By the time I showered and dressed and went to have breakfast, Mama told me Brenda and Celia had left.

"They left? But why didn't anyone wake me? I was supposed to go along," I whined.

"Really? I would have wakened you, but no one said anything," Mama told me.

"I'm not surprised," I muttered, even though if anyone really checked, they would know I hadn't told Brenda I wanted to go along for sure. I had been annoyed that she was even thinking of doing something without me, so I didn't act excited about the idea. I just had assumed she wouldn't leave without me. How could she not want to spend as much time as possible with me? After all, it had been months since we had seen each other.

"What do you mean, April?"

"Nothing," I said quickly. I didn't know what to say, since I didn't really know what to think.

"Well, we're all going out to dinner tonight. We all decided that we didn't want to eat leftovers after all," Mama said.

"We all decided? No one asked me."

"Don't you want to go out? Your father hates eating leftovers," she said, and then caught herself this time and added, "hated."

"Yes, I want to go out," I said.

I made some cold cereal and strawberries with skim milk, but I didn't finish it. My stomach was still twisted. Afterward, I put on a jacket and went for a walk with my hands in my pockets and my head down. I didn't even notice where I was walking. Direction didn't matter.

After Brenda had left for college, I thought about the day I would leave for college, too. Despite what I had said at the dinner table about going far away, I often fantasized that I would follow Brenda and go to the same school. I'd be there while she was still there, and my big sister would show me around. I'd be proud, because by then, she would surely be a star on the campus, and just being her sister would allow me to share some of the spotlight, the way it had when she was attending public school. I'd be thinner by then and maybe would have a boyfriend. There was even the possibility Brenda and I would go out on double dates with our boyfriends. We'd finally become real sisters in every sense of the word, confiding secrets about our love lives to each other, looking out for each other, loving each other the way sisters should.

How childish all those fantasies seemed now. As we grew older, the distance between us would only grow as well, I thought. I could never catch up to her. Brenda would be off on a whole new path that didn't include me at all. I'd be just like any other fan in the stands watching her play. Maybe. Maybe I would gradually stop going altogether.

With Daddy gone, with Brenda moving off like a planet that had broken its orbit, and with Mama drifting, I felt lost and very insecure. I wished Uncle Palaver could run his hand over my head and simply make me disappear. I walked along, feeling sorry for myself. I didn't even notice that the sky had become thickly overcast and was threatening a cold rain. The wind strengthened, slicing through my jacket, but I didn't care about being cold. I wanted to suffer.

The blaring sound of a car horn jerked me out of my thoughts, and I looked up to see David Peet, Luke Isaac, and Jenna Hunter laughing hard in David's car. They were all in the front seat, Jenna sitting on Luke's lap. They had pulled alongside the sidewalk and apparently had been following behind me for a while, amused by my slow, thoughtful pace. The three of them were seniors, but I imagined it was questionable that any of them would actually graduate this year.

I really hadn't spoken at all to David since I met him in the dean's office last year. He would wink at me and tease me, asking if my father had taken away my scooter, and his friends would laugh along with him. I would ignore him and keep walking. Both Jenna and Luke had been in trouble almost as often as David. I would look at them and their friends in school and think how true that old saying was: "Birds of a feather flock together."

"Where's your scooter, Scooter?" David asked after he rolled down his window.

"I don't have a scooter," I said. "The joke is getting tired. I'm going to have to send it to a retirement home," I quipped, and Jenna shouted, "Whoa. I guess she told you, David."

David held his smile, but I could see he was surprised by my quick comeback.

"Where you going, Scooter? There's no Big Mac down this street."

Jenna giggled.

"Leave me alone," I said, and kept walking, but he continued to drive slowly beside the sidewalk, even though he was on the wrong side of the road.

"You need to loosen up, Scooter. Hang out with some real people for a change, and have some fun," David said. I kept walking. "I've been watching you, and so has Luke. Right, Luke?"

"Yeah," Luke shouted over him.

"We see you've lost weight. You might even turn out to be a good-looking woman, right, Luke?"

"Yeah."

I caught my breath and turned. "What do you want?"

"Just want to be friends, don't we, guys?"

"David is right, April. Relax," Jenna said. "Luke here likes you, so when we saw you walking, we thought we'd come by and see if you wanted to go with us to the mall."

I smirked. *Sure,* I thought, or, as Brenda would say, *Yeah, right.*

"It's the truth," Jenna insisted. She was leaning over David and looking out the window at me. Luke sat up so he could gaze over her as well.

Luke Isaac wasn't a bad-looking boy. He had thick black hair he wore long in the back and swept back on the sides, a dark complexion, and light blue, sexy, sleepy eyes. I suppose he was attractive to me and to most other girls because he just looked dangerous, as if he could rape you with his eyes. He wasn't the sort of boy you played eye tag with. Give him the sense you had some interest in him, and he would smile and leer and swing his eyes suggestively before he started in your direction. It was enough to make younger, innocent girls like myself turn and walk away as quickly as we could without attracting too much attention.

"Why do you want to tease me so much?" I asked the three of them.

David shook his head. "I told you she was too young, man. I told you we were wasting our time fooling around with her."

"We're not teasing you, April. Where are you going, anyway?" Jenna asked me. She surprised me by getting out of the car and coming around to talk to me.

Jenna was tall, as tall as Luke and David. She had light brown hair cut stylishly. Her mother was a beautician with her own shop. Jenna usually wore tight pants and a tank shirt with a leather jacket. Some days she had a ring in her nose, and some days she wore it in her belly button, especially when she wore low-hung jeans. She had already been suspended this year for smoking in the girls' room.

All I could think at the moment was that Brenda would be so angry if she saw me talking to these three.

When she was still at my school, she was always warning me about staying away from this one or that one.
She had picked up an expression from Daddy she
loved: "It only takes one rotten apple to spoil the
barrel."

"Keep away from the rotten apples," was her constant warning.

"I'm not going anywhere special," I told Jenna.
"I'm just walking," I said.

She drew closer and played with my hair.

"You know, you should let it grow out. You're like
me. You need some hair around your face, but you're
not doing a good job with your bangs. What are you
using for a shampoo?"

I looked at her to see if she was sincere. She looked
and sounded as if she was.

"I'm going to be a beautician, so I know about these
things," she said. "I'm already working in the shop,
doing the shampoos and stuff."

I told her what I used, and she said it wasn't as good
as what she had.

"I'll bring some to school for you so you can try it,"
she offered.

"Can we get along here, please?" David cried.

"Hold your water," she fired back at him. Luke
laughed.

Jenna put her arm around my shoulders and turned
me away from the two boys, who were sitting and
watching us, both smoking and smiling.

"You see, here's the way it is," Jenna continued.
"Luke has this thing for younger girls who are obviously inexperienced. He thinks they're fresher or
something, like ripe fruit. That's what he says. Did you
realize he's been watching you in school?"

"No."

"He's a lot of fun. I'm with David. You probably know we've been on and off for a long time. We sorta have one of those hate-love things, you know. We fight and then have a helluva great makeup date," she added, smiling licentiously. "You should come with us," she said. "Have a little fun. See what it's like. What do they say? Nothing ventured, nothing lost?"

"No, nothing gained," I corrected.

"Whatever. You know what I mean. Whaddya say?"

"I don't know," I said. As always, I was attracted and repulsed by them at the same time.

"You know the rumors always flying around about your sister," she said.

"What rumors?" I snapped at her.

"You know," she repeated, nodding. "Some people think it's inherited or something. You're not like that, are you? I mean, you don't like girls more than you do boys?"

"No," I said, "and neither does my sister. Those are just ugly, stupid stories."

"Good. So come along and prove it. We're just having a good time."

I looked back at the car as though it could transport me into purgatory as easily as Funland. Wouldn't the other girls in school be surprised to see me riding around with Luke, Jenna, and David?

"You're just going to the mall to hang out?"

"That's it. We'll go to the Music Hall to listen and shop or," she said, leaning in, "shoplift." She laughed.

"C'mon already," David called. "I got an appointment with my dentist."

"His dentist?"

"He's just kidding. Coming?" she said, stepping back and holding out her hand.

I looked at the car and at her, and then I reached out

and took her hand. It was like reaching across some chasm, at the bottom of which was a pool of boredom.

"Great," she cried, and pulled me along.

Luke crawled over the seat into the rear and opened the door. He fell back, his legs spread out.

"C'mon in. It's warm in here," he said.

I hesitated.

"Scoot in, Scooter," David urged.

Jenna got in and closed her door. I did the same, but before I could close the door, David stepped on the accelerator, and the door slammed closed behind me. I fell forward onto Luke, who laughed. Jenna screamed as we shot off down the street and turned the corner so sharply the wheels squealed.

Luke sat up and reached over to put his arm around me and pull me closer.

"The way David drives, I better hold on to you," he said.

Jenna looked back and flashed a smile at me. Her eyes were lit with excitement. David continued to accelerate when he turned onto a main highway. I could see we were going close to ninety miles an hour. I had never gone this fast in an automobile. My heart was pounding.

"Slow down," Jenna told David after she looked back at us again. "You've got the poor girl terrified. Don't worry," she told me. "David is used to driving fast."

"The problem is, he does everything too fast," Luke quipped, and they all laughed.

"How would you know that?" Jenna fired back at him.

It was David's time to laugh.

"Don't you remember, Jenna? You told me," Luke countered, and they all laughed again.

Teasing and insulting each other was obviously their idea of fun.

"Stop looking so worried, April," Jenna told me.

"Give her something to calm her down," David told Jenna, and jerked his head in my direction.

"Oh, sure," she said. "Here." She handed me a bag with an open bottle in it. "Take some of this."

"What is it?" I asked, without taking it.

"Just some good vodka. It'll warm you up and make you feel good."

"I don't drink," I said.

"Nobody drinks," Luke said, "but once in a while, it helps. No big deal. Go on, take a swig," he urged.

"You're not afraid of some vodka, are you, Scooter?" David taunted.

"No," I said. "I'm just not used to drinking."

Jenna held it out and smiled. "Get used to it," she suggested.

They were all watching to see what I would do, and I realized it was some sort of test. One sip can't hurt, I thought. I closed my hands around the bottle and brought the neck of it to my lips to take a very quick taste. It wasn't horrible, but it wasn't anything delicious to me, either.

"That's not a drink. Take a real drink," Luke said, putting his hand under the bottom of the bottle and lifting it so I would bring it to my lips again.

I did, and he held it there while I swallowed and swallowed until I started to gag.

"Great!" Jenna cried.

"Good work, Scooter," David added.

Luke smiled and took a long drink from the bottle himself. "Good stuff. Where's it from, your daddy's private stash, David?"

"Matter of fact, it is," he said. "I poured it into that

bottle and poured some water into his. He mixes it, anyway, so he won't know the difference," David said.

We were continuing down the highway and passed what I knew to be the exit for the mall. I looked back and nudged Jenna.

"I thought we were going to the mall."

"Yes, David," Jenna said. "I thought we were going to the mall."

"Later," he said. "I got a nice surprise for us."

"Oh, great," she squealed, and turned to me. "I love surprises, don't you, April?"

I shrugged. Luke handed me the bottle.

"Your turn again," he said.

"I don't think I want anymore," I told him.

"Sure, you do. It will help you relax." He squeezed my shoulders, drawing me against him. "I can feel how uptight you are. You have to loosen up to get with it," he said. "Join the party."

"That's the surprise!" David cried. "We're having a party."

Luke brought the bottle to my mouth. "Hey, you hear that? That's great. Open now," he said, laughing.

"Go on, take a little more," Jenna said. "You'll love how you'll feel."

I let Luke put the bottle's neck to my lips again and swallowed as he held it up. It was like a father feeding his baby or something. It made me feel foolish, so I took the bottle out of his hands.

"I can do it myself," I snapped at him.

"That's the spirit, Scooter," David said. "Don't let him push you around."

"Look who's talking like a big shot, Mr. Henpecked," Luke told him.

I did take another long sip, and then I handed the bottle back to Jenna, who immediately drank. I thought to myself, since they were all doing it, it couldn't be so bad. I could feel it traveling quickly to my head, and either because they told me it would happen or I wanted it to happen, I felt myself loosen and relax.

David pulled off at the next exit and sped around the curve. I didn't know where we were. He made another turn and then another, each one sharply, causing us all to scream. As silly as it sounds, I started to enjoy the wild driving.

"Where the hell did you get your license?" Luke cried.

"License? What's a license?" David replied, and when they laughed, I did, too.

He slowed down and turned into the driveway of a tired-looking two-story Queen Anne–style home. There was a small square of neglected lawn on each side of the driveway. David stopped before the detached garage. The house was dark, the windows looking stained and grimy.

"Where are we?" I asked.

"This is my granddad's house," David said. "He's in the hospital. He had kidney stones or something. I'm supposed to be looking after the place. Gives me a good excuse for getting my father to give me the car," he added. "Now you got the whole story, Scooter. C'mon," he said, opening the door.

"I hope there's something to eat," Jenna said. "I'm hungry."

"I have something you can eat," Luke said, opening his door.

"No, thank you," Jenna said. "C'mon, April. We girls have to stick together," she told me, and I got out.

I felt warmer and even a little numb all over. For a moment, the earth turned and then settled down. It made me laugh, the laugh coming unexpected, as un-expected as a burp. Jenna laughed, too. David went to the front door, looked under a mat, and produced a key. He held it up for Luke to see and then opened the door, and we followed him into the house.

The house had a musty odor that almost turned my stomach. It was gurgling anyway from all the vodka I had consumed. David turned on a lamp in the hallway and then another in the small living room on the right. All the furniture looked old and worn, the area rug threadbare.

"How long has your granddad been in the hospital?" I asked.

"I don't know. A few weeks. He had other problems. He's about eighty."

David flopped on the sofa, and it looked to me as if a small cloud of dust rose when he did.

"Make yourself at home," he told us.

"C'mon," Jenna said, tugging me. "Let's look in the kitchen and see what's to eat."

I followed her into the small kitchen. There was a pale yellow Formica table with four chairs. I could see someone had spilled sugar over the top of the table, and there was a party of ants enjoying their discovery. Whatever David was supposed to do at the house, he hadn't, I concluded. The garbage can was full, the sink still full of dirty dishes, some caked with food remnants, and there were dirty glasses on the counter. I saw an open pizza box with pieces of crust still in it. The ants were all over that as well. On the floor below the counter was a bag full of empty beer bottles.

Jenna opened the refrigerator and held up a package of what looked like some sandwich meat. She held it with two fingers as if it was contaminated.

"Ugh," she said. "It has some kind of mold on it." She dropped it into the sink.

Then she sorted through whatever else there was in the refrigerator and concluded there was nothing interesting or edible. The pantry proved as disappointing. She did reach into a box of crackers but determined they were quite stale.

"David!" she screamed. "There's nothing good enough to eat here, and don't make any wisecracks."

"We'll go for a pizza later," Luke said from the doorway. We heard music coming from the living room. David had a radio turned on to an upbeat station.

"We better," Jenna said firmly, and walked back to the living room.

Luke and I followed. David was sprawled on the sofa, smoking a cigarette. He smiled up at Jenna.

"Come to Papa, baby," he said, reaching up for her.

She laughed and fell over him. Then they kissed, and David put his hand on her rear end and looked up at Luke and me.

"C'mon," Luke said. "Let's give them some privacy," he told me, and took my hand. He had the bottle of vodka in his other hand.

I let him pull me along.

"Where are we going?" I asked as he started up the steps.

"Upstairs, where we can talk and stuff," he said.

I hesitated, but his grip on my hand was tight. We went up the short stairway, and then he turned into a room, obviously knowing exactly where to go. I thought it was probably David's granddad's room. I saw a pair of pants and a shirt strewn over a chair, a hair brush and a comb on the dresser, and a pair of shoes and some old slippers next to the bed. On the dresser was a picture of a couple embracing under a tree, the woman looking small and frightened, as if she had been caught doing something illegal. It was taken years and years ago, because David's grandfather looked not much older than David. There were some inexpensive prints of country scenes and a scene of mountains in frames on the walls.

The blanket on the bed was pulled down, the two pillows creased with the imprints of a head or heads. Luke sat on the bed, stared at the floor a moment, and then looked up at me. He smiled and handed me the bottle of vodka. I shook my head.

"I think I had enough," I said.

"No, you didn't. You didn't have more than a few shots. Believe me," he said, pumping the bag at me.

I took it and sipped some more.

"See? No problem."

He looked at me hard and then took another long drink. He wiped his lips with the back of his hand.

"This is the first time you been with someone, right?" he asked.

"What do you mean, 'been with someone'?"

He nodded. "It's the first time. You like being with boys, though, right?"

"Yes," I said, getting angry. "You don't have to ask me that."

"How do you know if you've never been with one like this?" he asked, and then laughed. "You have to experiment to learn what you like, don't you? If you never tasted butterscotch, you wouldn't know if you liked it or not, right? Huh?"

"I guess not," I said.

"Sure, it's only logical. No big deal. I'm an expert when it comes to experiments."

He reached into his back pocket and produced his brown leather wallet. "See this?" he said, holding it out.

I looked down at it. There wasn't much to see, I thought, except for what looked like tiny slices in the leather.

"What?" I asked.

"What? Look closely," he said, holding up the wallet. "Count the marks. Fifteen. You'll be sixteen," he said, pointing the bottle at me and then taking another drink. "It's a service I provide to the female population."

I shook my head. The room was spinning a little, and I was now feeling a little nauseated.

"I'm dizzy," I said.

He reached for my hand. "Here, lie down and you'll feel better soon," he said, pulling me toward the bed. He put his hands on my hips and guided me beside him. I sat, and then he lifted me under my arms so I was farther on the bed.

"Just lie back and relax. Close your eyes for a while. That's it," he said when I did it.

I felt his hand on my cheek. His fingers moved down to my neck while his other hand lowered the zipper on my jacket. Then he opened the jacket.

"That's it, relax. You're with Dr. Sex himself," he bragged. "Nothing to worry about."

I opened my eyes, but the room didn't stop spinning. It felt as if the whole bed were spinning, in fact. I quickly closed them again. I could feel Luke unbuttoning my blouse, but it also felt so far away, almost as if it were really happening to someone else. He opened my blouse, reached under my back, undid my bra, lifted and folded it until it was just under my neck.

"Um," he said, "just as I thought. We're getting a good start here."

The air on my naked breasts surprised me. I started to raise myself into a sitting position, but he pressed on my shoulders and kept me from doing so. Then he went down to my jeans and undid them quickly.

"No, stop," I said when he lifted my buttocks to slide the jeans off.

"This won't hurt . . . much," he said. "I've never lost a patient yet," he joked.

"Please," I cried when I felt my panties going down. My jeans were already below my knees.

I pressed down on the bed to get momentum and lift myself up, and then he surprised me by bringing his mouth to mine, so forcefully it drove me back to the bed. That startled and frightened me, but what shocked me more was the sensation of feeling his naked legs against mine and then his hardened excitement pressing between my legs. I screamed and tried to turn out from under him.

"Nurse," I heard him say, "I think I'll need some assistance here."

Laughter came from the doorway. I turned and saw Jenna and David standing there. David had his arm around her waist, and she was gazing at me and Luke with a dopey smile on her face.

Suddenly, David lifted his right arm, and I saw he had a camera in his hand.

"Smile," he called. The camera flashed, and I screamed. "Hey, it's just for Luke's scrapbook. No big deal."

I screamed again when Luke lifted my legs higher, and then I began to pummel him as hard and as fast as I could.

"Nurse!" he screamed.

A moment later, Jenna was holding my wrists and keeping me from striking him.

"Relax," she said. "It only hurts for a moment."

How I did it, I don't know, but I managed to jerk my left knee up sharply to strike him where it hurts a boy the most. It was his turn to scream. He fell back, lost his balance, and went off the bed.

David went into hysterical laughter. Jenna released my wrists. I reached down and grabbed my jeans, pulling them up as fast as I could, not caring if my panties came up as well. Then I turned and crawled over the other side of the bed. David had moved away from the door to stand over the squirming Luke, so I lunged ahead and charged out the doorway.

"Hey, where the hell you going?" I heard David call out. "The party's just starting."

I nearly lost my footing on the short stairway and grabbed the banister to prevent myself from tumbling. The turn wrenched my side, but I didn't stop. I regained my footing and continued down the stairway and out the front door. For a moment, I just stood there, unsure which way to run. Their voices and footsteps behind me spirited me to my left, and I ran down the driveway, charging along the side of the road, running as hard as I could. My jacket and blouse were still open, my bra unfastened, but I didn't stop to dress. I ran until the pain in my side was so sharp it took my breath away, and then I stopped and went off to the left, into a small patch of trees and bushes. When I heard the sound of an automobile, I crouched as low as I could.

David, Luke, and Jenna drove by. Jenna was looking for me on the left, and Luke was looking on the right, his face framed in the opened window, a face of rage. They went by and disappeared around the far turn. I fell back onto the ground and immediately began to throw up. Afterward, I couldn't stop sobbing. My side hurt so much. It felt as if I had cracked a rib. I don't know how long I sat there, but every time I heard the sound of a car, my heart thumped. I didn't see them go by again. I hoped they had given up on finding me.

It was already well into the twilight hour. Night was falling quickly, and with it the temperature. I stood up, steadied myself, fixed my clothing, and walked out to the road. I stayed as close to the side of the road as I could, so that I could go off to the side every time I heard or saw a car approaching. After a while, I was positive they had given up and were gone.

Of course, I had no idea where I was going. I laughed to myself, remembering how I had been when this had all begun. I was walking to get myself lost, to disappear. Well, now it looked as if I had gotten my wish. The houses on this road were few and far between. When I gazed at my watch, I realized Brenda and Mama were surely wondering where I was by now.

What would I tell them?

I was both embarrassed and frightened by what had happened and what I had done. How would I even begin to explain it? The sight of emerging stars put more panic in my chest. At least, the threat of rain had passed, but I had to get to a phone, and quickly, I thought, and broke into a jog. When the headlights of an approaching vehicle washed over me, I started for the side of the road, preparing to run into the wooded area, even though it was difficult to see where I would be going.

I heard the sound of squeaking brakes and glanced back to see a dark red pickup truck. I stopped. An elderly-looking man leaned out of the passenger's side window.

"Hey, you all right, miss?" he asked.

"No," I said, catching my breath. "I'm lost."

"Oh. Well, where you headed?"

"I have to get back to Hickory," I said. I took a few steps toward the truck. "To 777 North Castle Drive."

"Hickory? Well, what are you doing running along this road?" he asked.

"Some friends of mine thought it would be funny to put me out on the road and leave me," I said, thinking quickly.

"You damn kids," he said. He opened the truck door. "C'mon, get in," he urged.

All my life, I had been taught never to speak to strangers, and certainly never to go anywhere with someone I didn't know. It was practically a religious chant as I was growing up. Every time we saw a terrible story on the television news, Mama would turn to me and recite it. Daddy often did, too. But this was a special circumstance, I thought. I really was lost, and the man offering me a ride looked like someone's grandfather.

I got into the truck.

"How old are you?" he asked immediately.

"Fifteen, nearly sixteen," I said.

"Your parents know you're running around out here?"

"No, sir. That's why I have to get home as fast as I can."

"I bet you do," he said, and shifted into drive to start off again. "What's your name?"

"April. April Taylor."

"What kind of friends would do a thing like this to you?"

"Not very good friends," I replied.

"You got that right. I ain't in the habit of picking up stray teenage girls, but if I didn't stop, Mrs. Petersen would be awful angry," he said.

"Who's Mrs. Petersen?"

"That's my missus," he said. "We have a grand-daughter who's about your age."

"I do appreciate your stopping for me," I said. I was on the verge of crying but held my tears back and my sobs down.

"Yeah, I bet you do. Can you call someone to come get you?" he asked.

"Yes."

"Okay. I'll take you to the Four Corners strip mall just this side of the highway. You can call from there. You have money on you?"

I did. I always carried a ten-dollar bill in my pocket. It was something Daddy gave me and told me to do always.

"Yes, sir," I said.

"Sir?" He laughed and looked at me. "You look like you've been in some panic. Better straighten yourself up a bit before your folks come for you," he advised. "So, what is wrong with you young people today?" he asked, and then proceeded to give me his answers, which included lack of discipline, spoiling children rotten, parents who were too self-centered, and a reduction in church attendance. He lectured in a monotone that, strangely enough, had a calming effect on me.

I thanked him when he pulled into the parking lot.

"You watch who you hang out with, young lady," he warned. And then he added something that made me laugh. "It only takes one rotten apple to spoil the bunch."

I waved and rushed into the shop to use the pay phone. The cashier gave me change for my ten dollars, and I called home.

Brenda answered, and from the tone of her voice, I knew everyone had been worried. "Where the hell are you, April?"

I told her.

"What are you doing there? Do you know what time it is? Mama is beside herself. How could you do this to her?"

I started to cry.

"Well, are you coming home or what?" she asked.

"I have no way to get home," I said through my sobs.

"I don't believe it. Just stay there. Celia and I are coming," she said.

I thought about asking to speak to Mama so I could apologize, but Brenda hung up. Then I remembered what Mr. Petersen had said in the truck, and I went into the restroom to wash my face and straighten my clothing. I had one bad mud stain on my jacket sleeve, and washing it seemed to make it worse.

What was I going to tell them? When they heard I had drunk vodka and when Brenda heard I had gotten into David Peet's car, I would be blamed for everything. I was too embarrassed to tell the truth, anyway. Luke had nearly stripped me naked, and they were all looking at me. My eyes filled with tears again. I had to take deep breaths to stop myself from just bawling aloud in the restroom.

I went out and bought myself something I hadn't eaten for months, a package of chocolate-covered graham crackers and a bottle of Coke. Then I sat on the bench in front of the store and waited. I felt tired and achy all over, especially in my legs. My nausea was gone, and my stomach gurgled complaints about being so empty. I had practically thrown up my intestines earlier. It didn't take me long to gobble down the whole package of crackers. I was terribly thirsty and went in to buy another Coke. Still hungry, I bought another package of crackers and had just started eating them when Brenda and Celia drove up.

"What the hell are you doing here?" Brenda asked as soon as she got out of the car.

Celia got out, too, and they both approached me.

"Well?" Brenda demanded, her hands on her hips. "And what the hell are you eating that junk for?"

I looked up at her, and then I looked at Celia, who was gazing at me with some amusement in her eyes. Brenda's were filled with hot rage. I threw away the remaining crackers quickly.

I hadn't come up with any idea of how to explain what had happened to me.

There was nothing left to do but tell the truth.

8

Invisible Tears

※◆※

I didn't tell the whole truth. I couldn't talk about what Luke had almost done to me, especially in front of Celia, and even more especially because of the things they had said about Brenda. On the way home, I limited my explanation to getting into David's car, drinking some vodka, and their pulling a prank on me by leaving me on some back road. Of course, I had no idea what I would do if David developed the picture he had taken and then showed it to people. I talked mostly about Mr. Petersen in the hopes that neither Brenda nor Celia would ask too many questions about David, Luke, and Jenna.

Brenda and Celia sat up front listening. Both of them kept their faces forward, neither commenting nor asking a question. At times, I felt as if I were speaking to mannequins. It's so much more difficult to travel through troubled territory, tell half-truths, and leave out unpleasant information when you have to do all the talking, I thought. It's like swimming out in the middle of the ocean without anyone offering any sort of rescue. You just flounder about, hoping. When I finished with some sniffles, which I hoped would bring me some expressions of sympathy, Brenda looked at Celia and then looked into the rearview mirror at me in the backseat.

"I really thought you were a lot smarter than that, April. It's not that I didn't warn you about those kids, and why would you drink anything they offered you in a paper bag? How do you know what was really in it? You never drank any vodka before, did you?"

"No, but they drank it, too!" I whined.

Celia laughed.

"They did!"

"It was in a paper bag, you said, right?" Brenda asked.

"Yes."

"So they could have brought it to their lips but not actually swallowed any or very much, and you wouldn't know. It's a trick college boys pull on girls all the time. The girls end up drunk or worse, and then the boys take advantage."

Celia turned slowly and looked back at me.

"Did they do that?" Brenda asked.

"What?"

"Take advantage of you?" she asked.

I could see Brenda's eyes in the rearview mirror. She was waiting for my answer and watching my face.

"No," I said, and turned away quickly. I couldn't tell her; I just couldn't do it, especially in front of Celia.

Neither of them said another word for a while.

"We'll think of a better story to tell Mama," Brenda told me before we arrived at the house. "Okay. Here's what you'll say. You'll tell her you went for a ride with some of your friends, and the car broke down. Don't tell her about the drinking. She doesn't know much about the kids at school, so she won't know how bad the ones you were with are. It's not hard to see she's still as fragile as thin china. More bad news could shatter her."

"I know how Mama is," I snapped back. "I'm the one living with her now."

"Then you should know enough not to get into this sort of trouble," Brenda returned.

"Take it easy," Celia told her softly. "You and I are not exactly angels."

Brenda grunted and lowered her shoulders.

"Are we still going to dinner?" I asked.

"No, it's too late. She's fixing leftovers. My father hated leftovers," she told Celia. "He was a kook for fresh food. He used to say the only thing he wants warmed over is his feet in winter."

Celia laughed. Then she grew sad and said, "You were lucky to have him. The only thing I remember my father saying is good-bye."

Brenda glanced at her and slipped her right hand into Celia's. They held hands up until the moment Brenda had to turn into our driveway.

Why does she feel so sorry for her and not sorry at all for me? I thought sadly.

"April," Mama said as soon as I entered, "what happened to you?"

I glanced at Brenda and then related the fabricated story as quickly as I could. I was not a very good liar. Daddy used to tell me my face turned to glass whenever I tried, and he could see right through to the squiggly little deceptions. Mama wasn't as keen, especially these days. She listened, and then she felt sorry for me, which only made me feel more terrible. Brenda was satisfied with my performance, however. I was sent to shower and change and come to our late dinner.

I ate well, too well for Brenda, who watched me like a hawk every time I reached for something, but I couldn't help how much I ate. I had had no lunch.

"You want to know what disappointed me the most today, April?" she told me in the kitchen after I had brought in some dishes and silverware to wash. "Seeing you eat that fattening candy when we picked you up."

"It wasn't candy; it was cookies," I said.

"Yeah, right. Like that makes a difference. If you're just going to go back to your old ways, I won't bother trying to help you," she threatened, but quickly smiled when Celia followed us in with some more dishes. However, she had heard Brenda's warning and threat.

"Oh, don't yell at her about the cookies, Brenda. She probably ate out of nervousness more than anything."

"I wasn't nervous," I shot back. I didn't want her coming to my defense.

"Believe me, honey, you were nervous," she said, nodding. "We've all been there."

Brenda and she nodded. The two of them looked so smug, so confident. They knew everything; I knew nothing. I put the silverware down and left the kitchen.

"I'm tired, Mama," I said, returning to the dining room. "Do you mind if I just go to bed?"

"Oh, sure, April. I know you went through a terrible experience. Don't worry. Celia and Brenda will help with everything," she told me.

Yes, Celia and Brenda can easily replace me, I thought, and went to my room. I didn't do anything. I sprawled out on my stomach and pressed my face to my pillow so hard I nearly smothered myself. I thought about Daddy and how he was before he had turned into Mr. Hyde. How quickly he would have come to my defense in this situation. Everyone needed someone to champion him or her. Even serial killers had good lawyers these days, or they had mothers who couldn't imagine them being so terrible.

I thought about David, Luke, and Jenna and how they were probably off somewhere having a good laugh at my expense. Maybe they had met up with some of their other friends and were telling the story. Then they would have the picture developed and show everyone. Maybe they wouldn't, I thought hopefully. Maybe they would realize that I could go to the police if they did. It would be proof of what they had done. They couldn't be that stupid, I concluded, but then I wondered if I had made a terrible tactical error by not telling Brenda the whole truth, especially when it all came out later. What would I say? I forgot? She would be even angrier at me.

I was in such turmoil my head felt as if it had been used as a Ping-Pong ball, and my stomach started churning and bubbling again. I tried talking myself to sleep, and for a while, I actually did drift off, but then I heard my bedroom door open, and I opened my eyes to see Brenda silhouetted in the hallway light. She stood there a moment looking in at me.

"Are you asleep?" she asked, her voice sounding softer.

"I'm awake," I said, sitting up. "What is it?"

She closed the door softly and walked to the bed. She had her arms folded tightly under her breasts. I could hear that the threat of rain that had been over us earlier and then gone had returned with a vengeance to deliver its promise. Drops closer to sleet sounded like pebbles against the pane. With the door closed, I

couldn't see Brenda's expression, but the way she held
her body told me she was still very angry, very upset.

"What made you go with those kids, April?"

"I don't know. I just went," I said.

"You knew what they were like. How did they get
you into the car? What did they say?" she pursued, her
voice resonating with suspicions. I dared not tell her
about the accusations.

"I don't know. They said we'd have fun. Jenna
said . . ."

"What?" she snapped.

"That Luke liked me."

"Luke? Luke Isaac? You went because she said
that?"

I shrugged and looked away. I heard her sigh
deeply.

"What else happened to you, April?" she asked.

"What do you mean?"

"I know you aren't telling it all. I saw it in your face
when we first picked you up. Just like Daddy used to
say, your skin turns to glass when you lie, and it's like
looking through a window."

I was silent.

"Okay, April, if you force me to be specific, I'll
be specific. What else did they do to you after you
drank the vodka? Did either of the boys do something
sexual?"

I started to cry. Brenda, the petrified tree, stood
firm, waiting.

"He tried," I said.

"Who tried?"

"Luke."

"Meaning what?"

"He said he wanted to do me a favor and . . . do it to
me. He said he was an expert with virgins. He even

had his wallet marked with his conquests. I was so sick I didn't understand what was happening until it was almost too late."

"What do you mean by 'almost'?"

"The other two came into the room and . . ."

"What room? I thought you said you were in a car. April," she added when I was silent. "What room?"

"David took us to his granddad's house because his granddad is in the hospital. Luke took me to the bedroom. He was taking off my clothes when Jenna and David came to the door. David took a picture!"

"The bastard," Brenda said.

"I had a chance to escape, and I ran out of the house. They came after me, but I hid in the bushes, and then everything else I told you was true."

"You should have told me it all, April. Celia and I could have done something earlier."

"What can Celia do?"

"The bastards," she said instead of answering, and then, after a moment, she turned and marched to the door. She paused after opening it. "Never tell Mama," she said, and left, closing the door behind her.

I stared after her in the dark, and then I turned over again and buried my face in the pillow. A few minutes later, I heard Brenda and Celia in the hallway. I rose quickly and went to the door. They were dressed in their jackets and heading for the front door. I stepped out. Mama's bedroom door was closed. She was probably asleep.

"Brenda!" I called after them in a loud whisper just as she opened the front door. "Where are you going? What are you going to do?"

"Just go back to bed, April. Go back to bed," she said, and she and Celia left.

I ran to the door and looked out the side window.

They got into Celia's car, backed out of the driveway, and headed away. It was almost midnight, and it was still raining steadily. Where could they be going? I returned to my bedroom, but I was too nervous to fall back asleep, and I just lay there staring up through the darkness. Every sound made my heart thump. Finally, pure exhaustion slammed my lids shut, and I was dropped into a deep sleep.

It was so deep a sleep that I didn't hear Brenda come back into my room much later. I wouldn't have known she had come in at all if I didn't open my eyes and see David Peet's camera beside my pillow. It was early in the morning, barely seven, but there was enough light in the room for me to see it. It was one of those throwaway cameras. For a moment, however, I thought I was still asleep, dreaming. Then the realization that it was really there set in, and I practically leaped into a sitting position, gaping down at it as if it were a giant spider or something.

I picked it up slowly and turned it around in my hands. How could it be here? With the camera in hand, I went to my bedroom door and peered out, listening. The house was dead quiet. Mama hadn't risen. These days, she was sleeping longer and longer, and there were mornings when I actually had risen, had made breakfast, and was just about ready to leave for school by the time she came out of her bedroom, looking dazed and confused about the time.

The sight and possession of this camera were so shocking I couldn't wait for Brenda to wake up. I quickly crossed to her room, knocked gently on her door, and then opened it and looked in. My mouth was forming an apology for waking her when I froze.

She wasn't there. The bed was empty. In fact, it didn't even look as if she had been in it.

"What are you doing, April?" I heard her ask, and nearly jumped out of my skin.

She stood behind me in her nightgown. I stared at her a moment. She looked as if her cheeks had been brushed with wet red roses.

"April, what are you doing?"

"I . . . was coming to ask you how . . ." I held up the camera. "How did this get on my bed?"

She smirked and walked by me into her bedroom. I watched her crawl in under her blanket. She patted the pillow and then looked at me.

"You can thank Celia for that," she said.

"Celia? I don't understand."

"Before she decided to go into advertising, Celia was thinking of becoming an attorney. Here I am, the daughter of an attorney, and she's more equipped to act and sound like one. She took some prelaw courses."

I shook my head, still confused. "I still don't understand, Brenda. This looks like the camera David had. It is, right?"

"Yes. It's not brain surgery, April. We tracked down David Peet. I know the hangouts around here, and there was no doubt in my mind he and his crew of creeps would still be out and about. We confronted him, and Celia carefully explained how we could go directly to the police and have him arrested for attempted rape. The very fact that he had that camera in possession was evidence."

Brenda smiled.

"She was really very good at intimidating David. I was even scared," she added. "Anyway, people like David Peet have no backbone. They can take advantage of weaker, more vulnerable people, but when they're up against someone with strength, they wilt. He produced that camera out of thin air so fast I thought he was competing with Uncle Palaver," she added, and lowered her head. Then she raised it again. "Smash it, and the film will be destroyed. You can thank Celia in a few hours.

"In fact," she said, sitting up again, "you can prepare breakfast for us. Celia likes her eggs over easy. Orange juice, coffee, and some wheat toast with jam. Now, let me get some rest. We'll be up and about by eight-thirty. We're meeting some of my old teammates for lunch today, the ones who graduated with me last year."

She lowered her head again and then turned on her side and closed her eyes. I stared at her. Why was she first going to sleep?

"You just got home?" I asked. "You were out all night?"

She didn't reply. I waited a moment and then left her room and started for my own. The door to the guest room was slightly open. I peered in and saw Celia on her stomach, the cover down to her waist and her bare back shining in the morning light. I thought about speaking to her but decided against it, and instead I went into my room, broke open the camera, and exposed the film. I dropped the camera itself into my trash can and covered it with paper so Mama wouldn't see. Later, I would empty it into a bigger trash bag.

I was too awake now to return to bed, so I showered and dressed and did what Brenda asked. I went out to the kitchen and began to prepare breakfast. Mama was up before Brenda and Celia and was surprised at how I had set the table, made the coffee, squeezed fresh orange juice and grapefruit juice, and gotten the eggs ready to cook.

"Isn't this nice?" she said. "Thank you, dear."

I told her to go relax in the dining room and let me

do it all. She put up some resistance until Celia and Brenda appeared, and then she agreed. The three of them sat chatting and laughing while I worked up the eggs, made the toast, and brought in the juice and coffee.

I tried to avoid looking at Celia, because every time I did, I thought I saw her smug, know-it-all smile. Everything she had predicted about me came true in her eyes. Brenda was obviously watching every move I made to be sure I treated Celia like some sort of royalty out of appreciation. Everyone complimented me on the eggs, and I finally sat and had one egg with a glass of juice and some black coffee. I ate sparingly just to please Brenda. Mama kept urging me to have something more. I told her I had nibbled on a bagel in the kitchen. I hadn't, but I could see Brenda believed I had.

Afterward, Mama surprised me by agreeing to go for a walk with Brenda and Celia. The rain had stopped, and now it was a crisp, sunny, late-fall day, the kind of day Brenda loved to greet with a five-mile run. I remained behind to clean up. I was supposed to join them, but by the time I had everything done, I heard them coming back. Apparently, Mama had balked at walking too far and returned instead to make her bed and clean the house. She claimed it was her day for vacuuming, but lately every day was her day for vacuuming.

"She grew panicky as soon as we were five hundred yards from our property. Doesn't she go for walks at all anymore?" Brenda asked me.

"Not that I know. I'm in school most of the day."

"She's become agoraphobic," Celia said.

"What's that?" I asked quickly.

"She gets panic attacks, anxiety probably stemming

from deep depression. I learned about it in my introduction to psych course last semester," she added. "That's why she wasn't so upset last night about our not going out after all."

Brenda nodded.

"What should we do?" I asked, developing some panic myself.

"She might need some professional help, Brenda," Celia said.

"Yes. Before we return to school, I'll have a talk with her and try to persuade her to see someone," Brenda said.

They went to her room to talk about it, leaving me out as if I were too young to understand. I went to make my own bed and straighten up my things. Shortly afterward, Brenda pulled me aside and told me I should personally thank Celia for helping me last night. She practically pushed me in her direction. She was sitting in the living room, flipping through a magazine, and looked up when I entered.

"I want to thank you for helping me out and getting that camera and film," I said. It was still embarrassing for me to talk about it in front of her.

"Oh, it was nothing. I was happy to play a role in it," she said. "Besides, Brenda was the tough one."

I looked at my sister. She had given Celia all the credit.

"We're sort of used to taking on males like that, aren't we, Brenda?"

"Yes," she said. "But you better watch your rear end now, April," she warned. "Expect them to give you a hard time. Just ignore them, and after a while, they'll get bored and move on to drowning cats or whatever those sorts of people do."

Celia laughed.

"Come on," Brenda urged her. "Before we meet my old teammates, I want to go to the school. There's a special basketball practice today, and I want you to meet Coach McDermott. He's the reason I'm in college ball today," she added.

Moments later, the two of them were off again. This time, Brenda didn't even suggest I come along. I moped about all day. After she vacuumed most of the house, Mama sat in Daddy's old chair and dozed or glanced at the television set, vaguely interested in whatever was on. It didn't seem to matter much. When she saw me, she talked about making lunch, but I told her I was just having an apple, which was all I did eat.

About two o'clock, my phone rang. I was hoping it was Brenda telling me she was going to pick me up to do something with them, but it wasn't Brenda. It was Jenna Hunter. As soon as I said hello, she went off on me.

"Listen, bitch," she said. "If you or your dyke sister and her girlfriend take David's camera to the police, you'll be very sorry. I'll testify that you practically begged Luke to have sex with you."

"I'm not going to the police," I said, "but it was a terrible thing you did to me, and you'd better stop saying those things about my sister. Just because she's a great athlete, it doesn't mean . . ."

"You were just afraid because you're just like her. It wouldn't have been so terrible for you, and you might have learned to appreciate boys," she said, laughing. "Remember my warning," she added, and hung up.

My hand was trembling holding the receiver. There was one thing I sure wasn't looking forward to doing, and that was returning to school after the long Thanksgiving weekend. Just the thought of it made my stomach tingle with tension.

Brenda finally did call, but not to have me meet them. She wanted their last night to be special, as special as the night before was supposed to be until I ruined it. She didn't say that, but I read between the lines. Celia and Brenda had decided to take us all out to what once was our favorite restaurant, Dickson's Steak House. Mama agreed, but I could see the sadness flowing under her face as memories of Daddy taking us all there returned. She was actually trembling.

There were many times when he had called to have us meet him after some court action. Most of the time, he was jovial, having done well, and it was always a party. As I looked at Mama returning to Daddy's chair, I thought how horrible it must be for her now never to have that sort of happiness and excitement in her life. Unless she met and married someone new who was just as wonderful to her, she would be forever sitting and staring at her memories. She would become a different sort of couch potato. Her mind was jammed full of reruns and replays. Nothing new loomed on her horizon except for what we brought home to her, and I wasn't exactly winning ribbons and awards of any kind.

I felt so helpless, because I didn't want to cry in front of her or make her feel any worse than she already felt by sympathizing with her and pointing out her sadness. For me, it was like watching someone sinking slowly in quicksand while I was unable even to hold out a helping hand. All I could do was stand nearby and see her disappear.

Brenda and Celia both did all they could to cheer her up later. They had obviously planned some sort of strategy to help Mama overcome her agoraphobia. They burst back into the house full of energy and laughter. Brenda was more talkative than ever, describing her reunion with her old coach.

"I even coached the team for him for a while."

"She was great," Celia testified. "She gave one side a play she uses at college, and they were unstoppable. Mr. McDermott was pretty impressed. I hope you can get yourself and April to one of the games in Memphis, Nora," Celia told Mama.

"Oh, we will, we will," Mama promised, but it was so weak and thin that no one believed her.

Later, Mama tried to find every excuse for us going to dinner without her. She had nothing decent to wear. She was tired. She would only be a drag on our happy evening. Celia and Brenda invaded her room and actually picked out her clothing for her, chatting away all the while and drowning out any reluctance Mama could express. They practically carried her out to the car, laughing off Mama's reluctance.

They kept up their merriment at dinner. Every time there was a quiet pause, one or the other would jump in with a story, a joke, a comment, forcing Mama to participate, be happy, eat, and drink wine. Daddy was practically not mentioned at all, but that didn't stop Mama from gazing around as if she expected him to arrive any moment, just as he used to when he was meeting us after court business. Twice, Brenda caught my eye, and we both knew what she was doing and feeling.

We went home relatively early, but Mama showed fatigue and excused herself to go to bed almost as soon as we walked through the door. Brenda and Celia stayed up talking with me in the living room about Mama's condition and how I had to do all I could to keep her from shrinking.

"After a while, she'll even limit how much of the

house she'll go into," Celia predicted. Brenda listened intently to her every word, as if she were a licensed psychiatrist. "She'll get so she won't even come out of her room. She'll have you bring her meals there."

"No, she won't. That's not going to happen," I cried. It was on the tip of my tongue to add, *You're not a psychiatrist. Stop pretending to be one, and with my mother, too!* But I didn't say it.

"Just call us if anything like that starts to happen," Brenda said. "She promised me she would see some-one, and I'll follow up on that. You'd better make sure you're around as much as you can be, and don't get into any more trouble, April."

It was then that I told them about Jenna Hunter's calling me and threatening me. I left out the remarks she had made about her and Celia.

"Don't pay any attention to her threats. She's the frightened one who's just trying to put on a good front. It's over, April," Brenda said. "Consider yourself lucky this time. If you do something that stupid again, you might not be so lucky."

"If they do bother you to such an extent that you can't stand it, then go to the dean of students," Celia suggested.

"They'll get even meaner if I do that," I whined.

"So, don't do it unless you absolutely have to do it," Brenda said. "Just do what I said, and ignore them. You'll see. They'll get bored and leave you alone."

"We'll call you every week to see how things are going," Celia promised.

I didn't want to look grateful, but I was. I just wished it had been Brenda who had said it and not Celia.

Finally, we all went to bed. They were up early to have their breakfast and start back to college. They had things to do, they said. I couldn't blame them for wanting to get away as quickly as they could. It was too demanding to be in a house full of so much depression. After all, how much laughter and how many smiles could you force before being exhausted with the effort?

I stood by Mama as she hugged them both in the doorway. Celia promised to return but tried again to get Mama to promise to come to Memphis. I was waiting and hoping they would invite me. Finally, almost as a last thought, Brenda suggested it quietly, out of Mama's hearing.

"If things are such that you can get away for a weekend, April, we'll have you visit. But you've got to be sure things are okay with Mama first," she said. "She needs you. You've got to watch over her. I'm depending on you to do that, and that's why I don't want you getting yourself into any sort of new trouble, understand?"

I nodded.

"She's going to be fine," Celia said. "We'll call you," she assured me again.

In the end, I had to smile and kiss her good-bye. She surprised me by holding on to me and whispering, "You'll be okay, honey. You'll be okay."

I watched them get into their car, wave, and back out of the driveway. They were gone in moments, and suddenly, I felt cold and realized how dark and cloudy it had become. Mama had already retreated from the doorway. I felt like running after them. I felt like running away.

Those days of wishing time would freeze were long gone forever for me now. If anything, minutes took too long to become hours, and hours took too long to become days. I wished instead that I could close my eyes and when I opened them, I'd be Brenda's age, getting into my car and driving off to college or to anywhere but here.

By the time I walked back into the house, Mama was settled in Daddy's old chair. She wasn't crying, but she might as well be, I thought. Maybe there is such a thing as dry tears that trickle down your cheeks and settle around your heart, invisible tears, but just as hot.

I retreated to my room to complete my homework for the next day. We had a light supper. Mama ate less than I did. It had been only a few hours since Brenda and Celia had left, but she was already back to her meager appetite. Maybe out of nervousness, maybe to get her to see she should eat more, I ate everything in sight, even part of her portion. I offered to clean up, but she wanted to do it. She said she needed to be occupied.

Afterward, she joined me in the living room to watch television, but she showed little interest in anything I could find. Eventually, she rose and left. She didn't go to her bedroom, however. Instead, I found her sitting in Daddy's office, her back to the door, gazing out the window. In her hands, she held a picture of him and herself taken on their honeymoon, which she had found buried under a box of old papers.

"Are you all right, Mama?" I asked her. She didn't answer, so I asked again, and she turned the chair to face me.

"What? Oh, yes. I'm fine, April," she said. She forced a smile. "I'm just thinking about things. It's nothing. Go on to bed. Don't worry about me. You girls shouldn't worry about me."

I wanted to say, *But I am worried about you, Mama, and even more so with Brenda away and occupied with her own life, her sports, and her new close friend,* but I didn't say anything. I nodded instead and left her encased in her own melancholy. I sensed that there was little I could do to draw her out of it, and I hoped that somehow she would find the strength to put it aside and go on. Maybe it was right to pressure her to see a therapist, and soon, because maybe he could cure her. I realized my hope was selfish. I wanted her to go on for me now.

That night, I tossed and turned and fretted in and out of nightmares, worrying about my return to school and facing David, Luke, and Jenna. As it turned out, Brenda wasn't wrong. They looked my way, but, except for their smiles and whispers, they didn't bother me. Maybe they thought Brenda and Celia would be back immediately, or maybe, as Brenda said, I was already old news. They had other prey to feast upon.

I didn't tell anyone about my frightening experience, and maybe, because Luke had failed to seduce me, they didn't brag about it, either. Occasionally, Jenna would give me a shake of her head as if I were the one to be pitied. A week later, she was caught smoking marijuana in the school's basement and was expelled, not suspended. She had been suspended too many times, and the school had a no-tolerance attitude about drugs. Her parents didn't do anything to fight the suspension, and she was gone.

David got into a bad accident with his father's car the following month. He wasn't killed, but he was injured severely and spent the rest of the school year in hospitals and therapy.

Luke quit school before Christmas, and then I heard he had enlisted in the army.

None of this happened quickly enough for me. Time was not my friend, nor was it Mama's friend. I got so I hated looking at clocks. They always seemed to have stopped, or it seemed the hands were moving through glue. Mama resisted going to see a therapist. She made promises to Brenda over the phone but never followed through, even when Brenda located doctors and practically made the appointments herself. Mama always had some excuse not to go. I thought it might change when Brenda and Celia returned for the Christmas holiday, but they could stay only for a few days, and any doctor we could find was already on vacation. Brenda's team was remaining on campus and training since they were neck-and-neck for the league championship already.

Mama had lost more weight by the time they returned, whereas I had gained back most of what I had lost. I was eating more out of frustration and depression, but Brenda thought I was just being weak and unable to show any discipline. She didn't hide her disgust, and if it weren't for Celia, she wouldn't have said anything kind to me the whole weekend.

The only highlight of my life was passing my driver's license test. I had taken the driver's education course in school, and that helped a great deal. I had no other real experience. Other student drivers went out on weekends with their fathers or their mothers, but Mama was too nervous to do so with me. I was determined to get something right, however. The examiner gave me a compliment. He said I was very careful and mature.

In late February, the big game was held to determine who would be champions of Brenda's school's league. Celia and Brenda had been working on Mama to get her to attend. They had even arranged for us to have a hotel room nearby. Until the last minute, Mama had agreed to go. We were all suddenly filled with new hope. Perhaps Mama was emerging from her pit of depression on her own after all. She and I were driving to Memphis, and she was going to let me do most of the driving. I was actually excited about something for the first time in a long time.

Most of the new clothing I had gotten when I lost weight, however, no longer fit well. I couldn't even close up my jeans. I had to return to my closet and sift through older things until I found something nice enough to wear to what I was sure would be a victory celebration after the game. I regretted not sticking to my dieting and procrastinating when it came to exercise. I was sure Brenda would chastise me for it. Despite my promises, I never joined the girls' volleyball team, either.

The morning of the day of Brenda's big game, I woke up early. The night before, I had gotten the car all gassed up and ready. I had packed my little overnight bag. At dinner, I did almost all the talking. Mama sat listening. When Brenda called, she perked up a bit and once again assured her we were coming. She had lost more weight and had not been to the beauty parlor for so long they stopped calling to see if she wanted an appointment. She missed her regular doctor's checkup as well, and the dentist's receptionist called to see why she hadn't kept her appointment there. She told me she simply forgot, and I made a new appointment for her.

This trip to Memphis would mark Mama's first real excursion away from home since Daddy's passing. Some of her closer friends had tried on a number of occasions to get her to do theater trips or shopping trips with them. She always found some excuse not to go, and finally, they stopped calling altogether. In fact, it was rare to hear our phone ring at all these days.

When it did, it was often Uncle Palaver. If he called when I wasn't there, Mama did a good job of covering up her depression and loss of interest in everything. But if I answered the phone, I told him the truth, first in hopes that he would come visit, and second because I was really getting frightened for her.

He did plan on a trip to visit, but another cruise ship offered him an opportunity that he said would result in his and Destiny's most lucrative payday. He promised he would look into visiting us as soon as he was ashore again. He knew we were going to see Brenda's big game, and Mama had made it sound very exciting, so he was optimistic things would begin to change and work out for the best.

Did he really feel that they would, or was he saying it just so he would feel better himself? When people say, "Everything will be all right," are they really saying, "Stop bothering me?" Maybe Daddy was right about Uncle Palaver after all, I thought. Maybe he lived in his own world of illusion, saw everything through rose-colored glasses, and never really grew up.

"That wasn't it," Mama had insisted when Daddy said these things about Uncle Palaver. "This is just the life he has chosen for himself. It isn't that he is too immature to have a so-called stable life. It's hard, if not downright impossible, for him to develop a family and work on the road the way he does," she'd argue.

Daddy would shake his head. "You're just as bad as he is. Your family's last name should have been Rationalization," he added, but he smiled and shrugged and made no more of it back then.

Was he right?

Had Mama finally come to the same conclusion now?

"It's all right," she told me. "Everything will be all right," she chanted, her voice drifting off into the emptiness her own eyes saw for herself.

Little did I realize then just how far she had fallen into that big black hole.

9

Growing Up Fast

❧✦❧

I was surprised and disappointed to discover that Mama had not returned to her room after breakfast to dress and get her things together for our trip. Instead, she had gone back to bed.

"Mama! What are you doing? Why aren't you getting dressed?" I asked from her doorway. "We have to get started. We want to settle in and have some lunch with Brenda and Celia before going to the game. Everything is planned."

She groaned.

"What is it? What's wrong?"

"It's my back," she said. "I have a pocket of arthritis at the base of my spine, and it kicks up from time to time. I would be so uncomfortable sitting in a car and later in the stands, April. I'm sorry."

"You never told me you had arthritis."

"I didn't want to mention it to anyone. I don't need to have you and your sister worrying about it. There isn't much to do about it but take some painkillers and rest."

"How do you know? You went to the doctor?"

"Yes," she said.

I stood there staring at her, my face full of skepticism.

"I did," she insisted. "I had an appointment when you were at school. There are my pills," she added, nodding at a pill container on her nightstand.

My shoulders drooped. I had been so looking forward to this trip. I needed it almost as much as I believed Mama did.

"But I want you to go anyway, April," she said, surprising me.

"What?"

"Just go. Instead of staying at a hotel, you'll stay with Brenda and Celia. I've already called and spoken with Celia about it, and she said she would cancel our hotel reservation. They have a room next to theirs that they are permitted to use for their guests. She checked, and no one else on their floor has requested it. It all works out fine."

"You want me to drive to Memphis myself and stay in the dorm with them?"

"Yes, of course. You're old enough and responsible enough to do it, April. You have a good head on your shoulders. I trust you. You're not at all like so many of the young girls your age who let others lead them astray. I'm very proud of you."

What could I say? If she knew of the trouble I had been in with David, Luke, and Jenna, she wouldn't be so confident of my abilities. I felt like such a phony, and yet it was true that because of all that, I was far more careful and less innocent when it came to making decisions.

I thought about what she was telling me to do now. Go to Memphis by myself? What an exciting idea. I had driven around Hickory, of course, but I had yet to make a sizable trip of any kind—and to finally stay at the college dorm, too! But there was just no way I could leave Mama alone for two days. How could I even contemplate it?

"I can't leave you, Mama, especially if you're not feeling well."

"It's just some arthritis. I'll be able to get up and go about my business here just fine, April. I don't need you to babysit me. It will only make me feel worse to see you moping about the house. And I would hate knowing I'm keeping you from being part of your sister's success."

"Does Brenda know about this?"

"I'm sure Celia has told her by now or will very soon," she said.

"I don't know," I said, my reluctant resistance starting to crumble.

"At least one of us should be there for Brenda," Mama said. "If your father were alive, he would take you for sure, and if he couldn't go for some reason, he would surely send you."

"But you'll be all alone here, and . . ."

"I'm alone here most of the time, anyway, April. It's not going to be anything unusual. Of course, I want you to call me the moment you arrive at the dormitory and let me know you're there safely. Go on," she said when I didn't say anything. "You're a big girl now, honey. You've got to be more independent. Don't be afraid of it."

"I'm not afraid of being independent, Mama. That's not it. I'm worried about you."

"I know, but I'll be fine," she said. "It's really only for a day and a half."

"Are you sure you can't come with me, Mama? We'll drive slowly, stop if we have to and walk about, or have a cup of coffee in a roadside restaurant."

"No, that wouldn't help. And besides, I'd just make it unpleasant for everyone, and I want it to be wonderful for Brenda."

"She wants you there more than she wants me."

"Oh, no, honey. She talked so much about showing you around the campus."

"Really?"

"Yes. Please go. It will make me feel more terrible if you don't, and I can't stand feeling responsible for any more unhappiness in this family." She looked away and added, "I know how I've been a drag on both of you."

"No, you haven't, Mama. You haven't!"

"Okay." She turned back to me. "Just go, April. Please. If neither of us shows up, Brenda will be so upset."

"But . . ."

"I'm sure the other girls on the team will have their families watching. Brenda pretends to be self-sufficient, but she needs you."

"Brenda needs me?"

"Sisters need each other, April, especially two who have gone through everything you two have gone through."

If what she was saying were only true, I thought.

I nodded. Maybe I was rationalizing. Maybe I was being selfish, but the prospect of doing all this on my own was too exciting, and if I didn't go, Mama would be more depressed. I should go.

"Okay, Mama. I'll do it," I said.

"Good, April. Just be careful. Don't pick up any hitchhikers. Go directly to the dormitory. You have the directions Brenda sent us?"

"Yes," I said.

"Kiss me good-bye."

She held up her arms, and I went to her to hug and kiss her. She held me for a long moment and then smiled at me.

"My purse is on the dresser," she said. "There's a few hundred dollars in it. Take it. You shouldn't travel without money."

I did what she said.

"I'll call you as soon as I get there," I promised.

"Good. Don't forget. I know it will be very exciting for you to take your first big drive and be on a college campus, but I'll be waiting to hear from you."

"I won't forget," I said.

"I told you often that you would be a big girl soon. Well, soon is here," she said.

"Yes. Soon is here."

I went to my room, got my overnight bag, and stopped by her doorway one more time to say good-bye. She had her eyes closed but opened them and smiled at me. Then I hurried out to the car and just sat there for a moment, still wondering if I should go or not. It wasn't that far, I decided. If I had to come back, I'd come back. I turned the key, started the engine, triggered the garage door open, and backed out. I closed the garage and drove off, feeling like a student pilot doing his or her first solo flight.

Minutes later, I had the radio on and was cruising on the highway. It was truly as if I had crossed over some boundary and matured overnight. Although I was sure they weren't, it seemed to me every driver who passed by gazed at me with surprise and awe, impressed that I, April Taylor, who had turned sixteen just recently, was alone and heading for Memphis. One man passing me smiled at me the way I remembered my daddy smiling at me. He even looked like him, and for a moment I thought maybe the dead slip into the bodies of strangers just so they could experience briefly something significant their loved ones who were left behind were doing. Maybe that really was Daddy.

Or maybe it was only wishful thinking. It had been so long since I had done any of that. Life had become too dark and difficult to permit the entrance of fanciful dreams. Besides, Mama was right. *Soon* had come. I was older now and had to stop fantasizing, pretending like a little girl who pulled on wishbones and hoped she got the longer end. Adults don't have time to daydream. I had to deal with cold reality just as well as any adult dealt with it. I had to take responsibility for my actions.

I was so nervous when I reached the city limits that even though Celia and Brenda's directions were precise, I made one wrong turn. However, I was able to correct it quickly and pulled up to the dormitory building just a little before eleven. I saw the parking lot and drove in, stopping in an available space. When I turned off the engine, I let out my breath as if I had been holding it in the whole trip. I was here. It was easy. Proud of myself, I scooped up my overnight bag and got out of the car.

The dormitory was a three-story red-brick building with a four-column white portico. I entered a lobby that had a few groups of sofas and chairs, tables, and stands. The floor was a dark brown tile, and there were three good-size chandeliers. The walls were a pale pink with large windows facing the front and sheer white curtains framing them. Four girls were talking and laughing to my right when I entered. One was in a bathrobe, and the others were in jeans and long shirts. The girl in the bathrobe wore a baseball cap. They glanced my way but quickly returned to whatever they were discussing.

To the left was a desk with no one behind it, and directly in front of me was a set of double doors that led into the residence itself. I stood there for a moment, unsure where to go or what to do next. I had Brenda's room number, 207. I had been hoping she and Celia would be waiting for me in the lobby. Imagining it wouldn't be hard to find their room, I continued through the double doors to a pair of elevator doors and pushed the up button.

I heard a girl scream with laughter and saw a tall redhead coming down the hallway toward me, accompanied by another girl in an oversized pair of jeans and overshirt. She was short and buxom. They looked at me as they approached.

"Those elevators are so slow, you're better off taking the stairs, unless you're not supposed to arrive until tomorrow," the redhead said, and gestured toward a door that had "Stairs" written on it. Her companion laughed again.

Just then, the elevator door opened. I shrugged and stepped into it, pressing the button for the second floor. It did seem to take an unusual amount of time for the doors to close again, and then the elevator jerked and started up in what seemed inches at a time. It stopped, and I was afraid the doors weren't going to open. They finally did, and I stepped into the second-floor corridor. I was surprised to see a boy standing in a doorway, leaning over a girl in a translucent nightie. She looked at me, but he didn't turn. Instead, he brought his lips closer to hers. When they kissed, I looked away quickly and followed the room numbers down to 207, which was nearly at the end of the corridor.

I knocked and waited.

No one came to the door, so I knocked again.

"Brenda?" I called. Still, no one came to the door.

Where was she? I tried the knob, but the door was locked.

"Brenda, are you in there?"

The girl and her boyfriend looked down the hallway at me. Feeling silly standing there, I started back toward the elevator. The boy followed the girl into her room and closed the door. This time, I did take the staircase, and when I reached the first floor, I hurried out to the lobby again, hoping Brenda and Celia had returned from wherever they had gone and were now waiting for me.

Two other girls had joined the four I had first seen, but Brenda and Celia were not there.

"Can I help you?" I heard, and turned to the desk to see a slim woman with dull dark brown hair threaded with white standing behind the desk. She wore what looked like a dark blue uniform that included a jacket and skirt with a lighter blue blouse. The jacket had padded shoulders. Her cheeks were quite pockmarked, and she seemed to have no chin because of how sharply it sloped from her lower lips to her neck. Two untrimmed eyebrows hung over her small, dark gray eyes.

"I'm looking for my sister."

"And does this sister have a name?" she asked, tucking the corners of her lips into her cheeks.

I looked back at the girls, who had stopped talking and were now listening to me.

"Brenda Taylor."

"Um," she said, her face quickly filling with disapproval. Then her eyes focused on my overnight bag. "I want you to know right from the start that I don't tolerate alcoholic beverages, drugs, smoking of any kind in the rooms, or excessive noise."

"Neither do I, ma'am," I said, and a girl behind me yelped.

I turned and looked back at them. They were all smiling.

"All visitors must sign in," she told me, and pushed a clipboard toward me. I put down my bag and signed my name on the blank line, noting that I was the first visitor of the day, and yet that boy was upstairs in one of the girl's rooms.

She turned the clipboard toward her to check that I had written my real name, I guess, and then turned it back. Just then, the front door opened, and Brenda and Celia entered.

"When did you get here?" Brenda asked without even saying hello. She didn't look at the woman behind the desk, either.

"A few minutes ago."

"Come on, honey," Celia said. She put her arm around my shoulders and squeezed me against her. Then she kissed my cheek. Brenda just stood watching.

"This is our guest, Ms. Gitman," Brenda told the woman who had questioned me. "My sister, April."

"I already know that. She's signed in. I've told her our rules," she replied.

"Thank you," Brenda said. "Now, I won't have to."

Celia giggled, and they marched me though the double doors to the stairway.

"That's Ms. Gitalong," Celia said. "Now you know why we want your uncle to make her disappear. We should go up the stairs. The elevator takes . . ."

"Forever, I know. I went up on it before."

"Oh, you went up to our room?"

"Yes, but before I signed in. She wasn't there when I arrived."

"She was probably back in her quarters pulling the legs off grasshoppers or something. We didn't expect you would get here this fast, did we, Brenda?"

I looked at Brenda. She kept her eyes away from me and just walked on ahead. She was making me feel very nervous.

"Brenda's a little upset," Celia whispered. "Don't worry," she added.

Brenda didn't talk until we got into their room and I had put down my bag. Then she turned, her arms folded under her breasts, and looked at me.

"What happened to Mama?" she asked as if whatever had happened was somehow was my fault. "Why didn't she come?"

"I thought she was going to right up to the last minute, Brenda," I said. "She didn't say anything at breakfast, and then she went to her room, and I went to mine, thinking she was getting dressed, but when I went to get her, I found her in bed complaining about arthritis. She told me she had already called you. She said Celia spoke with her," I added, looking at Celia.

"How could you leave her?" Brenda snapped at me.

Before I could answer, I started to cry.

"Stop it!" Brenda said sharply.

"She made me leave," I said through my sobs. "She said you would want me here."

"Of course, I want you here. I'm just concerned, that's all," she added, softening a bit.

"Everything will be all right, Brenda," Celia said. "April will be with me."

"I'm not worried about her. I'm worried about my mother."

"So am I," I said, "but she said she would be very

unhappy if I didn't go. She said it was just her arthritis, and she had been to the doctor, who told her to rest and take some painkillers."

"She never told me that."

"Me, neither," I said.

"We'll deal with all that later, Brenda," Celia told her. "We'll just take a ride to your house later this week."

Brenda relaxed a little more and sat on one of the two beds. They were separated by a small night table on which they had a clock and a phone. Except for what looked like a print landscape on the wall behind the beds, the room was stark. There were no posters, no pictures, not even any on the dressers or the desk. The bathroom was half the size of any of ours at home, if that. I could see that it was an older building. I imagined the attraction was simply the excitement of being on your own. To me, it was a little disappointing. I imagined Mama wouldn't have been very impressed, either.

"I'm supposed to call Mama as soon as I got here," I remembered.

"Then what are you waiting for? Call her," Brenda said, handing me the phone.

I tapped out our number quickly and waited. It rang and rang. Brenda raised her eyebrows and stepped closer. Finally, Mama picked up.

"It's me, Mama. I'm here at the dormitory."

"Oh, how nice. You had a good trip, then?"

"Yes, it was easy. How are you?"

"I'm fine," she said. "The pain is not so bad now."

"Let me speak to her," Brenda demanded, and I handed her the phone. "Mama, what's wrong? Why didn't you come?" She listened. "You never told me any of this. No, no, I'm not angry," she said. "I will. She's fine. We'll take good care of her," she added, looking at me. "Okay, Mama. We'll call you right after the game and tell you about it. I hope so. Celia and I will come see you as soon as we can. I know, but we want to," she said. "Okay. Call you later," she concluded, and hung up.

"I'm sure it's all psychosomatic," Celia said.

Brenda nodded. Then she looked at me as if she had just realized I had arrived. "Look at you. A big-shot teenager now," she said, and poked me in the shoulder. Celia laughed.

"Let's get you settled in the guest room, and then we'll show you around," Celia said.

"Thanks." I looked at Brenda. She had a tight smile on her face.

"I'm glad you're here," she finally admitted. "You'll see us whip their asses good."

Finally, I could smile, too.

The guest room just had a single bed, a dresser, and a desk and chair in it. It had one curtained window. I put my bag in the closet, and we went off immediately to grab some lunch at one of their favorite places. Brenda ate lightly. I wanted to have one of the big burgers, but I ordered a salad as well. Brenda immediately started in on me about my regained weight.

Before I could offer any excuses, Celia went into a long explanation about why some people are self-destructive. She concluded by saying, "April's problem isn't hard to see, Brenda. She has low self-esteem at the moment and needs to be reassured about herself. It's a crazy cycle, April," she said, turning to me. "You don't receive compliments, so you don't take care of yourself, and therefore, you don't receive compli-

ments. You reinforce your low self-esteem without realizing you're doing that."

"Are you sure you don't want to go into psychology?" Brenda asked her. "You haven't met anyone you
didn't want to analyze."

"Maybe I will. Look, this situation is classic. Your
sister grew up in a house where you were the star. You
were getting all the accolades, Brenda."

"She could have tried harder. She was lazy. She's
still lazy," Brenda said. She didn't look at me. The two
of them were discussing me as if I weren't even there.

"It's not laziness, exactly," Celia said.

"Oh, what is it then, Doctor?"

"Well, you told me yourself how your teammates
wouldn't try very hard if they fell too far behind. You
said you felt all alone out there many times. Well, she's
just fallen too far behind."

Brenda thought a moment and then just shook her
head and smiled at Celia. "You're too smart for your
own good. You know that?"

"Of course, I know that. You just said I was too
smart."

The two of them laughed. Celia leaned forward and
wiped some salad dressing off Brenda's cheek. They
stared at each other for a moment and then, finally,
Brenda looked at me.

"I've got to rest a bit and then go limber up in the
gym. Celia will show you around."

"I don't have to see anything," I said.

"I'll just take you for a walk around the school,"
Celia said. "Brenda says you'd like to see the library."

I shrugged, and Brenda smirked. "You know why
you don't have any energy or interest in anything,
April? You're not trying. You're using Mama as an excuse not to join anything."

"No, I'm not." Tears came to my eyes.

"Do we have to do this now?" Celia said. "You have a lot on your mind."

"You're right. Okay, do what you want. Let's go," Brenda said, and signaled for the check.

Her mood changes were driving me crazy. I couldn't tell if she hated the sight of me here or was glad I had come despite everything.

"She pretends she's so cool, but she's really nervous about the game," Celia whispered.

When we returned to the dormitory, Brenda went directly up to their room. She hadn't said a word all the way back. Celia stood beside me in the parking lot, watching her go into the building. Her eyes narrowed with concern.

"I'm a little worried about her with all that's on her mind. I mean, your mother and all," she added. "I think I had better spend some time with her. I can tell when she's really uptight. There's a rec room on the first floor, two doors down on the right. Why don't you watch some television or read for a while, and I'll come down as soon as I can?" she said. "Is that all right?"

"Yes," I said, surprised. Brenda never had shown nervousness before any of the tournaments or big games she had played when she was at home. How was Celia able to tell what was under her skin if I couldn't or Mama couldn't? And why wouldn't she want me to be there as well to help cheer her up and comfort her? I really felt like an outsider.

The rec room was bigger than I expected, but there was only one girl in it, watching television. She sat on the settee with her feet up, her shoes off. She didn't look much older than I was, and I wondered if she was a student or a guest like me. Could she have a sister here who was also on the basketball team? I saw she was watching a soap opera, and she was so involved in it she barely gave me a glance.

I plopped into the chair near the settee.

"He's lying, you know," she said without taking her eyes off the television set.

"Excuse me?"

"Dirk," she said, looking at me quickly. "Amanda is carrying his baby."

I looked at the set and realized she was speaking about the characters on a soap opera.

"Oh."

"Don't you watch *Rainbow of Dreams*?"

The commercial started.

"No. I'm not familiar with it. I don't really watch much television in the afternoon. My mother used to watch soaps, but she hasn't for some time."

"I don't see how she could stop. It's like an addiction. I actually scheduled my classes around *Rainbow of Dreams*."

"Oh, you're a student?"

"Of course. What do you think, I just come here to watch television?" She laughed and tilted her head and looked at me. "Now that you mention it, who are you?"

"I'm Brenda Taylor's sister. I drove to Memphis to watch her play in the championship basketball game."

"Oh, Brenda," she said. "I didn't know she had a sister," she added, glancing at the set. "No one knows much about BC."

"BC? Why do you call her BC? Her name is Brenda Taylor."

"Brenda and Celia. BC. Everyone calls them BC around here. They stick to themselves. Literally," she added.

I felt the blood rush into my face. "What's that supposed to mean?"

"Nothing," she said. She held up her hand. "I never said a word."

"Maybe they just don't like the choice of potential friends," I snapped back, and got up.

She looked at me as if I were from another planet, but the commercials ended, and the building could be on fire and she wouldn't care or turn away again. I was annoyed with her and with being relegated to the rec room while Celia cheered up my sister. I marched out and went to the stairway. Mama had said that two sisters who had gone through as much as we had gone through needed each other. I should be the one up there with Brenda, not Celia.

I hurried up the stairway and down the hallway to their room. Maybe I should have knocked first. I wasn't thinking. Mama's sudden illness and change of heart, the drive, all the tension between Brenda and me, my feeling so lost, all of it put so much turmoil into my mind that I didn't know whether I was coming or going, and certainly not whether I had made a big error coming here myself.

Of course, I wondered why they didn't lock their door. When I turned the handle and it opened, the last thing I thought was that would be a problem. I didn't enter, however. I simply stood there stupidly gaping.

Totally naked, Brenda was on her bed, faceup. Celia was straddling her and rubbing some sort of cream into her shoulders and her arms and then over her breasts. What made it look even stranger to me was that Celia was in her panties and naked from the waist up herself. Neither of them had heard the door open. Brenda gazed to her left and saw me.

"April!" she cried. "Close the door!"

Celia shifted and turned to look at me. She looked quickly at Brenda and then back at me.

"Why didn't you wait downstairs in the rec room?" she asked.

"There's only one girl down there, and she's watching some stupid soap opera." I swallowed hard and then asked, "What are you doing?"

"She's giving me a massage," Brenda said. "Go take a walk or something."

The two of them continued to stare at me. I wanted to ask why the person giving the massage had to be almost naked, too. I wanted to ask if women usually had their breasts massaged as well. I wanted to ask if all college roommates were as physically intimate as they seemed to be. I wanted to ask so many things, but instead, I turned and left the room quickly.

It wasn't until I was standing in the hallway that I realized my face was flushed and my heart was thumping like a flat tire on a car, each beat ripping under and around my breasts.

Nasty things said to me at school began to submerge from the dark, dank pool of unpleasant memories. Jenna's threat returned. The girl downstairs in the rec room's remark about BC echoed. I actually put my hands over my ears, as though the words were returning from the outside instead of being resurrected from the cemetery of horrid thoughts.

I shook my head and charged down the hallway to the stairs, practically flying over the steps. Then I hurried out of the building and, without knowing where I was going or even thinking of any direction, just walked down the drive and continued along the street.

What was I fleeing? My brain reeled with memories and thoughts, images and tantalizing emotions. Was I shocked? Yes. Did it frighten me? A little. Did it excite me? I didn't want to answer, even if I was answering only to myself.

When Luke touched me in places no one other than my own mother had ever seen, I was shocked and frightened but not tantalized or in any way sexually excited. All I could think of was how to escape.

For a while up there in Brenda and Celia's room, I was mesmerized. I was filled with the erotic exhilaration of a voyeur, especially during those few moments when neither Brenda nor Celia knew I was in the room watching them. Shouldn't I have been disgusted? Why was I so flushed? Why couldn't I get the sight of them out of my mind?

Was I going to be like Brenda? Why didn't I have deeper crushes on boys at school? Why didn't I care more about my appearance, my figure? These questions circled me like a swam of mad bees.

None of us knows who we really are, I thought. My father became a different man. Mama had changed so much I hardly recognized her. Brenda was one sort of big sister and person to me, and now she was another. Who was I? Whom would I be most like?

I heard laughter behind me and saw a girl and a boy walking together, holding hands and swinging their arms as they walked. Suddenly, they stopped, and there on the sidewalk in broad daylight, they kissed as if they couldn't take another step forward without doing so. What was that sort of passion like? Would I ever find it?

On and on I walked, until I realized I was getting lost and nearly panicked. If there was one thing I didn't want to do, it was that. I traced my way back, hurrying along. This time, I knocked on the door, and Celia opened it. She was in a robe.

"Oh, we wondered where you had gone. You were away so long."

"Where's Brenda?" I asked, seeing she wasn't in the room and the bathroom door was open.

"She's off to the gym. She never eats before a game. Go change into whatever you brought, and we'll walk over to the gym. There's a sandwich shop on the way, and we can have a small bite to eat first, if you want."

"I don't need to eat before the game, either," I said.

"Whatever. That's fine."

She reached out to brush some hair off my forehead, and I instinctively pulled back. She held her smile and her hand frozen in the air between us.

"You could do some nice things with your hair, April."

"I'll change," I said.

"If you want to shower first . . ."

"No, I'm fine," I said.

She still held her smile. "Are you all right?"

No, I wanted to say. *I'm not all right. What's going on between you and my sister?*

"I said I was fine," I replied instead, and went to my room to change.

I took so long, she came to my door.

"Hey, c'mon, April. I want to show you the campus," she said.

She was dressed in a pair of jeans, with a design made of pearls along the calves, and a tight black top with a black leather jacket. I couldn't deny she was beautiful in a striking way. Anyone's eyes would go to her in a crowd. Why didn't she have a line of boyfriends at her door?

I decided to be petulant.

"How come you don't have a date for the game?" I asked her. I felt smug and confident. It was like tossing water in her beautiful face.

She just smiled back instead.

And she said, "I do. You're my date, April."

10

April's Date

Maybe it was my overworked imagination, but I thought everyone was looking at us. The young men on and around the campus were obviously drawn to Celia. Why wouldn't they be? She was so beautiful, and it was for sure they weren't looking at me. Celia didn't acknowledge their looks or their catcalls. She seemed to walk through it all like someone walking through fog. Yet that tight small smile never left her lips. I thought she enjoyed her effect on them, but that was all she seemed to do. How could someone so beautiful be so indifferent to them? Wasn't there one who attracted her? Why was beauty so squandered on her? Why couldn't I have that sort of beauty?

Out of the corner of my eye, I saw young men wave after us with disgust, clearly saying it was a waste of time to look, to call, even to try to catch Celia's attention. They knew. They knew what I had refused to know. Now, everything I saw and every word I heard reconfirmed the truth building inside me. *This isn't my sister's roommate; this is my sister's lover.* The constant question swirling around in my mind was, where did I belong in all this?

I felt truly dazed while Celia showed me things, described things, talked about the school, her classes, the city itself. I vaguely listened, like someone working with music in the background. I knew it was there, knew that her words were there, but I was somehow withdrawn.

It was different in the gymnasium. I couldn't ignore anything. It reminded me too much of the high school games I had attended, either by myself or earlier with Daddy and Mama. It brought back those memories, the building excitement, the noise, the cheerleaders. It always felt like an event, and with the emphasis this school placed on female athletics, it was no different.

There was a group of boys in the bleachers who were there simply to mock the girls. There were always some in high school who were like that, but these boys looked drunk or high on something, because they were so loud and conspicuous. I saw the referee warn them, and then a woman who was probably a teacher at the school chastised them as well. They calmed down, but as soon as the game was under way, they were back at their shouts and howls.

I had watched Brenda play in competition many times, of course, and I always noted how the other members of her teams treated her with deference and respect. Right from the beginning, it was clear that they were looking to her for direction and momentum. Her energy drove her teammates. She was making shots and intimidating the opposition so aggressively and determinedly that after a while, even the boys who had come to mock the game settled into a quiet appreciation. They simply couldn't take their eyes off her. I realized that in the short time she had been away at college, she had become so much better than she had been. The quality of the competition probably sharpened her skills. She drew fouls periodically, and every time she went to the foul line to shoot, she looked our way. Celia didn't wave or anything, but I could tell they were exchanging more than just a glance.

Despite Brenda's superior abilities, the game remained very close and exciting, because there were girls on the other team who were quite good as well. I forgot everything, lost myself in the battle, and grew hoarse shouting. It was in the last two minutes that the game was determined. Almost as if Brenda were the heroine in a movie, it fell to her to make the final shot. The ball teetered for a second or so on the rim and then fell through as the buzzer sounded. Her teammates converged on her. It was actually the most exciting game I had ever seen her play.

"Isn't she wonderful?" Celia said.

The fans were rushing down the stands around us, but Celia remained seated, calm, her face full of light, as she watched Brenda greeting people, hugging teammates.

"She's like some graceful new animal out there. She glides and floats and does such wondrous things with her body, doesn't she?"

"Yes," I said, amazed at how taken Celia was with my sister. I certainly appreciated Brenda's abilities, but Celia's reaction was more than admiration. She seemed to be in utter awe. She turned to me.

"I'm so sorry your mother couldn't be here to see this. Brenda would have been so happy, too."

"I tried to get her to come. I really did!"

"Oh, I'm sure you did, April. I'd be the last one to blame you."

"Brenda probably does," I muttered. "She looked so angry when she first saw me."

"No, she doesn't blame you. She gets that way when she is disappointed, but she loves you. She really does."

Yeah, right, I mouthed.

"C'mon, let's wait for her in the hallway. It's too hard to get to her right now."

We left the gym and sat on a bench outside the girls' locker room, where we watched the other students walking by and saw members of the opposing team rushing away with the shadows of disappointment splashed over their faces like ink.

"I feel sorry for them," Celia told me, "but Brenda never does. She says if she feels sorry after beating someone, she'll never be competitive enough. What strength she possesses."

"I know," I said, but I said it sadly, as though it were a disease she had and not a good quality.

Celia gave me a sideward glance and then put her arm around me and squeezed me to her.

"Don't worry," she said. "You'll find what you're good at, too."

She held me a little too long for my comfort. I looked nervously at the students who were gazing our way. Finally, Brenda came out of the locker room, and Celia jumped up.

"Hey, hey, hey!" she cried. They gave each other the high five and hugged.

I stepped up behind them, feeling overlooked and

tentative while Celia raved about the game. Other students passing by congratulated Brenda as well. If I didn't feel as if I were just tagging along before, I certainly did now.

"What did you think, little sister?" Brenda finally asked me.

"You were fantastic, Brenda. I never saw you do so well."

She laughed and gave me a quick hug. Then she and Celia put their arms around me, and the three of us walked out.

"I'm starving," Brenda declared.

"So are we," Celia said. "Doheny's?"

"You think you-know-who is ready for it?"

"Sure, why not?" Celia replied. "It's sort of a hangout," she explained to me.

Hangout for whom? I wanted to ask, but it didn't take long to get there and find out.

There wasn't a male in the place.

Everyone there knew who Celia and Brenda were, too. What struck me about the bar and restaurant beside the absence of men was that the women there didn't look at all like college students. Most looked older; some looked much older.

"Didn't you want to go somewhere to celebrate with your team?" I asked Brenda.

"No. I don't care to relive every moment. It's done and gone. On to the next thing," she told me.

We had taken a table to the rear in the right corner. From there, we viewed the crowded bar. Brenda and Celia looked at the menu.

"What do you feel like?" Celia asked her.

"I could eat a horse on a gallop. I'm going for the Philadelphia steak sandwich. I know you'll order the Oriental chicken salad."

Celia laughed and leaned toward her. "You know me too well."

Brenda smiled at her in a way unlike any smile she had given me or even Daddy during the good days. She put her menu down, and they touched each other's hand.

"You were amazing out there," Celia continued. "There were times I thought you had actually learned how to fly."

"You saw how that big, ugly blonde was elbowing me, I'm sure."

"I did."

"Too bad the ref didn't," Brenda muttered.

"Are you sore? I'll put some of that ointment on you later, if you like."

"I'm all right. I got one shot in before the end of the third quarter which kept her off me for a while."

"I was tempted to get up and scream at the ref myself," Celia said.

Brenda laughed. "Yeah, right," she said. "You come down on the court to yell at someone."

I felt I was outside looking in at them or maybe even invisible. Perhaps I had disappeared.

"I thought we were going to call Mama right after the game," I interjected the moment there was a pause.

They both looked at me as if they really did just realize I was there.

"She's right. Order for me. Draft beer, too. I'll go use the pay phone," Brenda said, and rose. She looked at me. "You want to talk to her, too?"

"Of course, I do," I said.

"What do you want to eat?" Celia asked.

"I'll have the same salad you're having," I told her, and followed Brenda to the rear of the restaurant, where the bathrooms and the telephone were located.

Brenda dug into her pocket for a coin and began to punch out our home number. She told the operator to reverse the charges and gave the operator her name. I stood by waiting.

A woman with a very closely cropped head of black hair, an earring dangling from her right lobe, and a tattoo of a necklace made out of what looked like snakeskin around her neck stepped out of the bathroom. She had to brush by us and literally pushed me back. Brenda glared at her and then turned back to the phone.

"Mama. We won!" she said. "By two points. I made the final basket," she added, and listened. "Are you all right? You sound sleepy. Oh. Well, I couldn't have called you much earlier. She's with me. She's fine," she added, looking at me. "She's right here. I'll call you in the morning. Yes. Okay, Mama."

She handed me the receiver and walked away.

"How are you, Mama?" I asked quickly.

"I'm fine, April. So it was very exciting?"

"Yes, it was, and Brenda was the star," I said. I watched her returning to the table, where the waitress was bringing them mugs of beer.

"I'm so happy you were there for it, honey, so happy."

"I wish you had been here, Mama."

"Me, too. But it was important that you were," she said. "Be careful driving," she added.

"I'll talk to you in the morning after we get up. I'm leaving right after breakfast."

"You don't have to hurry home on my account, April."

"I want to, Mama."

"Okay, honey. Have fun, Good night, Mrs. Panda," she said, and hung up.

I stood there holding the receiver. Mrs. Panda? Why did she call me that?

Brenda and Celia were laughing when I returned. They toasted with their glasses, and I sat.

"You want a Coke or a lemonade or what?" Brenda asked.

"Just a glass of cold water," I told her. She raised her eyebrows and turned to Celia. "I guess you're having a better effect on her than I've had. She orders a salad and a glass of water?"

"No one's having an effect on me," I said sharply. "It's all I want."

They both looked at me, at each other, and then laughed.

I wished I were home.

"Mama said a strange thing to me," I blurted to stop them.

"What do you mean?" Brenda said, winding down her laughter. "What did she say?"

"She said, 'Good night, Mrs. Panda.'"

"Mrs. Panda? What's that?" Celia asked.

Brenda lowered her mug. "That's something my father called her when she was little, his little panda bear. He bought her a panda bear, and she treated it like a little friend forever," Brenda explained.

"Oh, how cute."

"But why did she call me that?"

"I'm sure she was just being sentimental and loving," Celia offered.

How did she know so much about us all, about how we felt? It wasn't her business. She reached for my hand. I started to pull away, but she literally seized it and held it.

"Your mother sees you growing up, April. You

were the baby in the family, and you're moving on, becoming a young woman, driving, on your own. It makes her happy, but it makes her sad as well. It's just part of what it means to be a mother, a parent," she explained.

"How do you know all that? You're not a parent." I wanted to add, *And you probably never will be,* but I didn't.

"It's basic psychology, honey. You'll see," she said, released my hand, but patted it.

I glanced at Brenda. She looked mesmerized by Celia. The two held their gaze on each other for a long moment, and then the food and my drink arrived. Some of the other women stepped over to our table to congratulate Brenda on the game. They had heard about it and about her performance. I noticed how they looked at Celia, who glared back at them like a guard dog, observing every touch, every hug and kiss.

"Who are these people?" I asked, scowling when we were alone again.

They both laughed.

"What's so funny?"

"The way you asked," Celia said. "Some of them work at the college in the business department. That woman at the far corner of the bar is a drama and speech instructor, Ms. Formier. The rest are people who work in the area."

"How come you don't go where other college kids go?"

"We feel comfortable here," Brenda said. She glanced at Celia. I caught a slight nod. "Look, April, I think you're old enough to understand now. Celia and I . . ."

"I don't want to hear it!" I practically screamed.

"What?"

"I'm tired. I'm going back to the dorm."

I jumped up and started out of the bar.

"April!" Brenda called after me, but I kept walking. I really felt as if I couldn't breathe. The cold night air hit me like a slap, and I broke into a jog. I felt the tears streaming down my cheeks and blowing off my chin. I wasn't sure I was going in the right direction, but I kept going, anyway. After I rounded a corner, I stopped to catch my breath, and I heard Brenda coming up quickly behind me. She called out to me, and I turned.

"What the hell do you think you're doing?" she demanded as she approached in a walk now.

"I didn't like it in there," I said. "And I don't like Celia. She thinks she knows everything, everything. Especially about our family!" I screamed.

"Calm down, April," Brenda ordered.

I folded my arms and turned my back on her.

"You're acting like a spoiled, temperamental kid."

"I am not, and don't call me a kid. That's what she would say. I'm sixteen! I'm a young adult!"

I couldn't help shouting now. Like a coiled fuse attached to a time bomb, I knew that sooner or later, I would explode while I was visiting, and now I had.

"Then act like an adult," she countered. Her face softened. "Okay," she said. "I understand. This is all happening too fast, and it's too much in your face."

I didn't say anything.

"Come on. We'll walk back to the dorm," she said. She turned left. "It's this way. You were going in the wrong direction."

"I didn't care. I just wanted to get out of there."

We walked silently for a while. I looked back once

to see if Celia was coming after us, but I didn't see her. I was finally alone with my sister.

"Most people can't help being who and what they are," she began. "I also know that most people don't want to believe that. They want to be able to blame others for the things they do or for who they become. First, it isn't right for people to stand in judgment like that, and second, their anger or intolerance is usually born of plain ignorance.

"I knew you took a lot of ribbing and abuse at school because of me. You never complained to Mama or Daddy or even me about it, either, and I was proud of you for that."

My heart was thumping. Brenda had never spoken to me like this. It was all left unsaid, stored in a closet or in a trunk, words not even to be whispered, thoughts to be driven away like pesky bugs. Now, Brenda was opening the closets, opening the trunks. The thing was, I was tempted to throw my hands over my ears and scream, *Shut up! Shut up! Shut up! I don't want to hear any of this!*

"I was never with any other girl before Celia," she continued. "I knew I had feelings that made me different, but I buried myself in my sports and ignored them as much as I could. When I was younger, I tried to deny them. I went out on dates, as you know, and I can't say they were all with losers. Some of the boys—most of them, in fact—were very nice. Don't think I wasn't upset with myself for not wanting to continue a relationship, but for me, it was always taking a journey on a street that turned out to be a dead end.

"When I came to college, I didn't expect it would be any different. Celia believes it's kismet that we met, especially at this particular time of our lives. She had doubts about herself and went through an adolescence not unlike my own. She had similar questions about herself. We certainly didn't expect what happened to happen.

"The truth is, April, that I chose to room with Celia as soon as I set eyes on her, and not because I fell in love with her. Oh, no. I thought just looking at her that she was completely opposite from me and being with her might change me somehow. Imagine my surprise when I discovered who she really was and what she really felt.

"I know what you're thinking," she said, pausing to turn to me. "You are thinking, *I wish the things my sister is saying she was saying about some handsome college boy.*"

I didn't say yes; I didn't say no. I felt too numb to speak and also afraid that my words would be wrong, that I might ruin this precious golden moment between us, a moment in which I sensed we were finally becoming real sisters.

She continued to walk.

"Maybe a part of me wishes the same thing. I don't know. I know with Celia, however, I don't feel any of the old guilt. I don't avoid looking at myself. I don't feel bad about feeling good.

"Do you know," she said, pausing again, "that when Daddy was being so hard on us all, I thought he was being especially hard on me because he knew who I was before I did, and he was taking it out on you and Mama as well? Maybe he was taking it out on himself, blaming himself for permitting me to do what some old-fashioned people would call tomboy activities, encouraging me, in fact.

"And then, when he ran off, I was convinced I was the sole cause of it. Do you know how many sleepless nights I spent thinking that? I hate to admit it to anyone, but I had a sense of relief when we discovered the real reason for his deserting us, as terrible as that reason was. At least it wasn't my fault. Do you understand?"

I nodded.

"Anyway," she continued, walking again, "after his death, I had this feeling that chains had been lifted from me. I wasn't willing to go wild or anything. I had simply stopped all the denial. I looked at myself in the mirror one day afterward and said, *Brenda, this is who you are. Take it or leave it, and get on with your life.*"

"What does Mama know?" I asked.

She didn't answer for a long moment, and then she stopped.

"You know, April, I can't say for sure. Sometimes, I would catch her looking at me with so much pity in her face I nearly cried, and sometimes, I saw her looking at me with admiration. Whatever, I think it's time I was as honest with her as I am with you. It's something I have to do, something I have to find the strength to do."

"Mama thinks you're so strong. So does Celia, and so do I," I added.

"I put on a good façade," she said. "Someone once wrote that you should be careful of whom you pretend to be, because that's who you'll be. Maybe it's very true for me. I don't know. When I first learned that you were coming here yourself, I was both angry and happy about it," she revealed.

"How could it be both?"

"I thought if you came with Mama, you two would be away from us enough to remain in some dark place when it came to me and my identity and that the façade, the denial, could continue. It was comfortable and easier not to have to admit to anything. But there was and is a part of me that wants to be honest, April, and I thought to myself, maybe, just maybe, this was the time to reveal myself to you. I was afraid. That's why I was so angry for a while. Celia continued to prod me to deal with it, with you. Of course, she was and is right. I didn't handle it well. We didn't. I can understand why you got so upset back there. I'm sorry."

She reached out and brushed my hair back the way Mama always did.

"Am I going to be like you, Brenda?"

She held her smile. "Is that what troubles you the most now?"

"In a way, yes," I said.

"I don't know, April. It would be very convenient or simple to say no, but I didn't know about myself, so how can I predict what's in store for you? You'll have to examine and come to understand your own feelings. I don't believe you have to be like me because of some inherited thing, but I don't know."

I nodded. "I guess I really was behaving like a child back there. I'm sorry."

"Not at all," she said.

She put her arm around me, and we walked along for quite a while without saying a word. I felt she wasn't simply embracing me with her arm but was wrapping her heart around me as well. She had trusted me with her innermost feelings and revelations. She had bared herself in a way she hadn't in all our lives together. We were never closer as sisters than we were at this moment, and yet I felt we were also farther apart in a different sort of way. I had a chasm of misunderstandings about myself and about her to cross before we could truly say we accepted each other. That would take time, and maybe, maybe, it would never happen.

Celia was waiting for us outside the dormitory. "Hey," she called. "What happened to you two? I was starting to worry."

"We took a little detour," Brenda explained. Celia nodded and turned to me.

"I'm sorry if I made you uncomfortable in any way back there," she said.

"No, it's all right."

"Oh?" She looked at Brenda and in a moment knew all that had passed between us. "Great. Well, I'm tired, and I didn't play a second in that grueling game, so I can't even imagine how you feel."

"Tired. Let's all get some sleep," Brenda said. "We can have breakfast and maybe show April some of our more fun places in the city."

"I think I'd better set out for home right after breakfast. Mama makes me nervous," I said.

Brenda nodded. "Fine. We'll follow you next weekend, and we'll get her to go out to dinner again."

There were some girls and their boyfriends sitting around one of the settee and chair arrangements in the lobby. When we entered, one of the boys called out, "Great game."

"Thanks," Brenda called back, and we went up the stairs to the rooms. "Are you all right?" Brenda asked me at the door to mine. "Is it comfortable enough?"

"Yeah, sure," I said. "I'm really glad I came, Brenda."

"Me, too," she said, and we hugged. Celia watched from the doorway. She smiled at me, and I told her good night and went into the room.

Had I ever had a more complicated, full day? Even this very plain-looking bed in this Spartan closet of a room looked inviting. I couldn't wait to get into it and close my eyes. I could hear Brenda and Celia talking, but their voices were so muffled and low I didn't make out any sense of anything. I heard them laugh, and then they grew quiet.

For a moment, I was caught in a heavy contradiction. I was happy for Brenda. She had obviously found great contentment. But I was actually very jealous of her as well. She seemed to have it all now: her wonderful athletic talent and someone with whom to share it, perhaps share the rest of her life. She had truly found herself, and she was very comfortable with herself.

Would I ever be? What really lay in wait for me out there? What revelations, discoveries, realizations would I confront, and would I be as comfortable and as satisfied with who I was as Brenda was now?

I wondered about Mama. What did she really know? How would she face this along with all her other burdens? I was afraid for her. Maybe this was just too much weight to bear. Maybe Brenda shouldn't be so forthcoming when it came to her. Wasn't it better to keep this all a secret until Mama grew stronger? I decided I would discuss it with Brenda in the morning.

I didn't think I'd fall asleep for a long time, but I did, and Brenda had to wake me. She was already dressed and stood by my bed, gently shaking me.

"Hey, sleepyhead. Get up and dressed. We're hungry," she said.

I ground the sleep out of my eyes and looked around. The confusion on my face made her laugh.

"Forgot where you were?"

"Yes, for a moment," I said. "What time is it?"

"It's after nine. We overslept, too. We're usually out

and about by eight. We'll wait for you downstairs," she told me, and left.

I washed and dressed as quickly as I could. Brenda and Celia were sitting on a settee and talking to another girl when I appeared. The girl had short pecan-brown hair and wore her glasses down on the bridge of her nose, looking over them as she spoke to Brenda and Celia. She had a notebook in her hand and had been writing.

"This is Marsha Graystone," Brenda said, introducing us. "She's the editor of the college newspaper."

"Hi," I said.

"What do you think of your sister?" she asked in a demanding tone. She held her hand poised with the pen as though she were going to write whatever I said verbatim. I glanced at Brenda and Celia, who were both smiling.

"I think she's terrific," I said.

"Why?" she followed like a prosecutor in a courtroom.

"Why?" I looked at Brenda again. "Because no matter what you think or expect from her, she will always surprise you," I replied.

"I love it!" Marsha cried, and wrote.

"I'm starving," Celia declared, standing. She put her arm through mine. "C'mon, we're treating you to a Mom's Kitchen breakfast with all the trimmings. Eggs and grits and biscuits and ham."

"You're going to eat all that?" Brenda asked skeptically.

"Today, I will," Celia said. "See you, Marsha," she threw back, and marched me to the door. Brenda laughed and followed.

Mom's Kitchen was a small restaurant designed like a roadside diner. There really was a Mom, too, supervising a short-order cook. Everything smelled so good I couldn't help being very hungry. For once, Brenda didn't scowl at me when I reached for the biscuits and the jam. In fact, there was a wonderful lightness about the three of us. They had me laughing hysterically when they imitated Marsha Graystone. Celia had her down pat.

"What do you think of your sister?"

We laughed at that and much more. For the first time since I had arrived, I felt more than welcome. I did want to stay longer, but I was worried about Mama, too. After we finished breakfast, I went to the phone to call her. It rang and rang, but she didn't pick up.

"What's going on?" Brenda called from the table.

I shook my head. "She doesn't answer."

"Did you call the right number? Do it again," she advised, and I did.

Again, it rang and rang, and Mama didn't pick up. Brenda, now concerned herself, called herself and held the receiver, listening to the constant rings.

"Maybe she went to the doctor or something," Celia offered.

"I have the car," I reminded them.

"She could have taken a taxi."

"Mama? No, I doubt that," I said.

"Let's return to the dorm and call from there. I'm sure it's nothing. She could be in the shower," Celia said.

Brenda and I exchanged looks of concern but agreed to do what she said.

"You know," Celia said as we walked back, "now that you have attended the game and there's no more pressure on her to be here, she probably felt better and went out. Maybe she called a friend."

"How can you say that now? Because she was having so much trouble leaving the house and going anywhere, you said she was developing agoraphobia, right?" I asked.

"That's right, but that's only a suspicion. I'm not qualified to . . ."

"I looked it up," I quickly admitted. "She *is* getting that way. Exactly."

Brenda's concern grew stronger. We called again the moment we arrived at the dorm, and again the phone rang and rang, and Mama didn't answer.

"I'd better get started for home," I said.

Brenda and Celia looked at each other.

"I'm sure she just went out somehow, Brenda," Celia said. "Okay," she added before Brenda could respond. "We'll follow April back in my car if your mother still doesn't answer by the time April's ready to leave."

"Right," Brenda said.

I went up and got my things together. I moved as quickly as I could, but that didn't matter. More concerned than she had revealed, Brenda was waiting for me in the hallway, and I could tell immediately from the expression on her face that something was terribly wrong.

"What?"

"I called Dora Maxwell and asked her to check on Mama for us."

Mrs. Maxwell was our closest neighbor. She and her husband had been there as long as we had.

"And?"

"She went right over to our house, and she called me."

"What did she say?" I asked, feeling as if I had to pull every word off her tongue.

"She said, 'Brenda, get home as quickly as you can.'"

"What does that mean?"

"I don't know, exactly."

"Why not?"

"She couldn't talk," Brenda said.

"Why not?"

"She couldn't stop crying."

11

Sleep in Peace

❧❖❧

Brenda drove my car, and Celia followed us on our ride back to our house. Like Mrs. Maxwell, I couldn't talk, either, and I wasn't crying. My throat was just so choked up and my chest so heavy. I simply sat there staring out the side window at the scenery rushing by. Whenever I looked at Brenda, she was hovering over the steering wheel as if she were urging the car to go even faster. I didn't think she realized how taut she was holding her neck and shoulders. Occasionally, I turned to look back at Celia, who was trying to keep up.

"Don't you go blaming yourself for anything," Brenda chanted. From the way she said it, I wondered if she were talking aloud to herself or talking to me. "Don't you do it."

"Blame myself for what, Brenda?" I asked, my lips trembling.

"Whatever happens. Whatever we find out when we get home, April."

"What are we going to find?" I asked, now openly crying.

She didn't answer. She just shook her head and held herself taut over the steering wheel. She knew more; she just wasn't saying. I took a deep breath, closed my eyes, and sat back. *It doesn't matter what she says. Whatever has happened is my fault,* I thought. I knew I shouldn't have left Mama. I knew it even after I had gotten into the car. I knew it the moment I drove out. I was just too excited about driving myself and getting to go to a college dorm.

I was trembling inside just imagining what might be awaiting us. The dark clouds ahead were definitely a bad omen in my mind. Sprinkles began when we reached Hickory, and by the time we arrived at the house, it had turned to showers. Mrs. Maxwell obviously had been waiting for us at the front window and opened the door the moment we turned into our driveway. She was in her coat and had on a plastic rain hat.

Brenda hesitated after she opened the door and didn't get out of the car.

"The ambulance has taken her to the hospital," Mrs. Maxwell said as she hurried toward us. She opened the rear door and got in quickly.

Celia got out of her car and approached. "What's happening?"

"We're going to the hospital," Brenda said. "She was taken there by ambulance. Get in."

Celia got into the rear of the car with Mrs. Maxwell, and we backed out of the driveway, turned, and headed away.

"After you called me, I went to your house and rang the doorbell," Mrs. Maxwell began. "I waited and waited and knocked. I looked through the windows and didn't see any lights on or your mother. I almost went home, thinking she had gone somewhere, but I remembered your telling me April had the car. Of course, she could have been picked up by someone," she rattled on, terrified of the silence. "However, I thought I'd see if your rear door was open and it was. I walked in and called and called, and then I went farther into the house and eventually looked in your mother's bedroom.

"At first, I thought she was just sleeping. Again, I almost turned around and returned to my home, but I noticed her right arm was dangling off the bed and thought that was odd, so I called to her. I raised my voice, and still she didn't respond. I went to her and shook her. Her eyes didn't open, but I didn't think she was . . . she was . . . passed away. I never saw someone who couldn't wake up like that. Of course, I thought she was in a coma or something. Then you called. The sound of the phone ringing nearly made my heart explode. I'm sorry I was so incoherent.

"As soon as we hung up, I saw the bottle of sleeping pills and realized it was empty and she might have taken too many. I called 911, and the ambulance got here quickly. The paramedics couldn't make her wake up, either, so they took her off to the hospital. I told them you were coming here, and I told them I would wait for you.

"I don't know what to think. I don't know what else to say," she concluded.

Brenda didn't say anything.

"She got the idea from what I told her about my mother," Celia suddenly said.

Brenda grimaced and looked at her through the rearview mirror. "Don't be ridiculous, Celia. Your mother wasn't the first one to think of that."

"I know, but . . ."

"Look, everyone has got to stop looking for ways to blame herself!" Brenda shouted.

It was like an explosion. No one breathed loudly.

"You, of all people, should know how complicated this situation is," she continued in a calmer tone.

"I know," Celia said. "I'm sorry."

I felt myself close up, my body fold into itself. I wished I were a turtle pulling her head back into and under her shell. I wished I were anything or anyone but who I was. Our family had been in a free fall ever since Daddy had turned into Mr. Hyde. No matter how hard we tried, we couldn't pull ourselves out of it. There wasn't any one choice, any one decision, that any of us had made to begin all this. Bad Luck had just come sauntering down our street one day, looked at our house and us, and thought, *Here's a good prospect. These people will surely know how powerful I can be,* and then, like shadows that fall when a cloud slips over the sun, Bad Luck enveloped our house and sank into it, soaking us up in darkness, disappointment, and defeat. He was still with us. I felt all the strength seep out of me as we turned into the hospital parking lot as close to the emergency room as we could get. I wasn't sure I would be able to put myself together enough to get out of the car.

Brenda turned off the engine, took a deep breath, and nodded. We all got out and followed her quickly to the emergency room entrance.

"This is so terrible, so terrible," Mrs. Maxwell muttered beside me. She held my elbow so tightly it actually hurt, but I didn't say anything.

The sight of so many people in the waiting room depressed us all. There was a line in front of the reception desk like you might find in a post office or a bank. There were people who looked as if they were in pain

and people who just looked miserable. Every time you
start feeling sorry for yourself for whatever reason, I
thought, you should just stop by a hospital emergency
room and look at the people waiting.

Brenda caught sight of a paramedic walking toward
the entrance. She veered quickly to the left and
stopped him.

"Did you happen to pick up my mother today?" she
asked. "Mrs. Nora Taylor, 777 North Castle Drive?"

He looked at me and Celia and Mrs. Maxwell and
nodded.

"Yes, ma'am," he said. "She was taken to the examination room immediately."

"Well, who can we talk to?" Brenda asked.

He looked at the desk and the line and then nodded
and said, "Come with me."

We followed him through the doors and into the
hallway. A patient was on a gurney in the hallway,
the right side of his face bandaged so that it covered
the eye. He had his head turned away from us. A nurse
came out of one of the examination rooms and hurried
to the nurses' station, and then a doctor appeared on
our left, and the paramedic approached him.

"Dr. Mallen, these people are the family of the
woman we brought in about an hour ago, Mrs. Taylor."

The doctor looked at us and nodded at the paramedic. "Please, step in here," he said, indicating an
empty examination room.

I don't know how I walked or even stood straight.
My body felt strangely detached, floating. Brenda, in
her usual firm way, stepped in quickly, Celia beside
her.

"You are?"

"I'm Brenda Taylor, and this is my sister, April,"
she said, nodding at me. "Mrs. Maxwell found my

mother, and this is my close friend," she added, indicating Celia.

"Your mother took a considerable number of sleeping pills," he began. "As soon as she was brought in, we inserted an endotracheal tube and began to pump her stomach, but too much time had gone by, I'm afraid," he said with as much emotion as someone saying one of the lights in the hallway had blown out. Because of that, none of us really reacted. We stared at him in expectation of another sentence. He looked at all of us and then asked, "Was there a history of attempted suicide?"

"No," Brenda replied.

"I'm sorry," he said, finally showing some human emotion, if only in an automated form. "We did all we could. She expired about twenty minutes ago."

"Like a parking meter?" Brenda retorted. Celia moved closer to her instantly and took her arm. She knew how she would be. "So, what's the fine?"

"Excuse me?" the doctor said.

"Are you saying Mrs. Taylor has died?" Celia asked him.

"Yes, I am. I'm sorry," he said. He actually looked a bit frightened and shifted his weight. "I can have one of the hospital counselors here immediately," he added, looking toward the doorway.

"Where is she?" Brenda demanded. "Where's my mother?"

"She's still in room three," he replied obediently. "There's so much happening at the moment, we're terribly behind, and . . ."

Brenda pivoted and then, with Celia hanging on, marched out of the room. I looked at the doctor and then at Mrs. Maxwell, who was crying openly now. Then I followed Brenda and Celia out and down the hallway to room three, where Mama lay on a gurney, her eyes closed. There was still enough color in her face for her to look as if she were just sleeping.

He's made a mistake, I thought. *They've all made a terrible error. Mama's just asleep. She'll wake up any moment and wonder where she is and how she got here. We'll all laugh about it.*

Brenda stood looking down at her and then slowly raised her hand and put it gently on Mama's forehead, as if she were checking for a fever. Celia stood beside her, her head down.

"Mama?" I said. It came out of me like a burp. I didn't even think to say it.

Celia moved to put her arm around my shoulders, and we three stood there silently gazing at my mother, who had drifted off and out of this life, away from the sadness and disappointment, out of the reach of Bad Luck forever, perhaps in hopes of meeting Daddy in a place where he was no longer Mr. Hyde, where he was young and handsome and happy. The two of them would be as they were, and death would be defeated. At the moment, I could think only of joining her. How easy she had made it seem.

Brenda leaned in and kissed Mama's check. She said, "Good-bye, Mama. Sleep in peace."

And then, that body of mine that had been going from soft mush to hard numb muscle returned to mush, and my legs gave way. In fact, I felt as if my torso were sinking through them. I sat on the floor before I went dark.

I woke up in another examination room. A nurse was standing over me, checking my blood pressure and pulse. She smiled at me when my eyes opened, then turned and nodded at Brenda.

"She'll be fine," she said.

I'll be fine? You mean, because I have blood pressure and a pulse, I'll be fine? My whole life will be perfect now? My mother died. I fainted and woke up, and that's it? I'm fine?

Brenda read my thoughts and didn't smile or even thank the nurse.

"We've got to go home now, April," she said. "There are things to do. I want to see if I can reach Uncle Palaver, too. C'mon," she urged, helping me sit up.

The room spun and then settled down. I stepped off the gurney, and Celia rushed to take my other arm.

"Let's just get out of here as fast as we can," Brenda told her.

It was as though we were making some sort of escape, escape from the reality of Mama's expiring as the doctor had said, escape from the eyes and the looks of all the medical personnel who knew what terrible thing had occurred. People in the waiting room looked up at us, thinking I was the one who had been brought to the emergency room.

"Where's Mrs. Maxwell?" I asked.

"She had her husband come get her," Brenda said. "She said she'll be at our house later."

"How long was I unconscious?"

"Not long," Celia said.

"Mama died?" I asked. I had to hear it again, to hear it from them, to know it wasn't just a nightmare and there was absolutely no mistake.

"Yes, April," Brenda said. "Mama died."

They put me in the rear seat, and I lay back. Celia drove, and Brenda sat up front just staring at the dashboard.

"Are you all right?" Celia asked.

Brenda nodded. "Let's go home," she said.

We drove off, and I thought, *Oh no, oh no, we're going home and Mama won't be there. We can't leave her behind.* It put a panic in me.

"We can't leave Mama back there!" I cried.

"She won't be there long," Brenda said. "We'll follow the directions Daddy left long ago for what to do in the event of their deaths. My father was Mr. Efficiency," she told Celia.

"Sometimes, especially at times like this, you can't help but be grateful for that."

"No," Brenda said. "I don't agree. I'd rather muddle through it all, suffer through every step."

"Like pounding nails into yourself? Who's blaming herself now, Brenda?"

Brenda was quiet. Then she turned away and looked out the side window. "I knew it last night," she said.

"How?"

"When April told me she had called her Mrs. Panda. I knew it was coming, but I didn't do anything. I should have gotten into the car and driven home, but all I could think about was that damn game and our victory."

"Brenda, you're not making sense."

"I am." She turned and looked back at me. "You know I am."

I looked down.

"Go on, say it, April. Say it!" she screamed.

I started to cry.

"Brenda, please don't do this," Celia said.

She looked at Celia and then turned around. "You're right. It's stupid to have regrets. You play your best, and that's the end of it. Home team loses, period, end of sentence."

For the rest of the way, we drove home in silence.

I went to my room immediately to lie down. Brenda

started to make calls from Daddy's office, and Celia fixed something for us all to eat. Every once in a while, even though I was lying quietly, I felt my heart begin to race as though the reality came into my body in jolts and traveled with electric speed through my veins and bones until it reached my heart.

I heard the phone ringing. A few minutes later, it rang again.

Celia came to my door. "Come have some tea or coffee and a sandwich or something, April."

"I'm not hungry."

"I know, but you should eat, anyway. You need to keep up your strength. You don't want to faint again, and there's a great deal left to do."

I thought about that. It was just starting to sink into my brain, which was probably like quicksand by now. What sank in wasn't just the reality of Mama being gone but also the questions that came along with it.

What would happen to me? Where would I go? What would happen to Brenda's college career and her athletic career? Who would take care of us financially? Was all that still in place?

Was it selfish to wonder about these things? A part of me thought so and kept me from bringing any of it up when I went out and joined them in the dining room. Brenda sat sipping coffee and nibbling on a scoop of tuna salad and some crackers. I looked at my plate and sank into my seat. Celia brought in some ice water in a pitcher and her own plate.

"Were you able to locate your uncle?" she asked Brenda.

I looked up with expectation. Yes, Uncle Palaver. How we needed him now.

"My mother had his itinerary on the desk. He's in a place called Beaumont, Texas. Someone from the the-

ater went to his mobile home and got him to call me."
She looked at me. "You know what he said when I told
him what had happened?"

I shook my head.

"He said Destiny predicted it. He said she has clair-
voyant powers. Can you imagine?" she asked Celia.
"Talking about things like that at this time?"

"He was just in shock. People say strange things,"
Celia said.

"I guess."

"Is he coming here?" I asked.

"He's on his way. He has to make connections
through Dallas. He called back to say he would be in
Memphis early in the morning and would rent a car.
He should be here before eight."

She toyed with her tuna a moment and then rose.

"I've got to call the funeral home and the minister,"
she said, but the phone rang before she could return to
the office, and it was the minister, Reverend Hastings,
who had already heard. Apparently, all the clergy had a
direct line to the hospital emergency room and the
morgue. I listened vaguely, still dazed, as Brenda discussed the arrangements.

Celia listened, too, but with that soft, small smile on
her lips. "She's so strong," she said shaking her head
and looking toward the kitchen. "Like a thick tree
trunk in the wind, unmovable. But later," she added,
turning back to me, "later . . ."

Later what? I wondered, but I didn't ask. I could
only imagine what that meant. Brenda would break
down and cry on her shoulder? Or rant and rave and
need to be calmed? Would she be more like me and
maybe faint?

I rose and walked down the hallway to Mama's bedroom. Her bed was still unmade, of course, and the pil-

low still had the impression of her head. I went to the bed and sat and stared at the pillow. I saw a strand of her hair and carefully plucked it off the pillow, holding it in my hands. It was a part of Mama. Her DNA was in this, her physical identity. I wrapped it around my finger and kissed it.

Brenda came to the doorway. She didn't ask me what I was doing or why I was in there.

"Celia and I are going to the funeral parlor, April. We have to choose a coffin."

"I should go, too," I said, standing.

"It's not necessary. I think it would be better for you to rest."

Celia's going, I thought. *Why is that necessary and not my going?* Brenda hadn't even hugged me yet. She hadn't cried with me or held my hand. If anything, at this moment, she reminded me of Daddy when he had become Mr. Hyde.

"I could go," I said through trembling lips.

"It's very unpleasant, April. I can't take doing this and caring for you at the same time," she replied, almost snapping at me. "Just stay here and, if you want, answer the phone. As people find out, they'll be calling. The funeral will be on Tuesday at ten A.M. at the church. We're not going to entertain anyone after the internment. I'll announce some charity or something where people can make donations in Mama's memory. Probably the cancer society, where we had them donate for Daddy's memory. We'll be home as soon as we're finished," she concluded, and left.

I heard them walk out the front door. They closed it softly, but to me, it sounded like a gunshot echoing through the house. Being alone was never frightening to me, but I felt myself sink into a panic. Death, Bad Luck, all of it had been and was probably still in the house. It gave me the chills to think about it. My teeth actually clicked. I hurried out of Mama's bedroom, went to my own, and crawled under the covers. I wanted to pull them over my head. Sleep, at least, was an escape. The phone rang often, but I didn't answer it. I was drifting, and even though I heard it, the ringing sounded way off in the distance, easy to ignore.

I did hear Brenda and Celia return. Brenda didn't stop to talk to me. I heard her go directly to her bedroom and close the door. A few moments later, Celia did stop to look in on me. I opened my eyes.

"Are you okay?" she asked.

"No," I said in a small voice, and closed my eyes.

I heard Brenda's door open and close again, and then all was quiet. The phone rang and rang a number of times after that. It grew very dark, and finally, Brenda and Celia emerged and began putting on lights and preparing dinner. Celia came back to my room to tell me I should get up, maybe take a shower, and come to dinner. The minister was going to visit us in about an hour, and Brenda expected he might have something to eat with us as well. Shortly after that, Mrs. Maxwell arrived with a pot of her homemade stew and an apple pie. She had been working on food since she had returned from the hospital. She sat with us for a while and was there when the minister arrived.

Brenda listened to him talk to us about God's will, the end of Mama's painful journey, the blessings she had provided for us, the need for us to be strong. She was staring at him with such indifference she made me nervous. It was finally Celia who carried on some conversation. He didn't eat much with us; he discussed the arrangements again, and left. Brenda was unusually quiet, I thought. Her silence frightened me because she looked as if she were holding an explosion under a lid within herself.

"I'm going to bed," she announced, and left us.

"It's all really first hitting her," Celia explained. "She'll be better in the morning."

I helped her clean up. Every once in a while, I found myself looking for Mama, expecting her to appear in a doorway, or expecting to hear her voice. Celia talked about her own mother's death and how she had dealt with it.

"I wasn't in a situation much unlike your own," she told me. "It's impossible to make any sense of it at the time. Even now, when I think back, I find it hard to believe. Don't worry," she said, putting her arm around me. "We'll be here for you. We'll always be here for you."

How could that be? I wondered. They were college students. What would Brenda do? Where would I go? I couldn't live alone here in the house. Again, I felt terribly selfish for even having these thoughts at this time. My mind should be only on poor Mama and not myself. Feeling exhausted again, I excused myself and went to bed.

I didn't think I'd be able to do it, but my body fooled me, and I fell into a very deep and long sleep, not waking up again until I heard the doorbell ringing and Brenda's footsteps in the hallway. I sat up, saw it was a little past eight in the morning, and slipped my feet into my slippers. I threw on my robe and went to the door. The moment I heard Uncle Palaver's voice, I rushed out, too. He was standing in the entryway, hugging Brenda. Celia was off to the right. They were both in their robes as well.

He saw me coming and held out his right arm so that he could hold the both of us at the same time. I rushed in to hold him as well, and the three of us stood there.

"You poor kids," he said. "What a time, what a time. I feel so bad that I wasn't here for her."

"She would have chased you out, Uncle Palaver," Brenda said, pulling away and wiping her eyes. "You know that."

He nodded and looked at me. Brenda went for his suitcase, but he insisted he'd carry it himself to the guest room. It was then that Brenda finally realized she hadn't introduced Celia.

"I've heard so much about you," she told him. "I'm so sorry our meeting each other has to be under these circumstances."

"Yes," he said, and went to the bedroom.

Celia rushed off to start breakfast, and Brenda and I went to dress.

At breakfast, Celia recapped all the events as they had occurred. Before she was finished, the phone began to ring. Mrs. Maxwell was bringing over more food. Our attorney called to talk with Brenda. And those women who had been Mama's friends before she had retreated from society began to call as well, all offering their condolences. The news was really spreading quickly now.

People began to arrive. Uncle Palaver was wonderful when it came to handling all that. Most everyone brought something to eat, as well as flowers and candy. Soon the house was taken over by Mrs. Maxwell and some of the other neighbors. I wandered about, accepting sympathies, listening to advice and expressions of hope, collecting kisses like someone in a church with a plate for charity.

The day seemed never to end. Whenever there was a dry spell, an empty moment, I felt the weight of the fatigue in my body. I dozed off a few times, once in Daddy's office on his leather settee. Unbeknown to me, Celia and Brenda had sat down to have a serious conversation about me and what we would all do. They weren't troubled by feelings of guilt for doing so, as I was. After everyone left the house, the four of us settled down in the living room, and Brenda began.

"I've been speaking with Mr. Weiss, our attorney, who has been in charge of our financial affairs ever since Daddy left us," she began. "He agrees with me that we should put the house up for sale immediately. We'll sell all the furniture with it. All we need to pack are our personal things. I've already contacted the Salvation Army to come and get Mama's clothes and Daddy's as well."

I looked at Uncle Palaver, who sat staring down at the floor. He seemed so much younger and unsophisticated. It was as if the death of his sister had driven him back to being a little boy again. Brenda was the one in control, the older one, the wiser one at the moment, and that disappointed me. I had hoped and dreamed he would come flying into our home and lives with all sorts of magical ideas that would ease the burdens, the pain, and the worry.

"Mama's clothes?"

"Celia and I have talked about everything, April, and Uncle Palaver agrees with us."

"Why didn't anyone talk with me?"

"That's what we're doing now."

"I meant before."

"You weren't in any sort of condition to talk about these things, April. Don't make a big deal of it."

I pressed my lips together and sat back.

"Anyway, Celia has called a cousin of hers who owns a house in Memphis that he rents. It's fully fur-

nished. It's in a nice neighborhood near the Memphis
Country Club, an area known as the Historic District,
and it's not far from a good high school. You'll have
your car, so you can drive to school every day."

"I'll go to school in Memphis?"

"Of course in Memphis," she replied quickly.
"Where else would I mean?"

"You mean, I'd go live with you and Celia in Memphis?"

She shook her head and looked at Celia, who smiled
softly and closed her eyes and opened them. Brenda
softened.

"Look, April, I'm old enough to be your guardian,
legal guardian, thank goodness, or some government
agency might come waltzing in here and butting in on
our lives. I don't expect any of our disinterested relatives to come and offer to take you in to live with
them, and I can't think of any you'd want to live with.
Half of them have sent regrets, and only two cousins
have indicated they'll be at the funeral tomorrow. This
is the best solution, right, Uncle Palaver?"

He looked up quickly, as though he had been in a
daze himself. "Oh. Yes, of course," he said. "And I'll
stick around and do whatever I can to help with the
transition."

"Just run your hand over the house and make it disappear, Uncle Palaver," I said, my eyes filling with
tears.

"Stop it, April. You have to grow up overnight, and
that's that," Brenda said.

I bit down on my lower lip and nodded.

"We'll enroll you in the public school nearby, and
we'll manage. If everyone cooperates, it will go well
and quickly."

"Like nothing's happened," I muttered.

"You were never crazy about your school friends here. You're not giving up all that much," Brenda said.

No, not much, I thought. *Not now, not with both Mama and Daddy gone.*

"It'll be all right," Celia said. "We'll have each other; we'll take care of each other. You'll see."

I looked at Uncle Palaver. He looked relieved.

"I'll make it my business to see more of you girls," he promised. "That's for sure."

"The day after the funeral, we'll do what we have to do with the attorney. We'll begin to pack our things, give away what we're giving away. We'll need a good deal of our kitchen utensils, dishes, silverware, all that."

"I'll help. In fact, I'll start right away," Celia piped up as if this was some sort of wonderful new event. "Then I'll go on ahead of the two of you and get the house as ready as I can. It won't take much to get us all established," Celia said. "We should have it all done in a matter of days."

"Days?" I asked.

"It's better we do all this as quickly as we can," Brenda said, and then added, "It's less painful for us that way."

I simply stared at her, which I could see annoyed her.

"Okay, April. This isn't easy for anyone. Do you understand?" she asked.

"Yes," I said.

"Good." She looked at Celia. "I'm going to take a hot shower and go to bed. Do you need anything, Uncle Palaver?"

"No, I'm fine, honey. Thanks."

Brenda rose. Uncle Palaver stood up and hugged her. He hugged Celia, too. Then he looked at me.

"You going to bed now, too, April?" he asked.

"I guess," I said. I stood up, and he hugged me. "Try to get some sleep. It's a hard day tomorrow," he advised.

I nodded. I couldn't talk. My throat was too tight. He kissed me on the forehead and walked out. For a long moment, I just stood there, listening to their footsteps. Then I followed them all and went to my own room. When I stepped in, I closed the door and simply stood there gazing at everything. I had spent my life in this room, and in a few days, hours, I would leave it forever and ever. In some ways, I would miss it more than anything.

My eyes went to my bed, and I stepped up to it and picked up my Panda doll.

"We're going away, Mr. Panda," I said. "We'll never be back, and you probably know as much as I do about what that all means."

12

Don't Look Back

It did all go smoothly and quickly. A part of me hated that. A part of me wanted it to be difficult and painful. That part continually chanted that it should not be this easy to slip out of one life and into another. I felt like the snake I saw in a science class movie wiggling out of its skin. It didn't even look back at what it had discarded, despite the fact that what it left behind was once an essential part of who and what it was. All this in a real way fit Brenda's philosophy about her sporting activities: never mourn over a loss, and don't spend all that much time celebrating a victory. Instead, look to the future. What was over was over when the buzzer sounded.

Well, the buzzer had sounded loud and clear on our lives. This game was over. Lingering about to wallow in the memories, to mourn and cry and rage, was pointless to Brenda. *Bury the dead and move on* were words clearly written over her face. The other part of me actually envied her. I couldn't take my eyes off her the whole time. I so wanted to be like her, wanted to be able to talk to people without sobbing or choking up every thirty seconds, wanted to be able to take charge of every arrangement, answer every new question. Other people noticed it as well, and many commented to me about how lucky I was to have an older sister who was so competent, mature, and responsible.

"How proud your parents would be if they were here," they said. It made it seem as if they were just away and couldn't avoid missing their own funerals.

It was probably true that Brenda's control kept me from falling apart. When she had told me I had to grow up overnight, she was right. No little-girl antics were to be permitted, no ranting and sobbing and sulking. Then, of course, I thought about Daddy and how he hated to show his emotions or his problems in public.

"That's why we have houses," he said once. "That's why we have our own homes, so we can close the doors and cry, and laugh, shout or rage without anyone else witnessing it. The walls are falling down all around us, but not mine, not ours."

Mama's funeral was ironically larger than Daddy's. I understood that there were people who simply couldn't forgive him for leaving us under any circumstances. It was more comfortable for the mourners to attend the funeral of a woman whom they all saw as a victim. The church was nearly filled, in fact, and a surprising number attended the internment as well. I could see Brenda regretted not having something at the house afterward. It would have shown Mama more respect, but Brenda was too hung up on our moving on.

In her head, I suppose she actually heard a referee's whistle.

Matter of fact, she went right to the packing when we returned from the cemetery. Uncle Palaver and I worked on making something to eat. Celia had been packing the kitchen utensils, dishes, and silverware all along, and we had to dip into some of the cartons to get things we needed.

"Couldn't this have waited a day at least?" I wondered aloud.

Uncle Palaver didn't answer. I had spent most of my attention on Brenda, clung to Brenda, and I really didn't see how devastated Uncle Palaver was. He looked so lost and alone, dumbfounded and confused at times.

"I wish Destiny could have come with you," I said, and he looked up from the sandwich he was eating mechanically.

"Yes," he said. "I do, too."

"Why couldn't she?" I pursued.

"I didn't want to say anything. There's enough to deal with here, but she's ill."

"Ill? How ill?"

"She has lupus," he said.

"What is that, exactly?"

"It's an autoimmune system disease in which a person's own immune system attacks organs and cells, causing dysfunction. It flares up from time to time," he said, "and it just happened to her the day before . . . before Nora passed on."

"Will she be all right?"

"I don't know," he said. He looked away and squeezed his temples.

"I'm sorry, Uncle Palaver. I didn't mean to make you think about it."

He didn't answer. After a moment, I left him sitting there and went to my room to begin to pack my clothes and my possessions. Celia stopped in to say good-bye.

"I'm the point man," she declared. "You know, the one who goes ahead and makes sure things are all right for the others following."

I was sitting on the floor next to a carton I was filling with old letters, pictures, souvenirs from trips, each item attached to a memory that replayed before me. I hadn't realized it, but tears were streaming down my cheeks, zigzagging across my jaw bone.

"Oh, April," Celia said, kneeling down beside me to hug me. "You poor dear. It's all so much harder for the younger child, I know. Psychologists talk about the length of time between the cutting of the umbilical chord and the present. Brenda's already gone through something of a separation by attending college away from home, not that she's any less devastated. I just don't want you to feel like you're alone in the world, okay? I know how terrible that could be."

I wiped away the tears.

"We'll be there for each other now," she added, kissing me on the cheek. "We'll be like the Three Musketeers, okay?"

I nodded. Was she really this excited about it, or was she pretending for my sake?

"Don't expect me to be a good cook. I was never a good cook," she kidded. "Is there anything you need me to do for you?" she asked.

I shook my head. "No, thank you."

"Okay, then. I'll see you soon. You'll like this new neighborhood, and I'm sure the school is fine. 'Bye for now," she added, and left.

I sat there looking after her and then looking at the carton. It seemed I needed to continually reinforce reality, continually convince myself all this was really and truly happening. I returned to packing, and a little while later, Brenda looked in on me.

"How is it going?" she asked.

I shrugged. "All right, I guess. I don't really have all that much that I want to take."

"No, neither do I. We're leaving a lot here. Everything in the garage, all the lawn equipment . . . someone will get a very good deal, I'm sure. Uncle Palaver is thinking of leaving tonight," she added, and I looked up sharply.

"So soon?"

"There's really no point in his lingering around, April. I gave him some of Mama's things, their mother's cameo and an ivory jewelry case that had belonged to her. He's on the phone making his arrangements."

"I thought he'd stay until we left," I said. Letting him go was such a final and definitive thing. Maybe I would never see him again.

"There's no point in that, and anyone can see how painful it is for him to just sit around here watching us pack up to leave. We'll call him when we're established in Memphis and give him our phone number and address."

"How will we find him?"

"I have his itinerary, the one Mama had out on Daddy's desk," she said. "He told me he's sticking to it, and it's nearly a year's scheduled performances, places, addresses, even phone numbers of the theaters."

I dropped an old diary into the carton and stood up. "Maybe I should spend some time with him, then."

"It would be better for us if you get done what you have to get done," Brenda replied. "He's not running right out."

"I hate doing this."

"I know, but this isn't going to be the last time you or I do things we hate to do. It's a part of life we can't escape, April."

"What doesn't destroy me makes me stronger," I muttered, and she smiled.

"You remember that."

"I should. I've heard you say it a thousand times when you're nearly exhausted or in some sort of pain exercising and running."

"It's worth remembering," she said, and left to finish her packing, too.

Actually, Uncle Palaver's arrangements called for him to leave for the airport before dinner, which was another disappointment. I thought we'd at least have that time together. He was packing his bag in the guest room when I went looking for him.

"I'm sorry I'm leaving so quickly," he said, "but I think I should get back."

I understood what he meant and nodded, imagining he was worried about Destiny.

"You guys are going to be fine," he told me. "I wouldn't go if I didn't believe that."

"I know. Don't worry about us," I said. "I just wish we had more time together."

"We will," he promised, and he put his arm around my shoulders and held me against him for a moment. He wasn't looking at me, however. He was staring at the wall and smiling. "I remember when I was a little boy, only about seven, I think. I performed this trick for Nora. Our mother had bought me a magician's game, and I was able to make a coin disappear in a trick box. She was such a good actress, your mother, even at that young age. She put on a great show of amazement and made me feel like I had matched Houdini or something. No matter what I tried to do afterward, I always worked on my magic act. Something inside me told me that would be who I would be. Of course, everyone blew me up, raved about my acting and singing talents until I made a fool of myself on the stage. Sometimes, you have to go in a circle to get where you belong," he said. "Don't be afraid of it."

He kissed me on the forehead and completed his packing. We started out together. I called to Brenda.

"Uncle Palaver's ready to go!" I cried, and she appeared.

He paused at the door and turned to us. "I hate leaving you two," he said.

"We'll be fine, Uncle Palaver. I'll call with our new information as I promised," Brenda told him.

He nodded, and she stepped forward to hug him. My lips were trembling so much I just buried my face against his chest for a moment.

"Sometimes," he said when I stepped back, "I think death is like some magic trick God performs. It's just another illusion." He shrugged. "Who knows? Remember, good magicians, real magicians, never tell their secrets."

He opened the door, stepped out, smiled at us, and closed the door.

Brenda and I were silent for a moment, staring at the closed door.

"I think I'm a little hungry," she said. "Mrs. Maxwell left a roast turkey and some salad in the refrigerator. I'm going to heat up the turkey. How about you?"

"I'll have a little, I guess," I said.

I followed her to the kitchen, found some dishware and silverware for us to use, and set it up in the dining room. I brought out a jug of water, too. She brought out the food, and we sat across from each other, both Mama's and Daddy's chairs now empty.

"My coach called yesterday," she said after we had begun to eat. "He told me I've been chosen for the regional all-star basketball game. I have to go to practice day after tomorrow. Mama would have wanted me to do that," she added before I could even suggest it was too soon.

I nodded.

I couldn't blame her; I wouldn't blame her. She had something to turn to, something to fill her days and give her a reason to go on.

What did I have?

"I'm going to depend on you to help us get through this, April. Celia is very intelligent, but setting up a home is not exactly her forte. Despite her sad stories, she was always spoiled by someone. I need you to be there," she emphasized.

"Okay," I said. I loved the sound of it: *I need you.* "Okay," I repeated, and I ate like someone with a ravenous appetite.

It made her laugh, and then I did.

Uncle Palaver's right, I thought. *So much of it all is merely an illusion.*

It was the hardest of all nights to sleep. Not only did the realization of Mama's being gone forever set in, but along with it was this terrible sense of drifting. The future was so unclear for me now, not that it had ever been in any way definite. At least, I used to think in terms of Mama being there, being at my graduation, helping me plan a college life and professional life, guiding me, being my best friend. I hated this sense of loneliness. No matter what Brenda or Celia told me, I knew in my heart they would have their own busy lives occupying them. It wouldn't be long before I was just a burden they would not have had.

On the other hand, I thought, I'd been a loner most of my life, anyway. This all just meant I'd be one somewhere else. I never had that easy of a time making friends or holding on to the few I had made. None of my classmates appeared at the church for Mama's funeral, in fact, even though some of their parents attended. What did I really have to lose by moving away? Except for Mama, of course, this room was all that had mattered to me, and after all, it was just a room, just four walls I dressed with some of my identity. I could do that anywhere.

I hugged Mr. Panda to me, closed my eyes, and pushed myself into a pool of sleep.

Brenda was up before me in the morning. She went to get a U-Haul trailer for us to attach to the car, because the cartons we had filled would be too much for the car trunk. Later that day, the real estate agent, Camellia Dawson Davis, appeared to review the house with Brenda. She looked as if she had been formed out of plastic from a mold. Not a strand of her hair rebelled. Her makeup was thick and perfect, and she wore a brilliant blue suit with high heels and enough jewelry to sink the *Titanic* again.

"I swear, darlin'," she cried as she marched about the house, "this is goin' to be one of my cheery pick sales. Here today, gone tomorrah. Don't you go worryin' a minute about it all. I'll get us a top price. Sure, you're goin' ta leave all these pieces of art, the vases, lamps, all of it?"

"Yes," Brenda said so firmly it would have taken a Marine to ask again.

Camellia Dawson Davis just nodded and walked on, her eyes widening with every room.

"Well," she concluded, "we're going to figure at least another ten thousand for the furnishings and all. I'll start showing the house tomorrah, if that's all right with you."

"We're out of here late this afternoon," Brenda said. "It's fine."

"Well, don't you worry about it," she emphasized. She glanced at me, smiled, and then turned away quickly when I just glared back at her. "I'll be in touch with your attorney. He'll have your address and your number?"

"By tomorrah," Brenda replied, unable to prevent herself from imitating Camellia.

I had to hide a smile. After Camellia left, Brenda and I returned to packing. By lunch, we were loading the U-Haul. Celia called to tell us she had already set up the utilities, including the phone, so Brenda had a telephone number to leave with our attorney.

"Don't we have to call the school to let them know I'm moving away?" I asked.

"We'll have the new school contact them. By now, I'm sure the gossip phone's been ringing off the hook, anyway, and most everyone who matters knows, April."

After lunch, we swept through the house slowly, checking to be sure we had taken what was really important to us. I went outside and circled it for absolutely no good reason. I guess I was trying to commit it to memory forever. Brenda went through the garage shelves and boxes. I met her inside the house. She stood there with her hands on her hips, looking about for a moment.

"What do you say we leave after I take a shower?"

I shrugged. "I guess so," I said.

"We'll have dinner with Celia in Memphis that way," she said. "There's just no point in our hanging about any longer."

"Okay," I said in a voice smaller than I wanted.

I returned to my room to gather what was left to put in the car while she showered. Mr. Panda was on the bed staring at me. It was true that when I was little, I did speak to the stuffed animal as if it could hear and understand all that I said. Now I felt as though I had been thrown back through time and was standing in front of it as a five-year-old again.

"We've got to go, Mr. Panda," I said. "You're going to live in a new home and sleep in a new bed. Don't look so sad. You're making me feel worse. This isn't the greatest place of all to live, is it? This isn't some kind of paradise. Why should I care so much? People move all the time. I would have moved away from here someday, anyway. I don't care about this room. It's just a room. Stop looking like it's the end of the world!" I shouted without realizing it.

I heard Brenda behind me. She was in her robe and stared incredulously.

"I thought someone had come to the house," she said. "What are you doing?"

"Nothing."

She stared another moment. "Let's get the hell out of here," she declared, and returned to her room to dress.

I scooped up Mr. Panda, put on my coat, grabbed

my carry-on bag which held my final personal items, and marched out of the house. I threw Mr. Panda into a carton in the trunk and squeezed my carry-on bag between two cartons. Then I got into the car and sat with my arms folded, waiting.

A very slight drizzle began. The drops were as small as grains of sand and barely made a sound against the windshield. The sky wasn't all that dark, either. Maybe it was only raining over our house and driveway, I thought. Maybe these were the tears of the dead.

I turned when I heard Brenda come out. She put down her last bag, locked the door, picked up the bag, and hurried to the car. She put the bag on the rear seat and got in quickly. It started to rain a little harder. She didn't even look at me. She started the engine and backed us out of the driveway. Then she put the car in drive and accelerated.

"Don't look back," she warned. "Just look ahead."

I did what she said.

And we were on our way.

Celia had given her good directions, so that in a little less than two hours, we were pulling into the driveway of our new home.

It was much smaller than I had anticipated from listening to Celia talk about it. To me, it looked no bigger than a bungalow, and it didn't have a garage. It had a carport just big enough for one car. There was a screened-in front porch with a patch of front lawn about one-tenth the size of our lawn. Scattered in front of the porch and around the lawn were a half dozen evergreen English boxwood shrubs. A wooden landing that looked like an afterthought was spread at the front door.

As soon as we pulled up, the screen door opened

immediately, and Celia stepped out. She was in a pair of jeans and a blue work shirt with the sleeves rolled up to her elbows and the shirt tied at her waist. She had a bandana tied around her hair and held a mop like a jousting lance at her side. She placed it against the door.

"Welcome!" she cried, holding out her arms.

Brenda got out quickly and headed toward her. I stepped out just as they hugged and kissed. Then they both turned to me.

"Wait until you see my discovery, April," Celia said, turning to me. "You're going to have your own little place. There's a studio behind the house, and it has a bed in it. There's no shower or bath, but there's a bathroom, and you can just use the house shower and bath, of course. The important thing is it will be your place, your own little place."

I squinted skeptically. A studio with no bathtub or shower. What was it?

"I've already fixed the bed for you. I've been busy as a worker bee," she declared. "I bought us all new bedding, towels, linens, everything to start. I even stocked the kitchen! Let me show April the studio."

"Let's start unpacking first," Brenda said. "No sense wasting a trip."

It seemed to me she didn't even look at the house. We could have checked into a garage, and it would have been the same thing. Where we were now didn't matter. All that mattered was we were somewhere else.

"Aye, aye, General," Celia said, saluting and winking at me.

We returned to the car and began to carry cartons and bags into the house.

I had to be grateful there was a studio apartment, I

thought. The living room was a quarter the size of ours, and the kitchen was not much bigger than that as well. There wasn't a separate dining room, just a portion of the living room utilized as such. All of the furniture looked as if it had fallen off a truck on its way to a garbage dump. I could see the springs had popped out under the long dark blue sofa. It looked as if it had been there from the day the house was built and not moved an inch in any direction since. Whoever had set the living room up had designed the furnishing around an old television set. Celia immediately announced that it didn't work and we'd have to replace it.

The one nice aspect of the small house was its flooring, all a dark oak hardwood that was well crafted and of such good quality that time only made it look richer. There were a few area rugs scattered about. The kitchen sink had large yellow stains around the drain, and the faucet had a leak. There was a four-burner gas stove and a small refrigerator that sounded a minute or two away from heart failure. The Formica counters were a faded yellow, as were the walls in both the living room and the kitchen. An antique toaster was set under one of the two windows in the kitchen, both with drab white curtains hanging listlessly around them.

The cabinets were open and showed where Celia had installed new shelving paper and neatly arranged what dishware there was with the house. She had also stocked one of the cabinets with staple items.

What was the main bedroom was the biggest room in the house, nearly the size of my bedroom back home. Whoever had lived here before must have directed all his or her attention to it, because it had newer, better-quality curtains framing the two large windows at the sides of the large headboard. The bed itself was a four-post canopy. There was a vanity table on the right with a good-size oval mirror in a mahogany frame. Besides the two nightstands, the furnishing included a built-in armoire and another dresser that matched the canopy bed frame. There was only one closet.

The second bedroom of the house was half the size, if that, and now used as some sort of storage area where the owner had put some broken furniture, a hammock frame, and a folding table. There was no bed. Down from it and just before the back door was the bathroom. Instead of tile, it had cracked gray linoleum. The white walls were in desperate need of washing. There was no stall shower, and the tub needed a shower curtain. I wondered how the two of them would arrange their toiletries in such a small cabinet with two short shelves beneath. There was only one window in the bathroom, and it had no curtain, just a shade.

If this was the house, I wondered what the studio apartment looked like. Celia opened the back door and told me to follow her across the small backyard to the shack behind the house. The door of it stuck, so she had to pull it hard to get it open.

"We'll fix that," she told me. She reached in to turn on a light and entered.

I followed, looking back to see if Brenda was coming, but she was already returning to the car to get another carton. The studio apartment was just one room with a pull-out sofa she had fixed with new linens, pillow cases and a blanket, a desk, and a chair. The bathroom wasn't much bigger than the bathroom on a commercial jet. It had a cracked mirror above the small sink.

"I know it doesn't look like much," Celia said, "but just think how you can fix it up. You can do anything you like to it," she added, and it was on the tip of my tongue to ask, *Does that include setting it on fire?*

Her voice was full of cheerfulness and excitement in an attempt to compensate for the dreary lodging.

"The important thing is it's your private area, and I know how much that matters to a teenager. It was always important to me when I was your age," she continued. "I know it's not what you're used to, but we'll make this into something. You'll see."

"It's all right," I said. If I hadn't, she would have gone on and on about it. I set down my carton of personal things. "We'd better get back to the car and help Brenda."

"Right. After we get everything into the house, we'll freshen up and go to this great restaurant just a few blocks away, the Memphis Belle. The waiters and waitresses all wear these quaint old-fashioned costumes, and the place is decorated like the dining room of some antebellum plantation house. You'll have so much fun exploring this area of Memphis, and I'm sure it won't be long before you've made new friends."

"Let's help Brenda," I said in response, and walked out.

It wasn't necessary to go through the house to get to the front. I went along the south side of the house where the grass was spotty and around to the driveway. Brenda was already back at the car for another load from the U-Haul. I just pitched in behind her. She glanced at me.

"It's only temporary," she said. "After the school year, we'll find something better."

I shrugged, which I knew annoyed her. She put the carton down and turned to me.

"You've got to stop that indifference, April. When something bothers you, declare it, state it, take a position. Start letting people know you exist. Don't be afraid of annoying or angering people. You have a right to your opinion."

"Okay," I said, my eyes narrowing to squeeze the tears that were pouring into them. "I hate it here. I want to go home. I want Daddy to be alive and the way he was when he loved us, and I want Mama singing in the morning and all of us laughing at the breakfast table."

Celia came up behind me. I could feel her there, but I didn't turn.

"I want to start over so I care about myself. I want to have friends, real friends, and I want to dress up and go to parties and meet boys and have so much fun I'm sick of it. I want to be normal!" I screamed.

I screamed so loudly that some birds perched on a corner of the roof of the house leaped into the air, crying to one another that this was no place to light on for a late afternoon meditation. Maybe they'd tell the whole bird kingdom, and not a single one would perch on the roof or even nearby.

I spun on Celia. She had that damn face of understanding.

"Normal!" I shouted at her.

She blinked.

"Okay," Brenda said. I turned back to her. "Now I know we're really related."

She didn't bat an eyelash, but the silence that followed was so heavy none of us breathed.

And then she laughed.

And Celia laughed.

And I couldn't help it.

I laughed, too, right through my tears. I laughed harder than I thought possible ever again.

The three of us hugged and then returned to unloading the car, now with a spurt of energy Brenda would call a second wind and I would call a miracle.

13

First Steps

❧✦❧

Brenda left it up to me to decide when I wanted to enter the new school, but Celia thought I shouldn't wait at all. She lectured about how necessary it was for me to get back into the stream of life and not to loiter about thinking constantly of the tragedy. She continually referred to herself and her own similar experiences.

"I don't mean to diminish your personal loss. It's terrible, but it's so easy to surrender to sadness and self-pity," she told me. "They're actually comfortable at this point and safe. You're so vulnerable because you've been so emotionally damaged. It takes very little to hurt you and get you crying, even if it's only crying inside. The only way to build your strength is to get involved in something new, dive right in."

I did start working on my pathetic studio apartment. I picked out some curtains for the windows and some paint to use for window trim. I bought a bright pink, fluffy area rug to put beside the pull-out sofa and then went about washing and polishing whatever I could. I bought some things for the little bathroom, too.

I did most of this after we had gone to dinner at the Memphis Belle. We were all quite hungry, and they had a great menu with so much variety. Celia made a pitch for us sharing a dessert called a Mud Pie, which was chocolate and vanilla ice cream in a graham cracker crust. I looked at Brenda. With Mama gone and Brenda my guardian, I would feel her looking over my shoulder even when she wasn't with me, I thought. She glanced at me and then at Celia before reluctantly relenting, and we did share one. We would have had to share it, anyway, because they were too big even for me. Actually, I ate the least. Celia ate the most, and we left a quarter of it because Brenda ate so little, and I wasn't going to be the one to finish it off.

That night, after we returned from the department store where I picked up the curtains, paint, and rug, all of us were busy unpacking and setting up the new living quarters. Celia had to return to school in the morning, but Brenda was still on family bereavement leave. By midday, however, she had done as much as she thought necessary and decided to attend a late-afternoon class and then go to the special basketball practice for the all-star game. Celia was right about my needing to occupy my time. When we were all to-gether the second night for our first dinner in the new home, I announced that I wanted to register in the morning.

"I don't have a class until ten," Celia said. "I could take her."

"No, they won't let you sign things. I'm her legal guardian," Brenda told her.

Celia agreed, but she looked so disappointed I wondered if I had become a pet project for her, someone on whom she could practice all the psychological theory she had learned.

I was nervous thinking about attending a new school, confronting new teachers and new classmates. My shattering nerves made me tired. It didn't matter that we hadn't replaced the old television set yet and I hadn't bought any new books to read. I went to sleep early. The walls of my little studio apartment weren't very thick. I could hear street noises, muffled but still easily discernible. In a house nearby, someone was practicing playing the trumpet. How different this was from our home in suburbia. I used to dream about living in a big city, but now that I was here, I wasn't that sure. Finally, all of it drifted away, and I fell asleep. I woke to the sound of Brenda knocking on my door to tell me I had to get up, get dressed, and have some breakfast. She had already confirmed the school's address and made the appointment for me. Actually, I discovered, Celia had done all that even before we had arrived.

It was cold and cloudy. I bundled up before running across the yard to use the shower in what I would now call the main house. I chose an oversized black sweatshirt with the words "The Ungrateful Living" on the back because it had been my most popular garment at school, and put on a baggy pair of jeans. It all hid my weight well, although I'd have to wear a mask to hide my chubby cheeks. My hair felt like steel wool when I brushed it, and I didn't put on any makeup, not even lipstick. I was never confident about all that, and Brenda was never any help.

Celia was chatty as ever at breakfast. Brenda was all business, talking about keeping to schedules, setting up responsibilities at the house, and following up what legal work still had to be accomplished after Mama's passing. I didn't eat much. My stomach was gurgling with nervousness.

"For today, I'll take you, and Celia will pick you up," Brenda told me. "Tomorrow and from now on, you can drive yourself."

"I don't mind taking you and dropping you off if you're nervous about driving in the city," Celia offered.

"She'll be fine," Brenda asserted, sounding what I thought was the first discordant note between them.

"Oh, I'm sure she will, but I just thought that . . ."

"We don't want to become her crutches," Brenda emphasized. "And don't give me any psychological logic," she added quickly.

Celia laughed, but it was one of those thin, fragile, china-like laughs that choked up in her throat. She swung her eyes to me and then quickly looked back at her food. I actually felt embarrassed for her.

"Brenda's right," I offered. "I'll be fine."

"Of course you will," Brenda said. "We all will."

When Brenda said it, it sounded like a command. *We'll be fine whether we like it or not,* I thought.

The school was literally ten minutes away by car. It was in a building that looked much older than other schools I had seen in the city, but it was in a convenient location. It had a population of nearly twelve hundred students, grade nine through grade twelve. The principal was an African American woman named Dr. Carol DeBerry. She couldn't have been more than five-foot-one, but she had a no-nonsense, firm demeanor that left me thinking I had been speaking to a woman six feet tall. One of the most surprising things I learned immediately was that I would have to wear a school uniform. The shirts and blouses had to be white, which was my worst color. It made me look even more overweight than I was, so I always avoided it. The blouses had to have collars and sleeves. Dr. De-Berry thought white blouses with Peter Pan collars were the best. Peter Pan collars, she explained, were flat collars with rounded ends that met in front. She spent so much time talking about the uniform I thought it was more important than grades in her school.

"Sweaters, sweatshirts, cardigans, and lightweight jackets are now permitted to be worn over the uniform top, but they must be either white, tan, navy blue, or black. Skirts and jumpers must be black, tan, or navy blue. We expect them to be knee-length or longer. I can tell you now that denim jeans and tight-fitting or baggy pants are not acceptable," she said, looking disdainfully at mine. "Your shoes should not have heels higher than an inch and a half. You can wear tennis shoes. We do not want to see any manufacturer's logos, names, pictures, or insignias on the clothing," she added, which eliminated my favorite sweatshirt. "We do not permit our students to wear their heavy jackets or raincoats during the school day.

"Here is a list of items we do not want you to bring to school. Notice we've included radios of any kind. A sharp instrument of any kind will result in your immediate suspension and perhaps criminal prosecution. There is no point in bringing cigarettes into the building. Smoking is punishable with suspension, and any violation of our behavioral rules, vandalism, violent actions, and use of profanity could result in expulsion. Is all this clear to you?"

"Yes," I said.

"Good. We've ordered your transcripts, and your schedule is arranged. Since you're not in a proper school uniform, I cannot permit you to begin today," she concluded.

Brenda's mouth dropped open.

"But we didn't know, and . . ."

"Well, now you know. Here's a list of stores in the immediate area that will have the proper clothing." She looked at her watch. "If you purchase what you need and can return by noon, I'll permit her to begin her afternoon classes."

She smiled as if she had granted us pardon from a death sentence and expected exaggerated expressions of gratitude. Brenda took the list.

"C'mon," she said to me. "We'll be back before noon," she told the principal.

"Very good," Dr. DeBerry said, holding her smile.

"Uniforms!" I moaned as we left the office. "And white. I look terrible in white."

"It will give you more motivation to lose weight," Brenda commented. She looked at her watch. "Let's get this done. I want to get to my one o'clock today, and I have to see the coach after my last class in the afternoon."

When we arrived at the store, I wanted to buy an extra-large long-sleeve blouse with a Peter Pan collar, but Brenda insisted I take the medium, which was closer to my size. The rolls of fat around my waist were emphatically visible. I made Brenda buy me an "acceptable" vest that went with a navy blue knee-length skirt. I already had on a pair of tennis shoes.

We rushed back to the school to have Dr. DeBerry look at my clothing and give me the stamp of approval. She made us wait in the outer office for nearly twenty minutes. I thought Brenda would have an angry fit and let the principal have it between the eyes, but she swallowed down her rage when we were finally permitted to enter for my fashion show.

"Very good," Dr. DeBerry said, and asked her secretary to provide me with my class schedule card. Brenda rushed off without saying good-bye. Dolores Donovan, a senior girl on office duty during her free period, was then assigned to give me a quick tour of the building and escort me to my next class, which was American history.

To me, it seemed more as if her assignment was to write my biography. Practically every five feet, she had another question. Of course, there were the usual "Where are you from? When did you move here? Why? What was your school like? Your friends? Are you upset about moving?" I was as vague as I could be, telling her only that we moved because of family matters. However, she was relentless.

"Who was that girl who brought you? Why didn't your father or mother bring you?"

She cornered me into telling her some of the truth. I told her how Daddy had died and then how my mother suffered heart failure. Heart failure was a good description for someone's death, I thought. Everyone accepted it, and I certainly didn't want anyone here to know that Mama had committed suicide. I wasn't ashamed of her, but I knew how that would color the way everyone looked at me, and I already had two strikes against me because of my weight and because I had no living parents. Even now, I thought to myself, even under these circumstances, it was still so important to be accepted, to find friends, to not be the object of ridicule. It surprised me how much I really still cared.

"Oh. How horrible for you and your sister," Dolores said. Before the school day was to end, most everyone in every one of my classes knew what Dolores knew.

For the time being, at least, I thought, no one would make fun of my weight. I could hide behind pity and sympathy. Was that awful of me? Maybe I could drop some pounds before anyone mean could use me as a target, I hoped. Living with Brenda would make it easier. She was sure to inspect every food item in the cabinets. Who knew? She might even keep track of the sugar, measuring it nightly. Maybe that was what I needed in the end: someone to take control of me. Half the time, I ate out of boredom. It was up to me now to avoid being bored.

I considered the after-school activities and thought I might join beginners' chess. I favored board games but had never taken the time to learn chess. Daddy told me he played somewhat, but he was never eager to teach me, claiming he wasn't very good at it because he lacked the patience. The only board game I ever got Brenda to play was checkers, of course. However, she thought sitting on her rear end for longer than ten minutes was degenerative and blamed my failure to lose weight partly on that. Nevertheless, before the school day ended for me, I signed up to join the beginners' chess club, which was meeting the next day. It met twice a week.

None of the other students were in a hurry to get to know me, which didn't surprise me. I caught some vaguely curious looks in my afternoon classes. The teachers introduced me, but no one came rushing up at the bell to make friends. As in my old school, other students were comfortable in their little cliques. Some friendships had been built over time and were not easily invaded. I understood, but I couldn't help being envious. Other than my teachers, Dolores was practically the only one who spoke to me the entire afternoon.

Celia was waiting for me in the parking lot when the school day ended. She was bright and full of energy and excitement. I knew it was a show to help me feel good about the move and the new school. I was quite aware of what she was doing, but it was difficult for me to be cheerful. I imagined I looked pretty unhappy.

"This is a very nice place!" she declared, standing outside the car and gazing about. "And it's so close to us. You could practically walk here. When the weather gets better, maybe you should."

"Who told you to say that, Brenda?"

"No, why?" she asked, holding her smile.

"Another way for me to lose weight," I muttered, and got into the car.

"Brenda didn't say a thing to me. You're getting paranoid, which is usual in your circumstances. The truth is, subconsciously, you're the one after you, not Brenda and certainly not me. But don't worry about all that now. I'll help you."

"How?" I snapped back at her.

She smiled. "Just be patient. You'll see. You didn't tell me about the school. How was it?"

I gave her my famous shrug. "School's school," I said.

"Anyway, some of the other city schools are more rundown," she declared, getting in. "Wasn't it all right, at least?" she pursued. Somewhere, she'd probably learned it was important to elicit a response.

"No," I said, deciding not to pretend just to make everyone else feel okay. "Look at me. Look at what I have to wear. They have a dress code here."

"It's not that bad."

"You don't have to wear it, so you can say that," I shot back at her. "I have to go shopping and get a few more uniforms. I have a choice of two other colors for the skirt."

"Oh. Do you want to go shopping now?"

I shrugged. She looked at her watch.

"Why don't we just do it, and then we can pick Brenda up. She should be through with practice by that time. We can stop at this great Chinese restaurant for dinner."

"Are we going to eat out every night?"

"No, silly. I just thought it would be easier until we get situated."

"Situated," I mimicked, and turned to press my forehead against the window. The world looked so dreary and dark to me.

Why didn't Mama think of me before she took all those pills? She knew what I was like, what my life was like. Why didn't she take that into consideration? It seemed strange to think it, but I did. Mama was selfish in taking her own life. Sometimes, you have to live for someone else's sake, especially if you're a mother and especially if your child's father is already dead and gone. I didn't think it was possible, but I was angry at her for leaving me behind.

After we bought the clothes and picked up Brenda, we went to the Chinese restaurant. What didn't surprise me but disappointed me was Brenda's lack of interest in how I had enjoyed my partial school day. From the moment we picked her up until our dinner was nearly finished, she talked incessantly about the upcoming all-star game and the revelation that she was going to be under the direction of another school's coach, one she didn't particularly like. She had heard too many bad things about him.

"He has this thing about punishing you if you take a shot he deems unwise. It puts stupid pressure on us all. I can't play well like that."

"Just be yourself, and if he doesn't like it, that's his problem. They have to know you're the best player."

"I'm not the best player. I'm one of the best."

"No, you're the best. Right, April?" Celia asked. It took me by surprise.

I widened my eyes and started to agree.

"How would she know? I'm not fishing for compliments here, Celia, so stop it."

"Okay, okay. I took April to buy some additional uniform clothing," she said, moving our conversation into another direction like a traffic cop.

Brenda sighed and then finally asked me about the school.

"I'm joining the beginners' chess club," I said. She smirked. "I always wanted to learn. It meets tomorrow."

"That's wonderful," Celia offered quickly.

"Yeah, it's great. Between driving and playing chess, she'll get a load of exercise."

"Oh, she'll do all right," Celia insisted.

Brenda gave me one of her "She had better" looks and finished eating.

I ate about half of what I ordered. My stomach felt as if I had swallowed a dozen spoonfuls of cement.

"Let's buy a new television set on the way home," Celia suggested. "I know you're going to want to watch the international basketball competition."

Brenda agreed, and we returned to the department store. A salesman volunteered to carry the set out to the car for us, but Brenda let him know in clear and certain terms that we were quite capable of it ourselves. Celia was obviously disappointed and not eager to struggle with it. It wasn't as heavy as it was bulky, and I was sure that the three of us looked very silly trying to get it into the rear seat of the car. We finally had to take it out of the carton, and I was assigned to sit next to it and hold on to it as we drove home.

Brenda and I carried it into the house, and Brenda hooked it up. I watched some television with the two of them before going to my hovel, as I now called it. It really wasn't much more than an afterthought, a shack. The little electric heater didn't do all that much even for so small an area. I worked on my school assignments, which to me seemed behind the work I had already accomplished back in Hickory, and then I went to sleep.

Brenda had made it clear before I left the main house that she wasn't going to be waking me up every morning.

"You're now responsible for yourself," she told me. "You have your car. Get yourself up and at breakfast in time. I don't want to hear about your being late for school," she warned.

Taking on the role of legal guardian made her assume a wholly different demeanor. It amused me how whenever she sounded stern, Celia followed with a laugh or "She'll be fine. Don't frighten her." Whether I liked it or not, I was gaining an ally against my own sister. It irked Brenda, and she chastised Celia about it, but Celia laughed it off and clearly humored her. If I could see it, Brenda surely could, I thought, but Brenda was forgiving when it came to Celia, far more forgiving than she was toward me.

The school day began the way it had ended the day before for me. I was simply not interesting enough or pretty enough to interest any of the boys or the girls. The little curiosity about me that had begun in the afternoon the day before seemed to dissipate like smoke, and I soon felt invisible. It wasn't an uncommon feeling for me. Perhaps because it was comfortable and safe, I accepted it.

At lunch, three of the girls from my English class

did invite me to sit with them. They began by firing questions at me like prosecutors. I knew they were searching to discover if there was anything startling about me that they could wave about like the front page of a newspaper among their other friends, but my answers were too bland, too dull. I didn't have much to say about the social life, the boys and girls from Hickory, or the teachers. One girl, Nikki Flynn, had a relative in Hickory and had been there. She described it as "boring." Even the mall was disappointing to her. Their conversation quickly returned to themselves, and in minutes, I was more like a fly on the wall than someone with them at their table.

For me, the most exciting event of the day was attending the beginners' chess club. About ten minutes after the final bell, I wandered down to a room inside the school library, where I found eight other students and the school's business teacher, a tall, lanky man, Mr. Kaptor. He had stringy, light brown hair and beady eyes under a pair of wire-rim, thick-lensed glasses, but he gave me the best welcome of anyone since I had arrived. The other students were pairing off at the desks, but I noticed a tall, very dark boy with ebony eyes and long ebony hair walking about, studying the boards as the others began to consider their moves. He had a very sharp jaw line and a very tight, strong mouth. When I saw him closer, I saw his long eyelashes and admired his high cheekbones. He wasn't bulky or what Brenda would call buff, but he looked muscular, trim.

"Welcome to the club," Mr. Kaptor said, shaking my hand. "Do you know anything at all about chess?"

"No, sir," I said.

"That's fine; that's fine. It's why we call it beginners' chess club, so don't be discouraged. Take your time, and you'll be surprised at how quickly you can get into it. My student assistant here will start you off. Peter," he called, and the dark-haired, handsome boy turned to us, seeing me for the first time. He was so intense about observing the others that he hadn't noticed my entrance.

He walked over to us.

"This is Peter Smoke," Mr. Kaptor said. "Peter, meet a new prospect, April Taylor. She just entered the school yesterday and chose our club for her extracurricular activity."

Peter stared at me without expression. Then he finally nodded.

"Peter has this cynicism about new entrants," Mr. Kaptor explained. "We get a few every month who attend one or two sessions and then never return. He hates wasting his time, don't you, Peter?"

"That's right," he said dryly. "What do you know about the game?"

"I know there is a king and queen and knights, but that's about it," I said honestly. "I've just played checkers up until now."

He didn't laugh. I wondered if he was capable of smiling. What kind of a name was Peter Smoke?

"Let's get started," he said. He nodded at a chair. "Sit."

I looked at Mr. Kaptor.

"I'll circulate and return shortly, but Peter's terrific at the basics. He's very modest, but he's regional champion," Mr. Kaptor said.

Peter went about setting up a board, and I sat across from him. This was just chess, but my heart was pounding as if I were entering a marathon.

"Okay," he said, looking at the pieces and not at me. "The object of the game is to checkmate your opponent's king. Checkmate occurs when a king is attacked and the king cannot escape capture on the next move. He's trapped. Here's the setup. The rooks begin the game in the corners. The knights, which some people call horses," he said, smirking, "are next to the rooks here. The bishops start next to the knights, and then come the king and the queen. Notice that the white queen begins on a white square and the black queen on a black square," he said, lifting each queen to be sure I knew what a queen was. "To begin the game, white moves first and then black, taking turns until check-mate occurs."

He finally looked up at me. I couldn't help staring at him.

"Do you understand so far?"

"Yes," I said. "But you don't jump pieces like you do in checkers, right?"

"Hardly," he said. "Checkers is a joke compared to chess. Forget you ever played it."

"I didn't play it that much."

"Good," he said. He looked back at the board and then quickly returned his eyes to me. "There wasn't a chess club in your previous school?"

"No, but I was always interested in learning how to play. My father knew how but didn't play much and didn't have the patience to teach me. My sister hates board games. She's an athlete. We lived in Hickory. Maybe you know where it is." I realized I was rattling off like a car that had lost its brakes and immediately bit down on my lower lip to shut my spewing mouth.

"Of course, I know where that is." He returned his attention to the board, and I thought that would be it, but then he looked up again. "My people were the first citizens of this state. I know every place in it."

"Your people?"

"I'm Cherokee," he said. "I didn't grow up here. I

grew up in Oklahoma. I returned to live with my aunt after my father died. My mother died when I was born."

"Oh."

He looked at the board again.

"My parents are both dead, too," I blurted, since he didn't seem to know anything about me. I guessed he didn't have his ear to the gossip phone in the school.

He looked at me again, and for the first time, his eyes softened. He didn't speak. He lifted the king.

"The king can move one square in any direction and capture an opponent's piece if it's on one of those squares, assuming, of course, that the opponent is not defending this piece. The king can never move to a square that the opponent controls. Doing so will move the king into check. Suicide," he added.

He moved a few pieces.

"Here, see this. In this case, the rook is one square away and undefended. If I put these two rooks here like this, they can defend each other, and the king can only move one way. Am I going too fast for you?" he asked.

"Yes," I said.

He sat back.

"All right, let's just go over the moves each piece can make, and then we'll go back to what I'm saying. The rook can move any number of squares in straight line, horizontally or vertically, but the rook may not jump a piece of either color. Got that?"

I nodded.

"The bishop can move any number of squares diagonally, but, like the rook, it may not jump a piece. Like the rook, it can move forward or backward, but in only one direction at a time. Okay?"

"Yes."

"The queen combines the power of the rook and the bishop. It can move horizontally, vertically, or in the diagonal."

"Wow," I said.

He glanced at me but continued.

"It's like the king in that it can move in any direction, but unlike the king, it can move far in one direction so long as there are no pieces in its path."

He took a deep breath.

"The Knight's move is special. It hops directly from its old square to its new square. The Knight can jump over other pieces between its old and new squares. Think of the Knight's move as an "L." It moves two squares horizontally or vertically and then makes a right-angle turn for one more square. The Knight always lands on a square opposite in color from its old square."

"The last is the pawn, which is the only piece that moves differently from how it captures. The pawn, like a warrior in war, marches forward one square at a time. It can never retreat. However, pawns that have not yet moved have the option of beginning their forward journey with a double move two squares forward. They can't jump other pieces. The pawn captures diagonally only one square ahead. Think of it fighting with a knife rather than a sword."

"Is this whole game thought of as a fight?"

"Of course," he said. "Military tacticians love it. It's strategy, defense, aggression, entrapment, retreats, the whole gambit."

"Checkers is friendlier," I said.

He stared at me so hard I thought he was about to get up and desert me, but to my surprise, he actually smiled.

"You're not the competitive type, is that it?"

"I guess not. My sister has the monopoly on that in our family. She's a star basketball player for Thompson University. She's on the all-star team for the region and will be playing a week from tomorrow," I said.

"Very nice," he said, obviously not very impressed. He cleared the board of all the pieces. "Okay, I want you to set up the board again, and as you do, repeat as much of what I told you as you can."

I felt a wave of panic. Truthfully, I had sat politely listening, but I was sure I wouldn't be able to repeat half of what he told me. Nevertheless, I began, and to my surprise, he wasn't upset by my errors. In fact, I realized his quiet way was not because of annoyance but an inner peacefulness I had never seen in someone as young. There was a maturity about him I couldn't help but envy.

"Can I ask what happened to your father?"

"You just did," he said.

I bit down on my lower lip.

"He was an alcoholic," Peter said. "Unfortunately, that firewater thing is a stereotype idea about Native Americans that proves more the rule than the exception. Life on reservations, Indian land, is terrible. Poverty level doesn't begin to describe it."

"You're a full-blooded Cherokee?"

"Yes," he said. "My aunt isn't. The Cherokees were driven out of Tennessee in 1838 in a historical event we call the Trail of Tears. Some mixed-blooded remained, and some returned, and my aunt is one of them."

He leaned over the board.

"Don't worry," he said. "I won't scalp you."

I guess my expression was pretty funny to him. His smile widened.

"How is it going?" Mr. Kaptor asked.

"It's a start," he told him.

"What's that Chinese proverb, Peter?"

"A journey of a thousand miles begins with a step," he replied, looking at me. "She's almost finished with the first step." He looked at his watch. "Let's go over it again," he said, and returned to the chess pieces.

When the club hour ended, my head was spinning, but I had to admit I enjoyed it. Peter went to talk to Mr. Kaptor, and I started out. I walked slowly, thinking about the day, my classes, the place I was now in. I thought about Uncle Palaver, too, and reminded myself to remind Brenda to get in touch with him. I was almost to my car when I heard, "Are you coming back on Thursday?"

I turned to see Peter Smoke.

"Yes, I am," I said. "I'm going to get my own chess set, too, and practice whatever I learn at home."

"It's not too bloody a game, too violent?"

"Stop making fun of me," I said, and he actually started to laugh. He nodded at my automobile. "You have your own car?"

"Yes. It was my mother's car."

"What happened to her?" he asked. "You asked about my father," he reminded me quickly.

I thought a moment. There was something about him that commanded honesty.

"Like the king shouldn't do, she moved into a square that the opponent controlled."

He stared, the meaning registering. "I said my father was an alcoholic. It's a form of suicide, too," he remarked.

I nodded. For a moment, we were just standing there.

"Can I give you a ride home?"

He raised his eyebrows. "It'll be out of your way," he said.

"How do you know? I didn't tell you where I live."

"It's a distance. It will take too long."

"I have time. Your turn," I said.

"Huh?"

"Looks like checkmate," I said, and this time he really laughed.

He got into the car, and we started away, with him giving me directions.

"You're going to be able to find your way back and home, right?" he asked.

"Yes," I said, not worrying about it. "Can I ask you about your name?"

"Peter or Smoke?"

"I think Smoke," I said, laughing.

"It's my ancestral name. My family's name was given to my father's great-great-great-grandfather who was in the Civil War. They gave Indians names then, and they gave him the name Jordan. I wouldn't accept it from the time I was twelve, but I wasn't able to change it until after my father died. I discovered my grandfather's name was Tsu-S-di, which translated means 'Smoke' so I took that name."

"Why was his name Smoke?"

"It comes from the Smokey Mountains. My people were there in the year 1000, and there are many legends about the mountains, the smoke. It's mystical, powerful," he said.

I could feel his eyes on me, his concern that I might, as I supposed many young people our age did, laugh at him. Instead, I turned to him and said, "I wish I had a name that had such power."

"April is spring," he replied. "Rebirth, life."

"I mean my last name. There should be a name store so I could go choose a new one."

"There is," he said, and gestured at the outside. "It's called the world. Anyway, you don't choose your name. It chooses you," he said. "And don't worry," he added. "It will find you."

He told me to make a turn at the next intersection, and we'd be on his street. His aunt's house was at least two times larger than our bungalow. It had a bigger, wider lawn and nice magnolia trees in front.

"You can pull into the driveway," he said.

"How do you usually get home?"

"Bus drops me off two blocks south. No problem. Thanks for the ride."

"You're welcome," I said. "Thanks for the chess lesson."

"You're welcome. How does the queen move differently from the king?" he fired, pointing his finger at me.

"She . . . can move as far as she wants as long as there's no one in her path."

"Think about that," he said. "Think about how to move like the queen."

He closed the door, smiled, and walked to his front door. I waved, backed out, and drove away, pretending I knew just how to get back.

It was the first time I cared what a boy thought about me, really cared.

14

Smoke Signals

Eventually, I had to stop at a garage, get out, and ask for directions. I was that lost. By the time I got home, Brenda and Celia were there, both sitting in the living room, Brenda looking like someone with a nasty case of migraine headaches.

"We were worried about you, April," Brenda said the moment I entered. "Where were you? Your club meeting couldn't have gone this long."

"It didn't. I took someone home."

"You drove someone home already?" she asked, grimacing.

"Was it a boy or a girl?" Celia asked.

"A boy," I said.

"You have to be very careful, April," she followed. "Urban kids are a lot more sophisticated when it comes to taking advantage of people."

"He wasn't taking advantage of me. He didn't ask me to take him home."

"Oh!" Celia said, raising her eyebrows. "What's this boy's name?"

I looked away. The two of them were sitting there cross-examining me like detectives at a murder scene.

"The last time you were in a car with a boy, you got yourself into a lot of trouble, April," Brenda reminded me.

"This wasn't like that."

"I hope not."

"So, what's his name?" Celia pursued.

"Why? What difference does it make?"

"April," Brenda snapped. "Don't be so insolent."

"His name is Peter Smoke."

"Peter Smoke?" Celia smiled. "Are you serious?"

"He's a full-blooded Cherokee Indian living with his aunt here."

"Is he in your class?" she asked.

"No. He's a senior. He's the assistant chess instructor and the regional chess champion," I said. "That's how we met."

Celia raised her eyebrows again. "Oh, he's not a jock; he's a thinker, a Native American thinker."

"Don't tease her," Brenda said. "I don't want her to think we're trivializing anything. Just be careful," she reminded me. "People take advantage of someone new, especially a young girl with her own car."

"It's just human nature," Celia agreed. "You have a big, generous heart, and you're searching desperately now for some iota of happiness."

"I'm not that desperate," I fired back at her.

"We're just trying to look out for you, April. Don't be so antagonistic," Brenda chastised.

I sighed deeply.

"We don't mean to be intrusive or bossy. We're just

concerned for you," Celia added. "Neither of us wants to see you unhappy."

"Okay. I'm sorry. Did you call Uncle Palaver and tell him where we are and how to reach us?" I quickly asked Brenda as she started to turn away.

"Yes, I did."

"Where was he?"

"He was in Beaumont, Texas, and on his way to New Orleans."

"How's Destiny?" I asked.

She shook her head. "How should I know? Why?"

"I just wondered," I said, smiling to myself. Uncle Palaver had not told her about Destiny. He had confided in me only. It made me feel special.

"I'm driving back to Hickory this weekend," Brenda added. "I have some legal documents to review with our attorney. A trust fund is being created for you. And the real estate agent has someone returning for a second visit. It looks promising. I'm just going for the day. Do you want to come along?"

"No," I replied sharply. Returning to Hickory with Mama gone was a horrible idea for me. I certainly didn't want to look at our house again.

"Suit yourself," she said. "We bought a ready-cooked chicken for tonight. I thought we'd have some salad and that would be enough."

"Fine with me," I said. "I'll make the salad."

Actually, it really was fine with me. Suddenly, watching my diet and losing weight took on a whole new meaning. Celia gave me one of her all-knowing smiles, and before she could say anything else, I left the two of them, put my books in my apartment, changed as quickly as I could out of my school uniform, and returned to the kitchen to do the salad.

At dinner, I was happy the conversation centered

around Brenda's all-star game on Friday. Celia talked about the two of us going together. It was being held at a nearby neutral college's gymnasium. As they talked about it, an idea blossomed in my head. I wondered if Peter Smoke would like to go. Was it too optimistic to even consider, and, more to the point, would I have the nerve to ask him or even suggest it? Was it too soon to make such a suggestion to him? What if he laughed?

"Are you going to ask your new friend if he would like to go to the game, too," Celia asked as I was going out the rear door.

I hated that she could anticipate my secret hope. Was I really so transparent? Could anyone see through me, or was Celia someone special and extra bright? And why was it so important to her, anyway?

"I don't know. All I did was give him a ride home," I muttered, and left quickly without even looking at her reaction.

However, I couldn't stop thinking about Peter Smoke. Was it possible for a girl to develop a crush on a boy so quickly? Was it horrible of me even to have such thoughts so soon after Mama's death? I told myself that it wasn't, because in my mind, it was still hard to accept Mama being gone. I had pushed it down and held it there, forcing myself not to think about it. I dove into my homework, read until my eyes were foggy, and then tried to go to sleep. The trumpet player was at it again, only tonight his music was melancholy to me. It brought tears to my eyes and made me think of Mama, her smile, her laughter, and her wonderful way of building me up, giving me hope. How lonely I felt without her.

Did Peter Smoke have nights like this? I wondered. Did he miss his mother as much? His life seemed even worse than mine. How did he embrace his sadness? From what well did he draw the strength? What had he called that forced relocation of the Cherokee Indians, the Trail of Tears? I felt as if I were walking the same route. Nasty, horrible, and cruel fate had forced my relocation. Maybe he was right. Maybe my new name and my new identity would find me. I had to learn to have his patience.

I smiled to myself. When we met again, I thought, I'd know that chess board backward and forward. I decided to spend my study period in the library reading up on it.

I was hoping to see him in school the next day, but he was like a ghost. I was surprised not to see him in the cafeteria at lunchtime, at least. Where did he go? Curious, I approached Dolores and started the conversation by telling her I had joined beginners' chess.

"That's so boring," she remarked. Her girlfriends quickly agreed with their nods and moans.

"No one is in it but the school nerds," JoAnn Docken added. She was a tall, light-brown-haired girl whose obviously cosmetically adjusted nose looked like an advertisement for Snobs 'R' Us.

"There was this interesting boy helping the teacher. He said he was an Indian," I added, trying to sound as casual as I could.

"Peter Smoke?" Dolores replied.

"Yes."

"Forget him. He's weird."

"I don't even see him in school," I said, gazing around the cafeteria.

"He never eats inside. Even when it rains, he's outside under the overhang. I heard he sleeps with a wolf or something," JoAnn continued.

"He smells like he does," another girl, Enid Lester,

said. She was in my math class and sat across from me, with her little makeup mirror open as if she had to continually check her face for signs of some change. Girls like Enid were like air-traffic controllers searching their own radar screens for signs of some blip in their looks.

They all laughed.

"I didn't smell anything bad," I said.

"You didn't get close enough, probably. Why, do you like him?" Enid pursued.

"No, I just wondered . . ."

"Watch yourself," JoAnn said. "We heard he carved his initials between the breasts of the last girl he was with at his Oklahoma school. Some Indian thing to make sure your woman is yours and yours only."

They all laughed again.

"That's so stupid," I said.

"She likes him," Enid said, nodding smugly, and they all laughed once more.

I left them giggling at me and walked out of the cafeteria and out of the building. It actually wasn't a bad day to eat lunch outside, I thought. Spring was beginning to creep in, and today we had bright sunshine and higher than usual temperatures. I searched the school grounds, and at first, I didn't see him and thought those girls had just made something up for spite. However, just as I was about to turn and go back into the building, I saw his ebony hair and realized he was sitting at a tree with his back against it.

"Hi," I said, and he turned slowly as if he knew I was walking up to him. He showed no surprise.

"You always eat lunch outside?"

He turned further to look at me. "I spend as much time as I can outside. We're locked up in there too much of the day as it is. Why eat in a noisy big room when you have this?" he asked, nodding at the lawn, the trees, the birds, and the blue sky.

"You're right. Mind if I join you?"

"The world belongs to all of us if it belongs to anyone," he said.

I sat and opened my brown bag. All I had in it was a stalk of celery and an apple. He glanced at it, but he didn't ask anything or comment. I took a bite of the apple and then a bite of celery. I was sure he could hear the crunching.

"Noisy food," he said. "You wouldn't hear that in the cafeteria with all the chatter."

"Sorry."

"That's okay. I don't mind that sort of noise. It's the yakkity-yak that drives me mad sometimes. We should all be charged for how many words we speak a day. People would spew less nonsense."

I started to laugh and then thought about what I would say. Would he think that was nonsense, too?

"I read a little more about chess. Those descriptions confused me at first."

"What descriptions?"

"E2 to E4. Gl to F3."

"Oh. And what did you learn?"

I leaned over and with my pen drew a square in the dirt. "The left of the board is thought of as numbers one to eight, and the bottom is letters A through H, so when they say 'E2 to E4,' that would be the pawn moving two squares forward."

He stared at me suspiciously for a moment and then, with a half smile, asked, "And what's behind that pawn on letter E?"

I thought a moment, envisioning the board. "The king," I said, and opened my eyes to see a wide smile spread across his face.

"Very good." He sat back and continued to eat his sandwich. I thought that was the end of our conversation, but he extended his arm toward the sky and said, "We all tend to think the clouds are random, but if you study the sky long enough, you see patterns. That's why I love chess, too, the sense of order, the clean sense of order. So much around us is chaos. It's nice to find patterns and order in anything."

I sucked in my breath and sat quietly. It was one of those moments that required no words. He glanced at me, and then we ate without speaking until we heard the warning bell.

"I can take you home again if you like," I said quickly when we both stood up. "I know the way now."

"Why?" he asked, looking suspicious.

"Why? Because . . . I could get some extra help with my chess lessons," I offered, trying to make my invitation sound selfish.

He held his smile back, but I could see it in his eyes. "Okay. That's a fair trade. You'll come in and spend an hour on the board," he said.

Come in? Into his house?

Maybe in his mind, it was a trade or an assignment or work, but to me, it was like being on my first real date. We walked back into the building together and parted in the hallway after we arranged where and when we'd meet in the parking lot. I hurried to class, my thoughts only on Peter's soft smile. I didn't hear Dolores and her girlfriends come up behind and beside me.

"We saw you out the window," Dolores sang. "You and Chief Smoke."

"Don't call him that," I said.

"Why not? He's an Indian, and a chief is the top Indian, isn't he?"

"Because you're making fun of him, and he'll know it, too."

"Big deal," Enid said.

"What are you hoping to become, his squaw?" JoAnn asked, laughing.

"She could be a squaw," Enid followed. "Aren't squaws big and stout?"

My face reddened. The three of them walked faster, passing me by.

My weight will always be a target for vicious people, I thought. Brenda was right all along. *I'm going to lose these pounds or die trying,* I vowed to myself. For the rest of the afternoon, I caught their sneers and sly smiles whenever I looked at them or their other friends. My honeymoon period here had ended quickly, I realized. The only one who would feel sorry for me now was myself. Just like in Hickory, everyone was vying for top spots in the popularity contest, and if stepping on me to get a little higher helped, well, so be it.

Of course, I didn't mention anything about the other girls and their snide remarks to Peter when we met after school. I wasn't sure he would care, anyway. He seemed to have little or no interest in making friends here or keeping the ones he had made. We drove away before any of the girls appeared in the parking lot. Despite my claim, I actually had forgotten the way to his house, and he had to correct me on two turns.

"My aunt isn't home," he said when we arrived at her house. "She works for a dentist. She's the one who cleans and polishes people's teeth, a dental hygienist."

"What about her husband?"

"She's divorced. The marriage went sour before they had children, fortunately," he said, leading me to the front door.

His aunt's home was modest in comparison with the home we had in Hickory, but if I compared it with where we lived now, it was a palace. The living room looked cozy. The furniture was arranged with the fireplace as the central focus. It was a pretty fireplace built out of fieldstone with a mantel upon which sat a miniature grandfather clock and two vases with flowers made of colored glass. Above the fireplace was a portrait of an old Indian man wearing a cowboy hat, a blue shirt, and jeans with boots. There was a corral behind him and a pony to the left grazing. In the distance were mountains with a blue tint and a pocket of soft white clouds crowning the peaks.

"That's my great-grandfather," Peter said. "The Smokey Mountains are behind him."

"Who painted it?"

"My great-grandmother," he said, smiling. "C'mon. I have my chess board set up in my room. There's a game in progress."

"Whom do you play against? Your aunt?"

"No, myself," he said. "What you do," he explained as we walked down the short hallway, "is set up famous games and try to meet the challenge. This is a game that won the regional contest five years ago."

His room was very neat and simple. The bed was made like a military bed, the cover sheet tight enough to bounce a coin off it and the pillows were without a crease. Nothing in the room was out of place. The dresser had a picture of a dark-haired woman in a silver frame on top of it. I didn't ask him, but I imagined she was his mother. There was a table to the right with two chairs and the chess board set up on it. He had a desk against the left wall, with his books, notebooks, and pens neatly arranged. The closet door was closed.

The hardwood floors were polished and clean, with a light brown oval area rug beside the bed. I immediately thought my pathetic studio was a pigsty compared with this.

The only thing out of the ordinary was a light blue hoop with feathers, beads, and what looked like arrowheads hanging above his bed.

"What is that?" I asked.

"It's a dream catcher."

"Excuse me?"

"A dream catcher. We believe that the night air is filled with dreams both good and bad. The dream catcher hung over or near your bed, swinging freely in the air, catches the dreams as they flow by. The good dreams know how to pass through the dream catcher, slipping through the outer holes and sliding down the soft feathers so gently that many times the sleeper does not know that he or she is dreaming. The bad dreams, not knowing the way, get tangled in the dream catcher and perish with the first light of the new day."

"Boy, could I use one of those," I said.

He smiled, went to the closet, opened it, and took one that looked similar off the inside of the door.

"This will be yours," he said.

"Really? It's beautiful."

"Really," he said, and handed it to me.

"I have nothing to give you in return," I said.

"You have given your friendship. Go on, take it," he urged, and I did. "Okay, let's go to the board," he said.

He began to rearrange the pieces to set up a new game.

"I didn't mean for you to ruin your game."

"No problem. I have it all memorized."

"You do?"

"It's like a fine painting. You don't forget it so easily," he explained. "Sit," he said, pointing to the seat across from him.

I sat quickly. He folded his hands and leaned over the board.

"Let's get more into it now. You know the board, the way the pieces move, the object of the game, some of the rules. The pawn, as I began to explain, moves in a most unusual way. This is one of the trickiest moves to learn and usually drives my students nuts. We call it capturing *en passant*, which is French for—"

"'While passing'," I said.

He nodded, showing he was impressed. "You know French?"

"I'm in second year. I took it as an elective."

"*Très bien*," he said. "Okay. Here's the story about this move. During the early days of chess, pawns could only move a single square at a time. Some changes were created in Europe to speed up the game. One of these, as I explained, was that the pawn can move two squares if it has not yet moved. Now, I didn't explain that when a pawn moves all the way down to the last rank on the board, it becomes another piece."

"What do you mean, another piece?"

"It gets promoted, only you can't promote it to a king. A queen, yes, but not a king. Most of the time, it's a queen, so it's possible to have many queens on the board. And don't say something dumb like too many chiefs and not enough Indians."

"I wasn't going to," I said, laughing. He laughed, too.

"Getting back to the *en passant*. It became possible for a pawn to move all the way down the board without the opponent's pawn ever having a chance to capture it. Here's how the *en passant* rule applies. For one move, and one move only, the black pawn can respond by capturing the white pawn as if it had moved only a single square. To effect the capture, the pawn is moved forward diagonally."

He demonstrated with the white and black pawn.

"Only pawns can capture *en passant*, and only a pawn on an adjacent file or row, can capture in this manner. Understand?"

"I think so," I said.

"It's a hard one, I know. Just watch as I move the pieces and do it again."

I watched him play against himself. As he moved pieces, he announced what he was doing.

"See?"

"Yes," I said. It was still a little cloudy, but I didn't want him to get discouraged about teaching me. "Who taught you how to play chess?"

"My father."

"Your father? But I thought you said . . ."

"It was practically the only thing we did together. He could drink and still play well. After a time, I began to anticipate his moves, and he got so he started to forget. I stopped playing with him then."

"Oh. I'm sorry."

"There's nothing to be sorry about. It was what was and no longer is. My grandfather used to say that if you dwell on the past, it will capture you, imprison you. Go outside and bury the unhappiness. I remember once I hurt myself, tripped and slid and scraped my palms raw. I cried until I ran out of tears. Then I sulked until my grandfather took me out back and dug a hole. 'Go on,' he said. 'Throw your unhappiness into the hole.' I had no idea what to throw, but I made a gesture that meant it, and he said, 'Good,' and filled the hole. 'Now you will forget the pain,' he promised, and I did."

I smiled skeptically.

"Try it sometime," he told me. "Okay, let's return to the king."

"Actually, my sister thinks like you do. She says you can't dwell on the game before, no matter if you won or lost. You have to look to the next game. She's very strong that way."

He nodded.

"She's playing in the all-star game Friday."

"You told me that," he said

"It's sure to be an exciting game. Would you like to go?" I asked quickly. "We'd be going with my sister's roommate."

He stared a moment. I held my breath.

"I've never gone to a girls' basketball game."

"They don't play like girls. You'd be surprised how exciting it gets, and when you see my sister play . . ."

He started to laugh. "Okay," he said when my face began to sink into itself. I imagined I sounded like a little fool. "I will go, but I buy my own ticket."

"My sister gets six free ones. I'm sure there will be one for you."

"If there isn't, you tell me," he said. "Understood?"

"Yes, of course."

"Now we'll look at something called castling," he said. "The king is permitted to take part in a very special move, the only chess move that actually involves two pieces at the same time. To castle . . ."

"Move the king two squares toward the rook and then move the rook to the square immediately on the other side of the king," I recited.

He looked up with surprise, and I smiled at him.

"You did do some studying," he said, impressed again.

Mama used to say she won Daddy's heart through his stomach because of her cooking. Here I was hopefully winning Peter's heart through chess.

"When can't you castle?" he asked. He sat back, folding his arms across his chest.

"When?" I panicked. I had absolutely no idea. I had only memorized the term to impress him. I shook my head.

"Why do it, anyway? When does it make strategic sense?"

Again, I shook my head.

"Go too far out in a stream before you learn completely how to swim, and you'll get washed away with the current," he warned. Then he smiled. "It's all right. If you knew all that, I wouldn't be able to be your teacher today."

My smile returned. He rose and went to his CD player to turn on some music. It was very different but very interesting.

"What is that?"

"Cherokee music. Indian flute," he said. "Do you like it?"

"Very much."

"Good. Back to castling," he said, "now that I'm with an expert."

We went on for almost another hour before I realized how late it had gotten and practically leaped out of my seat.

"I've got to get home," I said, recalling how Brenda and Celia had given me the third degree the day before.

"I'm sorry. I get carried away myself," he said, rising. "Especially if I'm working with someone who is genuinely interested and listening."

I smiled, even though in my heart of hearts, I knew I was here not because of chess but because of him. If he had any such suspicion, he didn't reveal it.

"Don't forget your dream catcher," he said, holding it out.

He walked me to the door and out to the car.

"Now, are you telling me the truth this time?" he asked, and I blanched. Did he see through me and know that I was less interested in chess than I was in him?

"What do you mean?"

"Do you really know the way home?"

"Oh," I said, relieved at what he was asking. I showed him a paper on which I had written the directions I had gotten yesterday.

"Okay," he said, holding the door.

I stood there looking at him. In a burst of courage, I stepped up on my toes and gave him a peck on the cheek.

"Thank you," I said quickly, and got into the car. I was afraid to look up at him.

He wore a look of amusement when he closed the door. I started the engine, put it in reverse, and looked at him to wave good-bye, but he had already turned to go back into his house.

I'd made a dumb fool of myself, I thought. My eyes were so full of tears by the time I reached the corner of his street that I thought I would have trouble driving. I sucked in my breath, bit down on my lip, and tried to shake the feeling of stupidity and embarrassment off, but it was with me all the way home.

15

Us Against the World

❖❖❖

Brenda wasn't home when I arrived. Celia came out of their room as soon as I entered to tell me Brenda had gone with her teammates to practice and would have a light dinner with them afterward.

"You're pretty late," she said. "Peter Smoke again?"

"Yes. He taught me more about chess."

"Only chess?" she asked, swinging her eyes.

"Only chess," I repeated sternly.

"What is that?" she asked, seeing the dream catcher.

"Something Peter gave me. It's called a dream catcher. You hang it over your bed, and it keeps night-mares away."

"If only it worked," she said.

"Maybe it does," I told her. "Maybe you just have to believe in it. Maybe the trouble is you don't believe in anything," I added sharply.

She laughed after me as I charged through the house

toward the rear door. "What do you want to do for dinner?" she called.

I paused. "You go where you want," I said. "I'm just making a couple of eggs for myself."

I closed the door before she could respond and hurried across the small yard to my apartment. The first thing I did was hang the dream catcher above my pull-out sofa bed. I had just finished when I heard Celia knocking at the door.

"What?"

"Can I come in?" she asked.

"Come in," I said, and plopped on the sofa. I folded my arms across my breasts and glared ahead.

She stood in the doorway, looking at me.

"What's wrong, April?"

"Nothing."

"Look, I'm sorry. I didn't mean to make fun of the dream catcher. I actually know what they are and have a great deal of respect for Indian spiritualism. I took a course in comparative religions and was amazed at the similarities between Native American religion and Far Eastern religion."

"That's nice," I said.

"Something else is bothering you besides my flippant remarks."

I didn't answer. She stood there, holding the door open.

"I know how it is when you have no one to talk to. I had no one for most of my life. It's all right. I want to help you," she said.

"Yeah, right," I said.

She came in, closing the door behind her.

"You don't have your mother anymore, and Brenda was never the sort of sister who had the patience for your problems, I'm sure," she said, which surprised me. "It's all right. I'm not telling stories out of school. Brenda would be the first to admit it. Am I wrong?"

"No," I said, knowing well that Brenda would never pretend to be one thing when she was another. Often, I wished she would.

"It's terrible to be alone with your feelings, especially when they're coming at you fast and furious, and they're so new and even frightening," Celia said.

She sat beside me on the sofa. I glanced at her and looked away. She was right about that, too, of course. What could I say?

"You really like this boy?"

I hesitated for a moment, and then I relaxed my shoulders. "I think so," I said.

"It's confusing, I know."

"I might have made a big fool of myself," I confessed.

"Oh? How?"

"When we said good-bye, I just . . . just kissed him on the cheek quickly and jumped into the car. I probably looked like a real idiot."

"I'm surprised. Usually, it's the boy who looks like a real idiot," she muttered. "What did he do?"

"Nothing. He just turned away and walked back to his front door."

"Maybe he's very shy. There are still a few of them around," she said.

I turned and looked at her. "Do you really hate men that much?"

"Hate? No. I'm just, shall we say, a little cynical. I had a number of experiences when I wasn't much older than you are, and none of them left me satisfied. Most were quite upsetting, matter of fact."

"Is that why you like to be with a woman?"

"No, I wouldn't say it was only because of those experiences. It's not easy to explain what makes you feel this way or that. There's something inside me that takes me in that direction. And I'm comfortable with it," she added quickly.

"When did you first know about yourself?" I asked, feeling bolder. She was the one who had come into my apartment to talk to me, after all.

"I didn't."

"What do you mean?"

"I didn't first know about myself. Someone else did and showed me," she said.

"How did she know about you before you knew about yourself?"

"Sometimes, people can see you better than you can see yourself. You're not objective, and you have a number of issues that prevent you from facing up to the truth. I dated plenty in high school. I cared about my appearance. I was quite attractive."

"You're still quite attractive," I said with an underlying bitter tone. I couldn't help feeling her good looks were wasted on her.

"I developed a reputation for being frigid. It wasn't something I could help. I didn't enjoy necking and petting and going farther. I wasn't comfortable. The boys in school began to call me the 'No Girl.' They wrote it on my locker, made up jokes about me. One day, they even pasted a large 'NO' on my back in the morning without me noticing, and I was the laughingstock of the school without realizing why for quite a while."

"How horrible," I said. I couldn't help being impressed with her revelations. Here she had been presenting herself as Miss Perfect, brilliant, attractive, and stable even after a very sad home life.

"This other girl at the school, Donna Cameron, befriended me while my so-called best friends began to distance themselves from me. After all, I wasn't being invited to the same parties anymore or going on double dates.

"Talk about your man haters," she continued. "Donna would have castrated the entire male population if she could. She had been the object of ridicule most of her life and had developed a very hard crust. But she was very sympathetic to me and always willing to keep me company. Our friendship grew. We talked a great deal on the phone, shared homework, went to movies together. We never really talked about sex or how I was being treated. It was almost like a grade-school friendship, you know. Boys were still in the distance or considered competition.

"She told me about her own failed romances when she was younger, and one thing led to another. I began revealing more about my experiences, and then one night, when she slept over, we, she . . ."

"What?" I asked, unable to keep my curiosity under control.

"She touched me, and it excited me, and then she touched me again, and then we kissed, and then it just happened. Neither of us talked about it afterward. We began sleeping at each other's homes more often, and for the first time in my life, I felt complete, uncomplicated, at ease. I slowly sank into my true self, and I guess I have Donna to thank."

"What happened to her?"

"I don't know. After high school, we kept in touch for a short while. Then she joined the army, and we drifted apart. I'm sure she found someone else, and that was fine. I wouldn't have wanted to have with her what I have with Brenda."

She was quiet, just staring at the floor.

"Peter is the first boy I have ever really thought

about like that," I said. "Do you think that means anything?" I asked. "I mean, because it took me so long to have these feelings?"

She shrugged. "If I've learned anything, April, it's that questions like that are not to be answered flippantly. Anyone who gives you an answer is just parroting some child psychology textbook."

She patted me on the knee and stood up.

"Let things just happen. What's meant to be will be," she said. "Are you sure you just want two eggs for dinner? There's this interesting new Thai restaurant I've discovered, and those dishes are very low in calories and fat if you order correctly. They're very tasty, too. You don't have to suffer on a diet, despite what Brenda says about no pain, no gain."

"Okay," I said, smiling.

After she had been so forthcoming with me, I felt foolish being petulant. Considering all that occupied Brenda's mind these days, I realized I was lucky to have Celia.

"Good. I hate eating alone, and when your sister is involved in an event like this all-star game, she is horrible company. I might as well be sitting with a mannequin at dinner—or anywhere, for that matter. If I hear how stupid this coach's strategy is or how obvious his plays are one more time, I'll go down to the gymnasium and kill him myself," she said.

I laughed.

"Come in when you're ready, and we'll go to dinner," she said at the door.

"I asked Peter to join us at the game," I told her.

"Oh?"

"Brenda still has extra tickets, doesn't she?"

"Far as I know, she does. You'll have to check with

her and make sure she didn't give any to her old teammates. He's going, then?"

"Unless he thinks I'm an idiot and he doesn't want
to have anything to do with me."

She shrugged. "If he does, he does, and that's that,"
she said. She peered hard at me. "You move on, April.
You don't dwell on failures and regrets."

"Everyone says that in one way or another," I
replied, thinking about the advice Peter's grandfather
had given him.

"Then it must be true," Celia told me, and left.

I chose something to wear, washed my face, and
brushed my hair so it looked like something, and then
hurried across the yard to meet her and go to dinner. At
dinner, she talked more about her own youth, some of
the funnier things that had happened to her, the friends
she had in college before Brenda, and her ambitions.

The wall that I had been building between myself
and Celia began to crumble. It was horrible to think it,
but in some ways, I was beginning to appreciate her
more than my own sister. She appeared to notice it as
well and told me she wished I would think of her as
her new sister.

"We've got to remember that we only have each
other now. It's you, me, and Brenda against the rest of
the world, and you know what?"

"What?"

"We're going to do just fine. All of us," she said.

She reached across the table to squeeze my hand
gently and smiled.

Brenda was in a small rage when she returned home
after her practice. She said the coach had her boxed in
with his stupid plays. He was favoring a girl from his
own team, Charlotte Johnson.

"She's good, but she's not as good as I am," Brenda declared. "In just about every play he's designed, she finishes with the shot. I'm sorry I agreed to play in this game."

"I'm sure you'll do fine," Celia said.

"Aren't you listening to me? I hate playing under this man," she snapped back at Celia.

"She's only trying to make you feel better about it, Brenda," I said.

Brenda raised her eyebrows. "Oh," she said. "Thank you, Dr. Taylor." She looked at Celia. "You're beginning to rub off on people," she told her, and went into the bedroom.

"Don't worry about it," Celia said. "She'll calm down. She often goes through these sorts of tantrums right before the big game. It's pressure. Afterward, she'll hate herself for the way she was. I'll go talk to her," she said, rising.

"Don't forget about the tickets," I called.

After a few more minutes of television, which was really like a light bulb with moving shadows to me at the moment, I rose, too, and went to my apartment.

Brenda was calmer in the morning. Celia had asked her about the tickets, and she told me she had one for Peter.

"Let me know today for sure," she said. "Otherwise, I want to give it to Paula Grassman, one of my teammates."

"Okay," I said.

I looked for Peter during the school day and understood why it was always hard to find him between classes. He rushed out of his and was the first to enter the next class all the time. Other students lingered in the hallways, talking and socializing until the bell rang, and then rushed to their rooms before the late bell sounded thirty seconds later. He was on a different corridor most of the day, so I couldn't get into the hallway fast enough to catch him.

Lunchtime, however, I found him at his tree.

"Hi," I said. He glanced at me.

"Hi," he replied, turning his attention back to the sky.

"I didn't have any nightmares last night," I told him.

He looked at me to see if I was being serious.

"Of course, I didn't have any the night before, either," I added, and he laughed.

"Then we'll have to wait to see if it works for you or not," he said.

I sat beside him and opened my brown bag.

"Same lunch?"

"It's no secret I'm trying to lose weight," I told him. "I've been trying to do that for a long time. Every time I lose a few, I gain them back."

"You need to follow the medicine wheel," he said.

"What's that?"

"Everyone has four aspects to his nature. North is the physical realm; East is what we call the realm of knowledge, enlightenment; South is the spiritual realm; and West is the realm of introspective thought. When you walk the steps of your recovery, you choose a starting point and continue in a sunwise direction back to your origin. A circle has no true beginning or ending, so when you have traveled through the wheel back to where you started, you begin again, but with new understanding. It's something you do all your life."

"I don't understand how it works," I said.

He turned and drew a circle in the sand where I had drawn the chess board.

"The North is a place of beginning because it is a place of rebirth. You make a decision here to stop abusing your body. First, you have to recognize that you are damaging yourself. You can't do this until you see the connection between your physical and emotional self. You abuse yourself because you are angry inside. Attack this anger."

I nodded. "Yes, I am angry inside. How do I stop it?"

"Go to the East, the morning direction. Tell yourself you are worthwhile, that you have been given a sacred gift, life, and you have a right to be you. You need to find a balance between yourself and others, a harmony. Once you are aware of what is causing you to abuse yourself and others, you can begin to stop it.

"Look to the South," he said, nodding at the sky. "Recognize that there is a power greater than us. Turn to it for help. You must connect inside with yourself, with the most private part of you, and admit to your fears, your desires and emotions. This way, you will care for your own spirit.

"When you look to the West, you will see that the path to recovery, to your solving your problems, comes when you admit to yourself that no one can change you but you. In the end, you're responsible for yourself."

"Have you done this, traveled the wheel?"

"Yes, and I'm traveling it now," he said. He unbuttoned his shirt and showed me a medallion he wore around his neck.

My grandfather gave me this," he said. "This is a traditional medicine wheel." He turned it over. "On the back is a prayer to the Great Spirit."

I didn't understand it, of course. "What is the prayer?"

"This is a four-wind medallion. It says, 'Whose voice I hear in the wind.'"

"I wondered how you dealt with all your problems," I said.

He closed his shirt.

"Oh? So, how have I done it?" he asked.

"By being comfortable with who you are," I said, and he smiled.

"Start your own journey, April."

He went back to his sandwich, and I bit into my apple.

"Oh," I said. "My sister does have a ticket to the all-star game for you. Will you go?"

"I will go," he said.

"Good. I'll pick you up. I mean, we'll pick you up, Celia and I. She's really very nice, I've decided."

He laughed. "That's good."

We sat eating quietly. The first bell rang, and we rose to go into the building.

"I'll see you at chess," I said.

He nodded and walked off to his class. I stood watching him for a moment and then turned to go to mine. Dolores and her friends were grinning at me again. I smiled back at them.

I'd already learned a lesson from Peter Smoke. *If I'm comfortable with who I am*, I thought, *they'll never be able to hurt me.*

Peter and I had another good session. I was surprised myself at how much I remembered and some of the ideas I had for moves. I saw he was pleased. He didn't want me to take him home after school, however. He had other things to do that day for his aunt. We parted in the parking lot with plans to meet for lunch again. I told him what time I would be by to pick him up for the basketball game, and he made me reassure him that it was all right.

For the first time since we had left Hickory, I felt

excited and happy. I was determined to travel the medicine wheel, too. Neither Celia nor Brenda was home yet. I changed into a jogging suit and went on a run. I nearly got lost because I wasn't paying attention to where I was going. This time, when I arrived home and Brenda and Celia were there, they were both pleasantly surprised, especially Brenda.

"You started doing something intelligent without my telling you or nagging you," she said.

"I'm turning north," I said.

"Huh?" She looked at Celia to see if she understood. Celia shook her head. "What's that supposed to mean?"

"You'll see," I said, and went to shower and change for dinner.

Now that I had begun this circle, I hoped I would finish.

16

The Big Game

Peter and I had another good conversation at lunch, and this time, we went inside early enough for him to walk me to my classroom. After school, I took him home and then hurried home myself to prepare for what I considered now to be our first date. Celia was already giving Brenda her massage. Only Celia appeared to notice or care how excited I was about bringing Peter to the game. Brenda left first. She never ate much before a game, and I didn't want to eat much, either. My stomach was swirling, and I felt as if I had swallowed a hive of crazed bees.

I showered and washed my hair. While I was working on some makeup, Celia came to the door and surprised me with a tray of cheese and crackers and a glass of white wine for me as well as herself.

"A little can't hurt you," she said when she saw how astonished I was. "It will relax you. I know you're nervous. You're worried about making a good impression, hitting it off. First social occasions are always the most testy. Unless, of course, you've already established some intimacy with Peter," she added, studying my reaction.

"We're just friends right now," I said.

"Good. You're not sure if it will turn out to be something more. It's natural."

She handed me the wine. I sipped some and nibbled on a cracker and cheese while she sat on the tub and watched me decide how to wear my hair and do my face. She began to make suggestions. Except for Mama's occasional coaching, I had no one to guide me about my looks. Brenda never wore makeup and always kept her hair short.

"You have some very nice features, April," Celia said. "You have to learn how to highlight them, how to emphasize your eyes, for example."

"What do you mean?"

She took the eyeliner and mascara out of my hands and had me sit on the tub while she worked on my face. As she put on my makeup and chose what she thought was the right shade of lipstick for my complexion, she lectured about cosmetics. It was on the tip of my tongue to ask her how she knew so much about it and why all this was important to her if she wasn't interested in boys, but once again, she anticipated my questions.

"The truth is, we look good for ourselves. It makes us feel better and more confident about ourselves. Girls who dress and fix their faces just to please boyfriends are often not true to who they really are inside. It's like putting on a mask as far as they're concerned. They might have a boyfriend who hates their hair one way, even though that way really enhances their looks. I guess the trick is not to see yourself as someone else sees you but how you, yourself, see yourself. Does that make sense?"

"Yes," I said, thinking about Peter and the medicine wheel. "You have to be comfortable with who you are."

"Exactly. There," she said. "But before you look in the mirror, let me pluck these eyebrows a bit. You've never trimmed them?"

"No."

I waited while she did it, and then she said, "Okay, look in the mirror, and tell me what you think."

I stood up and gazed at myself. There was nothing I could do about my chubby cheeks, and I hated the way my nose looked so swollen because of the extra weight I carried, but Celia had done wonders with me. I never thought I could look glamorous, but the makeup did draw attention to my eyes, and somehow, I didn't look as obese as I felt. *Do I dare think of myself as pretty?* I wondered.

"There is an attractive girl in there, April. You've got to get down to her," she said.

Perhaps nothing else that was ever said to me, all the warnings and threats Brenda lay on me, for example, all the pleadings in Mama's eyes, all the nasty things Daddy had said during his Mr. Hyde days, had as much effect on me as Celia's words. *Yes, I've got to get down to myself. I've got to let myself out from under all this . . . fat.*

"Thank you," I told her.

She smiled and hugged me. I felt I had a friend, a real girlfriend. She even followed me into my little apartment to help me choose what to wear. I always favored black because of how much thinner I looked when I wore it. Celia was hesitant about it. She didn't like anything I had in black.

"Nothing does your figure any good," she said.

"What figure?" I asked, smirking.

"You'll see," she said. "Just a minute."

She ran out and returned with a light black sweater with a deep V-neck collar she said would be attractive with my black skirt. She brought along a pair of gold teardrop earrings and a pearl necklace she thought would complement the clothes.

Normally, I was very shy and self-conscious about anyone seeing me undressed, but Celia seemed not to notice my bulges. Her interest was solely in what made me more attractive.

"You're not wearing the proper bra," she decided when I was down to my bra and panties. "When was the last time you bought one?"

"I don't know. A few months ago, maybe more like six months ago."

"You've developed since. That's for sure," she said.

"Here's a way to test." She put her finger on the cleavage area of my bra and pressed. "See how my finger bounces in and out. The cups are too small."

She ran her finger along the front edges of my bra and down the seams of my arm. I felt a tingle shoot through my body to my spine, but I didn't wince.

"You have bulges all along here, April, and it's not only because of excessive weight. You've outgrown this. Damn, you should have let someone know so we could have taken you for some new undergarments. I hate those loose-fitting bloomers, too. They belong on old ladies. We're going shopping tomorrow, but for now . . ."

"What for now?"

"I'm going to lend you one of my older bras. It'll fit you. I'll be right back," she said, and hurried out again.

When she returned, she brought a black, strapless Wonder Bra.

"Go on," she said when she saw my hesitation. "Try it on."

I unfastened my bra and slid it off my shoulders and arms.

"Didn't you notice these stretch marks?" she asked me as I made the change and she studied my bosom. "You're really developing quickly, April. You've neglected yourself," she said, brushing her hand over my hair and cheek. "It's not your fault, though. You've been through so much. For a long time, you've really been alone. Go on. Put on my bra."

I did as she said and then looked at myself in the small mirror above the sink. The bra lifted my breasts and made my bosom looked twice as big. She came up beside me and handed me the sweater. When I put it on, my cleavage showed deeply in the V-neck collar. Wasn't that too revealing?

"Very attractive," Celia said before I could ask.

"I don't think Brenda's going to like it," I said. It did make me feel quite self-conscious.

"Brenda is too occupied with Brenda to even notice," she replied. "And you're not Brenda. You're you. C'mon, finish dressing. We have to get started and pick up your date."

I gazed at myself again and then finished dressing. If my nerves were on edge before, they were over the edge now, I thought.

"I just hate it when men claim a woman is too sexy or too provocative as an excuse for their own overt and obnoxious behavior. If you don't look like someone's granny, they are justified in groping and even raping you. The best to me is when these husbands criticize their wives for being too obvious but just drool over someone else's wife or some other sexy-looking woman," Celia lectured.

"Don't some women drool over men?" I asked.

"Sure, but nowhere in proportion. Gawking, leering, and lustful eyes are mainly male characteristics."

Thinking about some of the girls I knew at Hickory, I wasn't prepared to agree with her, but I said nothing. After all, she was the one with experience, not me.

Peter came out of the house the moment we turned into his driveway.

"Anxious boy," Celia said. "He must have been waiting at the window. That's positive."

I quickly introduced the two of them when Peter got into the car. In the shadows, he didn't quite see how I was made up or what I was wearing. Celia moved into the backseat. I was so nervous I accelerated without putting the car into reverse and almost drove into the garage door.

"Hey, relax!" Celia cried, laughing. "Do you always have that effect on women, Peter?"

"I don't know as I have any effect at all," he said. He kept his face forward.

"Oh, I'm sure a good-looking young man like you has an effect on the opposite sex."

He turned and looked at me rather than reply to her. I saw his eyes narrow as he drank me in. Then he turned away quickly, and this time, I backed out well and started away.

"April tells me you transferred here recently, too," Celia said.

"I've been here nearly a year," he told her.

"Do you like it here?"

"Yes," he said, "but I'm at home wherever I am."

"Really? What's that mean?"

"It means I see the earth as my home. Anywhere you go, you're under the same sky," he said.

Celia laughed. "You haven't been to some of the places I've been, or you wouldn't be so quick to say that."

"Maybe not," he said. "We travel different roads, but we usually end up in the same place."

"Very provocative," Celia continued. "I see why you're a chess expert."

"I'm not an expert."

"That's not what April tells me."

"It's all relative. She's just starting. A mediocre player looks like Mikhail Botvinnik."

"Who?"

"A Russian chess champion I admire," he said.

I gazed into the rearview mirror at Celia. She was shaking her head and laughing.

"Do you go to basketball games often?" Celia asked.

"This is my first here," Peter told her. "And I don't think I attended more than two at my previous school."

"It's a lot different from chess," she muttered.

"Not really," Peter said. "Strategy is strategy."

She began to ask him questions about his Indian heritage. I was happy when we pulled into the parking lot of the school where the game was being held. I knew what it was like to feel you were being interrogated.

"Sorry about all that," I whispered when we got out and started toward the gymnasium entrance. There was already quite a crowd at the door.

Peter said nothing. He didn't look at me, either.

We entered and took our seats in the bleachers. Now that we were under the bright lights, I couldn't help feeling self-conscious again. I was waiting anxiously for some comment from Peter about my hair, my face, anything. Instead, he concentrated on the game, the players.

"Who is your sister?" he asked.

"Oh. I'm so stupid not pointing her out. She's number eighteen," I told him.

He watched her warming up. "She looks strong," he said.

"Just wait until you see her in action," Celia bragged.

As it turned out, however, this was not one of Brenda's best games. I could see from her expressions and the way she moved at the start of the game that she was still quite upset with the coach. The plays he designed and the position she was in often caused her to be in awkward or more difficult places for her shots. The other team had a very quick series of successful plays, and as the game progressed, the distance between them and Brenda's team grew wider and wider. Twice Brenda was taken out and sat on the bench. She was there for almost the entire third period, in fact, and when she was put back in, she was raging and so aggressive she quickly fouled her opponent.

Peter said little about it. I made some comments about Brenda's unhappiness and how it was affecting her performance. Celia kept saying, "Oh, we're in for it now."

When the game ended, Brenda's team had lost by twenty points.

"Your sister is going to be fit to be tied. This is the worst. It would have been better if she hadn't been chosen," Celia said.

She turned to us as we were leaving the gymnasium.

"You two, just go off. I don't think it's a good time to have Peter meet Brenda."

"Okay," I said. I was eager to be alone with Peter, anyway, and I agreed with Celia. Brenda wouldn't be good company. "I'm sorry about all this," I said as we walked to my car. "It was supposed to be a fun night. Brenda is a much better player than the Brenda you saw playing this game. She hated her coach."

"Focusing on her dislike of him did nothing to help her," Peter said. "If a branch doesn't bend, it breaks."

"Brenda is very serious about her career in athletics. She could be in the Olympics," I said, a little annoyed with his comment.

"All I mean is she will have many coaches or people she dislikes, and she has to learn how to compromise and deal with it so she can still do her best," he said.

We got into the car. It wasn't until then that I realized I didn't know where we were going.

"You want to come to my place for a while?" I asked. "It's not much to see."

"Then why do you want me to see it?" he asked.

I suddenly felt so small. I could feel his attitude toward me changing. Whatever warmth there had been between us seemed lost.

"Let's go to my house," he said. "It's my aunt's bridge night, and she's out."

Well, that's good, I thought, and drove out of the school parking lot. Feeling even more nervous than I had at the start of the evening, I began to talk a blue streak about Brenda's athletic achievements, her trophies and honors, the scouts who had visited in Hickory, her plans to be a physical education teacher in a college, and the possibility that she really would play in the next Olympics.

"It's good that you have respect for your sister and

are so interested in her," Peter said. "Now you must have respect for and interest in yourself," he added.

I know he meant well, but the remark brought tears to my eyes because he sounded so critical.

I drove into his aunt's driveway, and we got out and entered the house.

"Would you like something to eat or drink?" he asked.

"Just some cold water. My throat is dry from cheering, I think."

He nodded and got me a glass of ice water and one for himself. Then we went to his room. He sat on his bed and looked at me.

"Why did you dress like this?" he asked.

"Dress like what?"

"Like you are dressed. The makeup, the clothes. Is this who you are?"

"I just tried to make myself look nice," I said.

He sipped his water. "I'm just surprised," he said, putting the glass on the nightstand.

"Don't you think I look nice?"

"I'm not sure if *nice* is the right word." He patted the bed. "Relax."

There was something about his expression that sounded alarm bells in me. I moved hesitantly to his side.

"We really don't know all that much about each other, do we?" he asked. "Every moment is a new discovery. It's not unlike competing against a new player in chess. You wait to see his or her moves and learn how he or she thinks. Only then can you make your own moves wisely."

"You can't compare everything to chess," I said.

"Why not? The world is a great board game to me, and most people in it are merely pawns."

He took the glass from my hand and leaned over to place it next to his own on the nightstand.

"So, I am to discover the real you tonight, is that it?" he said, smiling lustfully and bringing his face closer to mine.

"No. I wanted you to go to the game and see Brenda and . . ."

"You talk too much about your sister," he said, and then he kissed me.

He pulled back, grimacing at the taste on his lips.

"That lipstick," he said. "It's on you like a few layers of mint or something."

He leaned over to pluck some tissues out of a box and brought them to my lips, wiping hard.

"Hey," I said, pulling back when he actually began to hurt me.

"You don't need so much," he said. "And why did you put on so much eye makeup?"

"I thought I looked good."

"For a clown," he said. "You don't need it, in my opinion."

I turned away, and he reached out and put his hand under my chin.

"Just be yourself, April. Don't try to be anyone else."

"I am myself!" I declared firmly.

"Oh? Maybe you are," he said, and he kissed me again, this time bringing his hand off my shoulder and alongside my arm. The kiss was longer and harder. He then kissed me on my neck and moved his hand over my arm and then over my breast, pressing himself against me as he did so.

I lay back on the bed, and he surprised me by lifting my sweater and kissing me on my stomach, moving the sweater up to make a path for his lips. My heart was thumping so hard I was sure he could feel the beat in his face. When Peter reached behind to undo my bra, the memory of Luke's sexual attack came rushing back. For a moment, I actually saw Luke's face instead of Peter's. I couldn't help it. I began pushing him away.

"What is it? What's wrong?" he demanded.

"I can't. I . . . can't," I said, pulling my sweater down.

He got up and glared down at me, his face filling with blood. He looked more embarrassed than I was.

"You know, there is a name for girls who do what you do," he said, quickly exchanging humiliation for anger.

"What did I do?" I wailed.

"You take me home after school, you kiss me after meeting me only twice, you invite me out with you and dress like this, and then you come to my house, and when I try to be intimate with you, you push me away. You're playing with me," he accused.

"No. I don't mean to. I'm sorry."

"Forget it," he said, turning away. "You'd better leave. My aunt might be home soon, and she might not like me bringing a girl here at night."

"Don't be angry at me, Peter."

"I'm not angry at you. I'm angry at myself," he said.

"Go on home. It's better if you go," he insisted.

I rose, the tears floating over my eyes now finding the strength to climb over my lids and streak down my cheeks. He kept his back to me.

"I'm sorry," I said. "I really am."

He said nothing, and the way he kept his shoulders up made me think every word I said, my very presence, was unpleasant for him.

"Good night," I mumbled, and hurried out of his house.

Just as I was opening the car door, another car pulled up beside mine. I saw his aunt looking at me with great interest. She was a dark-haired woman with a face rounder and more chubby than mine. Before she could get out of her car and ask me anything, I got into mine, started the engine, and backed out of the driveway. The tires squealed as I accelerated and pulled away.

I don't know how I drove home without getting lost or getting into an accident. I was crying so hard at one traffic light that I missed the change, and the drivers in four cars behind me sounded their horns. The angry blasts shot me forward again.

Neither Brenda nor Celia was home when I arrived, which pleased me. I hurried into my small apartment and scrubbed every bit of makeup off my face. I took off Celia's sweater and bra and sprawled on my bed, burying my face in the pillow to stop my sobbing. All I could see in my mind was Peter's look of condemnation and disgust.

Why had I pushed him away so hard and so frantically? Why couldn't I see him and not Luke? Why had I gone to his home, to his room, if I didn't want him to kiss me and make love to me? My own actions confused me as much as I imagined they confused him. *I'm such a little idiot,* I thought. *I'll never be happy.*

I didn't fall asleep. I just lay there staring at the ugly bland wall with the glow of my small ceiling fixture spilling gauzelike shadows down to the floor. I felt numb, almost as if I had left my own body, a body I had come to despise. Not only was my body awkward and heavy, it was full of betrayal. It let me dress it up so I could be optimistic about Peter's affections toward me, and then as soon as he showed desire, my body reacted with reflexes of rejection. It snapped like a body of rubber bands to retreat from his touch, his kiss, his caresses. What good was a body like mine? If I could take a knife and trim it down like a piece of soap being sculpted, I would. I was raging inside, my hands fisted, my teeth clenched, my eyes bulging with anger.

Suddenly, there was a soft knock on my door. At first, I thought it was in my imagination, but I heard it again and again, and then I heard Celia call.

"April?"

"What?"

She opened the door and entered. I forgot I was lying on my bed naked. She stood there a moment staring at me and then closed the door softly.

"What happened?"

I turned my head away. "I made a fool of myself," I mumbled.

She came to the bed and sat beside me, putting her hand on my shoulder.

"How? Why? Everything seemed all right."

"It wasn't. Right from the start, it wasn't," I cried through my tears. "I shouldn't have dressed like that. He thought I was . . . was a tramp."

"Oh, that's ridiculous. You looked so attractive. Maybe he's just not right for you. This could have been a good thing, April.

"I had such a time with your sister," she continued. "I've seen her uptight before, but not like this. It took all this time to calm her down. Apparently, she had some words with the coach afterward, too. She didn't want anything to eat. She drank too much. I just left her heaving in the bathroom.

"So, tell me what happened, exactly. Where did you go after the game?"

I sighed, sucked in my breath, and turned toward her. "I asked him if he wanted to come here, but he didn't. We went to his house. His aunt wasn't home yet."

"Oh. So he invited you to his home."

"Only to bawl me out and then to . . . to . . ."

"To do you, as they say," she filled in, and twisted her lips with sarcasm. "Take advantage?"

"He thought it was what I wanted. I thought it was, too."

"So, what happened?"

"I couldn't . . . I panicked. I . . . I don't know."

"You're at the age when those feelings are so confusing," she said, her voice softening. "Your body and your mind can easily be on two different tracks, going in different directions. I remember too well having experiences just like the one you had tonight."

"I doubt it."

"Oh, no. There's nothing unusual about what you've just gone through, April. You're actually just exploring, discovering. Don't be discouraged."

"Some exploration. I practically leaped out of my skin when he started to . . . to really touch me."

"It just wasn't the right fit," she said, smiling at me, brushing my hair away from my forehead. "Except for yourself and that terrible incident you experienced back in Hickory with those disgusting boys and that girl, no one has ever touched you in these places, right?"

I nodded.

"First, there is the surprise and then the confusion about how you should react. Everyone you speak to and everything you read tells you one thing, and then, perhaps, you discover something new about yourself you never expected. Am I right?"

"Yes," I said, nodding.

She smiled. "The worst thing is, some parents, many people, self-important religious people, especially, tell you these feelings are evil. They make you think your body is dirty for having these feelings. They lay such guilt on you, which only makes it all more confusing and in the end drives people crazy or into doing things that are bad for them. You must not be afraid of yourself," she said.

She stroked my cheeks and then leaned down and kissed me on the forehead. "In your face, I see myself as a young girl," she told me.

She put her hand on my neck and squeezed between my neck and shoulder. "You're so tight. Your body is like a brick right now."

"I know," I said.

"Close your eyes, relax. Let me help you the way I help your sister," she said, and moved so she could help me into a sitting position while she massaged my neck and shoulders. "How's that feel?"

"Good," I said.

"Sure it does." She surprised me by kissing my neck. "Just relax. Let yourself drift. Let your body soak in its own capacity for pleasure and comfort."

She spoke so softly, her words and voice hypnotizing. I did relax. Her hands moved over my shoulders, kneading my muscles, softening where I was hard and tight.

"Did he touch you here?" she asked, her fingers moving down over my breasts to my nipples. They hardened instantly.

"Yes."

"And that's when you pushed him away?"

"Yes."

"But right now, you don't want to push me away, do you?"

I thought I was losing my ability to breathe. I couldn't even speak. Her fingers were over and under my breasts, her lips grazing my neck.

"You need to know what this feels like. You need to be prepared," she said. "Just relax. Try to enjoy the feelings. You do enjoy them, don't you?"

I still didn't speak. Confusion made me mute.

She moved so I would lie back again, and then she lifted her blouse, undid her own bra, and sat beside me again. I was unable to speak or take my eyes from her breasts. She lifted my hand and brought it to her breast, moving it over her nipple. My arm tightened, but I didn't pull my hand away.

She moaned. "See? See how this can be wonderful if the match is comfortable. You weren't comfortable with him."

I wanted to tell her that wasn't it. I wanted to tell her how I had relived Luke's attack on me and how that had most to do with it, but she was moving over me, kissing me where Luke had kissed me, until she was nearly down to the small of my stomach.

Her fingers moved over the sides of my hips and came around to touch me where, as she had said, only I had touched myself.

Just at that moment, the door opened, and Brenda stood there wavering.

I was positive that when someone was shot with a gun or a rifle, this was how they felt. The electric spike that went through my heart and into my spine made me gasp and cry out. Celia sat up, surprised. She saw where I was looking and turned to see Brenda glaring at us.

"Oh," Celia said, "we were just . . ."

"You don't have to tell me what you were doing, Celia. I think I know what you're doing. You're both . . . disgusting." She backed out, slamming the door.

I started to cry immediately.

Celia rose quickly, put on her bra and her blouse, mumbling to me that I shouldn't worry. She would explain everything.

"She's just still quite drunk," she added, and left.

I lay there unable to move, my body feeling as though it had liquefied into a pool of jelly. Until I sat up, I didn't even realize how hard and fast my heart was pounding. It was taking my breath away. I actually thought I might have a heart attack or my heart would just explode in my chest.

When I stood up, I was dizzy, so I had to sit again and wait. Finally, I was able to go to the bathroom and throw cold water on my face. I put on my robe and opened the door just to look at the house. I heard Brenda screaming at Celia, calling her names, and then I was shocked to hear her call me names, too. Her anger was spilling over everyone. She was running people together, cursing, berating my father, Mama, Celia and me, coaches, anyone or everyone she had any contact with. The shouting seemed to go on for twenty minutes before she stopped and there was a heavy silence.

Should I go to her? I wondered. *Should I explain?* This wasn't my fault. I hadn't asked Celia to come to me. *Why does she hate me so much? She'll hate me even more now. Every time she'll look at me, she'll see what she saw happening here.*

I stepped back and closed the door. Then I sat on my bed and thought.

Here I was in a school I hated to be in, living in a small shack, and now rejected by the one person at the school I thought would like me. Here I was living with my sister and her lover, and my sister, who was never really overjoyed about having to care for me, now saw me as someone evil and disgusting.

Whom did I have? Who was I, really? Would I ever find my name, as Peter predicted? He was so good for me. He made me think of so many wonderful things. Now, I couldn't see myself returning to the chess club and sitting across from him.

What should I call all this, checkmate? Had life, Bad Luck, proved too difficult to defeat? I had lost *en passant*. Just passing through here, I had been thwarted, vanquished, beaten again.

I don't belong anywhere, I thought.

And then I thought, *I know where I should be. I know where being nowhere is.*

I rose and dressed in a shirt, sweater, jeans, and sneakers. Then I packed my small bag, making sure to include Mr. Panda.

It was hours later now, close to four in the morning. I moved very quickly but very quietly, crossing the yard and then opening the back door of the main house as quietly as I could. I tiptoed in and listened. Brenda was probably dead to the world now, sleeping off her drunken stupor. However, she would never sleep off her anger. I knew how she could harbor hate and wrath so well and for so long. She was, after all, always a competitor. What had happened between Celia and me was clearly a defeat in her eyes. She would never forgive. Her philosophy was to defeat, defeat, defeat, and never look back at the enemy you've crippled and smashed.

I moved softly past their bedroom into the kitchen and, as quietly as I could, opened the drawer that I knew housed some of the important papers. The one I was looking for was in there. I had seen it before. It was toward the bottom. I found it easily and clutched it in my left hand. Then I went to the pantry and found the can on the shelf that had our household funds. There was nearly five hundred dollars. I took it all.

They'll get more in the morning, I thought. *They don't need it.*

Again, moving as though I were walking on a shelf of air, I went down the short corridor. I was shocked to discover Celia sleeping in the living room on the sofa. I paused and stared at her for a moment, and then I slipped out the front door and hurried to my car.

When I got in, I took another deep breath and asked myself if this was truly what I wanted to do.

It is, was my reply.

I turned the key in the ignition, and, without putting on the headlights, because I knew the glow would light up the living room and maybe wake Celia, I backed out of the driveway. Then I turned on the lights and drove slowly to the corner. I made a right turn onto the boulevard and headed toward the highway that would take me west.

On the seat beside me was the paper I had needed. It was Uncle Palaver's schedule. I knew where he was now and where he would be tomorrow.

Tomorrow had become the most important word in my mind, because tomorrow, I would be where I belonged.

Nowhere.

Traveling everywhere. This is why Uncle Palaver was so happy on the road, I thought. No one could claim him, and he didn't have to set roots down anywhere. He moved with the wind, when he had a whim, and it was in that movement that he found comfort and security.

What was it Peter had told Celia when she asked

him if he liked being where he was? "I see the earth as my home. Anywhere you go, you're under the same sky."

That's all that mattered, being under the same sky. The rest of it was just . . . just window dressing.

It had to be wonderful to leave the past behind and look only to the future.

I used to hate the word *soon.* I used to hate to have to depend on tomorrow.

But at this moment, it was the only word that was full of promise.

Everything else was spoiled by defeat, by sadness, by mistakes.

So, good-bye, Brenda. Good-bye, memories of Mr. Hyde. Good-bye, the horror of Mama's death. Good-bye, the discomfort of an unpleasant new home. Good-bye to it all.

And hello to tomorrow.

In fact, as I drove on, I could see the light of a new day creeping up the horizon, driving the shadows and darkness back into hiding.

Was I just fooling myself one more time?

17

April's Adventure

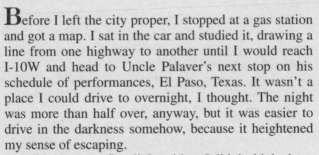

Before I left the city proper, I stopped at a gas station and got a map. I sat in the car and studied it, drawing a line from one highway to another until I would reach I-10W and head to Uncle Palaver's next stop on his schedule of performances, El Paso, Texas. It wasn't a place I could drive to overnight, I thought. The night was more than half over, anyway, but it was easier to drive in the darkness somehow, because it heightened my sense of escaping.

I didn't stop at first light, either. I didn't think about being tired, but when it was nearly midday, I realized I was very thirsty and even a little hungry. I pulled off at the next exit and found my way to a fast-food restaurant where they served breakfast in the form of eggs in a muffin. I had some juice and coffee and took a coffee to go. I wanted to drive and drive and drive, because as long as I was moving, I wasn't thinking about what I had done.

By now, I realized both Brenda and Celia would have discovered I had gone. They would have no idea how far I had driven or what my intentions were. I could just hear Brenda saying, "She'll be back. She's just having a tantrum. I don't want to waste any time worrying about her."

Or maybe they would have another row and would break up over what had occurred. In Brenda's mind, I would surely be the cause of it somehow. She was always fonder of Celia than she was of me. I'd have to have been the cause of the unhappiness. If I had remained in that house after Celia left her or she had left Celia, it would have been horrible. I was very wise to leave, I concluded.

When I was on highway I-20W, I realized I was weaving too much from lane to lane. Despite my determination, fatigue was settling in so deeply it had reached my bones. My eyelids were continually drooping. It was nearly five o'clock, and I had to think of stopping to eat something, anyway. I was angry at myself for not being able simply to drive all day and all night until I had reached El Paso and found Uncle Palaver. Once again, this hateful body of mine was disappointing me. I took the next exit, and this time, I had to drive a few miles before finding what looked like an old-fashioned roadside diner. I saw the trailer trucks in the parking lot and imagined it was a popular stop. I remembered Daddy telling us that when you travel on highways in America, you should look for parking lots full of tractor trailers.

"Those truck drivers know where the good food is," he said.

That seemed so long ago now. It was truly as if I had led two lives. I listened hard and closely to everything my daddy said during those days. He was truly a heroic figure to me, handsome, successful, and strong in so many ways. I thought there was nothing he didn't know and nothing he could not do. When little girls discover their fathers are just men, it's the first step toward the end of innocence. We don't want to take that step. We resist, but it's a battle fought in vain. I had to wonder, though, if Brenda had ever gone through it. Maybe that was the biggest difference between us after all. Brenda never had any childhood faiths to be broken. Brenda was born with realism in her eyes. Make-believe and fantasy were a waste of her time, detours that made no sense to her.

In the end, perhaps she was right, I thought. She faced no disillusionment, and the only disappointments she had were of her own making. There were no mornings filled with dark depression and fear when bubbles of dreams popped.

I pulled into the parking lot, parked, and got out after gazing at myself in the mirror and doing the best I could not to look totally disheveled and wild. It would be enough that I was a young girl traveling alone. I didn't need to do anything else to attract attention. When I entered, I tried to be as inconspicuous as I could be, keeping my eyes low, my head down, following the hostess to a booth way in the rear of the diner.

The place was very busy and occupied almost exclusively with truck drivers. I saw two women who looked as if they might be riding along with their husbands, but otherwise no other females. Three counter men and two short-order cooks were working feverishly to keep up with the orders and demands two very overworked waitresses shouted. The din of conversation was so loud I didn't realize there was country music playing over the speakers until I had sat myself and gazed at the menu.

The moment I did so, I saw Brenda's critical eyes watching me while she was waiting to hear what fattening food I would order. It was ironic how even after all that had happened and even though I was in flight from her as much as from anything, I could still hear her advice and her criticism and care about it.

I ordered water to drink and the roast chicken and vegetable plate with no bread. My waitress nodded almost as if she had expected no less and scooped up the menu before I could have a change of heart. I noticed one of the younger truck drivers gazing at me from the next booth. He smiled, and I quickly shifted my eyes to the window.

Night was falling faster because the sky was growing increasingly overcast. It's going to rain, I thought. I hated driving and riding in the rain. It always made the trip seem longer to me. There wasn't a sound more monotonous than the sound of the windshield wipers going steadily. Without realizing what I was doing, I closed my eyes and leaned a little more against the imitation faded red leather back of my seat. The drone of conversation, the clank of dishes and silverware, and the vague background of the country music worked like a lullaby. When the waitress returned with my dinner, I heard laughter and snapped my eyes open. All the men with the young truck driver were gazing at me and smiling.

"Are you all right, honey?" the waitress asked.

"Yes," I said quickly. "Just a little tired."

"Where are you going?"

"To see my uncle," I said.

"You better be careful driving in this weather if you're that tired," she said.

The demands of the other customers prevented her from asking any more or giving any more advice. I was happy about that but disgusted at myself once again.

I began to eat. The young truck driver slipped out of his booth and came over to mine. He was tall and lean, with very dark brown eyes and a sharp nose and jaw line. I saw he had a small scar on his chin. His brown hair was cut very close on the sides.

"You were dead asleep a few moments ago," he said. "You feeling sick?"

"No," I said. "I'm fine. I was just a little tired."

"How far have you driven?"

I glanced at the other drivers in his booth. They were all looking at us and smiling.

"She's too young for you, Dirk," one of them called, and they all laughed when someone else said, "That's how he likes 'em. Fresh eggs."

Dirk slipped in across from me and folded his hands on the table. "How far?" he asked.

"From Memphis," I said.

He nodded and looked impressed. "Where you going?"

"I'm going to El Paso," I replied. I was too tired to think of any lies, and I didn't care about what he thought, anyway. I continued to eat.

"All by yourself?"

I thought about Brenda and especially about Celia and how she would react to some man just making himself at home in her booth and poking into her business.

"You see anyone else with me?" I shot back at him.

"Whoa," he said, looking away. "You're a tough one, huh?"

"No. I didn't ask you to sit here," I added. My blood

was rising into my neck. I was very frightened but battled down anything that would show it.

"I'm just making conversation," he said. "You know how to get to where you're going?"

"Yes, thank you," I said.

"It's not a few hours away, you know. If you want a suggestion about where to stop, there's a motel about seventy-five miles west of here I'd recommend. It's inexpensive and clean. It's called Dryer's. Owner's name is Fred Dryer, and either he or his son Skip runs the office."

I didn't say anything. I kept eating. The food was okay but quite bland. It was nothing special to me. Daddy wasn't right. His rule wasn't always true. Was this what would happen to me my whole life, making discoveries that contradicted the things my daddy had told me and I had treated like gospel?

"How old are you?" Dirk asked.

"Do you mind?" I answered, and glared back at him, trying to look as tough as I could.

"Suit yourself. Just trying to be helpful," he said, rising.

His friends rode him with jeers and laughter as he returned to their booth. I was happy to see them all leave before I was finished.

"Happy trails," Dirk told me. I didn't reply.

"Can I get you anything else, honey?" the waitress asked. I ordered a coffee to go, and then paid and got into my car.

It was much darker now. I turned on my headlights, and just as I pulled out of the parking lot, the drizzle began. I turned on the radio to drown out the sound of the windshield wipers, sipped on my coffee, and continued down the highway. The rain got heavier and heavier. The wipers had trouble keeping up, and for long periods, I had to really slow down. When a car pulled in front of me abruptly, I hit my brakes and skidded to the side, drawing blaring horns from the cars whipping past.

All I needed now was to get into an accident, I thought. I practically crawled along when I resumed. The rain was not letting up. Finally, I gave in and decided I had to stop somewhere. I took the next exit and saw a billboard advertising the motel Dirk, the young truck driver, had recommended.

At least something good came of his poking into my business, I thought, and pulled into the motel driveway, stopping under the overhang in front of the office. I got out and went inside. I had to hit a bell to bring out an older balding man who had bushy gray sideburns and a light rust mustache.

"I need a room," I said. "It's raining too hard."

He squinted at me and then stepped up to the counter.

"We don't rent to anyone less than eighteen," he said. "You got proof you're more than eighteen?"

"Why is that?"

"Too many runaways these days," he replied.

"I'm heading to visit my uncle in El Paso. I'm not running away," I offered. He bit the side of his mouth and looked as if he were chewing on my answer. "I met Dirk at a diner, and he told me to stop here," I added quickly.

"Dirk Pearson? You know Dirk?"

"I just met him, but he thought this was a good stopover."

"Oh. Well, if Dirk recommended you, then I guess it's okay," he said.

I let out a breath and signed the book. When I paid him in cash, he looked very suspicious again. He gave me the key to room 8C and told me where it was. I had to drive around the corner of the building to an adjoining section that looked like an after-thought. I saw two tractor trailers parked in the lot and about four other cars. It was raining so hard now I was nearly soaked to the skin just going from my car to the motel-room door. The key didn't work too easily, either, and it took a few tries to get the door opened.

When I got inside, I went right to the bathroom and wiped my soaked hair. The room did look all right, even though the furniture was very worn and faded, and the lighting was dull, giving everything a yellow-ish glow. The table by the bed was stained with ciga-rette burns, but the sheet and the cover sheet were clean. The sight of the pillow and mattress was so inviting it wouldn't have mattered much if it was filthy, I thought.

I put on a long nightshirt and, without brushing my teeth or anything, crawled into bed. The rain on the roof sounded like flocks of birds pecking away. It was constant enough to drone me into a deep sleep, how-ever, and moments later, I was drifting into a wel-comed silence.

Before morning, I was visited by terrible night-mares. The one that snapped my eyes open and made me shudder was the vision of that young truck driver, Dirk, sitting in the chair across from my bed, watching me sleep and smiling. When I did open my eyes, I was so unfamiliar with my surroundings I was sure the sil-houette I saw was indeed him. I couldn't breathe. After a moment, I realized it was not anyone. It was the standing lamp.

I turned on the lights and gazed around. The rain had stopped or nearly stopped. The clock at the side of the bed read five-twenty. I was still quite tired and decided to sleep a few more hours, so I turned off the light and lay back again.

I'm alone, I thought. *I might be alone for a very long time. I had better get used to being frightened, and I had better get tougher inside, or I'll have to crawl back to Brenda and Celia.*

It was actually hunger that woke me again. I had slept more than a few hours. It was nearly nine o'clock. My stomach growled, and visions of eggs and bacon, soft rolls and butter, juice and coffee came rushing at me. I had eaten so little. It didn't surprise me, but I was determined to control my hunger.

The next time Brenda sees me, I thought, *she won't be able to recognize me.*

Interesting, I realized as I washed and dressed, how I expected to see Brenda again and even soon. What kind of a runaway was I?

I got into my car quickly, and stopped at the office to return the room key. This time, there was a young man behind the counter. He had beady black eyes and hair down his neck and over his ears that actually looked like a black mop had been draped over his head. He was unshaven and had a cigarette, unlit, dangling out of the corner of his mouth.

He looked surprised when I appeared. Then he remembered what I imagined his father had told him.

"You're 8C," he said.

"Not anymore," I told him, dropping the key on the counter. "Where's the closest place to get some breakfast?"

"Child's, between here and the highway," he replied. He looked either so bored or so exhausted himself that he would have to keep his eyes open with paper clips.

I thanked him and left.

At Child's, which was a very busy little restaurant, I ordered a glass of orange juice and two soft-boiled eggs. The aroma of bacon and ham and the sight of stacks of delicious pancakes with syrup running down the sides made my stomach twist and turn in agony, but I held to my dieting and even decided to drink my coffee black. I ate as quickly as I could, so I wouldn't be confronted with all the good food, and got back onto the highway after I got gas again.

I got onto I-10W and felt more energized knowing I was closing in on Uncle Palaver's location. Before I reached El Paso, I stopped again and this time had a salad with a glass of water. My stomach was beginning to rebel, demanding more and not letting my hunger pangs stop, but I just drank more water instead of ordering anything else.

When I reached El Paso, I pulled into a gas station and got directions to the theater where Uncle Palaver was performing. It turned out to be out of the city, farther west on the I-10 highway. I made a few wrong turns and didn't reach the theater until it was nearly six-thirty. The box office wasn't yet open, but there was a big poster of Uncle Palaver and Destiny.

The theater itself looked like a converted old warehouse. I had no idea where Uncle Palaver might have parked his motor home, so I thought the best thing to do was wait for the box office to open to see if I could get any information. I sat in the car and watched people begin to arrive. Finally, the box office opened, and I got out.

The woman inside was finishing organizing her change when I stepped up.

"Can you tell me where I could find Palaver?" I asked her.

"Inside at seven-thirty," she replied dryly without so much as glancing at me.

"No, I mean now," I said.

She looked up, annoyed. Her hair looked as if it had been molded out of wire and glued to her head. She had so much makeup on that anyone would have assumed she was part of the show.

"What?" she asked, squinting.

"I need to see him beforehand. I'm his niece, and I just drove in from Tennessee, actually."

She raised her eyebrow and pulled her lower lip back and in so far it created two thin gullies along her chin.

"Drove in from Tennessee?"

"Yes, ma'am."

"Well, I have no idea where he is. I just sell tickets here. He'll be here at seven-thirty. Do you want a ticket, or don't you?"

Four people had come up behind me and were waiting. Other people had parked and were entering the theater.

"Yes," I said quickly, not knowing what else to do.

I paid for the ticket and entered the theater. This wasn't the way I wanted to surprise him, but perhaps it would have to do. Unfortunately, the first five rows were already filled. I found the closest seat I could and sat waiting. The theater probably didn't hold more than three hundred or so people, so it filled up quickly. I guessed that Uncle Palaver's television appearances and other publicity must be working for him.

I realized, of course, that I had never seen one of Uncle Palaver's shows. None of us had. We had only the news clippings and pictures. I was very excited and eager for him to know I was here. I sat waiting for the curtain to open. I had worn the watch he had given me some time ago at Brenda's basketball game. There was only ten minutes to the start of his and Destiny's performance. Everyone around me seemed genuinely excited. I was proud and happy for Uncle Palaver. He was a success after all.

Just before seven-thirty, the curtain began to inch open, and the lights dimmed around us. A spotlight widened on the center of the stage and then suddenly went off and then on like a blink of an eye. There before us was Destiny, seated on a chair, only . . .

I leaned forward. *What was this? Some gimmick?* A hush came over the audience.

This wasn't Destiny herself. It was a life-size doll. A moment later, Uncle Palaver stepped out dressed in a tuxedo and top hat. The audience applauded, and he smiled, bowed, and looked at the doll.

"Nice crowd, Destiny," he said.

The doll's head turned ever so slowly as if it were panning the audience. Then the doll nodded, and its mouth moved. We heard, "It's a crowd. How do you know they're nice?"

People laughed. *He's a ventriloquist, too,* I thought. Funny how we never knew and he never did any of that at our house.

"Well, we'll soon find out," Uncle Palaver said. "Let's get some of them up here."

He stepped off the stage and picked out a half dozen members of the audience and had them go up to the stage. As he had them introduce themselves, he performed his sleight-of-hand tricks, pulling what would be embarrassing things out of their ears, and somehow, out of their jacket and pants pockets. He had an elderly man reach into his own pocket and come out with a folded-up *Playboy* magazine centerfold. The man's face turned red-dye-number-eight red, and his wife, who was in the audience, howled, causing the audience to roar. He swore he hadn't put that in his pocket. Uncle Palaver turned to the doll and asked its opinion, and it said he should have the gentleman look in his rear pocket now. Nervously, he did, and when he produced another folded centerfold, the audience applauded vigorously.

Every time Uncle Palaver performed a trick, he turned to the life-size doll of Destiny, and it moved its mouth and offered a comment. Where was Destiny herself? I wondered, and looked to the corners of the stage, expecting her to step out any moment.

She didn't.

Following the tricks, he then somehow managed to hypnotize the entire group right before our eyes. He had them do very silly things which Destiny suggested. The audience loved it. After that, he woke them all, and they looked sincerely confused. He thanked them, and they returned to their seats.

His ventriloquist act continued, with Destiny singing while he drank a glass of water. Almost everything he did now drew applause. The next part of his act involved what he called his psychic memory. One of the ushers in the theater went down the aisle, choosing people to stand. Each person recited his or her name, and then he guessed their ages within a year or two. My heart thumped when the usher reached our row, but he didn't choose me. After no fewer than fifty were chosen and had recited their names, Uncle Palaver asked them to sit.

He put his hand on the doll's shoulder and leaned down to hear what looked like a whisper. He turned back to the audience and began calling out the names of each who had stood. When he or she stood, he, leaning in front of the doll each time, then gave back his or her name and age. He didn't make a single mistake, and when all fifty were standing, the audience cheered and applauded.

He thanked the volunteers who sat and then began to brag about his capabilities. I thought he was being a little too immodest when, suddenly, the life-size doll screamed, "Aren't you being a little self-centered? You couldn't do any of this without me."

He then got into an argument with the doll about who was more important. Finally, he said, "Okay, smarty-pants. Let's see how you do without me."

He marched off the stage, and all we saw now was the doll sitting and staring out at us. Everyone assumed the same thing. Uncle Palaver would return, and the doll would have to admit it was totally dependent upon him. But that's not what happened.

What happened brought the audience to its feet, including me.

Suddenly, without Uncle Palaver there, the doll's head moved from side to side, it leaned a bit toward us, and its mouth opened.

"Is he gone?" it asked without him there.

The curtain closed to thunderous applause and then opened again for Uncle Palaver to take his bows. He pointed to the doll, and it leaned forward. We were actually applauding it as if it were alive.

Everyone began to leave. I tried to rush out to get backstage quickly, but people were moving so slowly. Finally, I did. A stagehand stopped me, and I told him who I was and asked to see my uncle. He said he was leaving from the rear door, so I crossed the stage and made my way back just in time to see Uncle Palaver carrying the doll in his arms and heading for the motor home, which had been parked behind the building.

I called to him, and he turned slowly. At first, he looked as if he didn't recognize me. I moved closer, and then his eyes widened.

"April? What are you doing here?" he asked.

"It's a long story, Uncle Palaver, a long, terrible story, but I've come to be with you because I have nowhere else to go," I said.

He looked at the doll as if he expected it to say something, to ask something, and I thought I saw him whisper in its ear.

"Come inside," he said, and walked up the short steps into his motor home.

I followed quickly and watched him carry the doll through the motor home to the rear, where his bedroom was located.

"Just a minute," he said, and went inside, closing the door.

I stood there gazing around. The motor home was as I remembered it, only it wasn't as neat. There were dishes in the sink and clothing strewn about the small living room area.

"Okay," Uncle Palaver said, coming out of the bedroom. "Tell me what's going on."

He sat on the small settee, and I sat across from him.

Where do I begin? I wondered. *How do I explain it without embarrassing myself?* I began by giving him details about our move, my entrance to a new school, my friendship with Peter Smoke. I rambled on and on, skirting the crisis that had sent me fleeing from Brenda. He listened politely, but I could see he was getting impatient.

"Why did you run away?" he finally demanded.

I took a deep breath and revealed the relationship Brenda had with Celia. He didn't look surprised. He nodded and listened.

"That's who your sister is. You shouldn't have run away from her."

"That wasn't the reason," I replied, and then told him about my last night. I didn't get into actual details, but I gave him enough to widen his eyes and get him to understand why I had to leave.

"I see," he said. "That is unfortunate. Well, we should call Brenda and let her know you're all right."

"No," I said sharply. "She'll only tell you to send me back. I don't want to go back, ever!"

He sat back, staring at me. I looked toward the bedroom and then asked him about Destiny.

"Where is she?"

He let his head fall back and gazed up at the ceiling with his mouth open so long I thought he had either fainted with his eyes open or fallen asleep.

"She's tired," he said, looking at me again. "She's exhausted, matter of fact. Remember the illness I described?"

"Yes. But where is she?"

"She's in bed," he replied, as if it were very obvious. "I've explained about you," he added.

I nodded. "I don't want to be any burden. I'll help you with her, with anything."

"That's nice," he said, looking terribly sad.

"How long have you had that life-size doll of her?"

"Forever, it seems," he told me. "We're an act now. We're inseparable."

"I never knew you were such a good ventriloquist," I said.

"I'm not," he replied. "Are you hungry? I usually eat something before I set out. I have crazy hours,

April. I don't live like most people. Sometimes, I drive all night and sleep all day until show time. I'll do that tonight. You can fix the bunk above the cab there the way you did when you were just a little girl," he said, smiling. "Until we decide what you should do, that is."

"I'd like to help you with your act, too, and be with you, Uncle Palaver. I can be your assistant. I'd like to be on the road. I have no place to call home anymore."

"Oh, I don't know about that," he said. "A girl your age on the road constantly. I don't know." He shook his head.

"You're the only one I have now," I whined. "Please. If you don't help me, I don't know where I'll go or what I'll do."

He thought a moment and gently nodded.

"Okay, we'll see," he said. "We'll see. Hungry?"

"A little, but I'm watching my diet."

"Well, I don't have much. I'm not the cook your mother was. I was just going to have some tuna fish on a bun and a cup of coffee," he said.

"I'll fix it for you," I offered quickly, and went to the refrigerator.

When I opened it, I was shocked to see how little he did have.

"You're not taking care of yourself, Uncle Palaver. Lucky I've arrived," I said, and he finally smiled.

I had to clean the coffee pot and wash some dishes first. While I did so, he returned to the bedroom. I heard him talking and thought Destiny was awake now. Perhaps he would finally introduce me to her. He came out and didn't mention her, however.

We sat at the small table and ate. I just had a scoop of his tuna and black coffee. He spoke about some of his shows, and I asked him questions about the tricks he performed. Once again, as always, he reminded me that a true magician never reveals his secrets.

"How did you get the doll to move its head and open its mouth like that?"

"It's never easy," he replied. "Sometimes, she refuses to cooperate."

I laughed, but he didn't crack a smile.

"What about your car?" he asked me. "Where is it?"

"In the parking lot," I told him.

"Okay. Drive it around. I have a hitch on the back of the motor home, so we can attach it easily enough."

"Thank you, Uncle Palaver. I'm so happy to be with you," I added.

"I'm sorry for all your troubles, April. Your mother would want me to do all I can. We've got to think hard about your future. This isn't a life for a girl your age. But for now," he added, seeing my disappointment, "we'll do what we can."

"Thank you," I said, and went to get my car. He was waiting outside when I pulled around the building.

"I can do this fine by myself," he said. "Take what you need into the motor home, and fix the bunk for yourself. I'll be right in, and then we'll be getting started. I'm to be in Phoenix tomorrow night."

"I know. I have your schedule."

"You do?"

"You gave it to us last time you were at our house."

"Oh," he said, remembering. "Yes."

I took out the things I wanted and went into the motor home. There wasn't much to do to fix the bunk. I changed into a long nightshirt, washed my face, and brushed my teeth by the time he came back in.

"All set," he said.

"Is there anything else I can do?"

"No. Just get some rest."

He got into the driver's seat.

"Are you going to drive all night?"

"A good part of it," he said. "It's how I do it. No problem for me," he added.

"Okay. Good night, Uncle Palaver, and thank you," I said, and crawled up and into the bunk.

"'Night," he called. He started the engine and slowly drove out of the rear parking area.

I lay back in the bunk bed, recalling when I had slept in it as a younger girl. If it seemed like a big adventure then, it was certainly one now. The trip and the tension had taken a bigger toll on me than I had realized. With that and the slight shaking and movement of the motor home, I fell asleep quickly.

Some time before morning, I woke with a jolt. It was as if someone had shaken me. I blinked and wiped my eyes, the realization of where I was slowly returning. The motor home was dark, but the glow from some pole light outside flowed through, outlining everything clearly. I saw Uncle Palaver slumped on the sofa, a bottle of whiskey before him. I watched him for a while, and then I thought I surely heard someone calling.

Destiny needs him for something, I decided.

"Uncle Palaver," I whispered, but he didn't move.

Again, I thought I heard something and this time decided to crawl down and see what was happening. I stood listening in the shadows. There was definitely the sound of someone talking, and it was coming from the bedroom.

"Uncle Palaver?" I stepped up to him and touched his shoulder gently. "Uncle Palaver?"

He moaned, but he didn't open his eyes. I looked at the bottle and saw it was nearly empty. I shook him again, a little harder.

"Uncle Palaver?"

He slumped to his right without opening his eyes. I shook even harder. He groaned and moaned but didn't open his eyes. He started to mumble something, and then he sank even lower on the sofa.

The sound of someone talking continued, but low. Was Destiny calling for him and too weak to raise her voice? I walked to the rear of the motor home and listened. It was definitely the sound of a woman talking, but she didn't seem to be calling for help. She was just whispering loudly. Maybe she was in a delirium or something, I thought, and knocked gently.

"Destiny? Are you all right? It's April, Uncle Palaver's niece. He's in a deep sleep. Do you need something?"

I looked back at Uncle Palaver. He wasn't moving. Slowly, I turned the doorknob and then inched the door open, calling softly.

"Destiny? Are you all right?"

When the door was fully opened, I gazed in and saw her lying in the bed. I could hear the whispering clearly now. She was talking about something she and Uncle Palaver had done together, some wonderful time they had near the Grand Canyon. When I heard his laugh, I felt chills in my spine. I looked back. He was still unmoving on the sofa. How could I hear his laugh?

"Destiny?"

I walked in. The light from the poles outside the motor home was not as bright as it was in the living room and kitchenette, but it was enough to clearly outline Destiny's head and body in the bed. I stepped closer and looked down at her.

My heart leaped in my chest.

It was the life-size doll. I looked about the small bedroom, but there was no real person in the room.

And the voices?

They were coming from a tape recorder beside the doll.

18

Follow the Wheel

❧

I made no attempt to wake Uncle Palaver. I didn't
think I could if I tried, anyway. He reeked of bourbon
and was snoring away now. I simply closed the door
on the bedroom and returned to my bunk. Sleep for
me was almost impossible, even though I was so
tired. The muffled sound of the voices on the tape
recorder leaking out of the bedroom kept me tossing
and turning. Toward morning, I finally passed out,
and I didn't awaken until I heard the engine start. I
listened hard for the voices, but I didn't hear them. I
lay there with my eyes opened, staring at the motor
home ceiling and wondering if what I had heard and
seen the night before was really just a terrible nightmare.

Gazing into the motor home, I didn't see Uncle
Palaver. The bottle of bourbon was gone. Suddenly, the
vehicle jerked and moved forward.

"Uncle Palaver?"

"Hey," he called back. "I'm just moving us along here a little ways. I parked in a supermarket parking lot last night, and usually their security comes around and raps on the door if they see I'm there too long. It's just another ten miles to a turnoff, and we'll stop and make some breakfast," he said.

He sounded clear-headed and okay. I climbed down from the bunk and looked toward the bedroom door, which was still closed.

He glanced at me. "Sleep okay?" he asked as he drove.

I held my breath and didn't speak, wondering if I should ask him about the tape recorder. Should I tell him I had gone into the bedroom? Should I ask him about the doll in the bed? Ask him about Destiny?

Something told me it was better to wait, to have him tell me everything.

"Yes," I said. "Fine."

"Great. We'll have some breakfast in a few minutes," he said.

I went to the bathroom, washed, and quickly put on my jeans and sweatshirt. I felt him pull us off the highway and park the motor home. When I came out, he was already in the little kitchenette, pouring me a glass of orange juice.

"When I park for a longer period, I expand the walls, but we'll be here only to have breakfast," he explained. "What would you like? I went out and bought some eggs early this morning at that supermarket, and some rolls and a few Danish."

"I don't eat that much anymore, Uncle Palaver."

"Oh. Well, it's here if you want it. What do you want?"

"I'll just have a soft-boiled egg," I said. "I can make it," I added quickly. "Go on and sit. I'll wait on you."

"Oh, I don't sit," he said. "I have to prepare something for Destiny. She likes a little hot oatmeal," he added, nodding at the range. He did have a pot on it and oatmeal cooking.

I stared at it and then looked at him, my heart skipping beats. Why was he doing this, pretending she was really back there? Was he doing it for my sake, hiding tragic news? He rattled on about her, stunning me so with the way he spoke about her that for a few moments, I couldn't move.

"She's upset that I'm doing all this, that I just don't put her in some facility and forget her. She thinks she's a terrible burden on me. It's been this way for some time, but if you really care for someone, you don't dispose of them just because they're in trouble.

"Your father didn't understand that. He thought he was doing you all a big favor by inventing that fantasy about his deserting you so you wouldn't suffer with him, but he broke your mother's heart. Loving someone means taking them on for better or for worse, just as it says in the marriage vow. People break their contracts with each other so easily these days. In every way," he added, turning to me. Apparently, he didn't notice my amazed look or read anything more in it than my surprise at his domestic abilities.

"They're quick to breach agreed business arrangements. People today say the contract's not worth more than the paper it's written on, and for good reason. No one lives up to his word, to his promises, anymore.

"Well, I'm not built like that. I make a commitment; I live up to it or break my neck trying, and I expect other people to treat me the same way. Of course, they don't. I can't tell you how many scheduled performances were canceled on me at the last minute.

"Destiny and I had an act that worked on the road. She was an integral part of it. When she got sick," he said, stirring the pot of oatmeal, "I came up with this idea to keep us going as an act. I had always used a little ventriloquism in my act, you know. You knew that, right?"

I shook my head.

"Yes, I did. And when we were in Atlanta, I got friendly with this puppet maker. I told him my idea, and he thought it was terrific, a challenge, so he worked hard on it. He actually visited us and took pictures of Destiny. The likeness is remarkable, just remarkable, don't you think?"

I nodded, still dumbfounded. What should I have said? I never met her, so how would I know?

"Anyway, we're still a hit on the road."

"How do you do it?" I asked finally.

"Do what?" He turned and held the spoon up. "Make oatmeal?"

"No," I said, smiling. "How do you get the doll to turn its head and move like that?"

"Oh, that. Okay. I'll tell you that because it's not so much a magic trick as it is a technical thing. I have this transmitter in my pocket, and the doll has little receivers in it. The puppet maker came up with that idea. Audiences just love the end of the act. Sometimes, I really overdo it. I run off the stage into the audience and out of the theater, or apparently out of the theater. I sneak around to get to the transmitter's range."

"But the voice, too?"

"It's on a tape recorder, and I trigger that as well so it plays over the sound system in the theater. Now you know the secret." He thought a moment. "You know, I just had an idea. Something for you to do. We'll have to practice until I'm satisfied, of course."

"What?" I asked, excited.

"I'll show you how to manipulate the transmitter. You can do it from the audience. That way, the audience will be even more impressed, because I'll make my exit very obvious and convincing. I'll go out a side door or something. What do you think?"

"Sure," I said. "I'll do anything to be on the road with you."

He nodded and then shook his head. "I'm just dreaming. You can't be on the road with me, April. You should be in school."

"It's all right. I'll do what's known as high school equivalency. You can be my legal guardian, Uncle Palaver. I'm sure Brenda won't mind or even care," I said.

"I don't know." He looked toward the bedroom. "With Destiny and all . . ."

"I'll help you with her, too," I blurted. "I mean, I'll do anything you need done."

What was I saying? I knew what I was saying to him, but what was I saying to myself? Simple, I thought. I was willing to go along with anything as long as I could stay with him and not be forced to return to Brenda and that life. What harm would it do, anyway? If he was happy like this, I wouldn't do anything to hurt him.

He considered. "Maybe," he said. "Maybe."

He poured the oatmeal into a bowl and put it on a tray.

"Fix your breakfast, April. I want to get started in about a half hour or so. We still have a distance to drive, and there's preparation before the show at the theater itself."

I watched him walk to the bedroom, carrying the tray. He opened the door and stepped inside, closing the door behind him. I heard his voice, muffled but sounding sweet and concerned. I heard my name mentioned, too.

Uncle Palaver's world is a world of illusion, I told myself. *To him, this all probably seems acceptable.* Of course, I wondered what really happened to Destiny and how long he had been carrying on the illusion, but I thought in time he would tell me all. He would sit and explain everything when he got to know me better, perhaps, or when he trusted me. I wouldn't betray him. Never. I knew what pain that brought.

I made my breakfast, and afterward, when he came out and told me she was asleep, I washed the empty bowl and other dishes and silverware while he went out to check the hitch and the car. Minutes later, we were on our way. I sat beside him and listened to him talk about his plans for the next show he would perform. He described some of the tricks and illusions and rambled on and on about some of the audiences recently and funny things that had occurred. Whenever he described an event or a place, he always mentioned Destiny and what she had thought or done. She was obviously woven so tightly into his memory and life now that it would take serious psychiatric surgery to get her out, and for what reason? He wasn't harming anyone, and it all made it easier for him to go on.

It reminded me of the play *Harvey* about the invisible rabbit. In the end, Dowd's sister realized he was better off believing and seeing the rabbit. All the psychiatrist could do was make him unhappy.

When we were young, we needed to believe in Santa Claus or some other wonderful illusion. When we were older, we fixated on movie stars or singers and built them up into people much greater than they were. We were always looking toward someone or something to give us some hope and excitement, to fill and complete our lives. So Uncle Palaver believed in his Destiny, so what?

I had nothing to believe in, and look how empty, how hollow and lost, I felt. Who was I to criticize and destroy his illusions?

No, I thought. If he wanted me to bring her the oatmeal tomorrow, I would, and I would pretend just as he did that she was there to receive it.

I would do anything to keep moving, because in my mind, I was moving away from all the sadness and disappointment that trailed behind. I longed to be able to forget the past and think only of what lay ahead.

When we arrived at Uncle Palaver's next venue, however, there was a message from Brenda waiting for him. Somehow, she had realized I would be going to see him. Perhaps she had noticed the missing schedule sheet. It surprised me that she could remember it, or else she somehow had located another. As it turned out, she had known how to contact Uncle Palaver's booking agent.

"Your sister is looking for you," he told me. "She left a message telling me you've run away and wondered if I knew anything. I've got to call her back."

"Don't," I said.

"We can't do that, April. You have to speak with her. Things could only become worse for you and even for me if you don't," he insisted. "Either you call her, or I will. What will it be?"

Reluctantly, I went to a pay phone near the theater and called Brenda.

"Just what do you think you're doing?" she asked the moment she heard my voice.

"What I want to do, what I need to do," I replied.

"What did you tell Uncle Palaver?"

"The truth."

She was quiet a moment. Then I heard her sigh deeply. "Celia left," she revealed.

"For good?"

"Probably. Look, April, you should come home and finish your school year. Over the summer . . ."

"It's not my home, Brenda. I hate it. I don't have a home, and maybe I never will. It's better to be like Uncle Palaver, be on the road, not attached to anyone or anyplace ever."

"Daddy used to call him a wandering gypsy, a hobo on wheels."

"Uncle Palaver's happy, and when I compare him to us or to the way we were, I'd say he was the lucky one."

"April, this is so crazy. You're not eighteen yet. Does Uncle Palaver realize he has to become your legal guardian?"

"Yes, he does. I'm going to help him in his act, and I'm going to go for my high school equivalency. I know what I'm doing."

"What are you doing in his act?"

I didn't want to talk about Destiny. It was better she knew nothing of that, I thought.

"It has to do with his illusions and such. It's too hard to explain, and besides, Uncle Palaver never talks about his tricks, and I can't, either."

"Yeah, right," she said. "Well, I'm not coming after you, April. You're going to be on your own. Let me know where to send you money, and I'll do that. All the paperwork has been set up for your trust, and the house was sold," she continued.

I didn't want to hear any of it. I felt like slapping my hands over my ears. Our house, our home, Mama, Daddy, all of it was gone.

"Good," I said. "I don't care about it anymore."

"I'm sorry about what happened with Celia. I know it wasn't your fault, April," Brenda said in a most uncharacteristically soft and tender way.

"It wasn't. I was . . . surprised, too."

"That boy called here," she also revealed.

"Peter Smoke?"

"Yes. He sounded very disappointed that you weren't here. I had to tell him I didn't know where you were or when you'd be back. He left you a message."

"What was it?"

"'I'm sorry,'" he said. "'Tell her I'm sorry.'"

"He did? Was that all he said?"

"No. He also said something peculiar. He said I should tell you to follow the wheel, whatever that means."

"I know what it means. If he ever calls again, you can tell him I am."

"Was he the one who told you to run away?"

"No. Mr. Panda did," I said.

She was quiet. Neither of us spoke for a long moment.

"I have an offer to join an international team this summer. I'm considering doing it. I was going to suggest you visit with Uncle Palaver then, anyway," she revealed.

"Then no harm's been done," I said. "I'm just doing it a little sooner. I'm happy for you, Brenda. Go do what you are meant to do. Follow the wheel."

"What the heck does that mean?" She actually laughed.

"Look it up. It's called the medicine wheel. It's an Indian thing."

"Okay, okay. Take care of yourself, April. I'm sorry we've never been closer than we are. Maybe most of this is my fault."

"It's no one's fault. It just is," I said.

"Will you call me once in a while and tell me how you are?"

"Yes," I promised.

"And don't forget to get an address from Uncle Palaver for where I can send you money."

"Okay," I said. I could feel the line between us beginning to thin out and drift off. It felt as if we had unclasped each other's hand.

"Good-bye, April," she said.

"'Bye," I replied.

She hung up first. I stood there with the dead receiver in my hand. I felt cold and numb, and for a moment, I couldn't breathe. I was like an astronaut who had stepped out of his space vehicle and was just hanging in space. Despite it all, she was still my sister. She was the last tie to what once had been a wonderful family life.

"Good-bye," I said again, even though I knew she was gone.

Then I hung up the phone and returned to the motor home, where Uncle Palaver was preparing himself and his Destiny for the evening's performance. He was already dressed in his fancy tuxedo and top hat with his white gloves.

"What happened?" he asked, and I told him. He gave me an address for Brenda to use and didn't talk about my returning, which pleased me until he added, "Destiny is concerned about you but for now agrees it's all right."

He showed me his transmitter for the doll and explained how he used it.

"I'd want you to practice first. We don't want to mess up an illusion. Once you do that, you spoil the whole evening for the audience," he said. "We'll do it tomorrow."

I saw a costume draped over the sofa. It was a glittering silver-sequined bathing suit with a black sash. He told me it was something Destiny wore when she came out onstage with him during the early days of their act together. He said she would bring out some of the set pieces, and in one trick, she would crawl into a box that he would then take apart and show was empty.

"If I lose enough weight and fit into that, can I do the trick with you and bring things out to you?" I asked.

"Well, I don't know. I . . .well, I guess you could," he said, nodding. "Destiny would like that, too, I'm sure. But don't go starving yourself like some women do," he warned.

He checked his watch and decided it was time to get backstage. He went into the bedroom and brought the life-size replica of Destiny out in his arms. I opened the door for him and followed him to the rear entrance of the theater. As we walked, I heard him talking to the doll, describing the theater and reminding it of when they were last in the area.

"People are different all over America, but when they are in an audience watching a magician, hypnotist, and memory expert, they all become children," he said.

The way he reacted made even me feel the doll had agreed.

He told me to go out, watch the show, and be a critic.

"I want you to watch everything and see if you can tell anything I'm doing and also keep track of how the audience reacts to each thing. That way, I'll know what

I should keep for the next show and what I shouldn't.
Okay?"

"Yes, Uncle Palaver."

"Don't hold back," he said. "We can take criticism."
We?

"Okay," I said.

One of the stagehands came over to talk to Uncle
Palaver, and after hearing what he wanted done, he
stepped up to speak to me.

He was a young man with curly black hair and a
well-trimmed goatee.

"Are you one of Palaver's assistants?" he asked me.

"The only one," I replied.

"I was here last year when he performed. You
weren't with him then?"

"He's my uncle," I revealed. "I recently joined him
on the road."

"Oh. Are you a magician and hypnotist, too?"

"No, hardly. I don't do anything magical," I said
dryly.

He stepped more into the light, and I saw he had the
most strikingly black pearl eyes, a tight firm jaw, and a
perfectly straight nose. Why was he backstage? I wondered. He could be a movie star.

"How long have you been a stagehand?"

"My dad owns this theater," he said. "I've been here
since I was ten. I'm not a stagehand, by the way. I'm
the stage manager. I run it all. Dad's semiretired. Right
now, he's off deep-sea fishing with friends, in fact.
Your uncle's sold-out tonight."

"That's wonderful."

"Yeah. He's nearly sold-out for tomorrow night,
too. If it goes well tonight, I'm sure he will be. My
name's Russell, Russell Blackman," he said, offering
his hand. I shook it quickly.

"I'm April Taylor."

"Hey!" he screamed at a man pulling up a scrim. "Go easy with that. It's tight. You could rip it."

The man slowed down quickly.

"It's hard to get good help for something like this. Half the time, I'd rather bring in high school kids who are at least excited about being backstage." He peered at me a little harder. "How old are you, April?"

"I'm eighteen," I lied. "I'm just taking some time off to decide what I want to do."

"Yeah, good idea. Well, it's almost show time. If you get bored afterward, stop by my office. It's back there," he said, pointing toward the stage right wing. "Kind of a second home to me these days. I usually like to wind down for a few hours after a theatrical evening, order in a pizza. It's something I learned from my father. You have to relax after a night like this. Hey!" he screamed at someone else. "Tighten that floodlight. I can see from here that it's too loose." He shook his head. "The theater. Except for my cashier and my bookkeeper, I've got more turnover than the front wheels on a race car. See you," he said, and walked off.

Why would he invite me backstage? I wondered. I was probably too deep in the shadows for him to see what I really looked like.

I hurried out to the audience to take my seat and watch the show. It was much like the previous show, only Uncle Palaver added some additional and more spectacular tricks, the most amazing being levitating himself. He used Destiny, of course, and to the audience, the doll somehow was the one causing him to lift slowly off the stage floor and hover in midair. She raised her right arm slowly, and he moved upward along with it. When she brought it down, he came down. The audience applauded loudly, and I heard people asking each other how he could do that.

The great finish with the mock argument brought the audience to their feet again. I clapped harder than some of the members of the audience, and I knew how he did it. There was something about stepping out of reality and into the world of illusion that was so comforting and easy for me. *I belong with him,* I thought. *I really do. It's in my blood as much as it is in his, perhaps.*

Afterward, I helped him gather up his things to bring back to the motor home. He carried Destiny in and put her back in the bedroom.

"Well," he said, returning, "I guess we did all right tonight. Maybe we'll sell out tomorrow's performance."

"Russell thinks you will," I told him.

"Russell? Oh, the owner's kid. Yeah. You want something to eat?"

I thought about Russell's invitation. "I was invited to have some pizza backstage," I said.

Uncle Palaver looked surprised. "Oh, really. That's nice. Mingle with the theater people, and get a feel for it. I used to do that a lot, but with Destiny's condition and all, I don't go anywhere usually. Go ahead. Don't stay out too late," he said. "I'm just going to relax a bit myself, describe the show to Destiny. She loves hearing about it."

He went to the cabinet above the sink and took out a full bottle of bourbon. I saw he had two more as well.

"We'll practice the big finish tomorrow," he added, and went to the bedroom.

I hesitated, wondering if I should go backstage. Was that just politeness, or did Russell Blackman really mean it? It could be very embarrassing, I thought. I stepped out of the motor home and walked slowly through the warm evening. The excitement of the show, the wonderful reception Uncle Palaver had gotten, and his amazing performance filled me with hope. I could really become part of all this, I thought. I suddenly had a thirst for knowledge about the theater. I wanted to learn as much as I could as fast as I was able to, so I could impress Uncle Palaver and become truly an integral part of his act. Who knew? Maybe I could become a magician alongside him. It would be a real family show. Wouldn't Mama have been amazed?

There was no one backstage when I stepped into the theater through the rear door. The only light there was came from the emergency lights above exit doors, actually. I made my way across the stage to the stage-right wing, where I heard some music coming from a room toward the rear. The door was slightly opened. The sound of a girl's laugh made me pause. Then I heard Russell cry, "Terrific!"

I stepped up to the doorway and saw him sprawled on a sofa. An open pizza box was on the table before him with a six-pack of beer. A tall, thin blond-haired girl in a white halter and knee-length skirt was pouring a glass of beer. She was leaning against the desk. Russell saw me and sat up quickly.

"Hey, April, come in. This is Palaver's niece," he told the girl. She looked at me and smiled. "My cousin Tess," he said, introducing her.

"Fourth cousin, twice removed," she added, and they both laughed. "Hi," she said. "Want a beer?"

"Sure," I said.

"The pizza's still hot and pretty good," Russell said.

I looked at it with ravenous eyes. I had been doing

so well on my diet, but I hadn't eaten much today, I rationalized.

"Thank you."

I took a piece in a napkin and the glass of beer Tess poured and sat across from Russell.

"Your uncle had a great night," he said. "The feedback was terrific. We're expecting a sell-out tomorrow night. People around here love these kinds of shows. Right, Tess?"

"Oh, yes. I thought he was great. How did he do that thing where he just rises straight up?"

"I'm not allowed to reveal any secrets," I said, and they both laughed.

"I'll tell you something," Russell said, leaning forward. "I've seen a lot from backstage, of course, but the way he talks to that big puppet and the way it reacts had me going. I could almost believe it was real, right, Tess?"

She nodded.

"I mean, the detail in the face, the skin or whatever it is that's supposed to be skin, and those eyes, everything. It's the best mannequin I've seen."

"Me, too," Tess said. "So, where are you from?"

"Tennessee."

"How long have you been with your uncle?"

"A while," I said, trying to keep it as vague as I could. "I'm exploring my options."

"That's what Tess has been doing, too. For years," Russell added, and laughed. She punched him playfully in the shoulder.

"Is it true that show people are more promiscuous?" Tess asked after a moment.

"What do you mean?"

"Loose, fun, uninhibited," she added.

"I've always found it to be so," Russell said.

"Tell me about it," Tess commented. "You know what they call this office?"

"All right, keep it to yourself," Russell said sharply.

"We're not hicks out here," Tess continued. "People who come through always think we are. Are you cool?" she asked me.

"I'm not sure what you mean," I said cautiously. "I suppose I am."

They both laughed.

"She's a careful one," Tess said.

"Yeah, aren't we all."

He reached under the table and put a packet of what looked like folded wax paper on it. Then he smiled at Tess and me and carefully unwrapped it to reveal a layer of fine white powder. He reached into his shirt pocket and produced three very small straws. He took a razor and began to cut up the powder into lines.

"Tess," he said, pointing to the first line. He gave her a straw.

"April," he said, pointing to the second and handing me a straw.

I looked at them and took it quickly.

He held the third straw for himself.

"Ladies, shall we begin the festivities?" he asked, and Tess moved to the table, got on her knees, brought the straw to her line, put the other end in her nostril, and began to inhale as she moved it up the line, sucking up the powder like a miniature vacuum cleaner.

"Wow!" she cried, throwing her head back. "This is good stuff."

"Only the best for my cousin," Russell said. He looked at me. "You're next," he said.

How many times in our lives do we come to these sorts of crossroads? I could hand him back the straw, turn away, and walk out, I thought. It might make him angry or nervous, and he might take it out on Uncle Palaver somehow. Maybe he would deliberately ruin his show, and I would have been responsible for that. They both thought I was cool, street-smart, just because I was on the road with Uncle Palaver. Is this what it meant, too? I wondered.

If there was one thing Brenda used to rage about, it was young people and drugs, anything that deteriorated health and stamina. She also hated the use of enhancing drugs that made some athletes look superior. How many times had I sat and listened to her lectures and tirades, especially after she had seen a teammate use some hallucinogenic? I hadn't spoken to her twenty-four hours ago, and here I was confronted by the very thing she despised.

"C'mon," Russell said. "We have places to go yet."

Tess laughed.

I approached the table, got on my knees as she had, and put the straw awkwardly to the line of white powder. Instead of sucking it up, however, I accidentally breathed out too fast and hard. I was just that nervous. The powder lifted away from the bottom of my straw, and both Tess and Russell jumped back as though they were afraid to be touched by any of it.

"Hey! Jeez! Damn! That's expensive," Russell cried.

"I'm sorry," I moaned.

"She's never done this before," Tess declared, her eyes wide and bright.

Russell looked from her to me. "Is that right?"

"I'm sorry," I said.

"Get up. Get away from it before you ruin my line," he ordered.

I stood up quickly. He lowered himself and, with

his eyes on me, brought his straw to his line and inhaled it all so fast I thought it might blow off the top
of his head. He sat back on his haunches and shook
his head.

"You're not eighteen, are you?" he accused.

Tess moved around on my right and drew closer to
me. "How old are you? Huh?" she demanded, poking
me in the shoulder.

"I'm seventeen," I confessed.

Tess looked at Russell. "Maybe that's not really her
uncle, either," she told him.

He nodded.

"Yes, he is!" I cried. "He's my mother's brother."

"I don't know," Tess said, tucking in the right corner
of her mouth. "Something smells here, right, Russell?"

"Right," he said.

"How's a young girl live with a grown man in a
motor home?" Tess asked him.

"Makes me wonder," he said, staring at me. "If I
were you, I wouldn't say anything to anyone about
this," he added, nodding at the residue of white powder."

"I wouldn't," I said. I rose to my feet and stepped
toward the door.

"Where you going?" Tess asked.

"I thought you didn't want me here anymore."

"The fun's just beginning," Tess said. "Take it easy.
She's fresh fish," she told Russell, and his smile
widened.

He brought his razor back to the paper and created
another line with what he could scrape up.

"Try again," he said. "Hold your breath until you
get the straw on it, and then inhale."

I glanced at it and then looked at Tess, who was

staring at me with a strange, twisted smile on her face. What else did she have in mind? What did he mean when he said we had places to go yet?

"I don't think I should," I said. "I'd better get back before my uncle gets upset."

"We'd feel better if you did," Russell said firmly.

"A lot better," Tess said, drawing closer to me.

"I just don't want to waste any more."

"You won't," Russell said. He sat back. "C'mon. First time is often the most exciting."

Tess was right over me.

I returned to the table, put the straw to the powder, my fingers visibly trembling, and then closed my eyes and inhaled. The moment the first grains hit my nostrils, I panicked and fell back.

They both laughed. I got up quickly.

"I can't do it!" I screamed, and ran out the door, nearly running into a set of rope weight. I twisted myself, turned, and continued across the backstage, their laughter still following me.

"Keep your mouth shut!" I heard Russell shout.

I burst out of the rear door of the theater and hurried to the motor home. My heart was thumping. I desperately tried to calm myself before going in. I surely didn't want Uncle Palaver to see me like this and find out what I had done. He'd insist I go back, for sure.

Instead of going in, I circled the motor home. My body felt hot. As I walked, I felt more excited, stronger and suddenly very alert to any sound or light. When I looked up, the stars seemed closer, brighter. My heart continued to race, and I walked faster. I imagined myself walking so hard and fast that I was digging a ditch around the motor home. It made me stop and laugh.

I leaned against the side of the motor home, not realizing until I heard the sobbing that I was right beneath the bedroom window. I could hear every sound from within clearly. Uncle Palaver's sobs became louder. *I've got to go to him,* I thought. *Something terrible is happening.*

I charged toward the front door, opening it quickly and stepping into the motor home. Then I hurried down to the bedroom door and listened. He was still sobbing, but it was softer. I knocked.

"Uncle Palaver, are you all right?"

"What are you doing?" I heard, and spun around.

Uncle Palaver was sitting at the wheel, drinking from his bottle. I looked at him and then at the door and then back to him.

"I . . ."

"You'd better go to sleep," he said. "We have another big day tomorrow."

He turned away and stared out the window.

I could still hear what surely was his sobbing coming from the bedroom.

Why did he want that to go on? Didn't he hear it, too? He just sat there, drinking and staring out the window at the darkness. I felt my nerve endings crackling and stepped into the bathroom.

Afterward, I climbed into my bunk, but trying to catch sleep made me feel like one of those greyhound dogs on a dog racetrack trying to catch the mechanical rabbit. Around and around I went, exhausting myself, but not falling asleep.

Finally, a good hour or so later, I felt fatigue settle into me like water soaking in a sponge. Uncle Palaver was still sipping his bourbon and looking out the window below me.

Before I fell asleep, I sobbed silently myself.

Being on the road wasn't as adventurous and wonderful as I had expected.

It was just a different journey through a maze of disappointments and sadness.

Everyone, after all, was chasing that unattainable rabbit.

19

Uncle Palaver's
Final Act

I was tired and achy the next day. The bunk was cramped and uncomfortable for me because I had tossed and turned all night, apparently. I went through the same breakfast illusion with Uncle Palaver. He made the oatmeal and took it to Destiny in the bedroom. I drank more coffee and found I was too hungry to eat just my plain eggs. I ravished the Danish that was still there.

Just as before, Uncle Palaver seemed to have no hangover from his night of continuous drinking. He took out the Destiny doll in the afternoon, and he and I practiced with the transmitter until he was satisfied I could perform the tricks well enough for him to entrust it to me.

I had a chance to look at the life-size puppet more closely, and I was impressed with the detailed attention to her face, right down to a small birthmark right under her lower lip. Why would that have mattered? Who could possibly see such a thing from the audience? Uncle Palaver was able to have the doll in a standing position as well as sitting, and for the first time, I wondered if some of the publicity shots and posters pictures he had sent us weren't taken of him and the doll and not the real Destiny.

I avoided going to the theater and confronting Russell for as long as I could, but when it was time for the performance, I had to accompany Uncle Palaver. Russell was there backstage. He didn't say anything to me. He just smiled, wagged his finger, and walked off to give someone orders. I breathed a sigh of relief. At least he wasn't going to say anything to Uncle Palaver.

He ran through the same performance, only at the end, with me now activating the doll, he made a far more dramatic exit. Heads turned in surprised when he charged up the aisle and out the front door, slamming it behind him. He glanced surreptitiously at me as he flew by, but everyone's attention was centered on him, and then, in confusion, they turned to the doll. He had made a point of my counting to at least sixty. The audience actually began to stir restlessly. I could see it in their faces. They were all wondering what was going on. How long were they supposed to sit there? When would he return?

Then I pressed the first button, and Destiny came to life. To me, the applause that followed seemed louder and more vigorous than the applause the night before. Uncle Palaver returned and walked down the aisle bowing. He smiled my way, and I knew I had done well.

Afterward, as we were packing up, Russell approached from behind me and whispered, "I saw what you two did. Sneaky." He laughed at my surprise.

"Stay cool," he said. "Maybe when you return, if you return, you'll be more experienced."

In what? I thought. Destroying myself? No, thank you, Russell Blackman.

We got everything settled in the motor home, and Uncle Palaver decided he wanted to get under way as soon as possible.

"You did real good, April, real good," he told me. "I might start thinking of other ways to bring you into the show."

"Really? I'd love that," I told him, and decided I would get my weight down so I could fit into that silver-sequined suit soon.

He went to his cabinet and took out his bottle of bourbon. After a quick swig, he said he was going to drive most of the night. He saw my eyes go to the bottle of whiskey.

"Don't you worry about it. I don't drink much when I drive. Just one to get me calm is enough."

We had a number of performances on the schedule that would take us to Northern California, eventually reaching the Napa Valley area by late spring. The distances between venues were not great, but he said he liked to have time to relax before a show. I went to bed and let the movement of the motor home rock me to sleep. Sometime before morning, I woke and realized he had parked the motor home in another supermarket parking lot. I saw the light was still on in the living room and could just make out the bottle on the table and his legs on the sofa. The bottle looked nearly empty.

How long before I had arrived had he been drinking like this? I wondered. How long could he continue to drink so much every night? I was afraid to be critical of anything, but when I woke up again and saw him hovering over a cup of coffee, I wondered aloud if he were suffering from a hangover.

He laughed. "Naw, never do. I don't drink that much," he said. "Just enough to take the edge off. Don't worry yourself. I'm fine."

Nevertheless, before we left the area the next day, he made sure to buy himself six more bottles of bourbon and store them in the closet. During the days, he taught me some of his tricks, especially the simpler sleight-of-hand ones such as the self-tying handkerchief, the cut and restored string, the coin through an elbow, and something he called the Houdini Rubber Band Escape, which made it look as if he caused a rubber band to jump magically from his forefinger and index finger to the last two on his hand, and then he showed me the vanishing knot trick using a handkerchief. Finally, he showed me how to do one he had performed often at our house, delighting even Daddy. It was called the Unbreakable Match. He would put a wooden match into a handkerchief, ask me or Daddy to break it, and after we had, he pronounced some gibberish, and, voilà, the match was whole again. The secret to this was simply to have two wooden matches, one concealed in the hem of the handkerchief.

These weren't tricks he used onstage, but he explained that from time to time, he performed at conventions or was part of a group of entertainers hired for elaborate parties. The tricks, as old and as simple as they were, were still favorites, he said.

It took me a while to get them all, but they were just illusions and, eventually, easy for me to do. I had mixed emotions about it as he showed me the secrets or the techniques. When I was little, I loved believing in magic and in Uncle Palaver's powers. Now that he was revealing that it was all fake in one way or another, I felt disappointment slipping in under my sense of accomplishment.

In the end, there was no magic, no real wondrous events after all. Everything was simply an illusion. Uncle Palaver was falling off the pedestal on which I had placed him. One part of me clung to the idea that he was still exceptional. He had a talent for performing all the illusions well, and that was something of an accomplishment, but another part of me, perhaps the dreamer, the child in me, suddenly saw him as a phony, a liar, a deceiver. It was all false, untrue. I suppose the closest comparison I could make was when I, or any child, suddenly realized Santa Claus was a fiction.

"You'd better watch yourself. You'd better not shout," was no longer a viable warning. Gifts were just gifts. Wishes didn't really matter. Yet, ironically perhaps, when we became older and were parents, all of us would tell our own children the same stories, the same fantasies. Somehow, inside us, we knew that, for a while at least, it was precious and important to believe in fairy tales.

Watching Uncle Palaver drink himself to sleep every night, knowing the secret behind every illusion he performed on the stage, pushing the transmitter buttons, and fooling the audience myself into believing something wondrous had just occurred gradually hardened and saddened me. I gazed into the faces of the various audiences we faced night after night on the road. Grown-ups and children alike were so desperate to believe, to escape from the world in which they were living. I could almost hear them thinking, *Please, do something to help me believe there is more than this, so I can go home tonight dreaming and remembering my childhood faiths.*

In a true sense, Uncle Palaver was able to do that for them. *April, respect and admire him for that,* I thought and urged my inner self. However, there was another voice, bitter, laughing, angry, warning me to open my eyes and stop fooling myself. *The journey you're on has an end, too,* this voice said, *and one day, you have to look into the mirror and see who you really are and realize what you're really doing with your life. This isn't the medicine wheel, and it isn't the wheel of fortune, April. It's just a wheel. You're only going in circles and getting nowhere.*

At one of our stops, I sent Brenda a letter with the address Uncle Palaver had given me for her to send whatever she was supposed to send me. Things were forwarded from there to our stops in advance. The second check that arrived had a letter with it. I had been on the road with Uncle Palaver for months now. I had lost some weight and had tried on the sequin suit. Celia had been right about one thing: my body was developing rapidly, almost as if it had just remembered it should. The suit fit, but I didn't like the way my thighs still bulged, so I decided to keep it in the closet for a while longer and wait before accompanying Uncle Palaver onstage to hand him tricks or crawl into that magic box.

The letter from Brenda was short but left me feeling sad for her. I went up into my bunk and just looked at her handwriting on the envelope. Finally, I had the nerve to open and read it.

Dear April,

Enclosed is a check for your monthly allowance. I have arranged with Mr. Weiss, our attorney, to have these checks forwarded directly from his office from now on. The reason is, I have decided to drop out of college. I know you will be shocked about it, but I'm not giving up sports. I'm turning professional sooner than I expected, and I've decided I can always return to college to finish my degree when I want or need to do that.

I especially would like to avoid seeing Celia these days. She has found someone new, and it seems I can't avoid running into them all the time. It's not like me to run from anyone or anything, and I'm not. I've just decided I'm happier on a court floor than a classroom floor for now. And you were right about this house. To come home to it and be alone in it is very depressing. At times, I find myself envying you. Maybe you did make the right decision. Who knows?

Sometimes, I just sit and think about all that has happened to us so quickly. It seems like a dream. The other day, I saw a father and his young children playing basketball in their driveway, and I thought about Daddy and those days when he and I were at it with such fury. We exhausted each other, but somehow, afterward, I felt closer to him than ever. It was just a look in his eyes that to me was better than a kiss.

Anyway, watch for me on the sports pages. The next win is for you.

Brenda

It was nearly a full minute before I realized I was crying. The tears were streaming down my cheeks and dripping off my chin. I put the letter back into the envelope and then put it under my pillow. I would read it often, because when I did, I could hear her voice clearly in my head, and it was as if we were still living together, still sisters. A part of me longed for that life, regardless of how unhappy I had been and how far I had fled.

In spite of what I had always fantasized about Uncle Palaver's life, it became patently clear to me that he, just like people who were settled in one place, followed a daily and often monotonous routine. He often did most of the driving during the night but always seemed to pull over before morning so he could sit and drink or go back to the bedroom and replay the conversations tapes he had made with Destiny. Of course, I knew these were fictitious conversations. Her voice was his voice projected through the doll. Whether they were from memories of actual conversations or not, I did not know. Regardless of what I had anticipated and hoped, he did not volunteer information about Destiny and him. I tried through subtle questions to find out more.

"When did you meet her?" I asked, and he simply replied, "Sometime ago."

"Where?" I followed, and he said, "At one of my performances."

"What brought you two together?"

"It was magic," he replied. "Simply magic."

He would then take on a dark, cold look, as if he had somehow sunk deeper into his own body. He didn't reply to any additional questions, and the look on his face frightened me enough to drop the subject. After a while, he would snap out of his reverie and talk about the next town, the next audience.

He spent his days practicing his illusions and thinking up new ones.

"The good thing about being on the road," he told me, "is that for each audience, your show is brand-new. I either don't return for some time—years, in fact—or it's for the first time. That way, everything is a real surprise."

I asked him about his cruise trips and performances, and he did talk at length about them, the places he had visited and the friends he had made.

"But these are temporary friendships," he added. "The ship moves on after you disembark, and unless you get back on that ship soon afterward, the names and faces dissipate like smoke in a short time."

It occurred to me that he really didn't have any close friends. When I asked him about it, he nodded and admitted that was one terrible disadvantage to being on the road and being a performer.

"The only people I stay in contact with these days are my booking agent, my lawyer, my accountant, and some theater owners I know and will see from time to time. I don't really speak to anyone from my past. Destiny," he said. "She's the closest person to me now, now that your mother is gone."

"You have me, too, Uncle Palaver," I reminded him, and he smiled.

"Yes, I have you, too. But you can't stay with me forever and ever, April. After this performing season, you have to think about your own future. College maybe, huh?"

"Maybe," I said.

Even the idea of thinking about a future frightened me. What would I do? Where would I go? Why couldn't I do this forever?

As time passed, I realized Uncle Palaver was drinking more and more. His complexion took on a pale yellow glow, and he was not eating well, either. Even though his face was gaunt, his stomach seemed to swell. He complained about his pants not fitting him, as if it were the fault of his pants and not his fault, but I noticed his arms and legs were swelling as well. For hours during the days now, he would retreat to the bedroom and sleep beside his Destiny. I would peer in and see him lying there, his arm embracing the doll.

Once, I was embarrassed and shocked to discover him totally naked beside it. It actually frightened me more than shocked me. I closed the door as quickly as I could and made up my mind never to spy on him again. For his part, he didn't appear to notice or care about my observations. He talked about Destiny's illness as though it had just recently been diagnosed, and he always retreated to his lecture about people who loved each other standing by each other through thick and thin. If he realized he was living in an illusion, he drowned the realization in his drinking. For him, it seemed to be the answer.

One day, however, he drank a little too close to a performance. For the first time since I had joined him, he fumbled and messed up an illusion so badly the audience actually gasped. He got hold of himself and completed the performance, but I could see the theater owner looking at him suspiciously afterward.

I thought about warning him, talking to him about the drinking, but every time I started the discussion, he grew tight-lipped and slightly angry. I was sure that if I nagged him about it, he would surely choose the whiskey over me and ask me to go home. I even considered hiding his whiskey in the hopes he'd forget and think he had run out of it, but despite his stupor, he always was quite aware of what was going on around him. It was troubling, but I didn't know what to do.

And then, one night, after he had brought the doll back to the motor home and placed it in the bedroom,

an idea occurred to me. It was a little frightening even
to consider doing it. I was worried about his reaction.
He could easily think I was teasing or mocking him,
and it would surely make him very angry at me. It
could be the cause of his asking me to leave, but witnessing his continuous degeneration was enough to
give me the courage and the reason to do it.

We were sitting in the living room having a light
lunch and watching television. He had messed up one
of his tricks again the night before but had recovered
before the audience realized it. Of course, I knew immediately. It put him off his rhythm, and he actually
cut the performance short, going to our finish ten or
fifteen minutes before he was scheduled to do so. I
didn't say anything about it to him, but the theater
manager asked him if everything was all right. I
heard him say, "You seemed a little distracted
tonight."

Uncle Palaver assured him he was fine and blamed
any loss of rhythm on his introduction of a new trick.
Of course, there was nothing that new in the act, and I
could see the manager knew it, too. *He's going to lose
bookings,* I thought. It was inevitable.

My voice was actually trembling when I began, but
I was determined to try. "When you were at the supermarket this morning, I heard Destiny call for you," I
said, and he turned to me slowly, a smile freezing on
his face.

"What?"

"I was sure I had heard her, so I went to the bedroom to see what she wanted, and we had a nice talk
about you."

"What kind of talk? What are you talking about,
April?" he demanded.

My heart thumped, and my breath caught in my

throat, but I gathered strength and determination and continued. "She said she was worried about you, worried you were worrying too much about her and because of that maybe drinking a little too much."

He stared at me. I held my breath. Would he scream, shout, tell me to leave?

"Aw," he said, waving his hand. "She worries too much. I'll speak to her. She's always picking on that. I know when too much is too much," he said firmly.

I hoped I had put something in his mind, though. If he believed Destiny wanted him to cut down, he might do it.

He continued to eat and watch television and then suddenly stopped chewing and turned sharply to me. I held my breath again.

"Don't you go counting my drinks and telling her anything," he warned.

"I won't. She knows what she knows herself," I said.

He considered my answer, nodded, and returned to watching television.

My risky idea didn't have much of an effect on him, however. If anything, I thought his drinking got worse. I kept track by the number of bottles he drank and bought and saw it was increasing. Then I noticed something even more frightening. First, I thought it was just some ketchup stain or tomato sauce, but soon I realized he was spitting up blood occasionally. I saw it on tissues, and I saw it on his cloth handkerchief. He did his best to hide it from me, even though I had taken on the responsibility of doing our laundry. We had a small washing machine in the motor home, but often we took the time to stop at a Laundromat and do a larger washing.

The second thing I noticed that put alarm in me was his trembling. I watched him practicing his sleight-of-hand tricks one afternoon and saw that he was dropping things, confusing things. His hands were trembling. The only way he seemed to be able to stop it was to take another drink. It was developing into a mad, destructive cycle, and I was standing by watching helplessly.

Once, when I saw he had put half a bottle of bourbon back into the closet, I took advantage of an opportunity when he was out and emptied half of that, filling it with water back to where it was. I held my breath when he drank from it. He didn't seem to notice anything at first, but then he just drank it all faster and went to a new bottle.

Perhaps worrying about him was a reason for my losing weight even faster, but one day, I suddenly noticed I looked taller and thinner. I tried on the sequin suit and saw it fit much better and actually looked flattering. Perhaps if I told him I was ready to join him onstage, he would change his behavior, I thought. When he stepped back into the motor home, I was still dressed in the suit and showed him how it fit.

Instead of making him happy and encouraged, he grew sad before my eyes.

"Seeing that costume brings back some happy memories, some happy lost memories," he said, and went to the bedroom.

Ironically, what I had hoped would bring him out of the darkness had simply driven him down deeper into it. That night, he didn't even start our drive. He went right to his drinking. He was asleep on the sofa when I woke in the morning, his bottles emptied. I woke him, but he stumbled into the bathroom, where I heard him vomit. Later, I found he had spit up more blood. When he came out, he went directly to the bedroom and closed the door.

I realized we were not going to make it to our next show if we didn't start out immediately. I pleaded with him to come out and start the drive, but all I heard was some sobbing and muffled speech. I had watched him drive the motor home enough to know how to do it and decided to start us on our way myself. I was nervous. A few times, I annoyed some drivers behind us, but I managed to get us onto the right highways and move us along far enough so that when he did come out, we were within striking distance of the next theater. He was surprised, and he wasn't as angry as I'd imagined he might be. He blamed himself and told me Destiny had chastised him. He claimed he was making a promise to both of us to reform himself.

Somehow, despite his condition and despite his fumbling and tired, weary appearance, he managed to get through the show. When we returned to the motor home, he did not, as was his habit, immediately begin to drink. He said he would drive a little and get some sleep. I made him something to eat, a scrambled egg sandwich, and he ate and drank some coffee. Feeling hopeful, I went to sleep myself. Perhaps this near professional disaster indeed had woken him up to what was happening, I thought.

However, when I rose in the morning, I found him like always, sprawled on the sofa, his arms twisted and his leg dangling, the emptied bottle of whiskey on the table. We had one hundred seventy-five miles or so to drive, which wasn't all that much considering show time, but he was just as incapable of driving this day as he had been the day before. Once again, he went into the bathroom and vomited. Afterward, he stumbled back to the bedroom.

I cried to myself and waited, hoping he would rise, shower, dress, and drive, hoping he would somehow restore himself as he had miraculously done before. When he didn't come out, I reluctantly went to the driver's seat and started up the vehicle, hoping the sound of the engine and the movement of the motor home would raise him and bring him to his senses, but he didn't emerge from the bedroom.

I was following the map we had but realized about a half hour into the trip that I had missed an important turn and had actually gone a good forty miles out of our way. I pulled the van over and studied the map, searching for the best way to repair the itinerary. It meant taking a side road through what looked like farmland and the beginning of the vineyards. The road wasn't as wide as the main one, and the macadam was broken and full of areas where rain had washed out sections. The motor home bounced so much at times that I was sure he would emerge to see what was happening, but he didn't. I drove as slowly as I could, but the time was worrying me. If I got lost again or broke down, he would be enraged for sure.

I came to another crossroad and pulled over to study the map more closely and be sure I'd made the right decision. As it turned out, I hadn't. The road I chose was even worse than the road I had been on, and after ten miles, I saw a sign that indicated it was not a through road. Panic seized me, and I stopped. There was no place nearby to turn around. I was afraid that if I attempted a broken U-turn, I might get the motor home stuck in what looked like a soft road shoulder.

It's no use, I thought. *I have to wake him and tell him what's happened.* I left the engine running and went back to the bedroom door, knocking and calling to him. He did not respond. I knocked harder and lis-

tened. It was silent. He wasn't even playing his tapes. I
tried the doorknob but found the door was locked.

"Uncle Palaver, please wake up. I'm afraid we're
lost," I called, waited, listened, and knocked so hard I
was really pounding.

Still, there was no response.

I turned and twisted the doorknob and pushed and
rapped on the door. Finally, the tiny lock that held it
shut gave way, and the door flew open, with me stum-
bling awkwardly forward and into the room. I caught
myself on the edge of the bed and looked at Uncle
Palaver lying with his leg twisted over the Destiny
doll, his eyes slightly opened, a stream of dried blood
streaking down his chin from the corner of his mouth.

His fingers were locked on the transmitter we used
in the show, and the doll's head was moving slightly
from side to side as if it were saying, *No, no, no.*

I screamed, but he did not awaken.

Panic submerged me in a pool of ice. For a few moments, I couldn't move, couldn't get my arms or legs
to do anything. Then I reached out to shake him. His
body shook, but his eyes didn't change. They were so
glassy they resembled the Destiny doll's eyes. Slowly,
I brought my fingers to his face. When I felt the cold-
ness in his skin, it was as if I had swallowed a ball of
fire that immediately exploded around my heart.

"Uncle Palaver!" I shouted.

And then I did the strangest thing I thought possible. I actually turned to the Destiny doll, as if I believed it could somehow help me. The head continued
to move, but slower and slower. The batteries were
running down, I thought. It might have been triggered
hours and hours ago. I pried the transmitter out of
Uncle Palaver's frozen-tight, hard fingers, and the
doll's head stopped moving.

I didn't know what to do. I just stood there stupidly looking at my uncle and his life-size doll entwined on the bed like two lovers who had made a suicide pact and carried it through. The realization of what had happened sank into me, or rather, I felt as though I were sinking into it, reality climbing up my stunned body until it reached my chest and clamped itself around my torso, making it hard for me to breathe.

I stumbled back and ran out of the room, falling to the floor by the sofa. The motor home's engine was still running. I felt my stomach twist, and suddenly, almost without any warning at all, I began to heave. I crumbled on my side and lay there, nearly traumatized by my own hysteria. Finally, it eased, and I pulled myself to my feet, hovering and trembling. I cleaned up my mess quickly and then drank a cold glass of water.

This can't be happening. It just can't be happening, I chanted to myself, but the only sound being the sound of the engine brought home the reality of the dead who don't speak. Uncle Palaver was gone. I was not only alone. I was lost, lost in so many ways.

I took deep breaths, wiped my face with a cold wash cloth, and returned to the driver's seat. For a while, I just sat there staring out at the fields, the brush, and the trees on both sides of the broken road. I was still afraid of attempting to turn the motor home around. It was tricky with my car hitched behind it, so I started forward. I hadn't noticed, but the clouds that had been blending and turning darker had changed the sky to completely overcast. Rain was coming, and soon. I was nervous enough driving this big vehicle in good weather.

I drove at least another two miles, and still there

was no place to make an easy turn. Then I came around a long, winding curve and saw what looked like a very old but very big farmhouse off to my left. As I drew closer, my heart sank, because the three-story building, although very elaborate, with a triple-window high tower, double-door front entry, large full-width side porch, and what looked like two-story bay windows in front, appeared deserted. The wood cladding was a very dull gray in desperate need of painting. The grounds were overgrown, and the statuary all looked unwashed, stained, and forgotten. Weeds invaded the gazebo like green parasites smelling death. This property was a shadow of what it once was, I thought.

The long, straight driveway that led up to the house was as cracked and pitted as the road I was on. I was going to continue and almost did accelerate before I caught sight of a pickup truck parked at the side of the house. It looked relatively new. Someone was there, I thought. I slowed down and turned into the driveway. The motor home bounced and swayed so much as I made my way up that I was afraid my car would break loose. I saw no one at first, but as I drew closer, I could see that the windows were draped, and there was some light coming from within. Encouraged, I continued until I could park in front. Then I shut off the engine, took a deep breath, and stepped out of the motor home.

Before I reached the half dozen steps that led up to the portico, a tall, stout black man with silvery gray hair came around the corner of the building. He was carrying a shovel and a hoe over his right shoulder and wore a pair of high rubber boots. When he saw me, he paused and wiped his forehead and his eyes as if he couldn't believe his sight.

"I need help!" I cried.

"Don't we all," he replied, and walked toward me.

As he approached, I saw he had gray stubble over his chin and patches of it over his jawline and cheeks. Although his hair indicated he was along in age, his face was smooth, his eyes bright and friendly, like the eyes of someone much younger and more innocent trapped in an older body.

"What's the trouble?" he asked. He wore only a flannel shirt open at the collar. The sleeves were frayed. His jeans were mud-stained and worn through at the knees. He wore no watch, just a silver chain with what looked like a silver heart.

"It's my uncle. Something terrible has happened to him," I said.

He looked up at the motor home. "Like what?"

"I don't know," I said, now unable to hold back my tears.

He looked at the motor home again as if it were somehow forbidden territory. Then he dropped the tools, scratched the top of his head, and slowly approached the motor home door. Just as he did, the front door of the house opened, and an elderly lady in a faded blue housecoat stepped out. Her gray hair was whiter than his but brushed and combed neatly into a bun. She had a dark brown walking stick with a pearl handle. Her thick-lensed glasses slipped down over the bridge of her nose as she peered out at me.

"What's goin' on, Trevor?" she called, and took a few more steps forward. She was wearing what looked like a pair of fluffy white slippers.

"This girl says she's in trouble, Mrs. Westington."

"What sort of trouble?"

"She says her uncle is in a bad way inside here. I was just going to look."

"Well, we don't need no more trouble here," she muttered loudly enough for me to hear.

"Yes, ma'am, I know that," Trevor said, glanced at me, and then entered the motor home.

I stood outside. The elderly lady remained firm, frozen, leaning on her cane and staring hard at me.

"I'm sorry," I said. "I'm lost."

"Yeah," she said, nodding. "No one comes up here anymore 'less they are."

When Trevor came out, he looked shocked.

"Well?" Mrs. Westington demanded immediately. She approached the top step.

"There's a man dead in there, all right, and he's lying beside a giant doll."

"What?" she asked, recoiling. "What kind of a nonsense story is that?"

"I swear, Mrs. Westington," Trevor said, raising his hand.

I continued to sob and embrace myself. "My uncle's a . . . performer . . . and . . . the doll is part of our act," I explained breathlessly.

"How'd he kick the bucket?" Mrs. Westington asked Trevor.

"Don't know as I could say, Mrs. Westington. Must've been pretty sick. Looks to me like he spat up some blood," he added, looking my way.

"He drank," I mumbled.

"What's that?" she asked.

"My uncle was an alcoholic," I admitted.

"Oh. Well, I know a little about that. My husband drank himself to hell. It ain't no pretty kettle of fish. Well, don't stand there. It's going to rain cats and dogs shortly. We'll make the proper phone call. Leave that vehicle door open, Trevor. Air it out."

"Yes, ma'am."

She tapped her cane hard on the portico wood floor. "Come along. We ain't got all day," she said turning.

I looked back at Trevor.

"It's best to do what she says," he told me.

I followed Mrs. Westington into her house.

I didn't know it then, but it wouldn't be all that long before it became mine as well.

20

Desperate for Love

❧❖❧

Inside, the house looked as if it had been frozen in time, the owner stubbornly refusing to throw anything away. Whether it was a worn rug, a frayed sofa, a broken vase, or a cracked figurine on a rickety-looking pedestal, everything was obviously still cherished. The wide entryway had a mahogany coat stand and hat rack with garments on them looking as though they had been placed there fifty years ago and never touched since.

Up close, Mrs. Westington resembled her possessions. Her pale alabaster complexion had patches of tiny, spidery veins close to the surface, making her resemble a life-size cracked porcelain doll. There were some futile attempts at cosmetics, patches of face makeup applied too thickly in spots and completely absent from other areas. Her lipstick was thicker on her bottom lip for some reason than it was on her top lip.

However, in spite of her fragile appearance, her bony shoulders, long thin-fingered hands, and reliance on the walking stick, she had an air of firmness and grit about her, especially discernible in her dark gray but yet bright eyes.

"Close the door!" she shouted at Trevor, who was just behind me.

"It's closed, Mrs. Westington," he said.

She turned and looked as if she didn't trust a word he uttered, and then nodded. "House is coming apart at the seams. Wind blows right through these days."

"Yes, ma'am," Trevor said. "I patched up that window frame on the pantry."

"Um," she said. She pointed at the sofa with her cane. "You sit there, girl," she told me. "Trevor, you go to the phone and call the highway patrol. The number's on the board by the phone."

She was obviously used to giving orders. I sat, and she stared at me a moment and then went to the window to open the drapes. The grandfather clock in the corner groaned instead of bonging the hour. She looked at her watch and shook her head.

"Don't know where the time goes," she muttered, more to herself than to me. "Okay," she said. "Now, tell me what you're doing on this road, driving that big thing with your uncle dead inside."

There was something about the way she looked at me and spoke that compelled me to tell her my story. Perhaps it had all been bottled up inside me too long. I was surprised myself at how much came out, how much I revealed, and how fast I spoke. At first, she just stood there listening. Then she slowly lowered herself into her dark brown cushioned chair. upon which she had placed an additional cushion to keep herself higher and make it easier for her to get up when she wanted.

She leaned on her walking stick and looked at me as I continued, her face showing little emotion, surprise, or displeasure.

"Sometimes, I wonder if it was God or the devil who made us," she said after a long pause when I stopped talking.

The entire time I spoke, tears rained down from my eyes, and my throat opened and closed, choking back words and then freeing whole paragraphs in one breath. I didn't realize Trevor had been standing in the living room doorway awhile, waiting for permission to speak himself. Mrs. Westington finally nodded at him.

"They're on their way here," he said, "and so is an ambulance."

"What good's an ambulance?" she muttered back at him as if he had ordered it.

"Got to take the body to the coroner, Mrs. Westington. Ain't gonna take him in my truck."

I waited to see if she was going to chastise him for what he had said in reply, but she just nodded and looked as if she appreciated his cold, factual answer. She looked at me again.

"How old are you, girl?"

"I'm seventeen, nearly eighteen," I said.

She shook her head and then turned to Trevor.

"Seems like the world's going to end up filled with orphans. Women drop out children these days like field mice and as soon as they can walk on their own, leave them to manage for themselves."

"Yes, ma'am," Trevor said.

"Well, let's get the girl something to eat and drink while we wait," she said, rising out of the chair. "I'll make some blackberry tea and tuna fish sandwiches.

You can go down the hallway to the powder room on the right and clean yourself up some," she told me.

"Thank you," I said, and followed her out.

"I'll wait for them outside," Trevor told us.

I could see the bathroom fixtures were quite old, the porcelain sink spotted with rust. Everything worked fine but revealed the age of the house, which I later found out was built nearly eighty-five years ago when the property was a successful vineyard and the family had its own winery. It was not hard to imagine that at one time, the house must have been beautiful. There was so much detail in the wall trim and the fireplace. The chandeliers, although looking as if they could use a good dusting and cleaning, were quite elaborate. Quality materials had been used in the construction. The hardwood floors probably needed only a good polishing, even after all this time.

Mrs. Westington told me to go into the dining room, where she put the tea and the sandwiches, cut into small squares, on the long, dark cherry-wood dining table. I thanked her again and sipped the tea and nibbled on the sandwiches. She watched me eat for a few moments, and then she rose and said, "They're here."

I had heard nothing. It was as if she had radar that told her when anyone had stepped onto her property. I rose and followed her out.

The sight of the police and the ambulance put a new wave of chills and then numbness into my body, which had somehow taken an intermission from the sad and terrible events that had just occurred. The police went into the motor home, followed by the two paramedics. I watched from the portico. The rain had begun, as Mrs. Westington had predicted, and fell in a steady, dull drizzle.

One of the highway patrolmen, a stout, tall man

with light brown hair, sauntered over to us as though the rain wouldn't dare make him wet. He stepped up and reached into his back pocket to pull out a notepad. He flipped it open, tipped his hat at Mrs. Westington, and directed his attention to me.

"What's your full name, miss?"

"I'm April Taylor."

"That man in there was your uncle?"

"Yes, sir, Palaver."

"Palaver?"

"He's a magician, hypnotist. I was helping him with his show. We travel to different theaters."

"How old are you?"

I glanced at Mrs. Westington.

"She's eighteen," she replied for me. "The poor girl's been through hell and back. Get to the point."

"I'm just trying to do my job, Mrs. Westington. There's a man dead in there. This is an unattended death. There's procedure."

"Well, no one's telling you not to follow your procedures, officer. Just get along with it. I just gave the poor girl something to eat when you arrived. Tea's getting cold."

"Yes, ma'am," he said, and turned back to me. "What happened to your uncle?"

"He died," Mrs. Westington said as if the policeman were a total idiot. I nearly laughed. I was feeling so confused. I was drunk on the insanity of what was occurring.

The patrolman grimaced and looked at me.

"My uncle was drinking heavily for a long time. I think he finally got very sick from it," I said.

"That big doll in the bed was part of his act?"

"Oh, Lord have mercy," Mrs. Westington muttered. "What's that got to do with anything now?"

"Where is the rest of your family, April?" he asked, trying to turn away from Mrs. Westington.

"Back in Memphis. My sister is a professional basketball player."

"And your parents?"

"Both dead," I said.

"I knew it," Mrs. Westington told him.

The paramedics carried Uncle Palaver out of the motor home on a stretcher, his whole body covered, and put him into the ambulance. I started to cry again.

"Oh, dear, dear," Mrs. Westington said. She put her arm around my shoulders. "I'm taking her inside. You can come in and finish procedures or stop by afterward," she said firmly, and turned me.

"Someone will be by. Is she staying with you?"

"Of course, she's staying with me. What do you expect she'll do, get into that contraption and drive off?" she asked, nodding at the motor home with my car attached.

"No, ma'am, it's just . . ."

"It's just raining harder. Tend to your procedures," she said, and guided me into the house.

"I've got to call my sister," I said. Telling the policeman about her reminded me it was something I should do immediately.

"Well, you go right ahead. The phone's in the kitchen on the wall," she told me, and pointed her cane in the direction of the kitchen.

I walked down to it and sucked in my breath a moment, closing my eyes to gather the strength I would need to tell Brenda everything and to hear her chastise me for staying with Uncle Palaver so long. Then I picked up the receiver. The phone was a rotary type and looked as if it had been manufactured a day after Alexander Graham Bell invented the telephone. I dialed Brenda's number and waited. It rang twice, and then a mechanical voice said, "I'm sorry, but this number has been disconnected. There is no forwarding number." I held the receiver while the message was repeated. That was followed with some number code, and then the phone went dead.

Mrs. Westington was standing in the hallway watching me.

"My sister . . . is gone," I said. "She's moved out. Her phone's disconnected."

"Doesn't surprise me. Half the world's disconnected," she said. "Go in there and finish your sandwiches and tea. There's plenty of time to do what has to be done."

"I'm not hungry," I said.

"Don't matter. Your body's had a big shock. You'd better fortify, girl, or you'll get sick yourself and not be worth a plumb nickel to anyone. Go on," she commanded.

I returned to the dining room and continued to nibble on the sandwiches. She went to get the water hot again for my tea. As I sat there, I thought again about Brenda. I had to find her. I got an idea and went out to the motor home to get the papers that Brenda had forwarded to me after I left Memphis. Then I hurried back inside.

"What are you up to, girl?" Mrs. Westington asked. "You're letting the water get cold again."

"I realized a way I might be able to find my sister," I said. "Our attorney should know."

She nodded. "Yes, attorneys usually know everyone's business. Go on. Use the phone again," she said, and brought the kettle back to the kitchen.

I called, and Mr. Weiss came on after his secretary told him who I was. He listened and told me he did know where Brenda was. She was with a team about to leave for Germany, and he had just faxed some documents to her hotel in New York City. He said he would try to reach her immediately.

"What are you going to do?" he asked.

"I don't know."

"Call me for whatever help you need there, April."

He asked for the telephone number, and I asked Mrs. Westington, who stood by listening. She told me, and I gave it to him. He promised to get right on it and try to reach Brenda as soon as possible.

"There's nothing more you can do," Mrs. Westington said after I told her what the attorney had said. "The police know you're here. They'll call."

The rain began to fall harder. We could hear it dancing on the roof as the wind whipped it along.

"A good drenching," Mrs. Westington said, gazing out the dining room window.

I sat quietly, still feeling dazed. She considered me a moment and then nodded to herself.

"I want you to go lie down now, girl. I'll show you to your room. Don't worry," she said before I could raise any opposition. "When you get a call, I'll let you know. Come along," she ordered, and started out to the stairway. It went up and curved like a "J" onto the second floor of the house. She guided herself with the banister but seemed to have no trouble going up the stairs.

The heavy overcast and rain made the second-story landing seem even darker than it was. I saw there were no windows. The two chandeliers dripped shadows along the panel walls. She led me to a bedroom immediately off to the right and opened the door.

"I'm sure you'll find it comfortable," she said. "Used to be my daughter's room."

I looked in at a beautiful white and pink canopy bed. The matching dresser, armoire, and vanity table had the same pink swirls in them. A soft, milk-white area rug surrounded the bed.

"I got a Mexican woman comes to clean the house once a week, and she always does this room. Bathroom's in there," she said, pointing her cane at the door on the right. "Just make yourself at home. I'll shout up when your call comes, and you can use that phone," she added, pointing to an antique brass phone on the nightstand beside the bed.

"I'm not really tired," I said.

"You're more tired than you imagine. Your insides have been turned and twisted. Don't tell me what you are and what you're not," she added sternly. "Go on, take a rest, and we'll see about it all soon enough. One thing about tragedy. It don't forget you for a moment when it visits."

The bed did look inviting. I walked in and sat on it.

"Make yourself comfortable," she urged. "Get under the comforter. You been riding about in that contraption so long you forgot how to enjoy a real room?" she asked when I hesitated.

"No, ma'am."

"Well, then, do as I say," she said.

I pulled the blanket back, took off my shoes, and slipped in. The pillows felt like clouds beneath my head. I saw her watching me from the doorway for a while. My eyelids drooped and then closed. Minutes later, I was asleep. She was right. My insides had been turned and twisted.

When I opened my eyes again, I thought I was still dreaming. Standing right by the bed and staring down at me with wide eyes was a girl who looked no more than fourteen. She wore a dark blue one-piece dress with a frilly white collar. Her very curly black hair was chopped short and looked as if someone had put a bowl over her head and trimmed it. Even though she had black hair, her eyes were almost Kelly green. She had a rich, peach complexion with a small, slightly turned-up nose, soft, full lips, and a cleft chin.

I braced myself up on my elbows and wiped my eyes. "Hi," I said.

She continued to stare and then suddenly raised her hands and, with her right forefinger, circled her mouth and pointed the finger at me.

"I don't understand," I said, and she did both gestures again, only more emphatically. She looked as if she might cry if I didn't figure out what she was doing. I thought a moment and then smiled. "Oh. You're asking who I am?" I said, pointing to myself.

She smiled and nodded.

"You're deaf," I whispered to myself. "My name is April," I said. And then, for some reason, repeated "April" slowly, enunciating each syllable. She obviously studied my lips.

She pressed her fingers down and showed me her palm, then moved her fingers quickly. I shook my head, and she grimaced. Then she thought a moment, went to the drawer of the nightstand and took out a pen and pad. She wrote on it and handed it to me.

She had written "April".

"That's right," I said. "That's my name. Who are you?"

She moved her fingers rapidly three times, and when I shook my head again, she took the pad back and wrote "Echo".

Echo? Didn't she understand me? I pointed to her again and mimicked her signing "Who?"

She nodded and pointed to the pad.

What a strange name, if that was really her name, I thought, but I smiled at her and nodded.

She smiled back and then watched as I rose out of the bed and slipped on my shoes. Hadn't Brenda called yet? What was happening? Was this little girl Mrs. Westington's granddaughter? Where were her parents? I started for the door, and she immediately seized my hand. It took me by surprise, but I saw she meant only to walk with me.

Mrs. Westington came to the foot of the stairway when she heard me descending. She immediately began to sign with Echo. She looked angry, too. Echo let go of my hand and stopped descending. She looked at me and then turned and ran back up the stairway and down the hall.

"What happened? Who is she?" I asked.

"Never mind who she is. She knows better than to bother guests."

"She didn't bother me," I said. "Didn't anyone call back yet?"

"No. I told you I would call you when they did, didn't I? Come along," she urged. "You can help me prepare dinner, peel potatoes while I shell some peas. I have a roast for tonight."

She didn't wait for my reply. She turned and headed for the kitchen. I looked back and saw Echo peering out of a doorway. As soon as she saw me looking at her, she backed away and closed the door.

What was going on here? I wondered, and continued down the stairway and to the kitchen. The potatoes were in a bucket on the table, the peeler beside it. Mrs. Westington nodded at it. She sat and began to shell the peas.

"Who is she?" I asked as I sat to begin the work.

"She's my granddaughter. She's deaf. Was deaf at

birth. My daughter had her out of wedlock and then decided it was too hard to be gallivanting about with a handicapped infant. She lived here with her for nearly four years before she just up and walked out on the both of us one day, supposedly just to have a vacation. That vacation has gone on for nearly ten years next month. So, here I was, a woman in her early sixties, becoming a full-time mother again willy-nilly."

"Does she go to a special school?"

"Yes, here. I have a tutor come regular, a young man who is a specialist with the deaf." She paused. "What about your own schooling?"

"I'm going to get my high school equivalency," I said. "I guess I'll have to start thinking about it more seriously now, and what I'll do afterward."

"Well, I guess you will. Time to pay the piper and end this running away from your troubles, girl. You don't see them, maybe, but they're always right there, like gum on your heel. Trouble with young people today is they have no grit, no staying power. Some difficulty comes, and they give up and run off. My daughter is a prime example.

"Think I like being left with a little girl who's deaf to boot?" she asked before I could disagree. "No, but I don't whine and moan and wring my hands and cry, 'Woe is me. Oh, woe is me.' I do what has to be done. Always have, always will. Take a letter," she said.

"Pardon?"

"Take a letter, take a letter. Write that down and remember it." She started shelling the peas again and then stopped. "She tell you her name?"

"She said her name was Echo. Is that true?"

"Yes, it's true. Her idiot mother named her that because when she spoke to her, it just came back at her, being the girl was deaf. Thought she was being cute, I guess. As it turned out, I like it, and I think Echo does, too. Although it's not easy to tell when she likes something and when she doesn't."

Just then, the phone rang. We both looked at it.

"Finally," she said, rising and answering. "Yes, she's right here. Well, she ain't running off. Okay, I'll tell her that." She hung up and turned to me. "They begun the work on your uncle, and preliminarily it looks like an acute case of cirrhosis. You know what that is?"

"A liver disease," I said.

"Yep. Alcoholics get it. My husband died of it, which was ironic, being we owned a winery. He wasn't fond of wine. He drank Scotch like water. We're all our worst enemy and put ourselves behind the eight ball. Keep peeling. I'd like to eat dinner tonight, not tomorrow," she said, and sat again.

"How'd your parents kick the bucket?" she asked after a moment.

I told her about Daddy and tried to soften what Mama had done, making it sound as if she had simply made a mistake.

"Everyone stews in his or her own juices in this world, I guess," she said. "Ain't you been through a tunnel of hell, and now with your uncle and all," she added, showing some warm sympathy, but it didn't last long. She grimaced and finished the peas. "Hardships come and go. You just have to gird up your loins and push ahead. No sense crying over spilt milk."

The phone rang again. This time, my heart began to thump hard and fast. She answered it, listened, and then nodded and held out the receiver. I rose slowly and took it from her.

"April, what happened?" Brenda asked immediately after I said hello.

I told her how Uncle Palaver had been drinking and how I had tried to stop him or slow him down but nothing had helped.

"Where are you, exactly?" she asked. I really didn't know and turned to Mrs. Westington and asked her.

"About ten miles east of Healdsburg," she told me, and I told Brenda.

She was silent a moment. "Well, I don't know what we're going to do," she said. "I'm actually flying out in four hours for Germany. You can't return to the house in Memphis. I moved out," she added quickly. "I'll have to call Cousin Pete. He's the only one I can think of quickly. Mr. Weiss will help you, too. I'm on a two-month tour," she added.

"I'll be all right," I said, tears coming to my eyes. I didn't want her to give up her opportunity, but it hurt to hear that she wasn't even considering it.

"Of course, you will," Mrs. Westington mumbled behind me. I glanced at her and turned back.

"Oh, I guess I'll just have to cancel. Maybe I can join up later."

"No, it's all right, Brenda."

"You see what you did by running away," she snapped.

"I'll be all right," I said. "I'll call Cousin Pete myself."

"Good," she quickly replied. "And call Mr. Weiss again. He'll find a lawyer there to help you do what has to be done."

"Okay."

"I feel terrible about Uncle Palaver," she said. "I just didn't know he was drinking so much. Mama certainly didn't."

"I know."

"What about his lady friend, Destiny? Where is she?"

"She died before I joined up with him," I said. I decided not to go into the doll and all that had followed, especially in front of Mrs. Westington.

"Oh. Well, maybe that was what drove him to drink so much."

"Maybe."

"April, are you really going to call Cousin Pete? Just stay with him for two months, and I'll deal with everything when I get back. We'll set you up in a school and . . ."

"Okay," I said. "I will."

"Promise?"

What did promises mean in the world we lived in? I thought.

"Sure."

"I'll call Cousin Pete's house in two days from Germany," she said.

"Okay, but I have to stay here until everything is taken care of."

"If I don't reach you there, I'll call this number again," she said. "I'm sorry about all you've gone through, April."

"Me, too," I said.

"I'll call you," she replied, and hung up.

I just stood there holding the phone.

"She coming to fetch you?" Mrs. Westington asked.

I took a deep breath. I was going to lie to her, but the moment I turned around and looked at her, I could see she would read right through me.

"She's about to go to the airport to fly to Germany," I said. "She wants me to call a cousin of ours."

"Where's this cousin?"

"In North Carolina."

She smirked. "And what are you supposed to do, drive that monstrosity back to North Carolina?"

"I don't know."

"Well, I do. Finish the potatoes," she said. "You'll stay here until there's a sensible solution. Don't argue," she said before I could even think of doing so. "You'd be talking to the wall."

Not five minutes later, the phone rang again, and this time it was Mr. Weiss. Brenda had called him immediately after speaking to me.

"I'll get on the situation out there immediately," he said. "My secretary is placing a call with the police. After we spoke, I perused your family papers and found information pertaining to your uncle. He had made your mother his beneficiary and then you and your sister. I know what arrangements he wanted made in the event of his passing as well. You just take it easy, April. I'll handle the hard stuff from here. No problem. Now, what about this cousin? Brenda wanted me to be sure you called him. You want to do that, or do you want me to do it and have him call you?"

"I'll do it," I said.

Cousin Pete was just a little more than a stranger to me. I couldn't imagine throwing myself onto his doorstep, but I didn't want to think about it at the moment.

"Fine. All right. I'll be calling you at this number and letting you know what I've arranged."

"Thank you," I said.

After I hung up, I told everything to Mrs. Westington.

"Well, that's good your lawyer's doing all that," she said. "But I can just imagine what he's going to charge. My husband used to say they get a clock embedded in their hearts as soon as they pass the bar exam."

"I don't care about the money," I said sharply.

She looked up at me a moment and then nodded. "You will. Sooner or later," she said. She looked at the potatoes I had peeled. "Now, cut them into quarters," she said. "I'm cooking them in the gravy. That's the way Trevor likes them. Then go get whatever you need out of that monstrosity and take a hot bath. There's nice bath powder in the bathroom. One thing my daughter made sure of was that she was in the pink all the time."

I started to cut the potatoes. "Why did you send your granddaughter away like that when she was coming down the stairs with me?" I asked.

"She's too desperate," she replied.

"Desperate? Desperate for what?" I asked.

She hesitated, her eyes softening a bit. "For love," she said, and turned to put the beans in a pot.

Epilogue

When I was finished with the potatoes, Mrs. Westington again insisted I go up and take a hot bath. I went back into the motor home to get some clothing and other things I would need. The moment I stepped into it, I started to cry. Gazing about at Uncle Palaver's things made me feel so sad for him. Before I left, I did a strange thing. I went back to the bedroom and looked at the Destiny doll. The head was turned toward the door, and the eyes were open. Of course, I was projecting into the doll what was really in me, but it looked truly sad. It brought more tears to my eyes. I sighed and hurried out of the motor home.

When I went back upstairs, I saw Echo's door open slightly and caught her peering out at me. I smiled at her and then went into my room and ran the bath. I nearly fell asleep soaking in the warm, perfumed water. After I came out of the bathroom to get dressed, I found Echo sitting on the bed looking at my things. She smiled at me and began to sign. I shook my head.

"I'm sorry. I can't follow you," I said. I shrugged, and she looked disappointed. I was sure she was asking me a dozen questions about everything. Even though it seemed silly, I continued to talk to her, retelling my story, what had happened, why I was there. She looked as if she were listening, and I imagined that from time to time, she was picking up some of it by lip reading. I made a gesture to indicate eating, and she nodded and smiled. This time, maybe her grandmother wouldn't yell at her when we descended together, I thought.

Mrs. Westington had set the table and begun to bring in bread and butter, salt and pepper, and a jug of water. I saw there were four places. She looked at the two of us and then signed at Echo, who immediately went to the kitchen to help bring in the food. I joined her.

When we returned to the dining room, Trevor had arrived, wearing a clean white shirt and a pair of black slacks. His hair was brushed neatly.

"Everything smells as good as ever," he said.

"You'd say that no matter what," Mrs. Westington told him. She gestured at Echo, who sat across from Trevor. I sat next to her. Then she surprised me by gesturing again at Echo and lowering her head.

Echo then said grace through her signing. Mrs. Westington kept an eye on her, and when Echo was finished, both she and Trevor raised their heads and said, "Amen."

Echo smiled at me with pride at her accomplishment, and I smiled back.

"Thank you for your hospitality," I told Mrs. Westington as she began to pass the dishes of food around.

She paused, looked at Echo, who was beaming at me, and then shook her head.

"Everything in this world happens for a reason," she began. "We don't see the reason right away and sometimes not for years and years."

"Amen to that," Trevor said.

She looked at him and pulled her lips back so the corners deepened. He glanced at me and concentrated on his food.

"Often, one person's hardship is another person's blessing. The secret is to keep yourself open and willing to enjoy the mysteries of the Lord. You understand me?"

"Yes, ma'am."

"Maybe you do; maybe you don't. Right now, it doesn't matter all that much. When you're older, as old as Trevor and me, it will matter."

She stopped, turned sharply at Echo, who was still staring at me, and then poked her shoulder with a spoon. She signed something angrily, and Echo started to eat.

"I got a real burden here," Mrs. Westington continued. "I do the best I can, but I'm the first to admit, it's not enough."

"Oh, Mrs. . . . "

"No, Trevor," she said sharply. "I don't need to fool myself about anything at my age. You should know that better than anyone."

"Yes, ma'am."

"Trevor's been with this family for nearly fifty years."

"Forty-nine years, seven months, tomorrow," he said, smiling at me.

"So I put up with his bad habits and tolerate his inadequacies," she added, and he widened his smile.

"Anyway, I've given it all a good think. Fate put you on that road out there as clearly as it made that poor child deaf. You didn't ask for it; she didn't ask for it. My husband used to say you play the deck you're dealt, and that's that. You're an orphan now, and Echo ain't much more than one herself."

"Oh, Mrs. Westington," Trevor said. "No one can call that girl an orphan. Not with what you do for her and all."

"When I need a compliment, Trevor, I'll call on you," Mrs. Westington said.

Trevor shook his head and went back to eating.

"What I'm saying here is you're welcome to stay on. I can see where you'd be of real service," she added, nodding at Echo, whose eyes were on me again. "Of course, I'll provide for your schooling needs and all else until you get it in you that you have to go on somewhere."

I looked at Echo. She seemed to understand what Mrs. Westington was saying.

"I don't know what to say," I said.

"You just say thank you and move in," she replied. "I saw how much you wanted to go live with that cousin."

I glanced at Trevor. He was smiling but keeping his head down.

"You can be of great help to me as regards Echo," she added. "It won't take you long to learn how to sign. As I told you, I have a good tutor for her, but I realize she is isolated out here and could use some young people companionship now. Maybe this tutor can help you with whatever you called it."

"High school equivalency."

"Yes, that. Well, go on and eat. You don't want it to get cold while you think," she said.

She immediately began to talk to Trevor about some of the things they needed done on the property and the house. Afterward, Echo and I helped clear the table and do the dishes. When that was completed, she took me into the living room to show me her books. She was proud of her library, and I was impressed with how much she had already read. Some of the titles were ones I had been assigned in high school.

Next to the books on the shelf was a picture of Echo and a young, good-looking black-haired man with Asian features who had his arm around her shoulders.

"Who?" I signed to her, and pointed to the picture.

She replied in her language. It took me a few times to comprehend that she was saying he was her tutor.

"His name's Tyler Monahan," Mrs. Westington said from the living room doorway. I didn't know how long she had been standing there watching us. "I'm lucky to have him. He worked at a school for the disabled in Los Angeles before he came back here to help with his own family after his father died. He's a loyal son and gave up his work in Los Angeles to help his mother with their sauce business. Echo there provides him with a chance to keep his hand in his real life's work.

"You'll meet him in a couple of days," she said.

I glanced at the photo again.

The phone had rung while Echo and I were in the living room.

"Just got off the phone with the police. Your uncle's death is ruled caused by acute cirrhosis, as suspected. Your lawyer's already contacted them and set up the arrangements for the funeral, which isn't much. He left orders to be cremated. We can attend a quick ceremony day after tomorrow at eleven."

I didn't say anything. I lowered my head.

"I told Trevor to drive that big vehicle around back. The lawyer's seeing about all that, too."

"Thank you," I said.

Mrs. Westington went through a series of signing with Echo, and from the way she reacted, I concluded she was telling her all about me, my uncle, and what had happened. She finished by explaining I might be staying here with them. It brought a wide, hopeful smile to her face.

"I have some book work to attend to," Mrs. Westington said. "She doesn't mind watching television with you, even though she can't hear it. She clings to any companionship," she added sadly. "And I'm not much to cling to these days. I'm up at seven," she concluded, and left us.

Echo was determined to show me as much about herself as she could. She pulled out family albums, school papers, and other pictures. At one point, I found a book on sign language, and I sat with her and practiced some of the hand gestures. That pleased her the most and made me laugh as well. Finally, the full impact of the day's events settled on me, and I told her I had to get some sleep. She was disappointed, but she understood, and after I helped her put everything back, she ascended the stairs with me. At my door, she showed me how to say good night and then, timidly but eagerly, she kissed me on the cheek and went off to her own room.

At that moment, I pitied her for living in a world of silence. But I also envied her for not being able to hear the voices, the cries, and the sobs that echoed in my own mind.

There were two windows in the bedroom that had once been Mrs. Westington's daughter's bedroom. They looked out on the east end of the house, and when I gazed out of them now, I saw the back of the motor home and my car where Trevor had parked them. I could understand selling the vehicle and most of Uncle Palaver's things, but I decided I didn't want to see his magic equipment sold, and I especially didn't want to see the Destiny doll taken away. I had no idea now what I would do with it all, but I made up my mind to make that a requirement of my remaining here in Mrs. Westington's home. I saw no reason why she would be opposed.

As darkness thickened and the stars began to brighten, I thought about the journey I had taken to arrive at this place. Was everyone's life as convoluted? Did everyone travel through a similar kind of maze, where each turn caused us to go in one direction or another? It seemed chaotic to me, until I thought about the way each event determined the next. Maybe there was a pattern. Maybe Uncle Palaver's doll was aptly named, and we were all in the hands of Destiny, one way or another.

Wasn't that what Mrs. Westington believed? That fate had brought me here?

Perhaps it had. Perhaps Echo had signed a prayer to God asking for someone like me to be brought to her doorstep. Who was I to question anything anymore, whether it be Peter Smoke's medicine wheel, Uncle Palaver's obsession for a lost love, or Mrs. Westington's confidence in a reason for everything?

So much about our lives is illusion, I thought. Daddy had tried to create one to replace his tragic reality for us. Brenda had accepted one with Celia that became a bubble and burst. And I had run off pursuing my own shadows and wishful thinking. I quickly understood that Uncle Palaver was simply drawing from that well of fantasy and serving it back to his audiences.

One way or another, we all arrive here, I thought. We all stop and watch the darkness swallow up the shadows and the illusions. Then we turn to ourselves and hope to find the strength to look into the face of reality and go on. That's what Mrs. Westington was doing or trying to do. She had asked me to join hands with her.

I was about to begin another journey, make a turn in the maze.

What was at the end of it?

Happiness?

More sadness?

Or just another turn?

Tomorrow would be the beginning of my pursuit of the answer.

So, good night, Daddy, I thought. *Good night, Mama and Brenda and Uncle Palaver.*

I put my lips to the window and gazed at Uncle Palaver's motor home.

"Good night, Destiny," I whispered.

Somewhere inside me, I believed she heard.

SIMON & SCHUSTER
PROUDLY PRESENTS

GIRL IN THE SHADOWS

VIRGINIA ANDREWS®

Coming soon from
Simon & Schuster

Turn the page for a preview of
Girl in the Shadows . . .

"**W**ell, ain't this a pretty kettle of fish," Mrs. Westington said. She glanced at Echo and then relaxed her embrace. "You probably don't remember who that is, Echo. It almost takes a divining rod for me to determine her identity, but that there is your mother or what passes for her," she said.

"Now let's not start out on the wrong foot, Mom," Rhona said.

"We've been on the wrong foot for some time, Rhona. Too late to get off that," Mrs. Westington said.

"Hi, Echo," Rhona said. "I wouldn't have recognized you. You've grown so. Don't you want to give me a kiss and a hug?" She held out her arms.

Echo stared up at her, unmoving, her hand

tightly clasping Mrs. Westington's. Did her own mother forget her daughter was deaf?

A tall, thin man with a grubby beard stepped up beside Rhona. He was wearing a white button-down shirt that looked like it had last been washed ten years ago and a pair of torn, ragged jeans with black sandals. His toes were so dirty, it was hard to tell where they were and where the straps of the sandals were. The strands of his dull, brown hair resembled broken springs shooting off in every direction. When he smiled, his thin lips practically disappeared, producing a dull slice above his slightly protruding cleft chin. His neck looked like it needed a good scrubbing.

"This is Skeeter," Rhona said, lowering her arms.

"Hi there," he said saluting quickly at Mrs. Westington. I glanced at her. She looked like she had just swallowed some sour milk. "You have a very nice house and great property. Love this old door. Oak, isn't it?"

"Skeeter? Didn't your parents give you a real name?" she asked.

I laughed to myself. Mrs. Westington wasn't one to hold back her thoughts and criticisms, even when she faced a complete stranger.

"Well, my real name is Sanford Bickers, but I never saw myself as a Sanford."

"Everyone knows him as Skeeter, Mom. No one knows him as Sanford."

"Then you two have something in common. You're both running away from yourselves," Mrs. Westington told her.

"I never knew you to be inhospitable, Ma," Rhona said.

Mrs. Westington looked at her askance.

"You're happy to see me at least, aren't you, Trevor?" Rhona asked him, her voice sweet and syrupy.

Trevor's eyes shifted quickly to Mrs. Westington and then he looked away.

"All right, Rhona," Mrs. Westington said sharply, "to what do we owe the pleasure of this visit by you and Mr. Skeeter?"

"I've just been through hell, Mom. Skeeter helped me a great deal. I would have thought you would be a little more considerate since you knew what I've been through," Rhona whined.

"I'm sorry to say it, Rhona, but I doubt very much you're through with hell," Mrs. Westington said. She turned to Echo and me. "Let's get our things inside and up to your rooms, girls." I signed quickly to Echo who was just standing there and gaping at Rhona.

"Who is she?" Rhona asked, nodding at me.

"This is April Taylor. She's been helping me with Echo. You can thank her properly later," Mrs. Westington told her.

"Is she staying in my room? I see it's being used."

"Your room? You gave up that room and a lot more years ago, Rhona."

"Well, where are Skeeter and I going to stay?"

"Who says you're staying?" Mrs. Westington retorted, and urged Echo and me to get our things again. I moved quickly, taking it all out of the station wagon. I glanced at Rhona who had folded her arms petulantly under her breasts and stepped to the side, glaring at her mother. Skeeter kept a small smile on his face. They watched us enter the house and then followed.

"Now listen to me, Mom," Rhona began. "Please."

Ignoring her, Mrs. Westington turned to Trevor and nodded at the living room.

"Would you be so kind as to turn that television set off, Trevor? We don't need the noise right now. Seems we have enough static already."

"Yes, ma'am," he said, then glanced at Rhona and went into the living room to do it.

"Go on up, April. Help Echo put her things away, please."

"Okay," I said. I looked at Rhona again. Her eyes were inflamed with indignation and resentment and it looked like it was all directed at me, as if I were the cause of all her lifelong problems.

Trevor stepped back into the hallway.

"I've got something waiting on me back at the winery," he told Mrs. Westington, nodded at Rhona, and hurried out.

I gestured to Echo for us to go up the stairs.

"Wait a minute," Rhona said reaching for Echo, who couldn't take her eyes off her. "Don't you want to say hello to your mother, Echo? Give her a proper greeting?"

"You forget the little signing you knew?" Mrs. Westington asked her.

"She knows what I'm saying?"

"I doubt that," Mrs. Westington told her. "I'm not deaf and I don't know what you're saying."

Rhona held out her arms, again expecting Echo to come to her for an embrace. Echo looked at Mrs. Westington and then she turned and started up the stairs with her boxes and bags.

"Echo! Echo, you listen to me."

"Lordy Dee. Did you forget the child is deaf?" Mrs. Westington asked her. "She doesn't recognize you, probably. She was barely out of infancy when you deserted her."

"Look, Mom. I came here because I need you to help us. Since you helped me get past my recent troubles, I thought you would have a different attitude, especially when you hear and see how I would like to make things right and do the right things from now on."

"Mending fences, are you?"

"Yes."

"Turning a new leaf, are you?"

"Yes, Mom," she said in a tired voice.

"With Mr. Skeeter?"

"Can we sit down and talk like two adults, please?" Rhona pleaded.

"Two? Are you saying Mr. Skeeter or you ain't adult?"

"Mom?"

"I'll make some tea," Mrs. Westington relented. "You can use the guest room at the end of the hall upstairs. It's clean. My girl cleans it once a week no matter if anyone uses it or not, so don't mess it up so it looks like that pigpen you're driving out there. Put on some decent clothing, clean yourselves up so you're both fit to be in the same room with decent people, come down to the living room and I'll let you get down to brass tacks."

"Brass tacks?" Skeeter asked, smiling widely and looking at Rhona.

"Mom has a colorful way of speaking. We already brought our things to that room, seeing mine was messed up."

"Messed up? It's twice as neat as your best day in it."

"Okay, Mom. Just come on," she told Skeeter and headed for the stairs.

I had been climbing slowly so as to hear their conversation. I sped up behind Echo and continued toward her room with her to help her put away her new things. I could see she was quite stunned with her mother's unexpected appearance.

"That's my mother," she signed to me as soon as we entered her room and she had put her bags and boxes down on the bed.

"I know."

"She looks different," she told me.

"People change. You haven't seen her in a long time," I said. "Let's put your things away."

I began to hang up clothes for her and she began to put things in her dresser drawers. She was full of questions, of course. Her hands were moving too quickly for me to follow so she began to write.

"Is my mother staying here now?"

"I don't know."

"Who is that man? Is he my father?"

Again, I wrote, "I don't know. I don't think he's your father, however. I think she met him long after you were born, Echo."

"I don't like him," she wrote, and I laughed.

"I don't think your grandmother is particularly fond of him either."

She thought a moment and then wrote, "Why didn't Trevor say hello to us?"

"He was in a big rush. As I explained to you, something must have happened at their business," I told her. She thought about my answer and for the moment that seemed to suffice.

I was going to ask her about her nightmare last night and her coming to my bed, but on second thought, I decided she had been through enough turmoil already today. It could wait for a time when we had a quiet moment together. I told her I was going to put my new things away.

When I entered my room, I found Rhona there, rifling through her closet, tossing garments onto the bed. She turned as soon as she realized I was standing there.

"These are my things," she said. "I'm not taking anything that belongs to you."

"I know."

She stared at me a moment and then turned to me completely, her hands on her hips.

"Who are you, anyway? How come you're living here?" she demanded.

I began to explain, describing how I arrived at the vineyard after Uncle Palaver's death. I told her who he had been and what we had done together.

"So that's why there's a motor home and a car back there. My mother just took you in?"

"Yes," I said.

"What about the rest of your own family?"

I told her about Brenda, about my parents.

"This is ridiculous. Now she's turning this place into an orphanage," she said. Her eyes narrowed with suspicion again. "Did you touch any of my things, my clothing?"

"Your mother wanted me to wear one of the nightgowns, but other than that, I . . ."

"I don't know why I even asked. You couldn't

possibly fit into anything of mine anyway, but I assure you I don't intend to let you just take over my possessions," she warned. "My advice to you is to find another old lady to take advantage of."

"I am not taking advantage of anyone."

"Right. I've been on the road myself, you know. I know what's what. I'm sure it wasn't hard for you to pull the wool over the eyes of an old lady and a deaf girl, and Trevor Washington's head isn't exactly filled with lightbulbs."

She scooped up a pile of her clothing and started out of the room. She paused at the doorway and turned to me, her face flushed with fury.

"Now that I'm back, I can assure you that you're not going to stay here," she said. "I intend to take back custody of my daughter and get what's rightfully mine. If you know what's good for you, you'll just get out now before there is anymore unpleasantness."

She walked out of the room. My heart was pounding and tears had come to my eyes. I put away the clothes Mrs. Westington had bought for me and then I sat by the window, looking toward the motor home and thinking. I did have some money—Uncle Palaver's cash on hand still in the motor home. I could leave. Brenda was probably right. I should just return to a regular school and finish high school. The equivalency exam wasn't going to work out anyway with Tyler behaving as he was. Mrs. Westington would say *The writing's on the wall.* He'll be giving notice any day now and be gone. I should be gone along with him.

And then I thought how deserted and alone both Echo and Mrs. Westington were going to feel. Would Rhona and that man remain here? I had no right to interfere, of course, but I didn't have to be a fortune-teller to see what Echo's future would be like if Rhona did take custody of her again and Mrs. Westington was unable to prevent it. Who knows where Rhona would put Echo? How lost and alone she would be. No, I thought. Mrs. Westington needs an ally now more than ever and Echo needs a friend. Trevor Washington, as devoted to her and Echo as he was, wasn't enough. It seemed to me I had to stay. It would be totally ungrateful for me to just up and leave right now when they needed me the most.

I heard Rhona in the hallway talking to Echo. She was probably returning to the bedroom for more of her things, and she had stopped at Echo's room.

"I really can't get over how you've grown," I heard her say. "And fortunately for you, you look more like me than your father, whoever he was." She followed that with a thin laugh.

I stepped up to the doorway and saw her enter Echo's room. The door to the guest bedroom was open and Skeeter came out of the bathroom with a towel wrapped around his waist. I saw he had a tattoo of what looked like a dragon wrapped around a mermaid across his chest. He paused and looked out, catching me looking at him. Then he turned and unwrapped the towel from his waist, exposing his rear end, which looked like it had tattoos on each side of his buttocks, as well. I stepped back into my bedroom quickly.

Rhona came in behind me and walked directly to the closet again. She picked out some other garments, sifted through the boxes of shoes and then went to the dresser drawers. She didn't look at me at all.

"I can fit into all of this. I haven't gained a pound since I left here," she muttered. "I don't know how some women get so plump and lose all their appeal to men. Being fat makes you asexual, you know," she added finally, turning to me. "Skeeter came up with that in one of his poems. *Your sex sank into your fat like a foot in quicksand.* Men don't like fat women, of course, and even women who like women wouldn't look at them. So where are you? In lard limbo, that's where. How old are you, anyway?" she asked. "Were you always overweight?"

"I don't think it's necessary for you to know any more about me."

"You're right about that, since you'll be going now that I've returned."

"I'll go when Mrs. Westington tells me to go."

"She will. Don't worry." She saw my new black skirt and plucked it off the hanger. Then she held it up in front of herself. "I could get in this with you, I think." She laughed and tossed it at me. "Pack," she said.

Tears came to my eyes, but I drove them back. Brenda would make mush out of her, I thought, and stepped forward.

"I said I'd leave when Mrs. Westington asks me to leave."

"My mother is an old lady. She waited too long to have me and now she's too old for all this."

"She didn't wait long enough," I fired back at her. "She should have waited for menopause."

"Oh, you're a wise guy, too." She piled some undergarments together and smiled. "Did you see how Echo looked at me. It won't be long. She'll want me with her, want to be with me. It's only natural. Skeeter happens to know how to use deaf people's sign language, too. He was a street performer, a mime. He's very educated even though he hasn't been to college. He's smarter than most college graduates, anyway. He'll have Mother eating out of his hand soon. You'll see. He's a charmer."

"Yeah, I could see it the moment I set eyes on his filthy hair and clothing. Won me right over," I said dryly. Brenda would have loved that one.

"Skeeter is like a chameleon. He can adjust to whatever he has to adjust to in order to succeed."

"Yeah, he looks very successful."

"He happens to be. You can't judge a book by its cover."

"What cover? I'd say he's down to his last pages, chewed and stained."

She glared at me a moment and then she laughed, shook her head, gathered her things and left the bedroom. I stood there, trembling, but keeping it under control and undetected.